The Grace of Guilt

A Novel

by

Gareth Young

First published by Dog Ear Publishing
4010 W. 86th Street, Ste H
Indianapolis, IN 46268
www.dogearpublishing.net

ISBN: 978-159858-945-0

Printed in the United States of America

The Grace of Guilt

by

Gareth Young

Acknowledgements

While I can never adequately articulate how much I appreciate the kindness and talent of the many people who helped to bring *The Grace of Guilt* to life, it would be folly indeed not to try.

I begin with Holly, my patient wife, who has tolerated my considerable weaknesses for eighteen years, and inexplicably hasn't shot me yet. I love you dearly Holly, and appreciate everything you've done—and not done! I also want to extend special thanks to my great teacher and dearest friend, Zenkai Taiun Michael Elliston, without whose gifts of wisdom and patience, I would not have been able to begin this book. The Three Treasures thank you, Sensei.

My deep gratitude goes out to other family members, too: my daughter, Morgan, my sister, Meg, and my sister-in-law, Heather, all of whom have read critically and offered sound advice: thank you all. Thanks also to the many friends, especially Larry Kahn, Brownell Landrum, Laura Buege, and Denise McCurdy, who managed the delicate balance of providing emotional support while delivering critical advice. This is tough to do, and you have my enormous gratitude.

Particular thanks go to the experts who provided guidance along the way, Red Pine, who offered criticism and redirection at an early stage, and Kent Alexander whose insight into the workings of the FBI was invaluable.

Last I want to thank those responsible for the cover art, which was a team effort by the Portfolio Center in Atlanta. The winner of a contest to design the cover was Andrea Foster, but the other students—Patrick Copeland, Melissa Cullens, Ali Dick, Ryan Howard, Jackie Huck, Rachel Maximo, and Joe Smith—offered wonderful alternatives, and together with their teacher, Melissa Kuperminc, they gave me valuable new perspectives on the book.

There were many others along the way, too numerous to mention by name, who offered enormous help and support, and I appreciate everything you gave me. Thank you all.

The Grace of Guilt

Chapter One

Jessica stirred the remains of her twenty-ounce Slurpee with the straw, sipped, and gazed out into the pasture. Her eyes lost focus and her mind drifted to the farm and to today's visitor.

"Jessica, did you hear what I said?"

Jessica jumped. "What? Oh, you're ready to go." She swung her legs over the split-rail fence and slid to the ground. Balancing her cup against a fence post, she dusted off the seat of her sundress and watched Alison do the same to her jeans. She took a last look at the big chestnut quarter horse, the paint, and the black mare who had been their midmorning companions, then turned and followed Alison, who was kicking her way through unmowed grass that bordered the two-lane highway, drifting toward the turn-off a hundred yards ahead.

"That's a pretty dress," Alison said without looking over her shoulder.

Jessica smiled, stroked the cotton print ornamented with yellow and peach lilies and lime foliage that was her summer treat, and said, "Thanks. I like your shirt, too. It's cute."

"Did you get all dressed up just to go and get a MoonPie?"

Jessica glanced sharply at her friend's back. "It's just such a lovely day," she said and looked down, brow furrowed.

"Are you meeting a boy?"

Alison's voice rang with gentle humor, but Jessica blushed and kept her head low, hoping her friend wouldn't notice. Jessica was sure she was the only rising sophomore in Wilkeston who never dated, even among the congregants of the Church of the Epistles, but although Jessica shared with her parents the church's strict moral and religious beliefs, she still had the hormones of a fifteen-year-old girl. And although she and Alison shared everything, Jessica had kept private her feelings for Colby Kidd, who was not only two years older than her and, to Jessica, a man but was also the preacher's son. He was coming to the farm today to help her father, and Jessica planned to bump into him.

"You *are* meeting someone! Who is it?" Alison had stopped and turned to stare, but Jessica lowered her shoulders and shoved past. She heard Alison scurry to catch up as she persisted with her questions. "Come on, tell me: who are you seeing?"

"No one. Besides, who would I want to see?"

"I don't know. Jeff Parker?"

"Alison!"

Alison laughed. "Yeah, I guess that was months ago." Alison knew all about Jessica's crush on Jeff and had even tried to goad her into acting on it, but she also knew that nothing had happened and that Jessica had moved on. Alison lapsed into silence, though Jessica knew her mind was spinning for an answer.

"I wonder… "

Alison had been Jessica's best friend since kindergarten, and they had always attended the same church and shared a homeroom at school, but Jessica sometimes wondered what the popular girl still saw in her. Perhaps she gave Alison a place away from teenage cliques, somewhere safe to talk about tampons and periods, crushes and dates, and Alison's increasingly intimate sexual experiences. It didn't matter, though: Jessica was grateful for a friendship without which the classroom would be a lonely place and the long summer vacation boring.

"I know," Alison announced with a tone of confident discovery, "you're seeing Colby Kidd."

Jessica scowled, said, "Of course I'm not," and pressed her head lower as she accelerated toward the unmarked road on which Alison would turn off.

"You are, too. I've seen the way you look at him. Where are you meeting?"

Jessica reached the corner. Sullen, though not sure why, she turned to face Alison. "We're not. He's just coming over to help out on the farm."

"Wow." Alison paused, and Jessica felt herself being studied. "You know he hangs out with Robbie and them? He's… " Alison let the silence hang, then shook her head and said, "Are you sure you know what you're doing?"

"I'm not doing anything, all right?"

Alison's eyes were sympathetic, but Jessica didn't want to talk about it. She had an insane crush on a stud two years older than her who she barely even knew, and she didn't want Alison making her feel stupid. She glared back defiantly.

Alison eventually shrugged. "Just be careful, okay? And call me if you want to talk." With a toss of her head, her long curls bouncing, she swung her hips, turned, and walked up the hill toward her house on the main street of the small mountain town of Wilkeston, North Carolina. With a twinge of regret, Jessica watched her BFF drift up the middle of the road, a run-down trailer park fronted by beaten-up pickups on her left, a furniture outlet on her right. Perhaps she should have sought Alison's advice on how to handle Colby; maybe she should call her back? But when Alison passed into the shadow of a large oak tree, Jessica sighed and turned to cross the highway. She glanced both ways and saw nothing but a scooter fading into the distance, probably Danny Collins making a run to the state line. Danny had lost his license years ago for drunk driving but tooled around town on his 50cc bike and once a week crossed into Georgia to buy a case of beer and a stack of lottery tickets. Jessica meandered toward the farm, dreaming of Colby's green eyes.

On Sundays, Jessica usually managed to get her parents to arrive early for church and steered them into a pew toward the front and on the other side of the aisle from Colby, from where she could admire Colby's strong jaw and broad shoulders in profile. She caught glimpses of him at school, too, though they were generally fleeting: usually he was with his friends and she was with Alison, so the best she could do was steal sly peeks. Occasionally, she got closer, leaning casually on a locker and manufacturing a hallway encounter, or exchanging quick humor in the lunch line, but he probably had no idea that she liked him. How could he? She was younger and a prude, and he could have any girl he wanted.

Jessica's home was a small farm less than half a mile from the pasture where she and Alison had met for the day. The house, barn, and surrounding trees and shrubs obscured the farmyard from the road, so she couldn't tell whether Colby's car was there, but she craned her neck as she walked up the long driveway, her heart beating faster and finally leaping when she saw a big blue Buick. It was Pastor Kidd's car, and for an insane moment, Jessica wondered if Colby had borrowed it for the day to take her for a drive. She dismissed the thought, but a thrill lingered in her belly. She swallowed and resolved that today, she would talk to Colby, even if she had to wander out into the fields to find him.

But first she had to feed the kittens.

Four weeks ago, Maisie, one of last year's litter of barn cats, had birthed six kittens. She had been far too young, and the birth had been premature: one kitten had been stillborn, and a second had died soon thereafter. Even now, Maisie was not feeding well, so twice a day, Jessica took a bottle of warm milk to the barn to feed the survivors. They were making good progress, though her favorite, Ella, was still weak.

Jessica turned to the left, past her dream of being taken for a ride, and entered the old, stone house to fetch the milk. The kitchen's austerity, stark cleanness, and lack of ornamentation spoke of Ma and were enough reality to shatter Jessica's daydreams. A relationship with Colby could never happen, for Ma expected Jessica to live the same life of sacrifice that she had made her own, eventually marrying a man to whom she would offer unquestioning obedience; although Jessica did not know when she would be granted permission to find that man, she knew it was not yet. Not only had Ma and Dad never talked to her of the birds and bees, they never even held hands, and when it came down to it, Jessica was too embarrassed to even bring the topic of boys into the house. Succumbing to earthy desires would bitterly disappoint parents from whose example she had learned that pleasures of the flesh were for lesser people. She turned on the faucet, picked up a bottle, and fumed, wanting to rebel and have a boyfriend, but knowing she lacked the courage to do so.

A bottle of warm milk in hand, Jessica stepped into the yard and looked around hopefully but saw no sign of Colby. Her chin fell, and she crossed to the old barn, a faded wood construction with missing panels and a gaping hole in one side from a runaway tractor accident—Jessica had not been allowed near the machine since. But the barn was structurally sound and the tin roof was only ten years old, so the hayloft where the kittens lived was warm and dry. Jessica entered the barn and climbed the ladder. When her head poked above the line of the hayloft, her heart stopped. Maisie was licking Ella, who lay motionless beside her.

No!

Jessica scrambled up the last steps and stumbled to the kitten. Maisie didn't object to her offspring being picked up, but Ella didn't stir as Jessica lifted her. Jessica laid the corpse aside and picked up the mother to console her, but Maisie was uninterested, her eyes dull like the lifeless buttons on the face of a stuffed toy. Jessica put her down, and the cat returned to her offspring, licked her all over, and then wandered drearily into the back of the hayloft.

These were only barn cats to Ma and Dad, but to Jessica, they were more—more even than pets. They were her friends, and the hayloft, with its familiar smells of oil, animals, and hay, was a sanctuary she shared with them, a place she came to rest and dream. When she was a toddler, Dad had made her a cedar chest in which she used to hide, giggling when he found her among her clothes, and when had she had turned ten, he had brought it up to the hayloft, where it still resided and held her treasures: a ticket stub from the first time Dad had taken her to the movies; Cassandra, her childhood princess doll; magazine photos of Leonardo DiCaprio, Justin Timberlake, and other MTV and Hollywood stars she wasn't allowed to watch; and a collection of her favorite romance and fantasy novels. The chest was also where she stored her diary, and the hayloft where she came to write. Ella's death was a desecration of her sacred space.

Quiet conversation approached the barn, and Jessica straightened; that would be Dad, who would make the pain go away, just like he always did. She knew that she was the jewel of his life, and he had told her a hundred times how, for the first twenty years of his marriage with Ma, he had desperately wanted children and had felt as blessed as Abraham when, at thirty-six, Ma had, like Sarah, borne him the child that he had no longer thought possible. Jessica felt blessed, too, for she loved her father more than anyone or anything in the world. His happiness was the most important thing in her life.

But he must be busy on farm business right now. She cocked her head to listen.

"Okay, Colby," her father said, his voice becoming clearer as he approached the barn, "you fetch the pick and axe from in there and get started. I've got to go down to Cook Hardware for some odds and ends, and then I need to spend half an hour in my shop fixing the chain. I'll meet you at the stumps with the tractor in an hour or so."

"Yes, sir."

Jessica flushed, brushed the straw and cat hair off her lap, then shook out her long black hair and pulled it back over her shoulders. She grabbed the nearest of Maisie's frolicking kittens and raised him to her lap, looked down briefly as Spike reached for and grasped the nipple of the bottle, then tickled his neck and shifted slightly so she could see down into the barn.

She had watched Colby from afar for long enough that she could close her eyes and still see his swaggering stride, the sleeves of his shirt rolled halfway up his forearms and his jeans hugging his hips and running down his long legs to break on the cowboy boots he favored. But today she kept her eyes open and saw him stop in the barn doorway, his arms loose at his side and his shoulders swinging with his head as he peered around the tractor and agricultural equipment, looking for tools. She gazed at him from the hayloft, her chest thumping and her breath arrhythmic. But this was more than nervousness: something very uncomfortable was happening. She was drawn to Colby, yet she was too embarrassed to do anything. What if he didn't like her? She thought he was interested, but what if she was wrong? What if she made a fool of herself? And what would Ma and Dad think?

Colby's eyes latched onto something in the corner, and he started to move. If Jessica didn't act now, it would be too late.

"Hi, Colby," she called.

What had she done? Guilt accompanied embarrassment, and she waited as Colby's head moved quickly from side to side, confused and searching for the voice.

He's so cute!

He saw her and called out, "Hi, Jessica."

"I'm feeding the kittens."

You idiot! What a stupid thing to say.

"I'm helping your father dig up a couple of tree stumps. I have to get some tools to loosen up the roots first."

"I could use a hand. The kittens are hungry, and Maisie's not feeding. And Ella's dead."

"Ella?"

Jessica nodded. "She's one of the kittens."

After a brief silence, Colby shrugged his shoulders. "I guess there's no rush. Is Ella up there?"

"Yeah, she's right here."

Boys!

She had a litter of kittens to feed, tiny little balls of fluff, and all Colby cared about was the one that had died. But he was strolling across strips of sunlight to the short ladder. Butterflies fluttered in Jessica's stomach as she dusted the wooden floor beside her with the palm of her hand.

Just then, panic hit her.

Colby would want to explore the hayloft and would surely look in her cedar chest, where he would see Cassandra and read Alison's diaries. She would look so immature, sitting in her secret place and feeding the kittens. What was she thinking? And what could she possibly talk about to a boy two years older than her?

Colby's head appeared at the top of the ladder, and he looked around. "Where's Ella?"

Jessica nodded to the side. "I put her over there."

Colby stepped onto the hayloft, took a few steps, and crouched down. Jessica tried to swallow the guilt she felt from looking at the strong shoulders and back that pressed against Colby's shirt.

"Cool." He stood up and, with a smile, crossed the hayloft, lowered his back against the bales of hay beside Jessica, and stretched his legs out straight, almost touching her. When Spike released the bottle, Jessica set him down, and he wobbled back to the hay. Colby was so close that Jessica could hear his breath. Her mind swirled, and she felt giddy. She wanted him to smile at her and say sweet things, wanted him to look at her and touch her, but mostly there was just wild confusion. She scooped her hand under a kitten that rubbed against her leg and lifted him to her lap, where he kneaded her waist and rubbed his head against her belly.

"Bubbles is hungry," she said.

"Bubbles?"

"Yeah." Jessica smiled. "He's kind of round, and he bounces a lot." She lifted the small gray-and-white bundle and held him out. "Why don't you feed him?"

Colby held out his open hands, a confused expression on his face.

"Let me show you," she said and slid across the inches that separated them. Her bare shoulder pressed against the muscles under Colby's shirt. Surely he could feel her heart pounding, the heat radiating from a face fit to burst with excitement? When their legs touched, Jessica thought she would explode.

Jeff Parker, her freshman-year crush, had been in her grade and so had been easier to talk to, easier to touch. One time last year, she had leaned on him and pressed against his back as she had reached around for a book on the desk in front of him, and she felt embarrassed whenever she remembered letting him hug her from behind for a reason she could no longer recall, allowing his hand to rest on her butt for a few seconds. It had been thrilling, but it had been in the classroom and safe, and very different from what she was doing with Colby. Today, her touch was an invitation, that much she knew, but an invitation to do what, she wasn't sure. With her heart in her throat, she put her hand around Bubbles.

"You do it like this," she said. Surely Colby could hear her voice quaking.

She laid Bubbles on his back on Colby's hand and held out the bottle. The kitten grabbed the nipple and sucked.

"Here, you take it," she said, and with her chest pounding, guided the older boy's hand to the bottle.

Jessica remembered a fantasy that she had never told her father and that Alison would have forgotten. It was a fantasy she had outgrown but that in some strange way still hung on in the corners of her imagination, surviving the havoc that puberty had wreaked on her emotions. She had dreamed of a prince riding up to the farm on a white stallion and sweeping her off her feet—Pastor Kidd, leader of the Church of the Epistles in Wilkeston, was king of her community. Could his son be her prince?

She slid her hand down the bottle to rest on Colby's hand and didn't resist as his leg pressed back against hers. She studied his face, whose flatness offered simplicity and whose breadth spoke of openness and honesty. The red hair and freckles gave it an air of novelty and perhaps a touch of humor, but above all, the face was just Colby, and when he was around, she tingled all over and fumbled and dropped things. Her crush on him was six months old, and she still didn't really know why she liked him. Now that she thought about it, there were plenty of muscle-bound boys: the school fielded a whole football team of them, and many of them were taller. If it was "cute" or "handsome" that she was after, she should have been drawn to Philip Darcy or Josh Delegance, and yet no one made her feel the way Colby did. Was this what being in love felt like?

"How old is he?"

"Four weeks."

Colby watched the kitten suck for some time, then looked up at Jessica and said, "He's cute. How many have you got?"

"Three." Jessica gazed helplessly at Colby, paralyzed by fear and wonder. Even her monosyllabic answers made her voice shake. She tried to summon the courage to speak a full sentence, tried to compose one, but Colby spoke first.

"You've been crying."

His hand moved toward Jessica's cheek, and she flinched. She wanted him to touch her and yet was unbearably nervous. She forced herself to sit still in the thrill of anticipation. Tender and light, the back of a finger wiped away a tear and then stroked her cheek again, although no tear remained.

"I'm sorry. I've probably been really insensitive about Ella, haven't I?"

Swallowing hard, Jessica fought to keep her voice steady as she replied, "No, you haven't."

"Are you sure? 'Cause if I have been, you know… "

Jessica didn't know, but it didn't matter. "No, you're fine. I'm just glad you're here."

Jessica knew she was out of control and speaking gibberish, but she couldn't tear her eyes away from Colby's. No one had ever looked at her like this before: it was a look of want, of need.

"You know, you've got a real pretty nose. I don't know where you get it from. Your mom has that long ridge," he said, and they both laughed. "But yours is real cute."

He put the bottle and the kitten aside, and Bubbles scurried away. Colby's touch on Jessica's nose was tender, not at all what she had expected, and the little things he said were funny. He moved his finger up to her forehead and ran it back down her small, upturned nose. Jessica was suddenly conscious that her hand still rested on Colby's and that it felt fat and heavy, her leg awkward against his. Colby raised his finger and tapped the tip of her nose ever so gently, and then tapped again. They both smiled, and their eyes met again.

"I could gaze into your eyes all day long."

"Dad has hazel eyes, too." Jessica felt herself floating, the barn and her body strangely unreal. She was in the presence of her prince, and they were as one. Her hand was no longer numb, her leg no longer inadequate; instead, they were irrelevant, as the whole universe was reduced to Colby's gaze. His finger slipped from Jessica's nose to her lip. She laid her head back on the hay.

"You have beautiful hair." He ran his fingers through the dark mane that was Jessica's pride and joy, pulling it forward so it cascaded over her shoulders, blowing a soft breeze onto her ears. With a familiar smooth slipping sensation, her hair slid back off her cheeks and shoulders. She smiled.

Colby turned his shoulders, tilted his head, and eased his mouth toward Jessica's. Sitting on the loose hay, the sultry humidity of late summer clinging to her clothes, the smell of the farm filling her nostrils, Jessica realized that her moment of magic had arrived. Colby tipped her head back. Jessica closed her eyes, and their lips met, opening up a blissful blackness into which Jessica melted. She had not known such beauty or pleasure was possible and wanted it to last forever. The world disappeared, and she disappeared with it, into the unknowing cloud of the kiss. Her fairytale ending had arrived; her prince had come.

The hand on her knee slid up her thigh and under the hem of her skirt.

This was not the way it was supposed to happen. The mystery of the kiss shriveled, and Jessica dropped her hand firmly onto Colby's fingers as she pulled away from his mouth. Colby lifted himself from her and raised his head. Jessica expected to see the softness of his last gaze, but it was gone, replaced by an intensity that scared her. She started to sit up, but Colby placed his hand gently on her shoulder, arresting her movement without pressing. The softness returned to his eyes.

"It's okay, I'm not going to hurt you," he said, removing his hand. "I just want to make you happy." He brushed her hair from her face and stroked her cheek, then ran the backs of his fingers up her arms, straightened the hem of her skirt, and, with just the tips of his fingers, touched her thighs.

It was wrong, and yet she tingled.

"Colby," she said as she looked down at her crumpled dress, "I've never done anything like this before."

"It's okay to be nervous; I am too. I really like you, Jessica. You're cute and pretty and funny."

Jessica just sat, letting Colby stroke her arm. On the rare occasions her father had spoken of boys, he had warned her of their ways and told her that they only wanted one thing. But was this so wrong? After all, Colby had backed off when she had asked, and Alison had gone much further than this, anyway. Besides, the kiss had been wonderful. Jessica relaxed and laid back against the hay, allowed her head to fall back and her arms to drop to the ground.

"I'd like to kiss you again, Jessica; can I do that?"

She gazed up at Colby and nodded; that is exactly what she wanted. He rolled forward, and she closed her eyes, wrapped her arms around his shoulders, and let her mouth melt into his. Her arms tightened and held him close while she ran her hands up and down his back. She let him slide her down to lie on the floor of the hayloft, her right leg entwining with his left. She had not realized it was possible to join with another human being in such an intimate way.

Colby's hands explored, wandering to places that had never been touched by a boy before, but when they returned to Jessica's hemline, she resisted, pulling herself back from paradise, and pressed on his chest. She opened her eyes as Colby let her push him up to a kneeling position.

Then he reached down and undid his belt and zipper.

Jessica's hands rose to her mouth, and she gasped, paralyzed. When she was able to move again, she averted her gaze: she had never seen a man naked, not even in the movies her mother disapproved of her watching. "Colby, what are you doing? Stop it." She dropped her hands to the ground and started to push herself away, but Colby put his index finger on her lips.

"Shhhh."

His whisper was just enough to make Jessica think twice. She glanced at his freckled face before closing her eyes tightly and tucking her head once more into her curled-up arms. The Colby of her dreams who had promised a home far away where kittens did not die, where princes and princesses lived happily ever after, was fading.

"It's okay, Jessica."

She had only wanted to let him kiss her, and yet they had lain together on the ground. She had held him close and rubbed against him with that strange, rocking motion, and it had been wonderful, but she did not understand what was happening. Even Alison's intimate accounts of what boys did when she let them take off her bra and what had happened when Jake had put his hand down her panties had not prepared Jessica for this. She was terrified and wanted to stop, but she had led Colby this far. The prudishness of her upbringing met in terrible ambivalence with the need to sacrifice herself. It was because of her that they were lying on the floor, because of her that Colby wanted to continue.

"It'll be all right, Jessica."

Jessica was afraid and neither moved nor spoke.

"Let's just take it one step at a time, and you tell me when to stop, okay?"

The tips of Colby's fingers stroked her raised calves. She shivered and lowered her feet to the floor beside him, knees raised. His fingers ran past her knee and stroked her thighs, up to, but not crossing, the hemline. She laid her head back on the ground and tried to relax. Colby's hands rested on Jessica's hips, then circled her belly, his thumbs caressing her.

"I'm going to lie down with you, okay?"

She sensed Colby's weight shift and felt him sit down beside her. When his hand touched her cheek, he whispered, "You're so beautiful." The hand stroked her hair, and he cooed, "You're the most beautiful woman I've ever seen."

Jessica shuddered. Dad had been there for every difficult moment in her life, but he couldn't help now, and she had spurned Alison's advice. What was she supposed to do?

"You're crying again." The hand brushed her cheek once more, and she let her arms fall away, though her fists stayed clenched. Her eyes remained closed as Colby lowered his body to the ground beside her, laid a leg across hers. He stroked her cheek again, ran his fingers through her hair.

Jessica was terrified, yet unable to move.

Colby kissed the tears that trickled out of the corners of her eyes, and Jessica choked out the words, "Colby, don't." Then he kissed her cheeks, and, on the verge of sobbing, she begged, "Colby, please."

"It's okay, baby, just one step at a time."

When his lips touched hers, Jessica started to mumble in protest, but he pressed, and she relented. How could she not? She let his lips open hers and she even put her arms around his shoulders. She was losing the will over her body. Colby rotated in increments until he was lying on her once more.

Finally, Jessica's resolve hardened, and she decided she couldn't let go this go any further. She released her arms, relaxed her lips, and waited for him to stop.

But he didn't.

Colby's head slid beside hers, his hot breath now on her shoulder. He pressed his thighs hard against the inside of her legs, and Jessica started to struggle, slid her hands between their bodies, and pushed up on his shoulders, but Colby used his weight and balance to hold her to the ground. With one hand, he reached down and lifted her skirt. She felt his hand on her belly, his warmth below that, and she squirmed and tried to roll him off, but he was too strong. His hand slid off her belly and onto her hips.

He ripped off her underpants.

Eyes wide in terror, Jessica fought. She tossed her hips furiously and beat at Colby with her hands while her feet flailed and kicked, but she couldn't break free. Colby held her hips to the ground and her legs apart. Jessica wanted to scream, but what did she have to scream about? Had she not brought this on herself? If her parents found her like this, they would be horrified.

Nonetheless, Jessica's instincts took over, and she filled her lungs.

Colby placed a hand over her mouth and smothered her cry. She tossed her head and tried to bite his hand, tried to pull it away from her face with her own hand, but before she could do so, it was too late to scream. The sharp, unfamiliar, and almost unbearable pain seemed to last an eternity, though she knew it was only a few moments. Colby's weight lifted, and Jessica slid out from under him to shuffle the short distance into the corner, where she yanked her dress down over her tucked-up legs so violently that she felt the seams give. She wrapped her arms around her knees to hold them tightly against her chest and then curled up to die, her lips quivering, loose hay clinging to her clothes, her tousled hair, her skin. She glanced up and saw Colby fumbling with his trousers but looking at her, his eyes wide and his face white. When their eyes met, he staggered backward as if she had hit him.

"I'm sorry," he mumbled. "Jessica, I'm so sorry."

She didn't respond. He finished dressing himself, and after a moment, extended a shaking hand and stepped toward Jessica, but Jessica curled up more tightly and pulled away. Colby stared at her, his shoulders wilting and his mouth hanging open, before letting his arms fall, limp, to his sides. After an awful silence, he took two steps back, then turned and lunged for the stepladder.

Jessica heard a thump as Colby slid down the last few steps and fell to the floor, then a clatter and a muttered curse, presumably him dropping the implements he had come in to seek in the first place. A crash and another outcry sounded like him stumbling into the tractor, and then with fast footsteps, he was gone.

What did Jessica's prince think of her now? She had fought him at the last, but not until it was too late. She had allowed—invited—him to violate her and yet in the end had rejected him, and Colby's hasty departure told her that this prince would not be carrying her off into the sunset. Jessica no longer wanted him to do so anyway. Having flaunted herself and tempted the pastor's son to lie with her, she was guilty, like Eve, of original sin, and, like Eve, she would have to face the consequences of her disobedience.

Spike, Bubbles, and Blizzard nuzzled up to Jessica. Were they still hungry, or did they sense that something was wrong? They mewed and rubbed their noses on her legs, but rather than offering consolation, they only reinforced the emptiness of loss.

Chapter Two

The door of the hardware store jingled as Will Jackson opened it to leave, and Dwight, the storeowner, grunted and returned to his catalog. S-hooks and short lengths of rope were highly profitable items, but in such small quantities—eighteen dollars and sixty-seven cents—Dwight would need a lot of visitors to make money.

But he looked up again, excited, at the sound of voices, and saw Will Jackson holding the door open for another customer before exiting. Darlene, who was kneeling to tidy the window display, looked up at the visitor.

"Can I help you, sir?" she asked.

"Yes please, miss." The customer's smile was as wide as the sunrise, his voice filled with the cool of early-morning mist on the river. "My toilet-tank washer is leaking, and I think I need to replace it."

"Yes, sir, let me show you where they are." Darlene stood to lead the way, her short top grazing a butterfly tattoo that peeked above the back of her jeans. Dwight smiled at his young assistant as she passed the enclosed checkout area in which he stood, sentry-like, commanding the glass doorway and the displays in the store windows that flanked it. He mumbled an inarticulate greeting to his customer and watched Darlene lead him up the main aisle of the store.

One eye lingering on the swing of Darlene's hips, Dwight tried to concentrate on the shambling figure that followed her: Rugged and wiry, the visitor wore clothes that hung off him like a burlap sack. His jacket, once tweed, was now a nondescript brown, and its pockets were weighed down and misshapen by the miscellany that filled them to overflowing. The customer's jeans hung loose like an elephant's skin.

"Here you are, sir; this is the kit you want."

"Can't I just buy the washer, miss? Everything else is working fine."

"I'm sorry, sir, it only comes in a kit."

The customer reached out and tilted the package that she held in her hand so he could see the price tag.

"But that's almost eight dollars for something that should only cost a few cents."

"I'm sorry about that, sir, but it's an integrated unit. The valves aren't sold separately."

Dwight smiled as the figure rummaged in his pockets, shedding scraps of paper along with coins and notes. After a while, the customer appeared satisfied that he had assembled enough money in his hand and said, "Okay, miss, I guess I'll take it. Thank you." He bent down to pick up his debris, stood, and took the toilet-tank system from Darlene before moving toward Dwight, who watched, amused, as the man wearing grubby clothes and a bushy, graying beard approached.

Although Dwight occasionally encountered his visitor around town, he had not seen the man up close since they were both teenagers, and he was taken aback by a presence that the youth he had known had not possessed. Sam was taller than he looked from behind, though still not a big man, and he radiated the calm confidence of one completely contented with his place in the world. When Sam was almost at the counter, Dwight spoke. "Hi, Sam."

"Hi, Dwight; how's Cheryl? And those two boys of yours? They must be almost out of high school now."

"Cheryl's fine, thanks." Dwight was surprised that Sam remembered his wife and kids, but putting the thought aside, he took the toilet-tank system, rang it up, and placed it in a bag. "Clark's fifteen, and Robbie's seventeen; they're both as big as I am. With tax, that'll be eight dollars and forty-six cents." He held out the bag.

The bright eyes shining out from under Sam's hair, much darker than his beard, made Dwight sense that he had Sam's complete attention. He felt at once comforted and exposed as Sam studied his face—a face Dwight knew to be flat and featureless, softened by years in the store and too much good food, with eyes that the mirror every morning told him were dulled. After a long pause, Sam looked down, took the bag, and held out a handful of crumpled notes and coins.

"This is the right amount," Sam said. "I'm sorry things are difficult for you right now, Dwight."

Dwight clenched the money tightly, his throat constricting. How did Sam know? Dwight hadn't said a word. Without looking up, he shoved the money in the drawer and heard the store door jangle. Despite the effort he put into his appearance, keeping his graying hair neatly brushed and his face clean-shaven, the sorrow Dwight tried to hide must still be obvious.

With a rustle, Darlene stood across the counter from him. "Who was that, and what did he mean, 'Things are difficult right now?'"

Darlene's perfume filled Dwight's nostrils. He stared into her gray eyes, heavily decorated with mascara and just inches from his own, and felt himself slipping into a vortex of lust. With a resolute sigh, he pulled himself up straight and tidied the counter.

"I don't know what he meant," Dwight replied, "but yes, I do know him. That's Old Sam."

"Oh, Old Sam, I've heard of him. He's the weirdo lives alone out near the creek on the other side of town, right? Keeps to himself?"

Dwight shrugged. "About twenty years ago, he was really active in the Church of the Epistles."

"He doesn't go any more?"

"To church? Hardly." Dwight leaned on the counter, shook his head, and said, "I haven't spoken to Old Sam in a long time." His gaze drifted off into the store, and he continued, "You know, I don't even know why we call him that. He's not old and his name isn't Sam; it's Emmanuel. Manny, we used to call him. He's actually a few years younger than I am, and I used to know him pretty well. When he was baptized—that must've been twenty-five years ago, now—he was real clever and a fire-and-brimstone fundamentalist; looked like he might even become a preacher. But then he went to college, and everything changed. He left the church after a couple of years. What was it now?.... That's right, he said he'd found a 'deeper Christianity in everyday life,' or something like that. His folks were so disappointed that they cut off his funding. They didn't have much money anyway, and it had been a real sacrifice for them to send him. I think he went off to live in some monastery. Anyway, he came back to Wilkeston a few years ago when his parents got sick, but he never came to church, except to attend their funerals when they died. The poor things passed away within a year of each other. Then Sam bought that piece of land and put a cheap old trailer on it."

"So where does he work?"

Dwight looked up sharply, intrigued by the wistful tone in Darlene's voice. She was staring with misty eyes at the door, and Dwight's greedy gaze took advantage of her distraction. But all too soon she shook her head, and Dwight hurriedly looked back at her face. "I don't think he has a job," he said, "leastwise, he never used to. He lives on his own out there with that dog that he adopted, and he grows his own food."

"But he had some money?"

"He does odd jobs from time to time, and I think he may still have some of his parents' savings left over. You can see he hasn't bought any new clothes in years. Why are you so interested, anyway?"

Darlene shrugged. "Oh, I'm not, really; he just seemed liked he cared, you know? And he looks kind of weird, like that hermit on the cover of *Led Zep. Four.* I've just never seen him before, that's all." She stood up and pulled the bottom of her shirt down toward the ring in her navel, jostling her breasts and drawing Dwight's eyes to her cleavage as she did so. He looked back up at her face to confirm that she hadn't noticed his glance and changed the subject.

"It's quiet today, Darlene."

"Yes, sir. I think we've only had three customers who bought anything, including Old Sam."

"Why don't you go get yourself some lunch?"

She glanced at her watch. "Thanks, I will. I'm supposed to be meeting my roommates, so I'll be back in an hour?"

"That'll be fine," he said, nodding.

"Great. I'll see you later." Darlene strode around the front desk and toward the door, and Dwight studied her from behind as she left the store: Her jeans were low enough and tight enough to suggest the improbability of underwear; her small, navy-blue t-shirt was so thin that he could see that her bra, which held her breasts in what he found to be an offensively promiscuous manner, was itself insubstantial; and her blond, highlighted hair must have taken hours to brush and spray into position. Although she would never parade the runways of Paris or New York, Darlene still knew how to make a man's pulse race.

Dwight suppressed his lust and forced himself to think of Darlene professionally. He had given her a job seven years ago as a reluctant favor to her father, a fellow member of the Church of the Epistles, when she had dropped out of high school, and the wild and rebellious youngster had surprised him by being among the most sensible and conscientious workers he had ever had, even during the two years of her stormy marriage and sudden divorce. He would hate to lose her, but although she was cheap labor, unless his business picked up, he would have no choice. He kept putting off the decision to let her go, since it would appear to everyone, erroneously and despite everything Dwight would say to the contrary, that he had done so because she had slackened. Dwight did not want to subject his employee to unemployment in Wilkeston's slow economy, but he couldn't keep waiting for her to get remarried and have a kid.

With a sigh, Dwight straightened the register tape and confirmed that it had recorded only three transactions. He performed some quick mental math and shook his head: $75 for a sunny summer morning was not good.

The doorbell rang again, and Dwight looked up.

"Hi, I wonder if you can help me. I'm looking for a couple of things."

Dwight felt self-conscious as the visitor's eyes ran from what had once been sandy hair down his tall, muscular, if slightly overweight, figure. The visitor pulled a scrap of paper from his pocket. "I need a spray-nozzle for a hose, some picture hangers, and a set of screwdrivers," he announced in a flat accent that Dwight placed as Yankee.

"The picture hangers are right over there," Dwight said, pointing down a short aisle, "and the screwdrivers are down this way." He led the way through the store. "Are you new to town?" he asked over his shoulder.

"We bought a vacation home on the lake."

Dwight bit his tongue. Folks from the big cities, mostly Atlanta and Chattanooga, were building new homes at a rapid pace, but although this activity had stimulated certain pockets of the local economy, it had not helped Dwight's hardware store one bit. The contractors, like the proliferating real estate agents who grinned down from billboards and the lawyers and architects who drove in from Atlanta, hired cheap, transient labor and bought their materials and tools from the encroaching superstores. The new builders were the bane of Dwight's existence.

"Here are my screwdrivers. Hoses and nozzles are on that aisle right there." Dwight pointed again.

The smartly dressed man said, "Thank you very much," and began browsing through the screwdrivers. Dwight returned to the front desk and a few minutes later lifted his head as he heard his customer approaching the till. Gracious. The man's hands were full.

"Did you find everything okay, sir?"

"Yes, I did, thank you. It's a nice place you've got here."

"Thank you, sir." Dwight picked up the smaller items and rang them up. "I do my best."

The screwdrivers were an expensive set, and the vacationer had also picked up a top-of-the-line pair of garden shears. Dwight was going to more than double the day's take on this one transaction. He pressed the total key. "It's a pretty day out there to be trimming hedges. That'll be eighty-seven dollars and twelve cents."

"Do you take this?"

Dwight looked down at the hand being extended toward him and saw with a sinking feeling that he was being offered an American Express, which would not only cost him three percent off the top, almost three dollars, but would also subject him to slow payment and a heightened risk of chargebacks. "Do you have anything else, sir?" Dwight looked up, his blue eyes pleading, and explained, "Amex is very expensive for a small place like this."

The stranger smiled. "I suppose it is. Cash is best for you, isn't it?"

"Yes, sir, it is. Thank you, sir; I appreciate it."

Dwight watched the stranger leave, and as the door jingled, he sighed. He'd been open since seven-thirty that morning and had only taken in a little over one hundred and fifty dollars. A few disappointing calculations confirmed what Dwight already knew: This would likely be the third year in a row that his net take from the store had not covered his living expenses.

A few years ago, a Home Depot had been built fifty miles away, and Dwight had been concerned, but it hadn't affected his business as much as he had feared. The real hit had come two years later, when a Walmart had gone up fifteen miles away on this side of Baxton, a town which, with a population of five thousand, was twice the size of Wilkeston. Had the store offered only a narrow range of goods, his core customers wouldn't have made the drive just to save a few pennies, but Walmart sold everything, so it had not only siphoned off his core business, the large numbers of small purchases but had also changed people's habits. People in Wilkeston no longer spent their Saturdays working around the houses and yards, stopping by his store for the odds and ends that they needed at the last minute, but instead took the family out to Walmart for the afternoon, to spend hours browsing and buying junk they hadn't even known existed.

Dwight's misery was interrupted by the phone.

"Hi, Cook Hardware. Can I help you?"

"Hi, Dwight; it's Cheryl."

Dwight frowned. His wife never called him at the store, even less so now there was such a strain in their relationship, but he could hear fear in her voice.

"What's wrong, Cheryl?"

"Robbie's missing. I hadn't seen him all morning, so I just went to check in his room, but there's no sign of him." She sniffed and added, "Dwight, his bed hasn't even been slept in."

Dwight's frown turned to a scowl. This was the second time in the last year that their older son had been gone all night. The last time, Dwight had called the police and had been mortified when his son had turned up, unharmed and carefree, resolutely refusing to say where he had been.

"Dwight, I'm afraid. Did you hear about the bombing?"

Dwight gripped the phone tightly, though he was not sure what this could have to do with Robbie's disappearance. "What bombing?"

"It was an abortion clinic in Atlanta. No one was killed, though it sounds a miracle. Do you remember the last time Robbie went missing?"

"Yes, it was the night before the fellowship supper." Dwight growled. He remembered the night well because his anger at Robbie's attitude on his reappearance had been so powerful that he had taken it with him to the supper and caused a major scene. When Tom Bates had spoken right after the blessing of the morning's news and said, "Last night's bombing was divine judgment for the sins of the abortion clinic," Dwight had lashed out with his tongue, so much so that Tom still bore a grudge. Though he had no idea what the coincidence meant—Robbie going missing two nights, and a bombing in Atlanta on each occasion—he recognized the connection that Cheryl was drawing and felt he needed to be with her. "I'm on my way home," he said. "No, wait, I'm on my own in the store right now. I'll have to wait till Darlene gets back from lunch, but I'll be there as soon as I can."

"You do that," Cheryl said and hung up.

The taste of bile rose in the back of Dwight's throat, for he had not missed the bitterness in her voice, nor the clipped end of their conversation, a result of his mention of Darlene. How did Cheryl know that Dwight's heart skipped a beat every time he saw his store assistant?

But his thoughts returned to his missing son and to the bombing. He reaffirmed his belief that murder was not an acceptable punishment for the sin of abortion, and his mind became increasingly frantic as it tried to find reasons not to link Robbie to the bombings.

Darlene returned from lunch twenty minutes later, and as Dwight rushed out to go home, his thoughts turned to his store assistant. He wanted to protect Darlene from her immoral lifestyle and to save her soul, but he could not see how radicalism would help. Despite Darlene's promiscuity and her stubborn refusal to come to church, his heart told him that she was a good person who cared for others and worked hard: surely she deserved to be saved? But Dwight wasn't sure that Pastor Kidd—or Cheryl—would agree. For the rest of his short drive home, he tried to shake images of Darlene cavorting licentiously in the backseats of cars with drunken men and then being blown to pieces as she entered an abortion clinic.

He pulled up in front of his house, slammed the door of his pickup, and leaned against it to finish his Marlboro. The front door opened, and Cheryl stepped out onto the small porch. Dwight pushed himself upright, and walked toward his wife. He took a final drag of the cigarette and ignored the disgusted look Cheryl shot him as he flicked it into the unkempt yard. She leaned into his chest, and he wrapped his arms around her, holding his head protectively over hers.

"Where's Clark?" Dwight released his wife, and they walked into the house.

"He's at the park, playing football with some of his friends, and they're going out for pizza afterwards. You know how he loves the summer vacation."

Dwight snorted. Thought he had asked the whereabouts of his younger son, he was not really interested in Clark right now. Clark was a polite, compliant boy lacking Robbie's zealous and intolerant streak and who planned to go on to college and become a veterinarian. Rather, Dwight was worried about what his older boy was up to and how he, Dwight, was going to handle it. He was not willing to let Robbie live under his roof if the boy was going to behave like this.

Cheryl asked, "What are we going to do?"

Dwight had already decided, and, without a word, he made for Robbie's bedroom. He sensed, rather than heard, Cheryl follow him and stop behind him as he placed a hand on the handle of the closed door. He waited, motionless, while he composed himself.

"Are you sure this is the right thing to do?" asked Cheryl.

"Yes," was his stern reply. "We don't have a choice. So long as he's living in my house, I'm responsible for his actions." He turned to face his wife, and she took a step toward him. He released the doorknob to hold her hands and spoke more softly. "This is the second time Robbie's done his disappearing trick, and we need to know why. Whether or not he's involved in these bombings, my guess is he's in trouble, or going to be." He forced a smile but knew it was a weak one. "We can pretend he's planning a nice surprise, but you don't really believe that any more than I do, do you?" Cheryl lowered her eyes, shaking her head, as Dwight's voice fell to a whisper. "Anyway, that's a risk I'm prepared to take. I'm worried that boy's headed down a bad path. We need to do this, Cheryl, okay?" He squeezed her hands.

She nodded meekly and looked up at him again. He released her hands and she wiped away the tears that were trickling gently down her cheeks. "Dwight, what if we find something?" she asked.

Dwight's jaw hardened, and he turned to open the door.

It was a small room, dominated by a single bed in the corner farthest from the door that wore a non-descript brown quilt. A cheap desk next to it, adorned with a makeshift wooden crucifix, and a straight-backed wooden chair tucked underneath, served double duty a work surface and as a bedside table. The only other piece of furniture in the room was a battered chest of oak drawers. Facing the bed, a faded painting of the crucifixion in a baroque frame hung incongruously beside a lurid "P.O.D." rack poster.

Dwight began with the closet, Cheryl standing behind him, arms folded, as he looked on the shelf and under the shoes and then rifled the pockets of Robbie's jackets and trousers. When he found only loose change and a pack of gum, he turned his attention to the desk.

The first of two drawers was full of pens and bric-a-brac, a legacy of the materials Robbie had accumulated over his high school years, and the other was home to only his well-thumbed Bible. Dwight closed the drawers and examined the mound of papers on top of the desk. Roughly a foot high in the middle and sloping toward its edges, the disorganized pile comprised magazines new and old, newspapers, even old homework, that had accumulated over a considerable period of time. It was an intimidating sight, and Dwight studied it carefully before beginning, hoping to keep his search secret so as not to antagonize his son. "I'm not going to move any of this, Cheryl, I'm just going to look at the papers on top," he explained. Cheryl nodded and put her hand on his shoulder.

Dwight flicked through the layers and, with great care, pried out a loosely arranged stack of white pages that he guessed had been printed at the public library. They were unsorted and had turned-up corners, clumsy creases, and even stains on them; Robbie had never shown respect for books or papers other than his Bible. Dwight laid the stack on his lap, smoothed out the corners, and started to read. The first few pages were blank, but the next was a printed email with the title "God Wants You to Kill Fags." Dwight's jaw dropped, and with a sense of horror, he glanced over his shoulder at Cheryl, whose fingers now dug into his shoulder blades. He returned his attention to his lap and, transfixed, read an argument laced with Bible quotes that God hates homosexuals, that they deserve to die, and that it is therefore the duty of any true believer to eradicate them.

When he had seen enough, Dwight looked over his shoulder at Cheryl, who nodded, and he continued leafing through the pile. After a few similar pages, he came to one headed, "God Hates Sweden" and could not suppress a burst of embarrassed laughter, which he stifled as Cheryl squeezed his shoulder. Discomfort turned to a churning sickness in his stomach when he came to a series of documents bearing titles including "Abortion is Murder," "Those Who Perform Abortion Deserve the Death Penalty," and "Our National Disgrace—The Slaughter of the Unborn."

Feeling dizzy, Dwight slipped the pile back under the magazines and followed Cheryl back to the kitchen. As Cheryl sat at the table and hung her head, Dwight fell into the chair opposite, facing her in awkward silence and studying her face. They had kept company in this room for half their lives; how could they not talk after what they had just seen?

Cheryl had been so cute at sixteen, when he had fallen in love with her. He had graduated from high school three years earlier—she was five years younger than he—and had been his father's full-time assistant when Cheryl had first come into the store with her friends. He had been so clumsy and awkward, helping Suzie select a hammer, but with eyes only for Cheryl. A few days later, she had returned with her friends, but it hadn't been long before she started coming alone, and soon after, they were dating. She had been so much fun—a bubbly, happy teenager—back then. It had been the happiest time of his life, and Cheryl's energy had continued into their marriage and through the early years of their children, but somewhere along the way, she had lost her spark. Although she still had the perfectly complexioned movie-star face of her youth, she took little pride in it, never wearing make-up and keeping her naturally blond, full hair short and straight. She favored drab clothes that revealed little of the flesh that was unusually well shaped for a thirty-eight-year-old mother of two, and she rarely smiled. Why did they never talk any more? How had they grown so far apart?

His reflections drifted to the night before, and the sick lump in his stomach swelled.

After another slow day at the store, he had consoled himself with couple of beers, and when Cheryl had sneered at him, he had said, "I don't do it often."

But Cheryl had jumped on him. "Do you think I haven't seen you sneaking beer out back and hiding six-packs from me in the creek these last six months?" she had said.

Dwight's cheeks flushed just thinking about it.

The first time he had brought home beer had been so innocent, just a flash of color that caught his eye in the gas station after a really bad day. Even when the beer had become a habit, it had been a long time before he had kept his supply in the refrigerator. Instead, he had savored his moments of secret rebellion at the creek. Yet Cheryl had known all along.

Later last night, he had walked up behind Cheryl while she was working at the sink and had put his hands on her hips, kissed her on the back of her head, and rubbed himself against her ass. He believed occasional, and usually spontaneous, physical union with his wife to be an important part of their marriage.

But she had wriggled away, turned to face him, and placed her palms on his chest. "You know I love you," she had said, "but unless you want a houseful of children in your old age, we can't do that right now."

He had groaned, "Not this 'birth control is a sin' nonsense again," and Cheryl had begun one of her lectures.

"It's not nonsense," she had said, "I've told you, it's quite straightforward. When God commands us, 'be fruitful and multiply,' he means that birth control is a sin. I don't know how I failed to see it all these years, but I'm grateful to Pastor Kidd for explaining it. We'll get the hang of this natural family planning soon enough."

Dwight smiled to himself as he remembered his persistence: "Yeah, well I think that if you look at Scripture the way you're interpreting it, you have to conclude that abstinence is a sin, too. Anyway, I'm prepared to take the risk of children tonight. Come on, let's go to bed," had been his riposte.

But Cheryl had not been interested. "These moments of weakness are sent to try us, Dwight," she had said. "I'm sorry this is so difficult for you, but we must be strong. I'm sure that if you pray for understanding, you'll receive it."

"How come it was okay all these years, and now it's wrong?" he had snapped. "You've tried to explain it before, but I still don't get it."

"It wasn't okay before, but we were led astray by that terrible woman, Margaret Sanger. She invented the birth control pill and founded Planned Parenthood, and then she split the church and started the 'right to privacy' arguments that led to Roe versus Wade. Her promotion of artificial birth control led directly to the abomination of legalized abortion. And they're doing it in Atlanta today."

Dwight felt a hand on his drawing him back to the present and looked up at Cheryl, who had reached across the table. He fought the instinct to withdraw his hand. So many little things about her had started to annoy him: the way she straightened his clothes before he left in the morning, the slurping noise she made when sucking hot chocolate off the top of her nighttime mug, the way she pampered the boys. And now it was her uninvited touch. Why was he alienated from her? Disgusted with himself, by force of will, he did not pull away but instead looked at her and forced himself to break the silence.

"I'm going to have a serious talk with that boy when he gets in."

"It'll be the first time you've spoken to him in years."

"What's that supposed to mean?" He pulled his hands away sharply.

"That boy needs a father."

"So all this is my fault?" Dwight's jaw tightened as he glared at Cheryl.

"You spend too much time worrying about that darned store."

"In case you haven't noticed, the store's not doing very well right now, and someone has to pay the bills around here."

Cheryl shook her head. When she spoke, her voice was tinged with sadness. "The man I married twenty years ago wouldn't have whined. He would have done something about it."

"Cheryl, I'm trying," Dwight pleaded, crushed by her disappointment. "What do you want me to do?"

She threw her hands in the air and tossed her gaze up to the ceiling. "I don't know: sell the store and get a job; rob a bank; anything. Just stop moping about how your parents left you for your sister."

"That's not fair." Dwight was angry now. "And anyway, that was ten years ago."

"But you can't give it up." Cheryl leaned forward and glared at him. "You keep trying to prove that you can run the store better than your dad did, and you can't. They're not coming back, Dwight; not now, not ever."

Cheryl had never spoken to him like this before. Perhaps the trauma of rifling in Robbie's room had animated her, but regardless, Dwight had to regain control of the conversation, had to direct it away from these uncomfortable subjects. "This has nothing to do with my parents," he said.

"You think Robbie can't see that you're weak and insecure? If you can't even face up to your *own* problems, how can you possibly understand what he's going through?"

"I don't want to talk about this anymore." Although it was only early afternoon, Dwight needed a break, and he stood up and stomped over to the refrigerator.

His movement was met with bitter laughter. "That's it, run away," Cheryl jeered. "And take your beer with you. Oh, a whole six-pack, and in the middle of the day, too. I've really gotten to you, haven't I?"

"To heck with you."

Dwight looked over his shoulder with alarm and cowered but saw to his relief that Cheryl hadn't moved. By some kind of miracle, the words that had sprung fully formed into his head as speech appeared not to have been spoken. Dwight needed to be careful, for his discontent was growing and his behavior becoming more rebellious, and it was only a matter of time before he did something to really shock his wife of twenty years. He grabbed his jacket from the hook by the back door and, after checking there were cigarettes in the pocket, spat out "I'm his father, and he will listen to me good and proper." The words were intended as bullets, but Dwight knew before hearing Cheryl's chuckle that he was firing blanks. He recognized his cowardice, but nevertheless, he rushed away from the discomfort of his wife's insights. He hadn't even reached the creek before he opened the first can, raised it to his lips, and let relief course through his veins. He put the rest of the cans in a pool in the creek to keep them cool, lit a cigarette, and settled in.

Cheryl was wrong. This had nothing to do with his parents leaving, though they had hurt him deeply. He choked back tears as he remembered the short-lived euphoria he had experienced those many years ago when Dad had told him the store was his. Dwight had taken it as a gesture of Dad's confidence in his business acumen and a reward for his loyalty to the family business, but the following morning, Dad told him the rest of the truth, and it had crushed him.

Raleigh!

He had always known that his younger sister Rose-Marie was his parents' favorite, but when she had stayed out east after finishing college and married that doctor, he had thought that his parents would recognize the loyalty of their oldest child and only son. Instead, they had spent three years secretly planning their own departure. Now they sent him pictures of his "gorgeous nephews" that he tossed in the trash and letters praising their talents that he threw away unread, though not without bitter thoughts of the opportunities Rose-Marie's girls would have in the university center of North Carolina that his own children would not. He remembered, too, his dream of opening a second Cook Hardware store in Baxton and of eventually building an empire that would stretch all the way to Raleigh. But he had abandoned his dream six months after the Walmart had begun its slow asphyxiation of his business.

None of that mattered now, though. He had to deal with his miscreant son, and Cheryl's misdirected rage at him wasn't helping. He didn't have the emotional energy to deal with her anxieties right now, so he lit a cigarette, opened another can of beer, and listened to the creek.

The sound of a car engine didn't disturb him, but the slamming door and familiar voice did. Robbie was home. Seething, Dwight put down his beer, dropped his cigarette to the ground, and stormed into the house. He marched through the kitchen, heading straight for Robbie's room.

Robbie's door was open, and he was lying on his bed. He lowered his Bible and looked over the top to greet his father with a smile. "Hi, Dad."

Dwight reeled, but not for the reason he had expected. His first glimpse of Robbie was like an old photograph of himself. His son had the strong nose and forehead that Dwight remembered from his own youth, the same narrow face, angular cheeks, and pure blue eyes. His sandy hair was thick and wavy, though much longer than Dwight had ever allowed his own to grow. For a split second, Dwight yearned for something lost: the sharp edges that had vanished from his own face, now flat and featureless, lost along with the thrill of living.

But then Dwight saw something alien staring at him from Robbie's face and recognized anger and intolerance.

"Where have you been?" Dwight demanded.

Robbie shrugged. "With a couple of friends."

"Where?"

"Sorry, but I can't tell you."

"What do you mean, you can't tell me?"

Robbie shrugged again. "It's pretty simple: I can't tell you."

"Your mother and I have been worried sick. So long as you live in this house, you'll follow basic rules of courtesy, and they include coming home at night." Dwight's temper had snapped, and his voice was rising. He felt Cheryl arrive behind him and place a quieting hand on his shoulder. "Now, where the heck have you been?"

"I told you, I can't say."

"Does it have anything to do with this?" In his fury, Dwight threw caution to the wind and strode to Robbie's bedside table. He grabbed the sheaf of pages that he had found earlier and waved them at his son.

Robbie sat bolt upright and glared at his father. "You've been searching my room?" He looked around wildly, his eyes settling nowhere. "What else have you done?"

"That's none of your business. Now tell me where you've been."

"No."

"Robbie, this is pretty simple." Dwight forced himself to speak calmly, though his voice was shaking. He felt Cheryl's hand squeeze his shoulder, whether to restrain or support him he neither knew nor cared. "Offering your parents simple respect is a cost of living under this roof, and that includes letting us know where you are and what you're doing. If you can't do that, you'll have to find somewhere else to live until you can." He tossed the papers back onto the pile, ignoring those that fell to the floor. As he stormed out, he spoke over his shoulder. "I want you to think about what I've just said and come find me when you're ready to talk. Come on, Cheryl, let's leave him alone for a while."

Dwight put his hand on the doorknob, stepped aside to let his wife leave, and closed the door with a crash. They retired to the kitchen, where Dwight slumped at the table, shaking, while Cheryl assumed her familiar pose at the sink. They remained silent, Dwight's mind a torrent of self-justification for his speech, composing and refining biting comments that he would throw at Robbie when the boy emerged.

After almost an hour, unusual clattering noises came from Robbie's room, making Cheryl and Dwight glance at each other with frowns. Eventually, Robbie's door clicked open and footsteps approached from down the hall. Dwight looked up at Cheryl with a smug grin, and together, they faced the kitchen door to hear Robbie's confession.

But instead of a contrite youth with a hanging face, they saw a young man with several extra layers of clothing, a fully packed rucksack on his back, his school bag on one shoulder, and a large, heavily packed sports bag on the other.

"Where are you going?"

"To live somewhere else."

"Why you… " Dwight slid his chair back and started to stand but was stopped by Cheryl's hand on his shoulder and the firmness of Robbie's retort.

"Dad, listen. You may not be able to understand why I can't tell you where I've been, but I can't, and I can't have you rummaging in my private things, so I think it's best for everyone if I leave. I love you all very much, and I'll miss you, but I have to do this. Some day, you're going to be very proud of me.

"I'm going to be staying in town, so I'll see you around. Maybe you'll even invite me over for dinner sometime?"

Dwight sat in stunned silence while Robbie walked past him, put his hand on his mother's shoulder, and reached round to peck her on the cheek. "Bye, Mom," the boy said, and then walked straight out of the house, closing the back door behind him. Cheryl's hand left Dwight's shoulder, and moments later he heard sobbing sounds. He rose.

"Cheryl," he crooned. Her hands covered her face, and her chest was starting to heave. He placed his hands on her shoulders, and repeated her name, "Cheryl—"

"Leave me alone." Her voice was harsh. She ripped herself away from his grasp to step back, and her hands parted, allowing her to glare at Dwight. Her eyes darted around as if looking for something and not finding it. Dwight waited, mute, and eventually took a step toward her.

"Just leave me alone," she choked, then turned and ran to the bedroom.

Chapter Three

Jessica awoke to the sound of conversation. Her eyes snapped open as she recalled her trauma, and they darted around to ensure her safety. She was sprawled on the floor of the hayloft but was alone and must have cried herself to sleep. Her mind was a jumble of confused and terrified thoughts, but she lifted her head to listen as she recognized her father's voice in the yard outside.

"Thanks, Colby. I couldn't have done it without you. Here, let me put those away."

The sound of Colby's name brought Jessica's feelings into focus and filled her with guilt. She pulled herself into a sitting position and crossed her legs, absently noting that the kittens had left her and realizing that if Dad and Colby had removed the tree stumps, she must have been in the hayloft for a long time. Jessica wanted to call out, but what could she say? I seduced Colby? I flirted with him and kissed him and pulled him on top of me until… Until *that* happened? Sure, she had resisted, but not until the very end, not until it had been too late. If she called out, Colby would denounce her for the slut she was. No, she couldn't say anything.

A car door slammed, an engine fired, and gravel crunched under the wheels of Pastor Kidd's large sedan as it tooled down the drive. Jessica's heart pounded, and her mind raced as she anticipated Dad coming into the barn; what would she tell him? She glanced down into the barn at his full head of gray hair and check shirt as he crossed beneath her, laden with pick and axe, and she banged her forehead against the heels of her hands, looking for inspiration, for hope. There was none; how could there be?

Dad's heavy boots chafed on the rungs of the ladder, and Jessica felt a thud as he fell to his knees in front of her. After a moment of silence, he asked, "Jess, what's the matter?"

She didn't respond.

He placed a hand gently on her chin and lifted her face toward his. Jessica let her hands fall away so she could look into the warm, round face with its familiar creases and deep hazel eyes. She raised a hand to Dad's cheek and cradled the face she loved, a face that radiated the compassion and comfort of years of confidences, the face from which she had inherited the small features that Colby had admired. She was almost smiling when Dad's brow furrowed and he sniffed, looked around, and took in the blood and stain on her dress. She followed his roaming eyes until they found the ripped underpants lying a few feet away, and any possibility of joy that had been left in her heart was torn out. After a moment's confusion, Dad looked at her with a question in his eyes, and Jessica buried her face once more in her hands. Dad threw his arms around her, and she responded, clinging desperately to him, but her soul was cracked, and the life he poured into her ran straight through. Soon—too soon for Jessica—Dad pulled back. Jessica let her arms fall to her sides again.

"Jessica, what happened?"

Poor Dad, he looked so hopeless, and she had no idea where to start. How could she tell him that his cherished child, God's gift to his middle age, had submitted herself, like Maisie, to the first male to smell her in heat? But it was even worse than that: Maisie was driven by pure animal instinct, whereas Jessica had intelligence and conscience and will. Jessica had not been a passive victim, but rather had called immorality forth with her own touch. She tucked up her knees and wrapped her arms around them, buried her head to hide. She had never known real guilt until now.

"Dad... I'm sorry... I'm so sorry," she said, and she was, but this time Dad couldn't help her. She was guilty and had to bear this herself. "I can't... I can't talk about it."

"Jessica, please tell me; I can't help unless I know. A man...or a boy, was here, wasn't he?"

Jessica's shoulders convulsed as she nodded. After a moment, she mumbled, "It was my fault, Dad; it was all my fault."

"No it wasn't. You wouldn't do that, Jessica, but I can't help unless you tell me about it. What happened?" He put his hands on hers, rubbing with his calloused fingers, abrading her skin with comfortable familiarity, but Jessica could offer only sobs.

"Who was it, Jess?" he asked again. "Was it someone you know?"

"Dad, I can't... "

Dad's grip tightened, and he spoke with a harsh edge to his voice. "Dear Lord, help and preserve us," he said. "Tell me it wasn't Colby." Jessica kept her head buried as her shoulders shuddered, and eventually Dad said, "Come on, Jess, let's get you back to the house."

Jessica curled up more tightly in her ball and shook her head violently. Ma would be there, and the prospect of that encounter terrified Jessica.

"We need to get you to the house," Dad said, trying to ease her to a standing position.

Jessica pulled back and shook her head again, her hair cascading to form a physical barrier separating her from the world. When she raised her head again, the hair clung to her wet face, but she could still see Dad through the jumbled strands.

He knelt down and parted the strands from her face with his thumbs. "You don't want to go and see Ma?" His hands cupped her cheeks, and he looked at her, uncomprehending.

The whisper barely escaped Jessica's quivering lips: "No."

"Your ma loves you. She'll make everything okay, you'll see."

"It was all my fault, Dad, and she'll know it. I don't want to see Ma, Dad." The silence that followed was a black hole sucking Jessica and her father in, and through the mist of tears, she watched Dad trying to pull himself out and failing, watched his eyes widen as the realization that Ma wouldn't make it all right dawned.

Ma had told Jessica many times that she had never wanted children, and she had always seemed to tolerate Jessica's intrusion into her relationship with Dad grudgingly. She was forever finding fault and blame, seeking ways to diminish and humiliate, and Jessica was confident she would do the same this time. In her mind's eye, Jessica saw Ma cocking her head at Dad, her ice-blue eyes glaring ferociously out of the sunken valleys of her ridged, narrow face, eyes calling, "See? Didn't I tell you she was no good?"

Dad lunged forward and grabbed Jessica's shoulders, jolting her so that her hair fell over her face again. "Tell me what happened, Jess."

"Oh, Dad, it was terrible. It was… oh, Dad." Jessica put her hands to her face and sobbed. Dad's arms around her shoulders weren't comfort so much as a temporary solace from the horror of Ma's reaction.

"Colby couldn't have done this," Dad said, sounding lost as he spoke his thoughts out loud, "but no one else has been here all day. Please tell me it wasn't Colby."

Jessica peered through her hair at Dad's face, but she didn't need to see him to know his emotions; her romance books spoke of the smell of fear, and now she knew it was not hyperbole, for Dad reeked of it. Her guilt deepened, and she pulled her legs tighter to her, pressing her back harder into the hay until she could go no further.

"Speak to me," he urged. "Was it Colby?"

Weakly, meekly, without raising her face, she shook her head and buried it in her hands.

Dad stood up and reached for her hand. "You can't stay here forever, Jess. I know it'll be hard, but we've got to go and see Ma."

Jessica pulled her hand back, for the first time in her life rejecting the support of a father of whom she was no longer worthy.

*   *   *

Jessica looked through the gap between her forearms and saw a pair of rubber-soled black lace-ups. Tilting her arms, she let her eyes run up knee-highs to the bottom of a blue pastel housecoat, and a shiver ran up her spine. It had not occurred to her that Ma would come into the barn; after all, she never did, for her place was the house. But today, of all days, Ma had not only come to the barn but had ascended into Jessica's desolation in the hayloft, and in her self-absorption, Jessica hadn't even heard shoes on the ladder.

Jessica was petrified. She tried to avert her gaze but was drawn to Ma's scrutiny. She lifted her eyes expectantly, feeling the blood drain from her cheeks while she waited.

Jane Cynthia Jackson was short and thin, and her bowed back and slumped shoulders, bent as if to carry the burden of her life of ostentatious piety, diminished her further. The skin on her deeply ridged and creased face, like the housecoat that she always wore two sizes too large, hung loose. What little hair she had was wispy and gray. She bore the marks of self-induced premature aging. Why Ma belittled herself every chance she had Jessica did not understand, but she did know that Ma sought every opportunity to humiliate Jessica into accepting her "station in life" as a child, a woman, and a member of "us country folk," who were somehow inferior to the rest of America. The dream that a fairytale prince would arrive on a white stallion with a glass slipper and sweep her off her feet had given Jessica hope, but today she finally understood that princes, too, are men.

"Ma?"

Nothing. Not so much as a flicker of the eyelids. It was as if Jessica hadn't spoken.

Jessica had never understood her parents' relationship. Both 52 years old, they had known each other since first grade and been married at the age of 16. Dad's love for Ma was expressed through reverence that verged on awe, but as Jessica had matured into her teens, she had found herself increasingly horrified by the soulless subservience that her mother offered Dad in return. How could either of them find this fulfilling? Though he had always let Ma perform the traditional woman's tasks—cooking, laundry, cleaning and managing the house—Jessica had seen no sign that Dad expected the slavish obedience that he received. Ma had made this hell for herself, but she had spent the last fifteen years forcing its expansion to include Jessica.

Jessica stared up, hopeless and helpless, into her mother's unresponsive face, which was frozen by glaciers deep in its crevices.

Lips hard, Ma's piercing blue eyes took in the torn cotton garment on the ground and the blood on Jessica's dress without reaction. She must have spoken to Dad.

"What have you done, Jessica?" Ma's voice was flat, non-judgmental, perhaps giving Jessica a chance to declare her innocence, and Jessica saw more clearly than ever why her heart had cried out for her prince, why she had lured Colby into her trap. Though she now knew her hero was not Colby, she still could not name him, for to do so would be to imply blame, and to blame Colby would be a lie. He was the pastor's son, anyway, so no one would believe her.

"I can't tell you, Ma." Jessica was terrified, but this was the best she could offer.

"Jessica, what just happened—what I think happened—must have been awful, but you need to tell me about it."

Jessica opened her mouth, but Colby's name stuck in her throat.

"However horrible it was," Ma continued, "to hide it is to lie about it, and that is not a path to repentance, forgiveness, and salvation. Talk to me, Jessica."

Ma's voice was stern, and she was in the fast lane to anger. Jessica did not want to make Ma angry, for that was when scary things happened, but she had no alternative. Not only could she not tell Ma of her guilt, but her mother's words had raised troubling thoughts about grace. Jessica had always known she was one of God's chosen, but was even her salvation now removed from her?

"I can't, Ma; I just can't." She pressed her face harder into her hands and sobbed again.

A bony hand grasped her by the wrist.

"How could you do this to your father?"

Ma yanked Jessica to her feet and hauled her to the ladder. Jessica stumbled down into a heap of bruised calves at its base, and without pause, she was back on her feet, being pulled into the lush, green yard. After hours in the shelter of the barn, the heat of the Southern summer sun beating down on her bare shoulders felt like the fires of hell.

"Ma, please," Jessica cried, terrified by Ma's rage, allowing herself be dragged, staggering and scraping her knees on the gravel, up the short path

to the house. The two young blue heelers who called the farm home were
drawn by the fuss and appeared from nowhere to run in circles around Jessica and Ma, darting in to lick and bounce, curious tails wagging 180
degrees.

"Splash, NO!" Ma commanded. Her free hand clenched into a fist and
lashed out, hitting one excited beast on the nose. Splash yelped and
stopped, his tail between his legs. Shep rallied round and sniffed him, and,
giving Jessica a forlorn look, the two dogs turned together to amble up the
path, abandoning her to her fate.

The sprawling single-level house with multiple outbuildings was built
of local rocks and was the only home that Dad had ever known. Ma and he
had moved into the spare room on their marriage night, and they still called
that room their own, even after Dad's parents' deaths had left the master
suite available. Jessica had stolen into her deceased grandparents' room
only once, when she had been only a young child, and could still remember
Ma's fury at her "desecration" of the place. The antiquity and deep familiarity of the house, offering communion with past generations of Jacksons
who had called it home, had always made Jessica feel secure, even in her
most desperate times. But today the thick stone walls and hardwood floors
were cold, and the solid mystique of heavy, paneled oak doors, the repeti-
tive tick of the family's old grandfather clock, her grandfather's ancient
rocking chair, all became nothing more than dead wood. Her soul had been
emptied, and there was nowhere for comfort to roost.

Ma hauled Jessica along at a furious pace, and the teenager struggled
to stay on her feet and to avoid colliding with the low coffee table and the
kaleidoscope of aged armchairs and end tables that were scattered through
the overly furnished living room. Ma wove through the densely cluttered
corridors and rooms of the house, until she threw open the door of the small
but well-appointed bathroom and cast her daughter onto the tile floor.

"Scrub yourself clean, child."

Before Jessica could compose herself and rise from the floor, Ma
returned with a pair of heavy-duty steel scissors, lunged forward, and
grabbed a fistful of Jessica's black hair.

Jessica cried out in pain. "No, Ma, not that!"

"Don't you dare fight with me." Ma's tone was severe as she released
the scissors, which fell with a clatter to the floor, and raised her arm as if to
backhand her daughter.

Jessica cowed and covered her face. Ma had never hit her before, but
then Jessica had never disgraced the family this profoundly, either.

Ma didn't hit her, instead retrieving the scissors, and, with three brutal hacks, cutting out a great clump of hair, which she threw into the toilet
bowl. Jessica lay sobbing on the floor, just aware enough to know that Ma
was crying, too, as she butchered Jessica's hair.

"Oh Jessica, I can't stand it," she said, dropping the scissors again
once her job was done. She knelt on the floor in tears then sniffed, wiped
her eyes, and inhaled deeply. After a long, slow exhalation, she spoke more
evenly. "Leave your clothes outside the door and I'll get rid of them. I can't
bear to look at them again." She turned on the bathwater and in a voice now
quiet, even gentle, she said, "Scrub yourself from head to toe and shave
your head." She grabbed her razor and shaving foam from the cabinet and
placed them behind the bath faucets, picked up the scissors, and stepped
around Jessica to leave. In the doorway, she stopped unexpectedly and
turned to face her daughter. "I'll have a talk with Dad, and we'll decide
what to do." She shook her head and crooned, "Oh, Jessica."

Hope welled in Jessica's heart that Ma was about to step forward and
hold her. Jessica's whole body tensed as she pulled herself up to kneel in
anticipation, watching Ma's eyes fill with tears and her hands return to her
mouth.

But instead of stepping into the bathroom to hold her daughter, Ma's
back stiffened and her head gave a small, dismissive shake. She closed the
door.

Jessica slumped to the floor and shuddered with despair as her
mother's footsteps faded away. Ma was right: What Jessica had done was
appalling. Still sobbing, she pulled herself together enough to get
undressed and obediently placed her soiled dress, neatly folded, outside the
bathroom door. With sudden resolve she closed the door for the last time,
determined that she could not continue living with this guilt. Taking her
own life would be a sin, but she was already damned. If only Ma had left the
scissors. Jessica knelt naked against the side of the bath in silent prayer,
then stood and slid into the deepening water. She hung her legs over the
porcelain rim, closed her eyes, and sank until her face was under the surface. The drumming water from the taps pounded against her ears, a physical sensation rather than a sound. The pressure in her face built and her
chest heaved as her body ran out of oxygen, but she would not move. Soon,
her suffering would be over.

She could not keep her mouth closed any longer, but she would not
give in and breathe. Her lips opened, reaching for life, but finding water
instead, and her lungs began to fill.

Jessica choked, her body lurching upright. Coughing violently, she
opened her eyes slowly. They came into focus, and she saw the surface of

the bathwater in turmoil and large puddles all over the room. Her gasps quieted, and she began sobbing again. She could not do it; her body's want—no, need—for life was too great. She was damned by the weak flesh that had received Colby and that would not let her soul escape this intolerable life to go to its rightful place in hell.

Jessica's despair was interrupted by voices in her parents' bedroom next-door. She could not make out what was being said over the noise of water running into the already over-full bath, so she turned off the faucets. Her sobbing quieted as her ears tuned in to Dad's voice.

"… look in your heart, Jane, and you know. Jessica's your own flesh and blood; she'd never do anything like this willingly."

"I know that the body is weak and that a young woman goes through great emotional changes, more than you could understand, Will. She may play the sweet little girl to you, but I've been telling you for years how manipulative she is, how much she's always going against my will."

"I know, I know, and I always side with Jess, but this… Jessica would never do this."

But Dad's voice was shaking. Was even he beginning to doubt?

"She's disobedient and disrespectful, Will; she always has been, but you close your eyes to it."

"She's always obeyed me. No, I won't believe it."

"Jessica has guilt written all over her, and she won't talk. That amounts to lying to us, Will."

"She didn't do… this *thing* on her own. Whether she's guilty or not, there was a man in the barn today, and the only person who's been here all day is Colby."

"I was busy all day, and you were out in the fields with a tractor. A chorus of demons could have been wailing outside without us hearing them. It would have been easy for Jessica to sneak one of those boys from school into the barn. Who knows how long they were in there and what they got up to before the Lord took you to find your daughter."

Jessica tasted blood and realized she'd bitten into her lip.

"I'll bet he did it while I was at the hardware store, or in the shop. I'm going to talk to Pastor Kidd."

Dad sounded desperate, as if this couldn't be happening. Jessica wanted to cry out, but fear of being caught eavesdropping prevented her.

"You will do no such thing, Will. The only proper thing to do is to find out from Jessica who it was, and when she's of a marrying age, we must give her to him. That's less than a year away, now."

Jessica's heart stopped. She had heard of such things: Didn't it say this in the Bible, perhaps in Deuteronomy? When a man lies with a woman—a woman who is not betrothed—he must pay the father silver and marry the woman.

A glimmer of hope appeared in her mind for the first time. Colby had lain with her, so perhaps he did bear some responsibility. But she dismissed the notion, for she had been the seductress, not the victim, and she could not marry Colby, for he was her prince no longer. Any thought of declaring his identity, however remote, must be abandoned.

"… but if she won't tell us, then we can't help her. She'll be living in sin. You've always been too forgiving when it comes to that daughter of yours, Will. She—"

"You are my wife, Jane, and I am your authority, and I need your support now more than ever." Such severity from Jessica's mildly spoken father was shocking.

"God is my ultimate authority. So long as you are the head of this household, the Bible says you intercede between us, but when you act disrespectfully, you blaspheme, and you lose that power."

Ma had never raised her voice to Dad like this before, had always preached to Jessica that the place of a woman was not to "usurp authority over the man, but to be in silence." Jessica buried her face in her hands and wept as her mother's footsteps stormed past the bathroom door. She slipped her cropped head under the water to hide in the dull echo of her racing heart. Just when she thought there was no more room left in her heart to be hurt any more, her parents' marriage was under assault and she knew she was to blame.

It was more than an hour later before Jessica opened the bathroom door. The flowery new summer dress she had folded so neatly and placed on the floor by the door was, like the innocent child who had put it on that this morning, gone, never to be seen again. She pulled on the clothes with which Ma had replaced it, a pair of jeans and an old t-shirt she had never liked, and braced herself to face the world. The cooler air from the hall felt like a breeze on her freshly shaved head, and she rubbed its smoothness self-consciously. Although she had scrubbed herself so hard that her skin was raw and, in places, bleeding, though her scalp was covered with cuts where she had shaved it, Jessica did not hurt. Instead, a dull gray numbness pervaded all. She trudged into the kitchen.

Ma's glare, the like of which Jessica had never seen before, stopped her in her tracks. "Jessica, I'm going to give you one last chance to tell me what happened and who you were with."

Try as she might, Jessica was unable to make herself speak.

I can't tell you, Ma. Don't you understand? I just can't.

The consequences of silence may be terrible, but to name Colby would anger Ma even more, and worse, it might lead to a lifetime living with her despoiler. Jessica stared with hopeless eyes at her mother until, with a grunt, Ma turned back to the counter.

Ma didn't answer when Jessica offered in a soulless voice to help prepare dinner. The silence seemed strangely fitting, but Jessica was still part, albeit an empty one, of the household, so she looked around to see what she could do to help. She didn't want to go elbow-to-elbow with Ma on the small countertop, but the colander of beans on the table in the adjacent dining room needed attention. Jessica fetched a bowl and sat in one of the six wooden chairs at the table to top-and-tail them. She watched Ma out of the corner of her eye the whole time, hoping for a crack in the armor, a little smile, even a glance, but Ma didn't look up from her work, moving directly from dressing the meat to preparing the fruit pie, then on to ironing the clothes.

After taking the bean ends to the compost bowl in the kitchen and washing the dirty dishes, Jessica gave up and went outside. The day was cooling, though it was still above eighty degrees, as it moved into early evening. The sky was clear, and there was a gentle breeze. Jessica thought of her kittens but couldn't make herself return to the kitchen for milk with which to feed them any more than she could bring herself to visit the hayloft, with its memories of Colby and Ella. She was in a daze, unaware of her purpose even as she opened the door of the workshop.

Built of the same stone as the house, the workshop was cool and uncluttered, and though it abutted the kitchen, it was quiet. It was here that Dad kept the modest selection of tools that he loved so much, where he repaired and tuned his farm equipment and worked on the household projects that he undertook as much for entertainment as for the end result. But most of all, this was Dad's sanctuary, the place where he came for privacy and contemplation. Jessica had spent so many quiet hours here in the warmth of Dad's company that the sounds and smells were solace for her, too. She closed the door behind her, descending on bare feet the five slab steps into the windowless cool of the room, and took two hopeful paces toward the front end of the truck, from which Dad's legs protruded.

"Hi, Dad," Jessica said, announcing her arrival. She looked around as she waited for him and took in the memories of the room: the cleared workbench on which Dad had first sat her with a penknife and a stick when she was five; the shelf beyond with a row of deformed grotesquery, the result of the next ten years of whittling; the table saw that, three years ago, had been Dad's proudest new addition and with which he had cut the wood for the desk he had made for her twelfth birthday. She picked up her knife and felt its comfortable weight in her palm, letting a crack of light into the numbness of her heart.

The wrench under the truck stopped rattling. Moments later, Jessica heard a clatter as the wrench fell to the floor.

"Dad?" Jessica called, worried by the noise, and covered the distance to the truck in wide strides. Now she heard a different sound coming from underneath: was Dad crying? Surely not. He was the strongest man she knew, the pillar that had always supported her. When life became unbearable, Jessica came into Dad's workshop, and he always made everything okay. But there could no longer be any mistaking the sound of sobbing emerging from beneath the vehicle.

"Dad, are you all right?" It was a ridiculous question, she knew, and Jessica's stomach churned.

The choking slowed, and, after a pause, Dad eased himself out from under the truck, his legs followed by his torso and then his tear-stained face. He sat up on the floor, and father and daughter looked at each other in desperate silence.

Jessica's hand followed Dad's eyes up to the head on which, only a few hours ago, her long black hair had flowed, and she rubbed her scalp self-consciously. Dad opened his arms, and Jessica fell onto his lap, throwing her arms around his neck and burying her face in his shoulder, sobbing uncontrollably.

When there were no more tears left in her, Jessica sat up and looked into her father's eyes again, smiled weakly, and slipped onto the floor in front of him. He had always been there for her, had found an answer to every insurmountable problem that she had encountered. He had always been able to pull something out of his hat, but in her heart, Jessica knew this time was different.

They stared at each other in silence for a long time.

"Dad, what's going to happen?"

Dad didn't say anything but gazed at his fingers as they stroked Jessica's cheeks.

"You and Ma… "

Dad lowered his fingers and, with soft, moist eyes, looked into Jessica's eyes. "Ma and I have been together for thirty-six years, and we've been through hard times before now. We'll work our way through this, too."

"But I've never heard you shout at each other like that before."

Another silence followed. The sparkle was gone from Dad's eyes.

"You heard that?"

"The bathroom is next to your bedroom, Dad." After a long pause, she added, "Ma thinks I'm damned."

"Your Ma loves you very much… "

"She doesn't love me at all." Jessica's interruption was vicious, but when she saw the shock in Dad's eyes, she looked down at her hands in shame. After a pause, Dad's quiet, patient voice changed the subject.

"If only I'd been with you, this would never have happened. If I hadn't worked on that tree stump, hadn't gone to the hardware store…" Jessica didn't say anything, and Dad's eyes softened as if recalling a childhood memory. "I bumped into Old Sam while I was at the store. He's a funny guy, but there's something about him… "

Jessica had heard of Old Sam; everyone had, though no one knew him. Folks said he was a wild man who went unclothed into the woods, that he ate roots and bugs, that he was antisocial, but they also said that, like St. Francis, he communed with the animals, that he could read people's hearts, that he had never raised his voice in anger. How strange that Dad should think of him now.

But Dad's distraction didn't last long. Shadows reappeared on his face, and he asked, quietly, "Who was it, Jessica?"

She replied with a scowl.

"Jessica, Ma loves you very much, but she loves the Lord and His Word above all. The way she sees it, if you won't confess your sin, you can't be saved. You've committed—or been party to—a terrible act, and you must confess. If you don't, you are sexually immoral and an adulteress, and it's written that we are not to keep company with such people. You're breaking her heart."

Jessica looked up in horror.

Not keep company…

What did that mean?

Before Jessica could ask, Dad put his hand to her cheek. She nuzzled into it, and he continued, "She'll probably stay up all night praying for you, but at this point, I think she believes your soul is lost."

"But Dad… " Jessica tensed, wanting to say something, to do something. Finally, she blurted out, "I can't tell you."

Dad's hand fell, his eyes following it to the ground. "It's always been so straightforward till now; it's been so clear what I need to do, but that was before it was about my own flesh and blood. Jess, I just don't know anymore… "

Jessica was storming around the workshop with her penknife grasped tightly in her hand and no idea how she had come to be on her feet. Dad's voice petered into silence, and she turned to face him, furious, hands on hips. Stamping her heel, she stuck her chin out and yelled, "Don't know what?"

Not looking strong any longer, Dad shrugged limp shoulders and said, "I don't know what we're going to do."

Jessica saw that what she had feared when she had heard the argument through the bathroom wall was becoming reality. Her guilt was going to destroy her family. The horror of her realization was interrupted by the sound of Ma's voice calling from the kitchen door. "Will, dinner's ready."

"Come on, Jess, we both need some food."

Jessica threw her knife at the bench, where it bounced once before sliding and falling to the floor with a clatter. She left it and followed Dad out of the workshop and back to the house, the words "not keep company" ringing in ear ears. She knew that dinner would be a meal of stony silence. Wherever she was predestined to spend eternity, she was in a living hell right now, and she could see no escape.

Chapter Four

"Happy birthday dear Simon, Happy birthday to you."

The five-part chorus faded, but the group erupted into applause as Simon, with one breath, blew out the seventeen candles that formed a circle around the rim of an otherwise unornamented chocolate cake.

"Well done, Simon; now you have to make a wish." Simon's friend Peter slapped him on the back while the birthday boy's mother turned the light back on, fetched paper plates and plastic forks, and took a knife to the cake. Simon grinned at Peter, closed his eyes for a moment to wish, then looked at the modest portion of cake offered by his mother.

"Do you think I could have a larger piece, please?" he asked, still smiling as he accepted the plate and turned to give it to Aunt Jodi.

"Oh, not for me, thanks."

"Go on, Aunt Jodi, you must have some. It's bad luck not to," Simon insisted.

It was important to Simon that his mother's older sister should have a good time. He had always been close to her, but when Uncle Walt—Aunt Jodi's husband, who had been committed to his role as CEO of a community bank until his last breath and who, as a result, Simon barely knew—had died six years ago, Simon had participated intimately in Aunt Jodi's grief, and the bond between them had tightened. They were no longer inseparable, as they had been for two years after Uncle Walt's death, but Simon still occasionally felt he was on the edge of direct mind-to-mind communication with Aunt Jodi. She had lost a lot of her energy the day Uncle Walt died, but she retained the curiosity in her beady eyes. As her body had slowed, her face, beyond her eyes, had lost the ability to express emotions, and today she sat, as she so often did, turtle-like, threatening to withdraw her head into her shawl at any time.

"Well, all right, just a small piece." Her eyes sparkled at Simon, their alertness hinting at the thoughtful mind that lay behind them, as she took the cake. With a forkful poised by her mouth, she added, "But then I must get back home and leave you children to play." She looked across the table at Simon's dad.

"Just let me know when you're ready, and I'll give you a ride," he answered.

Simon and Peter wolfed down large slices of cake and waited impatiently for Aunt Jodi to leave, then excused themselves to run into the woods behind the house to visit their tree house.

"See you later, Mom. We'll be back before it's too dark. And remember, Peter's sleeping over tonight. Bye, Dad."

Then Simon was free.

It had been a wonderful birthday. His parents had bought him a master's guide to karate in a three-DVD set—he had no idea how they'd found it, and it must have cost over $100—as well as the really cool pair of running shoes that he was now wearing. Aunt Jodi had given him a popular science book with the explanation, "This should help you with your AP." He had smiled indulgently, for it would not, but he would enjoy reading it nonetheless.

And the best was yet to come. Peter had ridden over on his bike midafternoon and had told Simon that he'd stopped off on the way to leave his present in the tree house. Simon had wanted to rush over, but Peter had told him he'd have to wait until after dinner. The look in his eye had told Simon that the present would be something special.

Simon let Peter take the lead. He studied his smaller friend from behind with great affection. They had been inseparable for as long as Simon could remember, starting at Wilkeston Elementary School on the same day, and several years later being baptized into Wilkeston's Church of the Epistles on the same day. Peter ate half his meals at the Cassells' house and slept at Simon's house as often as at his own. He was Simon's only close friend.

Occasionally Simon wondered about the affection he felt for Peter's elegant, slender fingers, about his fondness for the way Peter's black hair curled up and to the left just above his collar, and for the way his friend cocked his head, at once an act of curiosity and surrender. But mostly, Simon felt blessed to have a companion to make up for the brother he had never had.

They did not talk as they passed under the tree house to the ditch. The ladder was not well hidden, but the overhang under which it rested, and the couple of branches loosely covering it, protected it from accidental discovery. Its wooden predecessor had rotted long ago, and the boys had saved up to purchase a metal one, a necessary expense because the tree house was built twenty feet from the ground in an old water oak that had no low branches.

The two boys had built their tree house incrementally over five years and had intentionally picked a place off the beaten track, several hundred yards from the house and high up, so that it would never be seen, let alone invaded. The structure was equipped with sleeping bags, blankets, even an old gas stove, and there was a healthy store of canned foods. It was their very private club, a place where they had shared their successes and failures at school and the emotional struggles of life and where they had camped out many times. It had begun as a platform of odd planks they had purloined from garbage skips and earned by working on jobsites but had evolved over time into a three-level, weatherproof complex. It had a shingle roof that Simon had bought at a steep discount when he had worked at Cook Hardware over the summer two years before.

Simon let his excitement get the better of him and started to climb, but Peter stopped him.

"Let me go first. I want to see your reaction," he said.

So Simon watched Peter ascend before him. He had seen the excitement in his friend's face and now felt it himself: What could it be, that Peter was making such a big deal about? Simon's scalp tingled. Eventually, he followed and pulled himself through the hole in the floor to sit, cross-legged, facing Peter. Peter held a large, sheet-covered square that rested upright on the floor to his side.

"Ready?"

Simon nodded. When Peter pulled the sheet aside, Simon gasped at the portrait that was revealed. The canvas was huge, maybe four feet wide and almost as tall, and the painting was in bright oils. When the numbness of awe had passed and he was able to move, Simon crept forward to examine it more closely.

"You did this yourself?" He glanced up, and Peter nodded. "And it's for me?" When Peter nodded again, Simon said, "Oh, Peter, I don't know what to say; it's wonderful." He reached out with his fingertips and touched the rich texture of layered oils.

Peter had painted Simon sitting on a log, with the artist kneeling behind, his head higher than Simon's and his hand on Simon's shoulder. For the first time in his life, Simon saw himself through Peter's eyes, revealing a view radically different from his own. In the portrait, Simon had a powerful body and short neck that would qualify him to play football, a game in which he was profoundly disinterested, rather than a stubby, overweight body that embarrassed him, and the gap between his front teeth was not the unsightly center of attention that Simon saw every time he looked in the mirror. His unruly fair hair, which spiked like a field of wheat, was not just alive but was almost playful, and the round pudgy face that, in Simon's mind, made him look like an illiterate hillbilly was transformed by the smile Peter had painted into a face of simple joy. Even the brown spot in his left eye, a mark that he abhorred in his otherwise blue eyes, seemed to belong.

Peter's self-portrait was as technically accurate and yet revealing as the subject in the foreground. He had rendered himself much smaller than Simon, with bowed shoulders that diminished him further. His tousled black hair cast a shadow on his lowered face that softened his hollow cheeks and prominent nose, and only a trick of the light allowed the brilliance and joy of his hazel eyes to shine through from under his thick-rimmed square glasses.

Simon's wonder grew as he examined the painting. "It's incredible," he said, the words almost exploding from his chest. "It must have taken you ages." He looked from the picture to Peter, whose hanging head matched the picture and whose initial reply was a shrug and a coy smile. When Simon wrinkled his forehead and asked, "Well?" Peter shrugged again and spoke.

"It took about six months."

"Wow!" Simon sat back and looked at the picture again until another question arose and his brow furrowed once more. "When did you do it? I mean, how come I never knew?"

Peter gazed at the floor as he spoke. "I started last semester and spent an hour or two most mornings before school, and I've been doing it in the mornings most days over the summer. It was with all my other art at the back of the garage, but I kept it covered up so you'd never have even known I was working on it."

Simon was no artist, but he had always believed Peter to have talent. The rough texture of the oils gave the picture life and felt good to Simon's touch. The top of Peter's head and his left shoulder blurred into gray at the edge of the painting, and for a moment, Simon wondered whether Peter had run out of time, but then he realized all the edges of the painting seemed unfinished, faded, creating a soft frame inside a frame. Why had Peter placed himself so close to the edge that there was not room to fit in his shoulder?

But Simon didn't pretend to be an art critic. "It's beautiful, Peter; it really is."

"It's the best picture I've ever painted, and the most enjoyable."

Peter leaned the picture against the wall and slid round to look at it from beside Simon. After a moment's silence, he put his arm around the larger boy's waist and rested his head on Simon's shoulder.

No one had ever shown this kind of affection to Simon before. He loved Peter like a brother, would do anything for him, but for Peter to do this… Apart from those times when, as a boy, he had sought his Mom's comfort, the only time Simon had ever seen heads rested on shoulders was at the movies…

A flash hit Simon.

The sudden realization that Peter had painted them as partners, that his love for Simon was more than fraternal, was blinding. As the shock subsided, a deeper insight emerged—like that of the ugly duckling realizing he was a swan, of Mowgli realizing he was not a wolf—and Simon realized that his love for Peter was romantic, too. With this realization came great liberation. Simon's heart soared as he recognized at last the feelings he had for Peter, gave them a name and a place, and his thoughts came too fast to follow. He could now place his discomfort with football and boisterous locker-room games, his incomprehensible sterility toward attractive girls, his ache of not fitting in. The inexplicable thoughts that had confused him, the moments when he had stared just a little bit too long, they all made sense.

Peter lifted his head and hand and turned Simon's chin toward him. Simon looked into eyes, just inches away from his own, that he had never really seen before. The black pearl at each center was surrounded by a multicolored halo of greens and browns, woven together by a fine lace web, the hazel that he had taken for granted replaced by inconceivable complexity. But there was something else beyond the color, something soft and glowing, a love that defied description. Simon understood for the first time, and his heart soared.

But no sooner had his heart taken flight than it tumbled to hit the earth with a crash. His newly discovered love was one of the darkest of sins and would be a crushing blow to his parents. He was terrified.

"Peter…" he said, but, unable to articulate his fears, he looked down.

"Shhh." Peter took Simon's hand in both of his own and rubbed it.

Simon said nothing but waited, his heart pounding, his mind a whirl of confusion. What would his parents say? Dad, who had beaten him for splashing paint on the carpet, for breaking a chair, for spilling soda on the sofa, would try to kill him. Dad hated gays, blacks, Hispanics, and Arabs alike with zealous fervor, and had inherited his violence from an alcoholic father who had beaten his wife and three sons until dying after driving, drunk, into a tree one night. Mom's reaction would be more complicated, for though Simon thought she loved him unconditionally, her faith was deep and her conviction in the absolute truth of the Bible certain. He did not dare predict how she would react to the prospect of her son being damned.

Peter released Simon's hand and smiled, then stroked Simon's cheek with the back of his hand before cupping Simon's chin with the tips of his fingers. He reached forward and kissed Simon's cheek, then his lips. It was a wonderful, terrible moment, the realization of all Simon's suppressed love, but a violation of all of his upbringing and his beliefs. Peter kissed him again, and Simon's doubts were overwhelmed by love for his friend. He lifted his hand to the back of Peter's head to hold their mouths together. They shifted balance and held each other close before parting lips and hugging.

Peter sat back and put his hand on Simon's chest while Simon stretched out a hand to Peter's lips, tracing them with a slow finger. They were soft, moist and beautiful, yielding to the pressure of his finger and giving meaning to the confusing emotions he had often experienced as he watched Peter's lips. Simon took Peter's free hand in his own and stroked the fingers, understanding now why their slender grace had taunted him for all those years. Peter slid to Simon's side, and Simon let his friend ease him to the floor, where he lay on his back, one forearm under his head, forcing himself to remain perfectly still, to submit.

Peter unbuttoned Simon's shirt and pulled the tails out of his trousers, eased the shirt to the side, and sat back to look at Simon's chest. Simon was tingling with anticipation, fit to explode as Peter's fingers touched, then stroked, his chest, as Peter's lips—lips that he had loved all those years without knowing—kissed his pectorals and then his mouth again. Peter reached down to the buckle on Simon's trousers. Even in his naiveté, Simon knew he wasn't ready for that, so he reached down to still Peter's hands.

The gesture was enough, and the smaller boy nodded, took his own shirt off, and lay on the floor of the tree house beside Simon, head on one side of Simon's chest, his upper hand caressing the other. Together, they looked sideways at the portrait.

"You know why I've got my hand on your shoulder like that?"

Simon shook his head.

Lifting himself onto his elbow, Peter ran a finger along Simon's cheeks and lips as he answered his own question. "Because I'd follow you anywhere, and do anything you asked me, because I know I'm only in this world for you."

Simon wrapped his arms around Peter's shoulders, held him tight, and cried.

It was growing dark by the time Simon buttoned his shirt. He wrapped the painting in its sheet and lowered it with a length of rope that they kept in the tree house to Peter, who stood waiting on the ground. They dawdled back to the house, hand in hand, while Simon balanced the painting awkwardly with the other hand on his shoulder, and as they approached the lights of the house, Simon kissed Peter on the lips and let their hands part. Simon had expressed fear that his father would intuit the meaning of the portrait's intimacy, so the boys sneaked into the house through the front door, crept along the corridor to Simon's bedroom, and slid the painting under the bed before settling into the living room to watch TV and play video games.

For the rest of the evening, Simon self-consciously avoided touching Peter. He told himself this was to prevent his parents guessing what had transpired but realized that it sprang from his own guilt. He knew he loved Peter, and lying flesh-on-flesh with him for two hours had been the most wonderful experience of his life, but he also knew that what he had done, even what he felt now, was wrong. It was wrong, not only in the eyes of everyone he loved but, more importantly, in the eyes of God, and he was filled with self-loathing.

With Mom and Dad around, Simon found his conversation with Peter stilted, and eventually, when it was respectably late, Simon suggested they go to bed. He swallowed hard at the double-entendre and saw Peter smirk, but to Simon's amazement, his parents didn't notice. He brushed his teeth in silent terror, locking the bathroom door while he put on his pajamas, before climbing onto the top bunk. He pulled the blankets up high and faced the wall as Peter, less modestly, changed in the bedroom.

"Good night, Simon." The bed shifted as Peter slid into the bottom bunk and wriggled to get comfortable.

"Good night, Peter."

Simon buried his face in his pillow, bit it, and hit it with his fist.

You coward, Simon, you miserable shameless coward. Rolling over, he said, "Thanks again for the painting."

"You're welcome."

Now lying on his back, Simon pressed his eyelids closed and hit his thigh with clenched fist. *So that's it? He tells you he loves you, he gives you the most wonderful afternoon of your life, and all you can do is say, "Thanks for the picture?"*

But it's so wrong!

Fifteen minutes of anguish passed before Simon resolved to act. He climbed down from the bunk as quietly as he could and heard Peter roll over to watch. His heart was pounding so hard and fast that he was sure Peter must be able to hear it, and his head started to spin. It was all too much, and Simon's will broke. To cover up for his behavior, he walked down the hall to the bathroom, where he filled a cup with water, poured it slowly into the toilet bowl, and flushed. But as he made his way back to the bedroom, his resolve strengthened. He closed the bedroom door behind him and, as quietly as he could, took off his pajamas and lifted the sheet on the bottom bunk. Peter slipped over to make room for him, and they kissed and cuddled.

"I'm not ready to… you know… *do* anything. I just want to hold you."

"That's okay, take it at your own pace, Simon. I love you, so whatever you want is okay."

Several minutes later, Peter asked, "Is it okay if I take my clothes off, too? I won't do anything. I just want my body to touch yours."

Simon gave his permission with a kiss. After a few minutes, he found how comfortably their warm bodies fitted together and fell asleep in Peter's embrace.

* * *

The sound of Mom's footsteps coming down the hall entered Simon's dreams.

"Come on, Simon, its time to… " Her voice stopped in mid-sentence.

In the daze between sleeping and waking, Simon opened his eyes. The sun shone brightly through the bedroom window, the smell of breakfast wafting with his mother through the bedroom door, and Simon smiled at the dream that was fading fast. He completed Mom's sentence in his mind and frowned. Why had she not spoken the final words out loud? He moved his head to look at her and felt a body behind him.

Then Simon remembered.

Guilt hit him like a massive electrical shock, and he pulled away from his friend, jumping out of bed and into the room, as if separation would make everything okay. He faced his mother, a sick ache filling every cell, the churning in his stomach telling him that every organ in his body was rebelling, trying to jump out of his mouth.

His mother didn't move. The silence was terrifying. He studied the face he loved, the face that had understood and forgiven his failures through the years, but this time, he saw hopelessness. Mom was predisposed to smile, but not today. Her eyes were wild, and her mouth hung at the corners. Simon had seen her look this way only once before, the day Gramma had died. She stared at the bed where Simon had been, the bed where Peter still lay. Simon started to mumble something but stopped as his mother's eyes swung back to him and then dropped from his face to his naked body.

His horror deepened, and he lunged at the bed, snatching the sheet from the top bunk to cover himself. "Mom… " he stammered, but she did not seem to hear. A low wail came from between lips that started to shiver, the sound of the graveside, which took Simon back to Gramma's death. It was the sound of loss, of endless despair. After what seemed like an eternity, she staggered erratically back down the hall, appearing to have lost control of her limbs, bouncing off the walls, the mourning wail fading with her into the kitchen.

Neither Simon nor Peter moved for what seemed like an age, but eventually, Simon broke the silence. "I think we'd better get dressed. Dad'll go nuts." He glanced at Peter as they dressed. The wonder of long fingers, slender waist, and delicate touch was still in his heart, but it was strangely distant, inaccessible. All was cold. Leading the way to the kitchen with his head hanging low, Simon remembered with relief that his father would be at the church for an early morning class on "How to be a Better Dad," which Mom and Dad had agreed would be good for all of them. Although Simon, after years of abuse from Dad, did not anticipate it having any effect, it did mean that today he would be saved from his father's fury until later, by when Peter would be gone and would not have to watch, let alone experience, Simon's father's wrath. With trepidation, Simon led the way into the kitchen, where his mother was crashing dishes around in the sink. The smell of the grits, bacon, eggs, and hash browns arrayed on the table barely registered with him as he stared in terror at Mom's hunched shoulders. He had been collecting his thoughts, composing a monologue, but now that it came down to it, he was completely tongue-tied. His mother let the silence hang, occasional chokes accompanying the clatter of dishes, until she spun around with alarming speed to face the boys. Her eyes were swollen, red and bloodshot, her cheeks were stained with tears, and her voice quavered. She was a woman bereaved.

"Peter, I've loved you like a son," she sobbed. "How could you repay me with… with *this*? How could you lead my son into sin—"

"Mom, it wasn't—" Simon cut in, but was silenced immediately

"Don't interrupt me."

Simon fell back a step at the ferocity of his mother's voice. After a pause, she redirected her grief at Peter and continued, "Peter, I'm sorry, but you must leave this house." Her crying intensified so that it was harder for her to speak, but she struggled on. "You must leave this house and never return. And you can never see my son again."

Simon was horrified and heartbroken. "Mom—"

"I told you not to interrupt me," she lashed out, turning to face him as she did so, and showing Simon that her eyes held pain and conflict, not anger. Simon had broken her heart, and, crushed by the responsibility, he fell back, stumbling into a chair by the small table. He sat still, unable to move or speak. Mom seemed to understand, and her hand reached out to him, but it withdrew without touching, and she turned back to Peter, her voice more composed.

"This is between you, your parents, and your Lord and Master. I'm not going to interfere or tell your parents what you've done, but I hope and pray that you will seek their support and prayers." She raised her hands to her mouth, shook her head, and through her tears whispered, "Oh, Peter." After a pause, she added, "Please go."

The door swung closed behind Peter, and Simon watched Mom's eyes linger on his friend's departure. She didn't know what to do, that much was clear.

Finally, she heaved a long, shuddering sigh, and gazed at her son, her eyes a mirror for the guilt Simon felt. Unable to face it, Simon looked down at his hands.

"I just don't know what to tell your Dad," Mom said. "He'll kill you if he finds out." Sobs overwhelmed her again, and through them, she choked, "Oh, Simon." Even without looking up, Simon could tell that tears were flooding down her face again. "I can't tell him, I just can't." The pause lengthened. When Simon glanced up at his mother's now bowed head, he saw her shoulders starting to convulse. "I just can't do that to him, it would destroy him. His boy a … a homosexual." She whispered the word as if afraid the walls of the house would fall in on her. "Please go to your room while I figure out what to do."

It didn't occur to Simon to do anything other than obey. He trudged back down the hall, last night's euphoria a lost memory, his life in ruins. He closed his door and threw himself onto the bed where he had so recently lain with Peter. He was angry, but his fury was objectless; he was miserable, but tears would not flow. He knew he loved Peter, knew that it was a wonderful feeling, knew that with Peter, he was truly happy, but it was not allowed!

Though he knew his love was wrong, he realized that he did not really know why. Mom and Dad railed against homosexuality as if it were the worst of sins, and Pastor Kidd preached that it was a symptom of the terrible wrongs in modern American society, yet Simon could not remember where the sinful nature of homosexual love was taught. He knew, without her having to say it, that Mom thought he was damned, but hadn't Christ spent his time with prostitutes and tax collectors? He needed to know, and next to his parents, the Bible had always been his guide, so he picked up his well-used copy from the bedside table and thumbed through it. He sought clarity first in Genesis, surely the right place to begin anything. He seemed to remember that the first book taught heterosexuality unambiguously, but in the story of the Garden of Eden, he could find nothing to assert even the relative dominance of man over woman, let alone heterosexuality over homosexuality. Though God admonished man and woman—Adam and Eve—to be fruitful, He said nothing remotely helpful to Simon's predicament. Simon knew the Ten Commandments like the back of his hand but moved on to Exodus and read them again nonetheless, hoping they would say something new to him. "Thou shalt not kill. Thou shalt not commit adultery. Thou shalt not steal." What use was that to a seventeen-year-old gay boy?

It must be in here somewhere.

Then he remembered Pastor Kidd reciting from First Corinthians. When he reached chapter 6 verses 9 and 10, his jaw dropped, and he parsed two short sentences again and again: "Know ye not that the unrighteous shall not inherit the kingdom of God? Be not deceived: neither fornicators, not idolaters, nor adulterers, nor effeminate, nor abusers of themselves with mankind, nor thieves, nor the covetous, nor drunkards, nor revilers, nor extortioners, shall inherit the kingdom of God."

He threw his Bible to the floor in despair, buried his face in his pillow, and screamed into it. The divinely inspired words of Paul unambiguously damned him. But how could one sentence that came out of nowhere and returned to nowhere be central to the teaching of the Church? How could a handful of words in two thousand pages of text be enough to damn him? And yet whether they were enough or not, he had the guilt of his sin and of his mother's despair on his hands.

*   *   *

After sending her son back to his bedroom, Rachel Cassell had resumed cleaning the saucepan, but once she heard his door close, she let go of every semblance of self-control. The saucepan fell with a clatter, and she gripped the counter, overwhelmed with grief. Simon was damned, and she would be separated from him for all eternity.

Slowly, she raised her head and steadied herself: if she was careful, she would not fall over. She staggered to the table and collapsed into a chair, staring unseeing at the window above the sink. She was beyond emotion, beyond feeling, beyond the very possibility of tears; her heart was drained, and life as she had conceived of it was over. Until now, she had taken for granted that she would be with her family in heaven, but in one moment in Simon's bedroom, that possibility had ceased. What joy could heaven hold for her if her son would not be there with her? This mortal life had also lost all meaning and joy, for how could she find any pleasure in the prelude to eternity if she knew her own flesh and blood would be taken from her?

She wept, too, with self-doubt.

She had always known her husband, Brandon had a violent streak, even when Brandon had been a thirteen-year-old preaching in the school-yard. But she had needed him: she had been a thirteen-year-old girl whose father had abandoned the family two years previously and whose older brother was in jail on drug charges when Skip, the brother who was two years older than her and her closest companion during the family trauma of Joey's dance with the law, had died with two friends in a car accident. With no one to turn to and nowhere to go, she had been slipping in with a bad crowd when she had heard Brandon's preaching.

Rachel had been irresistibly attracted to him, and in the years that fol-lowed, they that worshipped together, dated, and eventually married. She had come to understand the terrible family circumstances that had given rise to his evangelism, and the torment that simmered underneath it. He had never raised a finger to her, but when he had shaken and thrown their six-month-old son onto the couch, she had been terrified and had vowed never to bring any more children into the world. She had been secretly practicing birth control ever since, though she knew it to be a sin, and lived in terror that one day Brandon, who had always wanted a large family, would dis-cover her secret. Had she done the right thing? Would Simon have turned out heterosexual if she had given him a brother? Would Brandon have changed, too? Was her birth control a sin that would damn her? She almost hoped it was, so she could be with her son.

She was just resolving that she could not risk Brandon's violence by telling him about what she had discovered when she heard his car pull up and glanced up at the clock. It was mid-morning. She had been sitting at the table for more than an hour. Disgusted with her self-indulgence, she wiped her eyes with her pudgy fingers, sighed, and stood. By the time Brandon entered, she was back at the sink, running the hot water and washing the saucepan she had dropped more than an hour before.

"Hi, sugar." The door closed behind Brandon, and three short foot-steps brought him up behind her.

"Hi," Rachel replied, accepting a kiss on the cheek without turning.

"I never had any breakfast before I left this morning. This looks good," Brandon said, turning and sitting at the table, and looking at the food heaped in front of him.

"Let me heat you up a helping, honey." Rachel wiped her hands, fetched a plate, and loaded it up with food.

"After I eat, I think I'll work on the car. It needs an oil change, and the timing's off," Brandon said.

Rachel put the plate in the microwave, leaned on the counter, and watched Brandon while she waited. It was inconceivable that he wouldn't ask her about a face that she knew was swollen, eyes that were certainly bloodshot, and she prepared her answer.

Brandon's blank gaze at the window dissolved, and his eyes drifted to Rachel.

"Are you all right?" he asked, frowning. "You look like you've been crying."

"It's Pastor Wood. You know, that preacher on TV? I was watching him this morning while you were out, and he has this beautiful way of saying things. He was talking about… oh, you're not interested." Rachel let her sentence fade as Brandon's eyes glazed and drifted back to the window.

The microwave pinged, and as she retrieved her husband's breakfast, Rachel smiled to herself. It would not be hard to keep Simon's homosexuality and Peter's banishment a secret from Brandon. But although she could not talk to Brandon about Simon's sin and expose her son to a beating that would help neither his soul nor his body, Rachel would consult with Pastor Kidd, who was the custodian of the family's souls. While she did not think he could do anything to redeem Simon beyond encouraging his repentance, Pastor Kidd ought to be told. Rachel held out a faint hope: She had to, or she would die right now.

Chapter Five

Life in the Jackson household quickly returned to a routine, but it was a routine that was not much fun for anyone, least of all Jessica. She resumed her usual chores and tried to help with meal preparation and house maintenance, but she received little or no feedback. Ma hardly spoke to her, and although Dad tried to act as if nothing had happened, it was a lame and soulless attempt. Her parents seemed to have lost not just the ability to smile—they had never been a wildly humorous pair—but also their spark of life, even their wills to live. They nursed their pain in silence, unable, or perhaps unwilling, to include Jessica in their suffering.

Jessica was ashamed and emotionally unable to face the world. She could not bring herself to be seen in public with her beautiful hair completely gone. She was ambivalent about the long weeks of summer vacation still ahead of her, vacation that would permit her to hide from Wilkeston and yet force her to be around her morose mother and broken father.

But gradually, although she continued to feel tired and to ache, she no longer thought of herself as suicidal or depressed, and her need for human and spiritual companionship began to grow. After ten days, soft stubble had grown on her head and her eyebrows had filled out acceptably, so she pulled on a pretty skirt and blouse and climbed into the back of the truck to accompany her parents to church. For a moment, life was back to normal: Dad stood in his Sunday best, freshly shaved with his gray hair slicked back and the silk tie that had once been his father's pulled tight against his throat. His hand rested on the door handle of his truck, and he looked around to make sure Ma and Jessica were ready. But when he smiled at Jessica, the moment vanished: His mouth twisted into a weak curve between sagging cheeks, and it was with wilting arms and an obvious struggle that he heaved himself into the truck's cab.

Ma did not even acknowledge Jessica's presence.

Jessica felt a nervous thrill as they approached the church, and she straightened out her red silk scarf, a childhood dress-up garment that she now wore in a conspicuous and ineffective attempt to hide the absence of her flowing locks.

Ma and Dad's morose behavior had been observed in town and at church, and as a result, she had received concerned calls from her friends, particularly Alison, wanting to know what had happened and why they had not seen her. Jessica had been polite but curt, not yet ready to reengage with the world, but now she was. She knew, however, that the red scarf she wore and her parents' funereal behavior made her stand out a mile.

The Church of the Epistles was a small community of a couple of hundred people, for whom Sunday service was the most important event of the week. Jessica had never before noticed the concentration of traffic—fifty vehicles arrived in the parking lot of the simple, white, wooden building just outside town at exactly the same moment. She fingered the knot of her headscarf nervously and pressed herself low and hard into the open back of the truck.

Soon enough, they had pulled to a stop, and she clambered down, though trying to do so carefully and elegantly, dusted off the straw, and straightened her skirt. She tried to maintain her dignity as she jogged a couple of steps to catch up with her parents and strode side-by-side with them, three souls lost in separate worlds, heads held high with silent pride. Jessica's isolation was exaggerated by the seclusion of the single-story church building, standing unornamented and alone among trees and hills, its sign set back from the road, the cross on its white steeple low as if trying to hide from curious eyes.

Out of the corner of her eye, Jessica saw Alison start to approach and then stop. Jessica kept her eyes straight ahead, walked in silence into the church, and sat on a middle pew next to her father. It seemed to her heightened sensitivities that the quiet conversation that bubbled inside the church for the next five minutes was all about her. She stared vacantly at the altar or down at her hands, and though she tried not to react to the conversation, tears welled in the corners of her eyes. She could feel stares burrowing into the back of her head and wondered what these people were thinking. It didn't matter to her, though; the truth was worse than anything they could imagine.

But she survived the next hour, and on the way out, she shook hands with Pastor Kidd. He held her hand a moment longer than usual until she looked up at his face, open and strong, topped by a semi-circle of gray hair crowning his freckled pate like a halo. He gave her a deep, rich smile that offered her the warmth and compassion of her Savior, a smile that indicated knowledge beyond the physical mark of her shaved head. Had Dad spoken to him after all?

"It's good to see you, Jessica; it's been too long. Come and see me sometime."

"Yes, sir, thank you, Pastor Kidd." The words slipped from her lips naturally, but as she looked into eyes, warm and green under the hint of red in his eyebrows, she started. In the pastor's eyes, she had seen Colby looking down at her. She released the pastor's hand in disgust but immediately felt ashamed. The pastor was a holy man who had just offered to help her.

Alison called Jessica that afternoon, and they chatted on the phone. Jessica couldn't bring herself to talk about Colby or her parents but arranged to meet Alison at lunchtime on Monday.

She had asked Ma if meeting Alison for lunch would be okay, but neither Ma nor Dad appeared interested in Jessica's comings and goings, so on Monday, Jessica left the house, unannounced, to meet her friend.

She glanced at her reflection in the door of the gas station, making sure the red scarf that she still wore was straight. The door jingled as she pushed it and stepped through. Alison was already there, leaning on the counter and talking to Shawn Hickman, a wiry youth who had dropped out of high school three years earlier. The door jingled again as Jessica let it close behind her, but neither Shawn nor Alison looked at her. Jessica cleared her throat, and when Alison still did not turn, she called out a hello. Shawn scowled at Jessica, and this time Alison reacted and came bounding across the store to hug Jessica, and lead the way to the food shelves, where they each poured a Slurpee and picked out a MoonPie while Shawn ogled Alison, who shimmied her shoulders and averted her eyes and tried to ignore Jessica.

The girls burst out of the gas station, which was too small to contain their teenage excitement, touching, holding, and giggling, and rushed across the road to sit on their favorite wooden rail fence.

"I don't know what you see in him, Alison."

"He's cute."

"Ew," Jessica said, pulling a face. "So not!"

"Is, too! Have you seen his butt when he's stacking the shelves?"

"Alison!"

Jessica was mostly role-playing, and she knew Alison was doing the same. They quickly put the topic of Shawn behind them and watched three grazing horses while eating their favorite lunch. Alison described the past two weeks at Braxton's community swimming pool, related the latest on the dating scene, and, more importantly, chronicled the flux of teenage female friendships. She also described with enthusiasm what the inside of her home would look like after she and her mother had finished decorating later in the summer.

After they had wiped their mouths and swilled their Slurpees, Alison reached over to loosen Jessica's headscarf. Jessica started to pull away but then stopped and swallowed and, with self-discipline that reminded her of when, as a child, she had let Dad pull a loose tooth, forced herself to sit still. As Alison loosened, then removed, the scarf, Jessica tingled and felt a pleasant thrill when her friend gasped at the spectacle of an eighth of an inch of fine black fur, and stroked her own frizzy, tawny ponytail as if to protect it.

Jessica realized that if she trusted Alison enough to let her look, then she surely trusted Alison enough to tell her what happened. She related first the incident with Colby, then her parents' reactions, and concluded with her ineffective attempted suicide. Alison was horrified but pressed for intimate details. Jessica blushed and squirmed as she answered her friend's questions, but after she had finished, she found that, instead of the negative judgment of which she had been afraid, she had achieved celebrity status and Alison's almost envious interest.

"He violated you!" Alison declared.

Jessica protested, but Alison persisted, and her questions challenged Jessica's recollection of the seduction.

Walking home alone after their lunch, Jessica reviewed her immorality in the hayloft in the light of Alison's comments, and by the time she arrived home, she had come around to Alison's thinking: Colby was partly at fault.

She closed the backdoor loudly, but there was no cry of, "Careful!" Rather, she could have sworn that her parents had not even noticed her four-hour absence. Confusion and anger made her restless, and she looked with disgust at the bookshelves, pulled out a couple of old romance novels half-heartedly, and replaced them. There was nothing in the house that she had not read, and she had already worked her way through all of the interesting books in Wilkeston's small library. She was well overdue for a visit to Baxton's larger library but didn't want to try to cajole Dad into taking her, so she poked around the house, trying to avoid Ma's glare. When she realized that she was standing outside the bedroom of the grandparents she had never known, she looked around. Neither Ma nor Dad was in sight, so she slipped in. Ma would be livid if she knew, but Jessica didn't care. Worse, she *wanted* to make Ma angry, to make her talk. But once in the room, with her back pressed to the door, Jessica's apprehension evaporated.

The room was spotless. Two engraved doves fluttered on the headboard of the high, four-poster bed, and half a dozen lace-trimmed pillows lay on top of an old handmade quilt folded perfectly square and smooth on

the bed. The solid oak furniture was dark, heavy, and beautifully ornamented. All the horizontal surfaces in the room were covered in china, photos, and mementos. Jessica stared in awe. She ran her finger along the
surface nearest her and then rubbed her finger and thumb together; the
room was a shrine without a speck of dust anywhere.

Jessica took a step to the nearest chest of drawers and examined the
large black-and-white photo in its center—a picture of Dad aged eight or
ten, sitting beside his younger brother, Uncle Terry. He had his arm around
the younger child's shoulder, and the boys flashed gappy smiles at the cam-
era. But the picture was tinged with the tragedy it anticipated: Anna, the
infant sister who lay across their laps, had died of a childhood illness, and
Uncle Terry had died five years ago, leaving a wife and four small children,
children that Dad loved but no longer saw because their mother, who had
never liked Wilkeston, had taken them back to her family home in Ken-
tucky. Jessica studied the sweet, innocent faces, and her heart ached for
Dad.

She made herself move on.

The next dresser held a picture of a couple in their mid-teens in wedding clothes, standing rather formally on the steps of the Church of the
Epistles. Jessica leaned forward to examine her parents as they had been
thirty-six years before. Dad had the same unusually small nose and ears,
and his plain face was a simple canvas for the joy radiating from his smile.
Ma had a narrow, angular face that held mystery and a haunting beauty. The
caverns and hollows of her mature face had not yet formed, and her eyes
had not sunk into their cold isolation; rather, they showed a joy that
matched Dad's. Why had she become so subservient? What had Jessica
done to make Ma so unhappy? Tears welled uncontrollably from her eyes
until Jessica could stand it no more and, choking a sob, ran out of the room,
leaving the door open wide as she raced for her own bed, onto which she
threw herself and wept.

*   *   *

Jessica and Alison met for the same lunchtime ritual two days later,
and it was almost like old times. They laughed about Shawn's butt, teased
each other, and tried to catch one of the horses, a big, brown quarter horse,
without any clear idea of what they would do if they succeeded. The loss of
innocence was beginning to recede as a memory into the past, leaving Jessica with nothing but a subtle melancholy and a growing disappointment
with her parents. She was beginning to look forward to school starting.

Exhausted from running around the field, Jessica collapsed on the ground beside Alison and laid her head on her friend's belly. "That was fun," she said, "but I'm exhausted."

"Me, too."

"You know, I get out of breath pretty easily these days."

"You eat too many MoonPies and don't get any exercise. You need to come to the pool."

"And have everyone laugh at my hair? No way. Besides, you know I can't swim. No, it's not that, anyway. I think I might be sick. I kind of ache... "

When Jessica paused, Alison asked, "Where?"

Jessica was emotionally stronger now than she had been right after the incident, though her parents were still a nightmare, but there was something wrong... This was awkward, even with her best friend, but she needed advice.

"It's mostly my breasts. They're sore... well... more like tender. Especially the nipples." Her neck twisted sharply as Alison jerked upright.

"What?" she asked Alison. Jessica didn't like her friend's stare one bit.

"You don't know?" Alison asked, appearing shocked.

"No, I guess it's just what happens when you... you know, when you *do* it." Jessica felt a little thrill: *I've done it, you've not.* "And when your parents disown you."

"Are you tired all the time?"

Jessica nodded. "I figured I might have that chronic fatigue syndrome thing. Maybe I won't have to go to school so much."

"Do you feel sort of queasy, maybe even a little sick?"

As Jessica nodded again, a sense of impending doom bore down on her like heavy thunderclouds accumulating overhead. How did Alison know all of this, and why did she look so anxious?

"That's what Trisha felt like last year."

A wave of nausea hit Jessica. Trisha, Alison's older sister, had married at eighteen and given birth to a baby boy eight months later.

"We talked about it just once, right after she got married. Jessica, could you be... pregnant?"

Jessica's head was spinning. How could this be? She was only fifteen, and girls in the Church of the Epistles just didn't have children at the age of fifteen. Even if she was pregnant, she wasn't of marrying age, so she couldn't, like Trisha, quickly tie the knot with the father. Not that marrying Colby was a possibility she would even consider.

Then another wave of nausea hit Jessica: Her period had been due a few days ago.

"Jessica? Jessica, are you all right?" Alison's hands were on Jessica's, but Jessica was only vaguely aware of them. "Say something, Jessica."

"Oh, Alison, my period's late. Do you think...? What am I going to do?"

"Well, first off, we need to be sure. They sell pregnancy kits in all the pharmacies, and they really work. At least that's what Trisha told me." Alison was talking confidently, proudly, her older sister's experiences vicariously restoring her stature. "We don't want to get one in town—people will start talking—but Ma and Dad are out visiting today, so we can borrow Dad's truck, and he'll never know." She hopped off the fence and faced her friend. "Let's go."

"You'll drive?"

"Sure."

Several years ago, Trisha had taught her younger sister to drive without their parents' knowledge, but Alison had never, to Jessica's knowledge, been on the highway. Jessica felt queasy at the prospect of being Alison's first real passenger but quickly decided that she had nothing to lose. "Okay," she said and followed Alison meekly back to the house to wait while her friend fetched the keys and brought the truck around to the driveway. She couldn't help smiling as she hopped in. "You look like a little mouse staring through the wheel. Do you want me to reach down and push the pedals for you?"

"At least I can drive," Alison snapped.

"You're sure you'll be all right taking the truck?"

Alison appeared to relax and smiled. "Trisha used to do it all the time, and she used to take me with her. Mom and Dad never found out."

They drove twenty miles, past landmarks familiar to Jessica from her regular trips with Dad to the library, a reminder of the life she had lost. A plain billboard that Jessica recognized but to which she had never previously paid attention cried out, "God, please send us a Savior to lead us to the Light," and answered itself with, "I did, but you aborted him." Jessica's stomach churned, and she pulled her legs up to her chest, resting her feet on the seat, her mind tossing terrible thoughts at her. The Walmart slipped past, another reminder of trips with Dad, and two miles later, they pulled into the parking lot of a small drugstore just outside Baxton. Alison reached around the steering wheel and slid the gearshift into park.

"You won't be recognized by anyone here," Alison said. "Just run in and ask at the pharmacy counter for a pregnancy test kit."

Jessica did as she was told and clung to her package in silence as Alison drove back, urging Jessica to come to her house to take the test. Jessica was terrified and refused, even when Alison parked in her driveway and took the key out of the ignition. The argument became more heated until Jessica eventually climbed down from the truck and left on foot, ignoring the pleas that followed her. Jessica's distress at the argument with her friend quickly evaporated in the anxiety of walking home, and for the entire thirty minutes, Jessica felt terribly conspicuous, certain that everyone driving past knew what she had in the little plastic bag clenched tightly in her fist.

But Jessica arrived home uninterrupted and, apparently unnoticed by her parents, locked herself in the bathroom and sat on the toilet seat, fumbling with the innocent-looking blue box with shaking hands as she opened it and read the instructions on the insert.

Remove the protective cap; expose the wick to a stream of urine for five seconds, then wait. If a blue line appears in the control window within ten seconds, the test has been correctly performed. If an additional blue line appears in the results window, the test is positive for pregnancy.

Jessica shuddered as she read and reread the insert.

Positive for pregnancy.

There was a lot more in the instructions about when to test, false negatives, and limitations, but at its heart, the whole test was described in this one short, simple paragraph. Jessica slipped her underpants down, raised the toilet lid, and sat down again, this time with the white strip in her hand.

Remove the protective cap.

She did so and stared at the thin wick, a cheap plastic device that held her fate.

But wasn't this against the teachings of her church? Hadn't Ma expressly denounced pregnancy tests when talking to her about the evils of birth control? Nervous, looking for a way out, Jessica's mind tortured her as she stared and wondered what to do. Eventually, she concluded that she had no choice, lowered the strip, and strained to pee.

She strained again. Her bladder was full of Slurpee, but she couldn't squeeze anything out, and her mouth was dry. She sat for ten minutes before the first trickle arrived. Once started, it became a flood that splashed onto her fingers. Jessica raised the strip and stared, her hand dripping slightly, while she counted, "One, two, three, four, five..."

If a blue line appears within ten seconds, the test has been correctly performed...

She rose and started pacing, her panties abandoned in her anxiety, crumpled on the floor by the toilet, while she stared at the white strip.

Eight seconds.

A faint blue line appeared as if from nowhere. She rushed to the counter, compared the wick to the box, and threw the box down. She did not need to read the instructions to hear them echo in her mind.

...the test has been correctly performed. If an additional blue line appears in the results window, the test is positive for pregnancy.

Jessica paced, staring defiantly at the strip.

Was something happening?

At first she tried to pretend it was an illusion, but after only moments, she could not deny the existence of a second blue line. She froze, the test gripped fiercely in her hand, and started to cry.

*   *   *

After two sleepless nights and another positive pregnancy test, Jessica remembered Pastor Kidd's offer of a visitation. Though she was not willing to tell him that she was pregnant, she needed his advice, so one morning when her parents were both out of the house, she phoned the pastor. Mrs. Kidd was sweet and told her to come around at two o'clock that afternoon.

At the appointed time, Jessica waited nervously on the front step of the imposing two-story house, staring through the large stained-glass panel in the center of the solid wooden door. It wasn't long before she saw blurred movement through the glass. With a click, the door swung away from her.

"Hello, dear. You must be Jessica? That's a pretty dress. Please come in... this way. I'll take you through into Harris's study. He'll be with you in just a minute. Would you like anything to drink?"

Despite Mrs. Kidd's compliment, Jessica did not feel pretty. But she had put on her nicest summer-print dress—older and not as nice as the one her mother had thrown away, but colorful and well-cut, nonetheless—and her only pair of heels, and she had made a real effort with the limited makeup in the house, so she appreciated the acknowledgment. She followed the large frame and loose, un-ironed khaki pants of her hostess, wondering whether the eyes held captive in bottle-bottom glasses were really as small and close together as they appeared, unsure what to make of the wide nose and square jaw underneath them. Mrs. Kidd was an enigma within the church, rarely seen or heard, yet ever-present in the background of the pastor's life. To Jessica, she looked like a cross between Mrs. Doubtfire and a Walt Disney washerwoman with rolled-down stockings.

Declining the second offer of a drink, Jessica sat in a high-backed chair facing the desk to wait. Book-lined walls and imposing piles of papers on the large Victorian desk and surrounding floor intimidated her. Coming over clammy and deciding that visiting Pastor Kidd had been a foolish idea,

Jessica rose to leave. She was just turning to the door behind her when it closed, and she found herself facing the pastor as if she had risen to greet him.

"Jessica, how nice to see you. Let's sit down over here."

Pastor Kidd was dressed for the library in a loose burgundy cotton shirt with a starched collar. His gray slacks were sharply creased, his bare feet nestled in backless leather slippers. He waved casually at a pair of dark-blue leather armchairs in the far, book-lined corner of the room. Jessica led the way and sat, her heart pounding and her lips dry. Pastor Kidd's short, yet broad, frame fit comfortably within the chair, and his forearms relaxed on its arms. Jessica's gaze flickered across his impenetrable deep green eyes and implacable face, her resolve and her prepared speech crumbling in his intimidating presence.

Pastor Kidd broke the silence gently. "So, Jessica, I suggested you come to see me, and I'm glad you have. I've got some idea what you want to talk about, but why don't you go ahead?"

Although his calm manner and soft voice made her feel more at ease, Jessica still didn't know where to begin. After an uncomfortable silence, she blurted out, "Colby raped me," then stopped, shocked at what she had said. It was the first time these words had formed in her head, and she knew at that moment that, although she was not innocent, Colby had also sinned.

Pastor Kidd remained upright and alert, a slipper bobbing on the end of a neatly crossed leg. "That's a very serious accusation, Jessica. I talked to Colby after your father asked some questions—which, incidentally, stopped well short of accusations of rape—and he denies that anything happened between you. Colby has his weaknesses, but he has always been a good boy, and an honest one. I don't think you can seriously expect me to believe you, especially after you've spent three weeks concealing whatever transpired from your parents.

"But asserting blame is not a fruitful line of discussion for us anyway. This is about *your* life and *your* soul, not my son's."

"But…" Jessica lurched forward to begin her protest, but as it failed to materialize, she slid back and crumpled in her chair. Her sudden certainty of Colby's guilt and discovery of his bald-faced lie made her angry, but the combination of her own residual guilt, the intimidating presence of the pastor, and her revulsion at the idea of having to marry Colby cut off her tongue. Her eyes drifted out of focus and stared at Pastor Kidd's chest; her hands clenched tightly, fingers twisting.

The pastor waited patiently. "You're upset, Jessica," he said eventually. "I understand, but it's not a helpful response. Colby has told me he didn't do this, and the matter is closed. What's important is that you repent and accept your sin, that you receive Christ in your heart as you've done before. With that, you can—you will—be saved, and we can all get on with our lives."

Jessica felt sick to her stomach. Although she was not innocent, she no longer felt that she should bear this guilt alone, but rather that Colby should take his share. And it was a big share.

But Colby was lying.

Jessica wanted to lash out at her one-time prince who had abandoned her, at his father who would not believe her, at her parents who were too quick to judge, but she knew that if she pressed Pastor Kidd about Colby's guilt, she could not win, for not only would he surely defend the family dynasty, but the only prize for her unlikely success would be marriage to a worm she now despised. Unable to find expression for her building anger and frustration , she started to shake.

After a few moments, Pastor Kidd spoke again. "Let's move on to the heart of the matter. It sounds like you have had sexual intercourse outside marriage, and we should talk about your sin and state of grace."

Jessica shivered.

"You say that it was not a willing act, which is important. We are all sinners, and it is never too late to repent and submit oneself completely to the Father. If you truly repent of your sin and completely accept Christ into your heart, then you will be saved."

Tears filled Jessica's eyes. She couldn't respond to the challenge of disclosure, so she moved past it and said, "Ma and Dad won't talk to me. They've changed so much; they won't tell me what's going on and what they're thinking."

Pastor Kidd considered her with his soft, green eyes and took a sip of his water. He lowered the glass, placing it carefully on the small table beside him, before he looked up and spoke. "I've talked to your parents both separately and together. Those conversations, like this one, are private affairs, and I cannot divulge what we discussed. However, I do want to help you get on with your life, so I will tell you what I can." He steepled his fingers, stared thoughtfully at the books over Jessica's shoulder, and spoke deliberately. "Despite my assurances of the consequences of sincere repentance, your mother cannot conceive of the possibility of your salvation. She will continue praying for you for the rest of her life, but I believe that she has given up on your soul. Your father is more difficult and complicated. Your parents have known each other a long time—as you know, I married them myself—and he's devoted to her at a level I don't think you can understand. He cannot be happy without her, so he's suffering from the dual loss of your soul and her spirit. I will continue to work with both of them, but I fear it will be a very long while before either of them smiles again."

"What if I have a baby?"

The words had flown out before Jessica could stop them, and she froze, stone-faced, wanting them back, but it was too late. Pastor Kidd uncrossed his legs and folded them the other way, then shifted in his chair as he studied her. Had she seen a flicker of emotion? It was gone before she could be sure.

"I don't know quite what to make of that question, Jessica. Treating it hypothetically, if you're pregnant, you will, of course, have a baby, and that would not change a thing I've said. How old are you?"

"I was fifteen last month." Jessica was aware that she was being downright surly at this point.

"Hmm. If you were pregnant, then things would be more difficult. Even if we are able to identify the father, which is unlikely, given your insistence on accusing Colby, you will not be of marrying age even when the child is born, and so your baby would be both conceived and born illegitimately. The visibility of this would be a terrible stamp of sin in the eyes of the community. I grieve greatly at your pain and with all my heart want to help you. All that I said before about what you have to do to be saved is still true, but I'm a practical man, Jessica, and I have a bigger responsibility for the well-being of the community of the Church of the Epistles. The members of the church are simple folk who want simple rules to keep their community clean and sanctified. An illegitimate child born in their midst of a minor who won't declare the father's name would be difficult for them to accept. If this were to happen, they might press me to cleanse the church of such a sin, and if they were to do so, then, to satisfy my larger obligation, I may have to listen."

Jessica started to protest, but Pastor Kidd continued. "I've said more than I should because I want to help you. You are a delightful, if very unfortunate, young lady, and I'll assist you in any way I can, within the constraints imposed on me by my office."

Jessica glared at the pastor in silence, his gentle green eyes seemingly unaffected by the fury in her sharp hazel ones, until she stood and stormed out, understanding neither the situation nor her new petulance, and leaving both the office door and the front door wide open on her way. She wanted to scream—no, she wanted to hit someone, to hurt someone—Colby, Pastor Kidd, her parents, anyone. They were all to blame.

Chapter Six

Eight days after her talk with Pastor Kidd, Jessica sat once more in the pew of the Church of the Epistles beside her father.

The sign on the road to Braxton—*I did, but you aborted him*—had haunted Jessica's nightmares for more than a week as she sweated over her pregnancy. Yesterday morning, after locking the bathroom door and testing positive for the fourth time, she had resolved to have an abortion. She had picked up the phone to call Alison and ask her to drive to one of the clinics in Atlanta, but her fingers wouldn't press the dial pad. Her shaking hand had fumbled the receiver back into its cradle, and she had collapsed in tears, tormented by images of an aborted Savior wagging an accusatory finger at her from heaven. Fifteen minutes later, she had pulled herself together. She could not—no, she would not—violate the life of her unborn child. She would have the damned baby. It was because she thought of her future child literally in that way—damned—that she swallowed her pride and returned to church, intent on saving his soul, even if hers was forsaken.

Although Jessica did not recall hearing a single word spoken in the Jackson household about her pregnancy and had certainly said nothing herself, she had no doubt that her parents knew. She could tell that her room had been searched and suspected that Ma had found the first positive test hidden in her underwear drawer; but it did not matter *how* Ma knew, what mattered was *that* she did and that Jessica's ostracism was now complete. Even the few words that Ma had previously offered to guide and instruct had been withdrawn, and Dad's despair was horrible to behold; he aped Ma's sunken cheeks and stooped shoulders. He must have lost ten pounds in the past two weeks.

"Dearly beloved, let us listen to the Word of the Lord. Today's reading is from the Book of Genesis, chapter 19." Pastor Kidd laid a large Bible on the lectern at the front of the church and with great deliberation opened it to the appropriate page. His eyes took in the congregation as he pressed the pages open, then looked down at the text, and after a long pause began.

"'And there came two angels to Sodom at even; and Lot sat in the gate of Sodom; and Lot seeing them rose up to meet them ...'"

Pastor Kidd read to a rapt congregation about the men of Sodom demanding that Lot hand over the angels sleeping under his roof and about Lot, after offering up his virgin daughters in the angels' stead with the instruction, "do ye to them as is good in your eyes," evacuating his family to Zoar while the Lord rained fire and sulfur from the heavens and overthrew Sodom and the surrounding cities. Once finished, Pastor Kidd left the Bible on the lectern and stepped around it, ostentatiously waving his note-free hands at the congregation.

"So what are we to make of this passage?"

The pastor looked around, an orator skilled at the use of long silences and eye contact. Jessica saw many pairs of eyes bow to his gaze, but hers were not among them. She stared at him defiantly until he moved on.

"Is this a tale of a distant time when people had different problems and morals? Can it be that the history of God's people that has been handed down over the centuries has no relevance to our lives? 'God forbid!' When we read from the Book of the Lord, we hear of the temptations and evils that existed in the past. But these are precisely the evils that exist today." His eyes roamed as he swept his arms and repeated emphatically, "Precisely the same evils."

He shook his clenched fist in the air, paused, and looked around. "And why is that? It is because Satan is still among us. In His Old Testament, God explains how we should behave. And do you remember what Jesus, who came after, said about the laws of the prophets? Do you remember?"

Pastor Kidd smiled as he looked around and waited. Jessica was sufficiently detached to observe his technique for the first time and smiled back, amused by the apparent inspiration and improvisation of a sermon he had certainly learned and tested with his family, the density of Biblical quotes that he used to gain credibility and authority, and the affected intimacy of standing in the aisle to be closer to his congregation.

At just the right moment, Pastor Kidd spoke into his own silence. "In Matthew five, seventeen, Jesus says, 'Think not that I am come to destroy the law, or the prophets: I am not come to destroy, but to fulfill.' You see? Our Lord tells us that the law of the Old Testament is precisely the law that we sinners are to strive to uphold."

So this was to be a lecture on Old Testament morality. *What's the Old Testament punishment for rape?* Jessica looked around for Colby.

"The story of Lot is one of sexual immorality and homosexuality and tells us of the punishment that God has in store for the wicked. This message doesn't just appear here in this passage from Genesis. Throughout the Old Testament, God admonishes us to be sexually upright. In Leviticus He tells us, 'Thou shalt not lie with mankind as with womankind: it is abomination.' And again he says, 'If a man also lie with mankind as he lieth with a woman, both of them have committed an abomination: they shall surely be put to death; their blood shall be upon them.'" Pastor Kidd paused again, then gestured emphatically with his arms. "Scripture is completely clear."

Colby was in the front row on the other side of the church, his face held high, his chin jutting out. Jessica wondered how her infatuation could have so quickly turned to hatred and contempt. And how could Pastor Kidd still plan to hand the ministry over to that revolting monster?

"And in the New Testament, we are told the same. Do you remember the words of the apostle Paul? I'm sure you do. In First Corinthians, he speaks very clearly: 'Know ye not that the unrighteous shall not inherit the Kingdom of God? Be not deceived.'" Pastor Kidd pounded his fist into his other palm and repeated, "Be not deceived, dearly beloved, and listen carefully, for what follows is important." Pastor Kidd looked around, his open palms extended to the audience. Jessica smiled again at the pastor's stagecraft and imagined the years he had spent rehearsing in front of a mirror. In her mind's eye, she saw the Kidd household at dinnertime, the pastor striding around the table trying new lines and new techniques on Colby and Mrs. Kidd while they chewed their pecan pie and offered pointers. But Jessica's smile turned to a grimace as she felt her parents beside her join the rest of the congregation and lean forward expectantly into Pastor Kidd's silence.

"'Neither fornicators, nor idolators, nor adulterers, nor effeminate, nor abusers of themselves with mankind, nor thieves, nor the covetous, nor drunkards, nor revilers, nor extortioners, shall inherit the Kingdom of God.' None of them! Do you hear? Not one."

Jessica had listened carefully to the list and wondered why rapists were not included. The thought made her feel guilty, for she was in church and it was unworthy, but she couldn't let it go: Colby surely shared blame with her. And she really did not understand why the Bible, time and again, offered rape as the spoils of war to the victorious Hebrews.

Pastor Kidd continued, "Paul says this again and again that fornicators—and by that, he means anyone having sex outside marriage—are damned to the fires of hell for eternity. In Romans, he says, 'For this cause God gave them up unto vile affections,' and again, 'Wherefore God also gave them up to uncleanness through the lusts of their own hearts, to dishonor their own bodies between themselves.' And in One Timothy, 'Knowing this, that the law is not made for a righteous man, but for the lawless and disobedient, for the ungodly and sinners, for unholy and profane, for murderers of fathers and murderers of mothers, for manslayers, for whoremongers, for them that defile themselves with mankind, for manstealers, for liars, for perjured persons, and if there be any other thing that is contrary to sound doctrine, according to the glorious gospel of the blessed God, which was committed to my trust.'

"Our Heavenly Father makes it perfectly clear—perfectly clear, dearly beloved, perfectly clear—that he abhors and will punish the sexually immoral. In Leviticus he tells us 'For they committed all these things, and therefore I abhorred them,' and the apostle of the Lord says in Romans chapter one, verse twenty-seven, 'And likewise also the men, leaving the natural use of the woman, burned in their lust one towards another; men with men working that which is unseemly, and receiving in themselves that recompense of their error which was meet.' Paul sees no alternative in the matter. When a member of the Corinthian church was guilty of a sin of sexual immorality, he told the congregation, 'Deliver such a one unto Satan for the destruction of the flesh, that the spirit may be saved in the day of the Lord Jesus.'"

Jessica felt reluctant admiration for the man's ability to deliver this fire-and-brimstone diatribe against loose sexual morals, precisely the kind of message that would resonate with this congregation. Three weeks ago, she would have lapped it up herself and would neither have noticed the carefully rehearsed rhetoric that he was using so effectively nor reflected on the reason for the vitriol, but as she did so now, the repeated homosexual theme made her realize that the message was not directed at her.

"The punishment in this world will come when the Lord rains down fire and sulfur on those who sin against him, as He did on Sodom and Gomorrah, but of far greater consequence is the eternal punishment. Do you remember the book of Revelations, chapter twenty-two? When John is telling us about the city of God, he says, 'For without are dogs,'—and when John says 'dogs,' he means homosexuals—'and sorcerers, and whoremongers, and murderers, and idolaters, and whosoever loveth and maketh a lie.' So beware; these people are not admitted to heaven. The sexually immoral are damned, and we must exercise great care not to let Satan slip into our midst and tempt us into sin.

"Now, please rise and turn to number four eighty-three in your hymnal." Pastor Kidd walked back to the front of the church as the congregation burst into song, looking rather pleased with himself.

Jessica did not think the pastor felt her eyes drilling into his back, and she doubted that he would have cared if he had. She was not so pleased. She reflected not on the content of the sermon itself, but rather on what had *not* been said. Why had God saved Lot after he had offered up his daughters to a town of sexually depraved monsters? Where was the morality in Lot's daughters getting him drunk and then becoming pregnant by him? Why had Pastor Kidd chosen to gloss over this portion of the story in his sermon?

Jessica knew full well why Pastor Kidd had skipped so much, and that was precisely what troubled her: He was picking and choosing only those passages that served his purpose. Whatever happened to "He that is without sin among you, let him first cast a stone" or love that "beareth all things, believeth all things, hopeth all things, endureth all things"? She had never heard him use the former, and had heard the latter only at weddings.

As Pastor Kidd's sermon had unfolded, Jessica's mind had been busy. She was unsure whether relief or despair accompanied the realization that her prior faith in her salvation had been an illusion, but now she knew she would have to find salvation for herself and for her unborn child elsewhere. She realized that all the flaws and prejudices of the Church of the Epistles which she had just seen laid bare had existed before, but that until she had been their victim, they had been hidden from her.

What did Pastor Kidd think: that after his sermon, everyone would suddenly start behaving like saints? Everyone knew about the secret lives of many of the congregation—everyone at high school, anyway. They knew about Mr. Yeats, the church treasurer and a good-looking general handyman, and what he got up to during the long afternoons he spent parked outside the homes of his repeat customers, housewives whose husbands were at work. Or Mark Pocock, a laborer and bachelor with a subscription to *Playboy* magazine, who went to Atlanta every few months with Jacob Day from Baxton for a long weekend at the strip bars, the kind in small, rundown buildings off the main streets that interpreted the laws liberally and had plenty of private rooms. Where was the moral consistency here? Why were the sins of old men ignored when her pregnancy would condemn her to hatred?

She wanted to rise and walk out of the church before the service was over, and had it not been for the years of love with her parents and the invisible bond between them, she would have done so. Instead, she spent the fifteen minutes that she lifelessly mouthed the hymns looking around and trying to understand. She studied Ruth Adamson, aged thirteen—though her make-up and extravagantly styled hair made her look older—in a pretty dress much like the one of hers that Ma had discarded. Ruth had surely never been touched by a boy, though she was dressed to turn old men's heads. And there was Karina Langley, sixteen years old and in a dress far too revealing for Jessica's taste, with her father's arm wrapped protectively around her shoulder. When she looked at Alison McCabe, her own best friend, holding her hymnal and sheltered by one parent on each shoulder, suddenly Jessica realized that there were at least six teenage girls whose fathers could not stand the idea that this might happen to them. Jessica was being made the scapegoat for the sins these men were afraid could be visited upon their daughters. In that moment, Jessica realized that the Church of the Epistles did not preach the universal message of love that she sought but was, rather, a private club promoting a doctrine of exclusion.

She looked around the congregation, trying to imagine what was going through other people's heads, trying to spot other targets for the sermon, and her eyes fell on her cousin Peter, who was staring at the pastor in what could only be defiance. He was close enough to Jessica that, as she watched him, she could see the sternness of his lips and the fierceness of his brow as he glared, unflinching. But why would Peter react so strongly to the sermon? Surely he was not gay. Jessica laughed at the idea, but then looked at Peter again wondered if perhaps he *was* gay. That would certainly explain why he looked angry and had not been singing. Peter had never had a girlfriend, though he was seventeen years old; he had never played sports or hung out with the boys; he always seemed on the outside. If Pastor Kidd believed Peter was gay, it would also explain the sermon.

Jessica had never, to her knowledge, met a homosexual before, and a wave of nausea passed over her. Nausea gave way to anger that he should bring his sin into the church. But the detached spirit with which she had observed the service returned and forced Jessica to scrutinize her reaction. Even if he was gay, which she didn't know for sure, Peter was still the same person whose artistic talent she had always admired, still the cousin she hardly knew but who was always so sweet and kind. The only thing that had changed was her perspective, which had taken on the very prejudice of which she was accusing the church. She was not able to completely conquer her reaction but bowed her head in recognition that it was her flaw, not Peter's, and vowed next time she saw him to let him know what he had just taught her.

The congregation stood, and Jessica's mind came back to the pastor. She dragged herself with dreary distaste through the remainder of the service, and she was made physically sick by the hypocrisy of the leader of the church placing Christ's flesh and blood in her mouth when he had only the other day told her that he would not help her.

When Jessica arrived home, she threw herself facedown on her bed and cried for hours. Eventually, she got up and, without speaking to her parents, walked alone to the gas station where she and Alison had spent so many happy hours. Feeling completely cut off from the world, she bought a MoonPie and sat on the fence, watching the horses graze. It started to rain, but she did not care. She was still wearing her pretty church dress, and it would likely be ruined, but she did not care about that either. Soon, her pregnancy would be known to the world, and it would not be long before Alison's mother would tell her daughter to have nothing more to do with Jessica. The full weight of the Church of the Epistles would come to bear, and she would be squeezed out without a spiritual home for her baby. In despair, she threw the second half of her MoonPie, still in its plastic bag, into the field. She was oblivious to the rain that made her dress cling and ran down her naked legs to pool inside her soaking tennis shoes. The chestnut quarter horse that she and Alison had tried to catch just a week ago ambled over, sniffed at the package in the middle of the field, and moved on, leaving Jessica completely alone. Her tears mingled with the raindrops running down her face and washed away the last traces of the hope that she had been foolish enough to allow back into her soul.

Chapter Seven

Simon and Peter had not spoken to each other since "the incident," and for the third Sunday in a row, they exchanged longing, hopeless looks as they entered the church with their families. Simon had not expected to hear such a clear exposition of Pastor Kidd's views of sexual morality, and the glares the pastor had directed at Simon removed any doubt about its targets. As Simon burned under the pastor's flaming words, his forehead beaded sweat and his mind raced, trying to work out how the pastor knew. Peter wouldn't have said anything, and he knew Mom hadn't even told Dad, for the belt hadn't come out. Simon concluded that Mom must have asked Pastor Kidd for advice, maybe for his prayers, a confidence that had been repaid with a vitriolic sermon. Well, at least Simon knew how the church felt about gays, and his question of Biblical references had been answered. His hanging head was spinning and his stomach churning as he walked beside his mother back to the car, now realizing he was truly damned, his life in this mortal world a miserable stepping stone to an eternity in flames.

"So shall we go to Hardee's for lunch?" Dad asked, pulling out of the parking lot and heading toward the restaurant without waiting for a response. He flicked the turn signal with his finger, spun the wheel to the left, and after a moment spoke again. "What about that sermon? Wasn't it great? I don't remember the last time I saw Pastor Kidd moved that much." After a pause, he added with a tone of revelation, "Say, you think we've got one of those monsters in the congregation?"

Simon jumped in his seat and glanced at the rearview mirror to see Dad's strong eyebrows furrow and the deeply set eyes darken. His mouth and forehead were always severe, intense, but now anger was rising in them. "You know, I bet that's it. Tarnation, a fag in the Church of the Epistles. Heaven protect us! But why is Pastor Kidd preaching to us about it; why doesn't he just kick him out? Or better yet, just tell us all who it is so we can

string him up." He shook his head. "You know, it makes me sick just thinking about it, all that unnatural evil right there in the same room as us. I bet
he even took the Eucharist. What do you think, Rachel, do you think there's
a fag?" He glanced at his front-seat passenger.

"Don't you think you're overreacting, sugar?" she asked.

Dad slowed down and waited for a gap in the oncoming traffic to
make his turn, calming down while he thought.

"No, I don't think so," was his considered reply.

"Maybe you're just reading more into it than you should."

"No, there's more to it than that." Dad was getting excited again. "Pastor Kidd was talking to someone back there, someone in the church. The
thing I want to know is who." His brow furrowed again, and he glanced at
Mom. "You know, don't you?" he asked in a firm voice.

Simon winced and stared at the mirror, captivated against his will.
The issue must have gotten right to Dad's marrow, for such perception was
unlike him, and Simon watched Mom trying to put a brave face on it.

But Dad didn't give her a chance, following up immediately and
harshly. "Who is it, Rachel?" he demanded, his eyes flashing back and forth
between the road and Rachel's face. He glanced in the rearview mirror and
into Simon's eyes before Simon could avert them.

"No!"

The car swerved, but Dad quickly regained control and pleaded,
"Rachel, tell me it's not…Simon."

Rachel stammered a couple of half words but then closed her mouth,
also caught off guard and unprepared to carry off a bluff.

Stern resolve replaced the confusion in his father's voice. "We're
going home right now. Oh mercy, what are we going to do?"

For the rest of the short drive, Mom sobbed and rocked back and forth
in the font seat while Simon shuddered in terror of the judgment that was
to be visited on him. He had been no stranger to beatings since he was a
small child and had learned that resistance itself was punished, for whenever he tried to run away or hide, he was caught, and when he tried to fight
back, he lost. He had learned to shut off his mind and live with his terror.

When they arrived at the house, Dad was a man possessed. He
grabbed Simon by the arm, hauled him into the house with the strength of
ten horses, and threw the youth on the living-room floor.

"So you're a fag. My own flesh and blood, corrupted by Satan. After
all these years, after everything Mom and I have done for you, you repay us
with this. How dare you!"

Simon rolled over and stared up hopelessly from the floor at the
gorilla-like violence gathered in his father above him. Dad tore off the wool

shirt that hung loose and unbuttoned over his t-shirt, his '60s-style greased-back hair bobbing up and down, comically out-of-place.

"Brandon don't, please don't. This won't help anything."

"Shut up, woman! The ungrateful whelp's got it coming to him." He threw his shirt on the couch and reached for the buckle on his belt.

"Dad, I just want to be normal. I don't want any of this; it's just the way I am."

Prior experience warned Simon that even verbal resistance would make things worse, but he had never seen rage like this in his father's eyes, and the terror that gripped him in its iron vice had squeezed the words out.

"How dare you! We've done everything to bring you up properly. We've given you the church and red meat and all the love a family can offer." His belt came free with a single long, firm pull. "How dare you talk to me about 'the way I am'?" These last words, spoken with a mock whine, accompanied the raising of the belt in Dad's hand. Simon cowered and hid his head behind his arms as his father's arm swung toward him. "Take this for 'the way I am.' And this... and this"

"Brandon, stop it. Stop it!" Rachel, becoming hysterical, ran forward and threw her large body over her son's. "Don't you remember those classes you've been to about loving your family and loving your child?"

"Get out of the way, Rachel. Those classes are for raising a Christian family, not the brood of Satan. This homosexual dog is no kin of mine; now get out of my way."

When Rachel gave no sign of moving, Brandon stepped forward and grabbed her wrist. "Rachel, this is God's will. You heard Pastor Kidd today: 'His blood shall be upon his own hands.'" He dragged his screaming wife by the wrist, oblivious to her blows and shrieks, and repeated, "This is God's will."

The shocking words that Pastor Kidd had quoted from Leviticus were seared permanently into Simon's mind, and despite his father's inaccurate recall, which Simon chose not to correct, he could read them on the back of his eyelids right now: "They shall surely be put to death; their blood shall be upon them." He opened his eyes and looked up at hearing his mother's screams. Dad had thrown her out of the room so hard that she had crashed into the far wall with a dull thud. Like a toy doll, her head flopped and made a cracking sound as it hit the plaster. She slid to the floor in slow motion. Simon recovered his breath, stood up, and yelled, "Don't you dare treat Mom like that." Defiance and shock at Dad's abuse of Mom transformed him into the powerful figure of Peter's birthday portrait, a hero in his beloved's eyes. He would protect Mom.

"And don't *you* dare talk to *me* like that, you faggot," his father yelled back, slamming the door and sliding a chair under the door knob. "'Honor thy father and thy mother.' As if it's not enough for you to become a faggot, now you're telling me what to do. Let's see if we can drive the devil from you, shall we?"

The belt fell across his shoulder and sent Simon reeling. In the face of Dad's righteous anger, the deluded self-image of oil and canvas fell apart, and Simon saw himself for what he was and always would be: a weak, disobedient boy fully deserving of his father's wrath. Worse, he was now wallowing in irredeemable sin. Dad's violence was beyond anything that Simon had seen before, but nonetheless, he was acting within his rights. Despite his mortal fear, Simon let himself be driven back until he cowered on the floor, curled up with his hands over his head. He was going to die, and maybe Dad and Pastor Kidd were right: maybe he deserved to. The agony of blow after blow raining down on an already-bleeding back became a numb persistence, and he felt the world slipping away, fading to white. Was that a choir he heard singing? Maybe this wouldn't be so bad after all.

*   *   *

Simon woke from a dream of bright lights and swirling colors and shapes to a soft, warm sensation caressing his back, interrupted by occasional bolts of piercing agony. When one of these sharp shocks finally woke him fully, he winced, yelling, "Ouch!" and opening his eyes to look around. He was lying on his belly on the living-room floor beside his kneeling mother, who was soaking a sponge in a bucket and mopping his back. His shoulders tensed as he remembered, and he started to sit up, but Mom placed a gentle, firm hand on his back to keep him still. Simon relaxed and let her continue, wincing occasionally, and though his thoughts were chaotic, he idly noticed that she must have removed his shirt to expose his beaten and cut back.

"Where's Dad?"

"At the police station. He's probably... probably in a cell."

"He's been arrested?" Simon tried again to roll into a sitting position, but Mom held him down.

Why would Dad be in a police cell?

Mom must have called the police on her own husband. Simon recalled Mom flying into the wall, and this time he resisted her pressure and ignored his pain to roll over and look at her face.

"Oh, Mom!" Simon was shocked. It was all he could do to string a coherent, if short, question together. "He did this?"

She shook a head whose right cheek and eye would not have been more puffed-up if Mike Tyson himself had hit her. "It happened when he threw me out of the living room. He didn't mean to hurt me, but he was angry. I was afraid he was going to kill you if I didn't do something." She stopped trying to minister to his wounds and sat back to look at her son. "He was scary, Simon, oh, he was so scary." She put her hand on his cheek. "I don't know what to do. I don't know how we can save your soul, but I do know that whipping you to death won't help." She stroked his hair and continued, "What if all we've got together is a few short years in this world? What if you stay gay, so when you die, you go to hell and I never see you again?" Her eyes filled with tears, and she pushed him roughly back onto his belly. "Now lie down and let me finish cleaning you up."

Simon obeyed her, his mind in a whirl. He had obviously passed out as a result of the pain of his thrashing, but what had happened then?

"So you called the police?"

She continued sponging his back as she talked. "I just wanted them to make him stop, but they got pretty serious. They came into the house with guns and everything, and when he still didn't stop, they kicked in the door." Simon looked across the room and saw that the door was leaning against the wall in approximately its usual location but detached from the frame.

"Then they threw him to the floor, put handcuffs on him, and dragged him out to their car. It was awful. But at least you're both okay." She paused to wipe her eyes and nose with the back of her hand before resuming cleaning and dressing Simon's back.

The sound of a car engine grew louder and idled outside the house. Rachel stood up and peered out of the window, then turned with a frantic look in her eyes. "Quick, go to your room and put on a shirt," she ordered as she snatched her materials up from the floor and raced out of the room. Simon did as he was told and had almost finished before he heard the knock on the front door. He finished buttoning his shirt and tucking it in as he ran into the bathroom while his mother, hand poised on the front door latch, waited for him to close the bathroom door. He did not know what was going on, but it was obviously important to Mom for him to be presentable, so he washed his face and forearms and ran wet fingers through his hair, the running tap obscuring the voices outside. His shirt was already sticking to his back, but if he was careful to face the visitors, no one would be able to see.

When he heard Mom calling for him, he replied, "I'm in the bathroom; I'll be there in a second." Taking one last look in the mirror, he ran a comb through his hair, dried his hands, and unlocked the door.

He made his way toward the unfamiliar female voice with an out-of-state accent that was drifting out of the living room. "Ah, you must be Simon. How are you?" the voice asked as he entered. A woman stood up from Dad's armchair and extended an arm. Simon looked at his mother, who was sitting on the couch, for cues, but she only offered him an insipid smile, so he stepped forward and accepted the proffered handshake, which was not only soft and ineffectual, engendering instinctive mistrust in Simon, but also clammy. He hurried to let go and sat next to his mother, suppressing his involuntary desire to wipe his hand on his trouser leg as their guest resumed her seat, facing them at a ninety-degree angle.

"Now, let me see, where were we? Ah, yes, you were just about to explain the door to me." The woman looked up from her notepad and waved a floppy hand toward the leaning door. Simon eyed their guest from top to bottom. She was middle-aged, moderately overweight, modestly unattractive, and had dull, uninteresting eyes. She wore baggy tan slacks under a buttoned brown shirt that was too small and exposed a sausage-string of white flesh down her front. All told, she was one of the most unimpressive people Simon had ever met.

Mom cleared her throat and caught Simon's attention, the mischievous sparkle in her eye telling him she was going to have some fun. "Simon, this is Mrs. Onions from… "

"Oh-NIGH-ons. My name is MIZZ Oh-NIGH-ons," the frumpy woman interrupted, wriggling uncomfortably in her chair.

"Sorry, I got that wrong again, didn't I? I just don't seem to be able to get the hang of it." Mom paused, cocked her head, and, with a deliberateness that made Simon want to laugh out loud, said, "Miss Oh-NIGH-ons." This time she pronounced the surname correctly, and with a huff, their guest let the error in her title go. "Miss Oh-NIGH-ons is from the Department of Social Services, and she seems to think we need some help."

"Why would we need their help?" Simon looked back and forth between them, feigning astonishment and confusion.

"Mrs. Cassell, can I have some privacy with your son, please?"

"Certainly. Simon, I'll be in the kitchen."

"Okay, Mom." Simon watched his mother leave, recognizing from her derision what was going on. He may be terrified of his father, but he certainly didn't need help from this outsider.

"So, Simon, how are you?"

"Actually, I'm a little flustered right now."

"How so?" Ms. Oh-NIGH-ons pulled herself forward in her seat, pencil at the ready.

"Well, I was just getting ready to go out, and I'm already a little late."

"Oh." Disappointment replaced her enthusiasm, and she sagged back into the chair.

Simon asked, "Is this going to take long?"

"Not if you answer my questions clearly and honestly."

"Good, because I'd hate for Josie to think I'd stood her up."

"Josie?"

"Yeah. She's my girlfriend...kind of." Simon glanced around and leaned forward with a conspiratorial air. "Mom and Dad don't know I'm seeing her, 'cause they don't like her dad. He's a bit sleazy. And they don't go to church, either. But she's kind of cute, and you know, she... she *goes*." Forgetting his tender back, he fell back in his seat. The pressure made him wince inside, but he was careful to show no sign of the pain and instead smiled broadly at Ms. Onions, then winked and watched with amusement as she flushed and looked down at her pad. "So, how can I help you?"

"Well, the police came around here earlier and arrested your father. I understand that he was beating you with his belt and that they had to kick the door in."

"Oh, you want to talk about Dad, do you?" Simon crossed his legs and watched Ms. Onions. His interviewer straightened up, pen poised over her pad, obviously expecting to get to the root of things. Simon was enjoying this game and paused for a creative moment, then tipped his head back and laughed. "He was drunk earlier, that's for sure, and he was pretty mad at me, too. See, I borrowed his car last night and made out with a married woman on the back seat. Only, her husband found out, and he called Dad this morning to tell him about it. Dad was furious, and was yelling at me like you wouldn't believe; he was using words I ain't ever even heard before, but he was so drunk, he could barely walk, let alone beat me."

"Simon, this doesn't make sense. Why did the police kick in the door and arrest your dad?"

Simon shrugged. "I don't know. Maybe they needed some exercise? Have you asked them?"

The social worker slammed her notebook shut and stood up indignantly. "Simon, I know I'm not from around here, but I'm not stupid. Your father wasn't drunk—from what I hear, I doubt if he ever drinks—and I know that your stories aren't true, but if you won't level with me, I can't help you. I understand that you've just experienced a great trauma and that you can't think straight, but I believe you're in danger here." She calmed down for a moment, and with artificial compassion thick enough to be scraped off with a trowel, placed her cold, damp hand on Simon's arm, saying, "If you want to talk to someone, please give me a call. Here's my card."

Simon winced at the touch and stood up to allow himself to slip out from under it. "Yes, ma'am, I'll do that. Hey, maybe we can take a ride together when Dad's calmed down enough to let me use the car." Simon winked.

Ms. Onions huffed, placed her card on the coffee table, and walked briskly to the door. "I'll let myself out, thank you," she said, and was gone.

As the door closed, Simon fell back onto the couch, wincing as he bumped his back, and collapsed in hysterical laughter. He looked up through tears of laughter at Mom, who came in to join him, laughing too.

"Simon, that was terrible."

"You heard?"

"Of course I did. You were awful to her."

They rolled on the couch, laughing for the next five minutes, but their humor couldn't last. As it subsided, it was replaced by a more serious and somber air.

"What's going to happen, Mom? What are they going to do to Dad?"

"Sergeant Wilson isn't just an elder at the church; he was in your Dad's grade at high school, so the police won't press charges. I'm going to let them keep him overnight, but he'll be home tomorrow." She was sitting upright, looking anxiously at her hands, rubbing them together. "Simon, with your father's temper, it's not safe for you around here right now. I think you need to pack a bag and go live with Jodi for a while. Brandon's always been terrified of her and wouldn't dream of going 'round there to get you."

"Okay, staying with Aunt Jodi makes sense, but Mom...?" Simon didn't know how to ask but had to do so; something was bothering him and wouldn't go away. His eyes scanned Mom's expectant and increasingly confused expression until he finally blurted out, "Has Dad ever hit you before?"

Mom laughed, and the tension evaporated. "Without your father, I'd probably be dead. He was there to save me in my darkest hour, when your Uncle Joey had just gone to jail for the first time and Skip had just died."

Simon wasn't sure how to handle 'I would probably be dead,' so he asked about her brothers instead. "No one's ever told me about Uncle Skip."

Mom stared into space, her expression blank, and spoke quietly. "Joey was always trouble, and he took to drugs early, but Skip was so much fun. He was two years older than me, and we used to play together all the time, but when he was fifteen, he started getting into the same stuff as Joey. Ma couldn't deal with it, and Dad had already left us: He took off right after Joey got sent to the big house, and that's when Ma lost it. I think you'd call it a nervous breakdown. Then Skip started getting really bad, and it was only three months later that he drove into the river with Bud and Mickey, and they all drowned."

She paused, but Simon didn't interrupt; he knew that Uncle Skip had been drowned with two high school friends, but this was the first chance he had had to hear the rest of the story, so he waited, hoping Mom would continue.

She sniffed, still staring into space, and did so. "I was thirteen years old; my sister had left home; my oldest brother had just been sent to jail; my other brother had just died; and Ma was having a nervous breakdown. My whole life was falling apart. I fell in with a bad crowd at school, the kids who did drugs and stuff, and I spent more time on the streets than I did in the classroom.

"And that's when I met your dad. One day, I was wandering through the schoolyard—I don't even know why; it seems like I hardly ever went there anymore—and he was out there with a Bible in his hand, preaching. There were a couple of kids listening, and it seemed like something I should hear. To this day, I don't know why, but I stopped and told my friends to go on without me, and that was it. I was hooked on the Bible and hooked on Brandon at the same time.

"He's had a horrible life, too. His dad beat him all the time—beat him and his mom. She started coming to the church when your Dad was born, but she doesn't come anymore, hasn't for years. Your dad realized before he was ten years old that he couldn't rely on anything in this world, that all he had was the Lord, and, God bless him, he took it into his heart to preach about it. I don't know what would have happened to me if I hadn't heard the Word of the Lord right then.

"No, Simon," Mom said, smiling, as her eyes refocused and she turned her head to him, "he's never laid a finger on me before, and he didn't mean to hurt me this time. I know he'll never touch me again, but he gets mad at you… " She covered her face, sobbed, then looked up at Simon again. "I don't know why, and he doesn't either, because he knows what it's like to be beaten. He swore he'd never be like that, but he just can't stop himself."

The silence was long, but eventually Mom spoke again. "I'll call your aunt Jodi and tell her to expect you."

Simon stood. "I guess I should get packed to go. I need to get my school stuff together for tomorrow, too."

Simon was already looking forward to a prolonged stay with his aunt. He would be able to talk to her, tell her about his love for Peter, and he knew that she would listen. He even hoped that she might be able to help.

"Mom, there's one other thing."

"Yes, dear?"

"I don't know how to make you understand. It's, it's… " Simon looked around the room, searching for inspiration, and suddenly looked back at his mother. "It's like the way you can't help loving Dad, no matter what he does, or the way you love chocolate ice cream; this is just the way I am. I can pretend to be something else and be miserable, but you just have to accept that it's who I am. I'm sorry if it's not what you want, if I'm just a huge disappointment, and I'm really sorry if it means I'm going to hell, but there's nothing I can do about it."

"Oh, Simon, if only you understood what you're saying." She pressed her hand to his cheek and rubbed with her thumb.

"But I do, Mom, I do."

"Just go and pack your bag before you break my heart."

Chapter Eight

Dwight sat cross-legged on the floor of aisle 11B and counted seven electric fence kits. He ran the tip of his index finger along the top surface of one, then rubbed the finger against his thumb and examined it. He grimaced at the grime and wiped his hand on his jeans, an empty ache churning in his belly as he thought of the amount of money he had locked up in inventory.

His eyes slipped out of focus, as they did so often these days, and he relived the days before Robbie had moved out. It had been Dwight's curiosity—or doubt—that had led him to search Robbie's room, his sense of righteousness that insisted on confronting the boy. Cheryl didn't have to say anything for Dwight to know that she blamed him for driving their son away. After Robbie had walked out of their lives two weeks before, Dwight had tried to support Cheryl and had sought her support in return, but it hadn't worked. Her movements had become increasingly lethargic and lifeless, and she had hardly spoken to him. She did not so much look at Dwight as *through* him when he talked to her, as if he were no more than an irritating fly buzzing around the room. Dwight was trying to come to terms with the loss of not just his son but his wife as well.

And he had done so by drinking. His occasional evening bottle of beer had become a nightly craving and, within a few days, an addiction. His stops at the gas station had become more frequent, and introspection at the creek with cigarettes and beer was now a lengthy, nightly routine. The last two weeks had been terrible.

Dwight tried to shake off his malaise. He pulled himself upright, looked around the shelves, and scuttled to the next aisle. He had arrived at the store today before Darlene but had barely seen her as he spent the morning darting from aisle to aisle like a cockroach, pretending to himself that he was performing an informal inventory check, though he knew that he was really punishing himself. He looked for expensive items to question how long they had been in the store and why he had bought them in the first place. He was horrified at just how much of the cash that he needed to support his family was tied up on the shelves.

But worse than that, he was haunted by what he had seen during Pastor Kidd's fire-and-brimstone sermon yesterday. Its intolerant message troubled him deeply, but more importantly, the fervor in Cheryl's eyes had revealed something he should have recognized weeks, even months, before—an emerging intolerance consistent with sympathy for bombing abortion clinics.

By unspoken agreement, they had taken Clark home after the sermon and had each eaten their lunch privately, their communal trip for a family Sunday lunch a thing of the past. After lunch, Dwight had wanted a beer, but when he had reached into the refrigerator, he had found it bare, and there was not a drink to be had for miles around on a Sunday, so he had sat outside by the creek with his cigarettes, blindly watching the water run by, oblivious to the beautiful afternoon and the sound of the birds and insects around him. His mind had tossed and turned on why there was no beer in the refrigerator, for he was sure he hadn't drunk it all last night. Eventually, he couldn't escape his initial conclusion that Cheryl had thrown it away, but he knew that confronting her would lead to denial and an unproductive argument, so he had instead fretted about the financial problems of his store and broke out in a cold, panicked sweat. He had finished the last cigarette in the pack, viciously ground out the sparks on a rock, and slipped the butt back into the empty pack. Resisting the temptation to fetch another pack, he had crumpled the one in his hand and walked back to the house, throwing it into the trash on his way to the shed to fetch a shovel and work in the yard.

Sunday afternoon had passed in misery, and Dwight had eventually succumbed to the oblivion of uneven sleep, and today promised to continue the deepening of Dwight's despair. In the swimming supplies section of the store, Dwight stumbled upon a $300 pool liner that he did not remember buying. He was slumped on the floor, removing it from the dusty box, when a cough made him jump. He turned to see Darlene standing over him. His heart beat a little faster as his eyes ran from kitten-heeled leather boots and up the curves of her calves and thighs before he checked himself and looked at her face.

"Yes, Darlene?"

He privately acknowledged that over the last couple of weeks, his assistant had been doing an admirable job of single-handedly holding the business together while he felt sorry for himself. He would have to find an appropriate way to thank her.

"It's lunch time. I don't need long today, but there are a couple errands I'd like to run. Are you all right, Mr. Cook?"

Dwight smiled. "I'm not having a good day, Darlene. Actually, the truth is, the weekend was pretty bad and I'm having a hard time getting over it. You know, I'm really looking forward to having a couple of beers tonight."

Darlene looked intrigued and a little surprised. "I didn't know you drank, Mr. Cook."

"There's a lot about me you don't know."

Like what I'm thinking right now.

Involuntarily, he glanced down at long legs beneath the skirt that was only just long enough to be decent, but quickly caught himself and looked back up. "I shouldn't drink; it's against my religion, but I started a few months ago, and I must admit beer's pretty good. And I didn't have any in the house yesterday when I really needed one."

That tyrant threw them away.

Why was he telling Darlene this?

"Well, you look depressed. You've been real good to me, and I know business has been pretty bad, so if there's anything I can do to help…"

"You're a real cutie… I mean, sweetie, Darlene, you really are." He blushed at his slip, but Darlene didn't seem to have noticed. "You run along for lunch; I'll be fine."

"Thanks. I'll see you later."

She turned and was gone, but not before Dwight had taken a lingering, lecherous look at her body from behind. He turned back to the shelf and, disgusted with himself, punched the floor so hard that his knuckle bled.

He had spent a lot of time fantasizing about Darlene since Cheryl's rejection had deepened, and he now looked at her young body with growing frequency and desire. He knew she was off limits, but the attention she lavished on decorating her face to give prominence to its small, smooth features had become an infatuation, and he relished the moments when she stood close enough for him to smell her perfume and shampoo. He loved the way her hair bounced on her shoulders and the light veil of bangs that covered her dark eyebrows. Most of all, though, he loved the tight, revealing clothes she wore.

But what about her reputation?

Darlene had married at seventeen, less than a year after coming to work at the store, and Dwight had watched her mature from teenager to full womanhood. The greasy youths who had hung around her in the store during her short marriage had, in the four years since, matured into grown men who came in on Saturdays to drool over Darlene like dogs over raw meat. Dwight had a fair idea how she spent her weekends: how could he find such a licentious creature anything but revolting?

Yet her reputation was also an invitation.

Dwight slipped back into his morose contemplation, too depressed even to raise his head and look at Darlene when she returned from lunch and slipped past him into the back room. He mostly ignored the handful of customers that made up the afternoon's business, leaving them to Darlene's care and stealing the occasional glance at her from behind, especially when she bent down and her short denim skirt rode high up her thighs.

When the distinctive click of the door locking attracted his attention, he glanced at his watch and read that it was five minutes before six o'clock. Cook Hardware closed at six, but the store was empty, and the house rule was no new customers after 5:55. Dwight stood up and brushed off his jeans, which were dirty from a day on the floor, and went to the front counter, arriving too late to help Darlene close the register but in time to take the cash tray from her and carry it through to the narrow utility room at the back of the store where he would reconcile the day's takings. He left Darlene to finish pulling down the blinds and turning out the lights and was sitting at the desk, about to start pulling the money from the drawer, when he sensed Darlene looking over his shoulder. He turned toward the perfume and inhaled.

"Thanks, Darlene, I can finish up here. You take yourself home now."

"That's okay, I'd like to help you count up. And besides, I've brought you a little something." In two steps, she crossed from the desk to the particle-board bench that ran the length of the opposite wall. The countertop, fixed to the wall with cheap brackets above two filing cabinets and a compact refrigerator, was strewn with miscellaneous boxes and papers.

"Have you ever drunk vodka before?" She bent down and opened the door of the refrigerator.

Dwight spun his rotary chair around completely to face her. "Vodka?" he repeated in disbelief.

"Uh-huh." She removed two glasses filled with ice from the small freezer compartment and placed them on the counter above her head, then stood up and turned from the refrigerator with a full bottle of cold liquor in one hand and a small carton of orange juice in the other. "It's best to keep the vodka in the freezer, but you don't have room for it in that little one in there. Here, have a Screwdriver."

Darlene sloshed a generous helping of vodka into each of the glasses while Dwight studied the butterfly tattoo just above the waist of her skirt. Though he had seen the tattoo hundreds of times before, Dwight had never before studied the light fur in the grooves of her smooth back and the way the painted wings nestled under the hem of her shirt, and he felt an unusual thrill as he noticed them now. Darlene added a splash of orange juice to their glasses and returned the ingredients to the refrigerator. She kicked the door closed, stirred the drinks with a pen that was lying on the counter, then licked her makeshift stirrer dry. With a flourish, she dropped the pen, picked up the drinks, and turned to face him. "Here, this'll help you relax. I think you need it." She held out a glass.

Dwight held the crude cocktail up to his nose and took a sniff. His head jerked back.

Darlene tossed her head and laughed. "You're funny."

As the fire in his nostrils and eyes subsided, Dwight furrowed his brow and asked, "Where did this come from?"

Darlene shrugged. "You looked like you needed to chill real bad, so I stopped by the house at lunchtime."

"Well, that's mighty nice of you, Darlene." Dwight looked at the drink, his brow still furrowed, and repeated, "Mighty nice." He braced himself and took a sip, determined to keep his composure.

He managed to, but only just. It tasted like he imagined paint-stripper would, and had it not been ice-cold, he would probably have choked. He stared at the glass while he composed himself and recovered his breath. When he was ready to talk, he looked up at Darlene to find that she had been watching him. She smiled, took a sip of her own drink, and pulled herself up to sit on the counter above the refrigerator. Her skirt rode up, exposing flesh that Dwight's eyes found irresistible. Darlene had already pulled the fabric back down to cover her panties and crossed her legs before Dwight blushed and looked at his lap. He rested his glass on his knee and stared at it while he tried to compose himself, then rocked back and looked up at her.

"So what are you doing, bringing a bottle of vodka to work to share with an old man?"

"You're not an old man." Darlene laughed, and with a mocking tilt of her head and shimmy of her shoulders, added, "Anyway, I like my men mature." Resuming her upright pose and more serious demeanor, she continued, "Like I said earlier, you've been good to me. I know you don't need me in the store. There's not enough business to support you right now; hasn't been for months, so after all these years, giving you a couple of glasses of vodka and trying to cheer you up when you're having your last look around the store is the least I can do."

Dwight let out a snort. "Is that what you think I've been doing today, having a last look?"

"Look me in the eye and tell me it's not," Darlene challenged, resting her hands on the edge of the counter and leaning forward on them.

Dwight stared back, unable to answer. Was it that obvious to everyone except himself? He grunted and looked at his vodka before downing it in one gulp, grimacing and baring his teeth. Darlene slid off the counter. Her fingers touched Dwight's as she took the empty glass from his hand. He swallowed hard, and his greedy eyes watched her bend to retrieve, use, and then replace the Screwdriver ingredients in the refrigerator. She placed the refilled glass on his knee, let her hand linger against his, and resumed her position on the counter.

"So what are you going to do tonight?" she asked.

"Oh, I don't know," he said, but as he looked at Darlene, he knew what he wanted to do. "I guess I'll go home to my broken family and try to hide from them." He knew he shouldn't discuss such things, but not only did he not care, he was glad to get them off his chest, glad to have someone to talk to.

"What do you mean?"

Dwight laughed and sipped again. "You got a cigarette?"

"You drink, you smoke, what other little secrets have you got hidden away?" Darlene gave him a quizzical look as she reached into her purse and tossed him her pack and the lighter.

"Like I said, there's a lot about me you don't know." Dwight reached forward with the lighter resting on top of the pack, placed them on the counter, then settled back and sucked his cigarette. He exhaled and watched the smoke spiral for a moment before continuing. "I just smoke in the evenings to relax, you know. Cheryl hates it, of course." After another pause he returned to Darlene's question. "You don't want to know what's going on at home, it's not that interesting. Actually, it's pretty depressing." Dwight took another long sip of his Screwdriver between drags of his cigarette, sat back with a sigh and closed his eyes briefly. "This is really good," he said, then opened his eyes, raised his glass, and added, "It's just what I needed."

But as he lowered his glass again and looked at Darlene, young and tempting in front of him, the blood rushed to his head and his stomach churned. Dwight Cook was a married man with children, and a respectable member of the community, and to indulge his lust in this way, even as a voyeur, was deeply wrong. Besides, what would people say if they knew he was drinking vodka with a young woman of Darlene's reputation?

"I really ought to get off home."

Dwight sat up, spun his chair and put his glass on the desk.

"Why don't you stay just a little longer? I could use some company myself."

Dwight glanced over his shoulder and stopped, his glass still in his hand. Darlene had leaned forward so that her skirt rode up her long legs and her cleavage was thrust up, and she had cocked her head, looking at him with doe's eyes. She couldn't be flirting with him, could she? Dwight retrieved his glass and took another sip as his ambivalent heart pounded in his chest, the morals of a lifetime at war with the promise of physical gratification. The alcohol must be making him imagine things, but he was enjoying it.

"I'm kind of mad at my roommates," Darlene explained, "and I don't want to go home yet. Besides," she said as she leaned a little further forward, "you look like you still need cheering up some."

Dwight forced his eyes to stay on her face and swallowed hard. "Well, it's mighty nice of you. Maybe I can stay for just a little longer." He made himself comfortable once more and returned his glass to his knee.

"Say—" Darlene jerked upright, her eyes sparkling with an idea, "you want to play a game?"

"What kind of game?" Dwight curled up, laughing at a private joke that seemed riotously funny, and Darlene joined him, but he stopped when he realized he had no idea why he was laughing.

"Isn't there a pack of cards around here somewhere?" Darlene offered.

"You know, there might be." Dwight's eyes scanned the room, his brow furrowed in thought. "I've seen them somewhere... I know," he exclaimed, "they're in here!"

Dwight slid his chair the short distance to the filing cabinet beside Darlene, put his drink on the counter beside her, and opened a drawer. He rummaged around in it, distracted by Darlene's dangling legs and the tantalizing smell of their owner hovering over him. "Ah, here they are." He pulled out a handful of loose cards. "But they've been here forever, so there's probably not even a full deck." He rummaged a little while longer and recovered three more cards. Satisfied that he had completed his search, he closed the drawer and sat back in his chair to count them, but his inexperience with cards and the effect of the vodka rendered him ineffective and clumsy.

"Here, let me have a go." Darlene reached forward for the cards, and Dwight's eyes popped as her cleavage was thrust right under his nose. She sat up, straightened and shuffled the cards, then started to count, and Dwight watched, mesmerized, as her red fingernails worked quickly through the deck in threes, until she looked up and said, "Forty-seven."

"Well, shit." Dwight put his hand to his mouth in shock, then looked at Darlene, who was laughing.

"Mr. Cook, you really are full of surprises tonight. Well, with forty-seven cards, we're not going to be able to play anything serious, but we can have some fun. Why don't we play some poker? You know the rules?" Dwight shook his head while she shuffled the cards. "It's easy," she began. "We each get five cards, then we bet a while, then we change our cards once and bet some more, and the best hand wins the money. That's all there is to it. The betting's easy, too: You just put as much money in the pot as the other player, or put in more to raise, or you fold your hand." Darlene looked around, searching for something, and said, "If you've never played before, you need to know the hands." She reached for her makeshift stirrer, stood up, and crossed to the desk, where she rummaged for a blank piece of paper, and leaned beside the cash drawer to write.

The smell as she brushed past Dwight made his head swim. He hadn't felt like this in a long time, maybe even his whole life. He was intoxicated by the alcohol, by the idea of poker, and by the smell of the beautiful young woman who was flitting around him. He spun his chair around and pressed up against Darlene's arm to watch her write.

Darlene narrated as she tabulated the hands. "A royal flush—that's the ace, king, queen, jack, and ten of the same suit—is best, then comes a straight flush. You know what that is?" Dwight nodded. "Then comes four of a kind, then a flush, then... no, wait, a full house comes next, then a flush... then a straight... then three of a kind... then two pairs, a pair, and last, the high card. Okay." She slid the paper toward Dwight. "Is that clear?"

Dwight nodded and picked up the list.

"Good. Now we'll need some money to bet with." She frowned and looked around, then her face lit up, and she burst out, "Hey, let's just use cash from the store. Here, let me count some out." She pulled the cash tray toward her and, as if it were Monopoly money, counted out and gave them each three twenties, two tens, three fives, and five ones. "Minimum bet is two dollars, okay?" She thrust one hundred dollars in Dwight's hand and stepped back to the refrigerator. "Let's top up our drinks before we start."

The drinks refreshed, Darlene slid back up onto the counter and brushed the debris away from the area beside her. "Let's play right here. You want me to deal?"

Dwight nodded again, slid his chair closer, and put his money and the list of hands on the counter. Darlene lit two cigarettes and gave one to Dwight, then picked up the cards and placed the toe of her boot on his knee. Dwight knew he should push it off, knew that he should go home, but why go back to a morgue when he could be having fun with someone who wanted him around? Being touched by Darlene, even if it was just her boot, was thrilling.

"Okay," Darlene pressed on, "before I deal, we've both got to put in the ante—that's two dollars. Good. Now I deal us both five cards. One... two... three... four... five. Okay, now look at your cards. You're going to have one go at changing the cards you don't want, but you have to bet first."

Dwight fumbled with his cards. He had the queen of diamonds, the ten of spades, the seven of hearts, the six of clubs, and the two of hearts, and after he spent a few moments sorting them with reference to the list of hands, he realized that he had nothing.

"What do I do if I can't make one of those hands?" he asked.

"First off, you don't tell me." Darlene's giggle gave Dwight a fleeting glimpse of Cheryl twenty years ago. "What you should do is place a bet to stay in, then I either match or fold. If I fold, you keep the pot; otherwise, we change cards. You must keep at least one, which means you can change up to four, so with what you've got, you just keep your highest card. How many do you want?"

"Four." Dwight kept his queen and picked up a pair of fours. Darlene also changed four cards. Excited, Dwight put in ten dollars. Darlene matched him and revealed a pair of eights to win.

Dwight's next few hands went just as poorly, and it wasn't long before Darlene had all of his money.

"I guess that's it, then," Dwight said, disappointed that the thrill was over, but ready to call it a day.

"It would be if it was real poker, but since this is just for fun, how about I buy your boots and socks for twenty-five dollars apiece? Take them off and throw them over there," Darlene said, gesturing toward the corner of the room, "then I'll give you $100 and we can start again."

Darlene removed her foot from Dwight's knee and crossed her legs, and, jolted by shock, Dwight saw where this game might be headed. He looked up at Darlene, sure he couldn't be right, but his insides squirmed at the conspiratorial gaze she returned.

Maybe he would stay a little longer.

With Darlene's boot on his knee above a bare-foot and a replenished Screwdriver beside him, Dwight played more cautiously, trying to concentrate on the game and fighting to overcome the effects of the alcohol, and though he lost the next four, hands he didn't lose all his money. Slowly, he surged back, and though he had a feeling Darlene was playing to help him, was thrilled when he won a big pot and left her penniless.

"Well, I guess that's it," she said, chuckling.

"Hold it," Dwight said, confused. "Don't you want to play some more?"

"Well I'd love to, Dwight, only I don't have any money left."

Dwight's frown turned to a smile. "Well, you know I'm enjoying the game, and I'd hate to stop just because you've run out of money. I tell you what I'll do: I'll buy that shirt for $100." No sooner were the words out of his mouth than Dwight's amusement turned to embarrassment. He had spoken involuntarily, had overstepped the mark.

"Why, Dwight, that's quite a price for a little old t-shirt," Darlene said, and the challenge in her eyes made Dwight's intestines tie themselves in knots. He was sure he had crossed the line and was about to blurt out an apology when she smiled, crossed her arms over her belly, and, in a snap, pulled off her top and tossed it toward his boots. Dwight's embarrassment fled in the face of his racing pulse, and he stared at her flesh and the flimsy black bra for an eternity before looking back up at her face.

"Sorry, I don't mean to stare... I mean, it's rude... I mean... I'm sorry, Darlene. It's just, I never... "

"That's okay, Dwight." Darlene's voice was gentle, soothing. "We're just having a little fun here. You need a break, something to cheer you up, and besides," she said, her eyes darkening, "I've seen the way you look at me in the store." Her tinkling laughter shattered Dwight's awkwardness, and she added, "Now top up the drinks again, will you, and let's play another hand."

Fortunes ebbed and flowed as Darlene teased her boss. She lost her skirt, but he quickly lost his shirt, and after taking an early lead in the next round, Darlene lost but refused to sell her underwear before her shoes. Dwight protested when she insisted on selling him the ankle bracelet he had never seen before for $100 but backed down quickly and played along. He was upset when he lost his trousers, and even more so when, immediately afterward, his four-of-a-kind lost to a royal flush and cost him all his money in a large pot. Down to his underpants, with no money left, he had nowhere else to go.

"So I guess that's it," he said, a statement, not a question.

Darlene laughed. "It can be if you want, but I can see everything that's under there anyway." She slid her toes up his leg and stroked his erection through the fabric of his y-fronts. "I'll give you a hundred if you let him come out to breathe, and then we can keep playing."

Dwight was unable to move. He felt like a troll, ugly and unworthy and turned to stone by the sunlight, and the moral fabric of a lifetime shuddered at this wrong.

But no one had expressed this much interest in him in over ten years, and anyway, he had crossed the line a long time ago. Eventually, he regained control of his senses and spoke, his voice quaking. "Okay, let me top up the drinks first." He broke open the second Vodka bottle and could feel his heart pounding, fit to jump out of his chest, as he lit them both a cigarette. Unable to put it off any longer, he looked at the floor in embarrassment and removed his underpants as quickly as he could.

"Well now, that was worth playing for," Darlene said as Dwight sat back down.

Dwight looked up to see her staring down between his legs, and his embarrassment transformed into pride. He smiled self-consciously at her as he said, "You're the first woman—apart from Cheryl, that is—who's ever seen me naked. Well," Dwight paused to look at the ceiling, "I guess technically, Cheryl really hasn't *seen* me, 'cause we do it in the dark and under the covers."

"And you haven't done it with Cheryl for quite a while, have you?"

Dwight looked up sharply. "How do you know?"

"Oh, let's just say I can just tell." Darlene dismissed his question with a casual air, took a swig from her refreshed drink, and said, "Let's play a different game." She slid off the counter and stood in front of him for what seemed an age, then in quick movements popped off her bra and stepped out of her tiny black underpants. She glided forward, straddled his legs, and lowered herself onto his lap, then rested her arms on his shoulders and slowly, inexorably, moved her face toward his. Conflict raged inside Dwight, but only for a moment. He wrapped his arms around Darlene, pulled her close, and pressed his lips to hers.

Chapter Nine

The day after Pastor Kidd's sermon on sexual morality, Jessica bathed, dressed, and prepared her breakfast in silence. She looked around the kitchen for any sign that Ma and Dad had realized this was the first day of her sophomore year at high school, but there was none.

Jessica had been anticipating the opportunity to leave the crushing depression of home for weeks, but since any attempt at talking to her parents seemed to invite scorn and derision, she had not spoken of it. Instead, she had circled the date on the kitchen calendar with a bold red marker pen and had written beside it in large capitals, "BACK TO SCHOOL." No new bag or supplies had shown up, so she had scavenged as best she could from last year's materials and from odds and ends she had found around the house.

She was finishing her cereal and about to give up on her parents and walk to the bus when Dad came into the dining room, looked at the clock, and stood facing Jessica, his hands on his hips, waiting. Jessica took a last spoonful, rinsed her bowl in the kitchen sink, and, without a word being spoken, followed him to his truck.

The drive to school with Dad had always been ten minutes of fun, an opportunity for babbling early morning confidences, but today, they sat in the cab of the pickup a million miles apart, Jessica's bag clasped tightly to her chest as she stared through the windshield, numb and empty, until Dad pulled the truck to a stop and dropped the stickshift into neutral. Jessica cast a forlorn, unreturned glance at him, slipped out onto the sidewalk, and watched the truck drive off. With an ambivalent sigh, she turned to the noisy schoolyard. Although school would be a welcome relief from the depressing silence of home, now that it stood before her, she was terrified of the scorn and derision of her peers.

Jessica tossed her bag on her back and strode into the red brick building, thinking of Alison. They had met only once since the pregnancy test, at which time Jessica had shared her story of the two blue lines over a Moon-Pie. They had, however, talked several times by phone, and in yesterday's conversation, the enormity of returning to school pregnant and with a shaved head had hit Jessica. After they had hung up, Jessica had gone to the barn, but the two surviving kittens and their rapidly recovering mother no longer needed her help to nurse and had soon disappeared behind the bales of hay, leaving Jessica alone to weep.

Jessica wove along corridors to homeroom, anxiety mingled with pleasure, both at being away from her parents and at the prospect of time with Alison. A familiar voice called out, "Hi, Jessica," from behind, and her heart lifted as she turned to face her friend.

But her smile quickly disappeared when she saw that Alison had company.

"Hi, Alison. Hi, Rosalie."

"What happened to your hair?" Rosalie's question had a harsh edge.

"I had it cut off and gave it to charity for a wig." Jessica had prepared half a dozen stock replies that also included, "I had an accident with a harvester on the farm" and "I got it caught in an electric pencil sharpener."

"Really?"

Rosalie's sharp tone intimated that she had a follow-up. Jessica bit her tongue and braced herself.

"I heard that you had a boyfriend over the summer and that you both shaved your heads before you... before you made love." Rosalie giggled, embarrassed.

Jessica's laugh was bitter. "Yeah, we shaved all over. In fact, we shaved each other; you should try it. Come on, Alison, we don't have to put up with this."

But Alison looked back and forth between them sheepishly. "Rosalie and I were just talking about something. You go ahead, and I'll catch up with you."

Jessica pulled her head down low onto her shoulders, turned, and stormed off, furious.

How dare she side with Rosalie!

"Save me a seat," Alison's voice drifted after Jessica.

Though she didn't respond, Jessica did save a seat and was grateful when her best friend collapsed beside her, panting, just as the teacher arrived for the roll call. The morning passed quickly, though Jessica found the social interaction of the organizational sessions oppressive and raced through them, signing up for the bare minimum. She had returned to homeroom and was sitting alone, absorbed in her social studies textbook's narrative of the founding fathers, when Alison returned to drop off her things and fetch Jessica for lunch. They walked to the dining room together.

After six weeks of practice, Jessica had learned to ignore her environment, and as she walked, she cut off everything beyond the friend beside her. But the world intruded all too soon.

"So tell me what really happened." Rosalie had caught them up.

"I told you," Jessica snapped, resenting not just Rosalie's persistence, but even more the intrusion into her time with Alison, "I'm giving my body to charity one part at a time. They're giving a good deal on kidneys, too—you want the phone number?" She turned her back on Rosalie.

"Why are you hanging out with that miserable slut?" Rosalie asked Alison and brushed past, bumping heavily into Jessica on the way.

"Why do you have to behave like that?" Alison hissed at Jessica.

Jessica scowled into space and bit her tongue. She didn't have to explain herself. Besides, it was Rosalie's fault, anyway, poking her nose in like that.

When they reached the dining room, Jessica noticed with gratitude that a group of sophomore boys in the line separated her from Rosalie, meaning she would be left in peace with Alison while they waited for their food. She glanced around the room and noticed Colby on the far side, already eating his lunch with boys from his homeroom. She was still staring at him when he looked up and caught her eye. He immediately looked down at his plate, and Jessica felt a mean grin crease her face. She was glad that he was not in her grade—he was a senior—and hoped that he would maintain his apparent desire to avoid her. Jessica was still staring at the top of his head when another giggling voice intruded from behind.

"Want happened to your hair, Jessica?"

Was there a conspiracy to pester her? She turned to the two girls from her grade who had joined the line behind them, and snapped, "It's none of your business. Just leave me alone," and spun to face forward again. She ignored the embarrassment radiating from Alison, though out of the corner of her eye, she did see her friend shrug at the sniggering girls and hang her head.

Alison and Jessica ate their lunch in near silence. Afterward, while they were in the bathroom, Alison slipped away unannounced. She reappeared at the beginning of afternoon classes and once again sat beside Jessica, but over the next few days, she spent more time with Rosalie and other girls in the class. Jessica bitterly resented Alison's lack of loyalty, and as her isolation grew, she realized she was becoming surly and antisocial, behavior that she attributed to the hormonal changes that accompanied pregnancy.

"Why are you ignoring me?" she challenged Alison on Thursday morning before classes started.

Alison was sitting in the seat Jessica had saved on Monday and turned her head away to look out of the window. Jessica muttered a curse under her breath, intentionally loud enough for her friend to hear. Alison's head snapped back, her eyes ferocious and her gestures animated.

"Right now, you're the most horrible person I know, and you're so ungrateful. I drove you all the way to Baxton and you went home on your own, and now you're being rude to all my friends and making them mad at me. You look stupid without any hair, but you're making everything worse. It's just embarrassing to be with you; I don't know why I ever liked you."

Alison puffed her chest out and turned her face to the window again. Jessica stared at the back of Alison's head. She wanted to grab that frizzy ponytail and tear it out; perhaps then Alison would understand. Her fists clenched and unclenched under the desk, digging grooves into her palms, until the teacher arrived and distracted her.

Then the rumor-mill started to grind.

Jessica first overheard the poisonous stories in her homeroom on Friday right after she had seen Alison in a fiercely energetic conversation with Rosalie, and by Monday of the second week of school, it seemed that the whole sophomore year—the whole high school—was talking in whispers of a month-long secret tryst that she had kept with an unknown married man, and of the six-fingered, brain-damaged love-child that she was carrying.

What had Alison said to Rosalie? How could she have violated their confidence and turned the entire school against her? Jessica's bottled-up rage grew, and with it, the tension between them, until on Tuesday they had an ugly argument in the cafeteria and Jessica screamed, "I hate you," threw a glass of Coke over her friend, and stormed out, head down, knocking two trays flying from their astonished holders' hands on her way. She felt better for a while, but her actions got her suspended for two days—after all the years in which she had not resisted her parents' conforming pressure, she had found Ma's mute astonishment and silent anger almost funny—and completely ostracized her from the only person with whom she had been on speaking terms. When she returned from her short forced break on Friday, no one spoke to Jessica, but she overheard conversations at the lockers and in the hallways that seemed intended for her ears. She heard that her lover was black, or physically deformed—perhaps even both—that he was her pimp, that she would *do it* after class for $10. She wondered what to buy with the money that the rumors asserted she had been paid for her long and physically challenging summer services.

But when she entered her homeroom to see Alison sitting with Rosalie and the chair beside her own empty, tears sprang into her eyes. Jessica had not acknowledged to herself Alison's very special role as her only confidant and believer, and her best friend's absence was crushing. Alison was not only no longer available but had betrayed Jessica's trust. Jessica didn't think she could stand the pain. She ran to the restroom to hide for a period, skulked around for the next couple of lessons, then dragged herself to lunch, not wanting to encounter a hostile Alison, and stood alone in the line, silent amid the bubbling conversation, head low to avoid glances. She sat alone in the corner with her tray, poking her food and distracting herself with memories of childhood princesses. She decided to start bringing a book to read during lunch, but all her own books were dog-eared with use, and she had she read everything of interest at the Wilkeston library. Perhaps she could contrive a way to get to the Baxton library tomorrow, which would be Saturday.

Jessica was just starting to eat when a tray appeared on the table opposite her, accompanied by a male voice that asked, "Is it okay if I sit here?"

She muttered, "Sure," barely glancing at her companion, and returned to her food and her problem. While eating, she decided to forego Baxton and visit the Wilkeston library. Apart from the logistical simplicity, the reassurance of reading old favorites was what she wanted right now, anyway. Satisfied with her decision and having eaten her fill, she placed her empty plates on the tray and glanced again at the youth opposite her. He was familiar, though she didn't know him well, a boy in her class with an ordinary round face that lacked prominent features, the plastic kind of face with tan hair that reminds you of half a dozen acquaintances but leaves no lasting impression of its own. He looked up at Jessica and smiled, and his bright blue eyes lit up, but Jessica broke eye contact and moved on with a scowl.

That weekend—Jessica's second after returning to school—was a hard one, lonely and isolated. She was sure that, as Pastor Kidd had said, Ma was praying every night for her soul, but all Jessica experienced was icy coldness. She wanted to grab the miserable woman and shake her.

It's not about you, Ma, I'm despoiled and I'm pregnant, and I need you. Don't you understand, Ma? I need your help!

But Jessica was tired of trying to engage Ma, whether by persuasion or anger, and didn't have the energy to fight with her. Instead, she took her Bible—she smiled to herself and wondered whether "old habits die hard" or "hope springs eternal" was the more appropriate epithet—and sat on the bench along the back wall of Dad's workshop, interspersing romantic fiction she had borrowed from the Wilkeston library Saturday morning with her spiritual reading. Dad was there some of the time, too, and though he had lost his aura of invincibility and barely spoke, Jessica still found reassurance in the familiarity of the room and his occasional presence.

He had returned from church on Sunday and settled in to work under the hood of a tractor, apparently oblivious to Jessica's presence in the corner, when the sound of vehicles approached. Jessica put a finger on the page in her book and looked up at Dad as car doors slammed and the gentle murmur of voices bubbled outside.

"I wonder who that can be," Dad said to himself, wiping his hands and stepping out into the sun. Jessica didn't follow, but from the introductions and familiar voices, she recognized a delegation from the church. The noise quieted as the group entered the house, but Jessica's escape into romantic fiction had been disturbed, so she walked to the gas station for a lonely MoonPie. When she returned to the house an hour later, the visitors had left, and though neither of her parents spoke of what had transpired, Jessica knew it was something unpleasant, for their silence over dinner was oppressive, and Dad, who was a charter member of the clean-plate club, poked at his food and barely ate.

After dinner, Jessica toyed with the idea of going to the barn to see Maisie and her growing kittens, but the likelihood that they would have little interest in her presence, and the terrible memories of the place, sent her instead to Dad's workshop. He was already there, his head bowed over the workbench, a broken chair that he was repairing on the floor beside him.

"Dad, what's wrong?"

He shook his head and fidgeted with the wood on his table-saw, his shoulders hunched, and hiding from Jessica the sorrow that she knew was in his eyes. She wanted her old Dad back, the Dad who laughed and smiled and played. Jessica remembered the happy pictures in her grandparents' room, an array of Dad as a child with sparkling eyes and a broad grin, and a portrait of joy on her parents' faces on their wedding day.

And there was so much left for him to enjoy. Ma's parents had passed on many years ago, but her two sisters still lived nearby, and both had children. Aunt Meryl was even a member of the Church of the Epistles, and their son, Peter, was only a couple of years older than Jessica, and in the same high school. Aunt Emmy wasn't much further away in Baxton, with four younger children who could bring much joy to Dad. But Ma never associated with either of her sisters, and Jessica and Peter barely knew each other. Why was Ma so cut off? What sense of self-sacrifice or lack of self-worth pulled her into such morbid isolation? What right did she have to impose her rigid, antisocial self-loathing on this family?

Jessica wanted to slap Dad, tell him to pull himself together. She was no longer angry with Ma, on whom she had given up, but Dad… Dad! He should be strong, should be there to help and encourage Jessica, but instead, he was letting Ma drag him further down the path of exclusion and misery.

Wake up, Dad! Don't do this to yourself—to me.

In disgust and despair, Jessica left her books on the bench under the shelf that held her childhood carvings and ran out of the workshop, not knowing or caring if Dad was watching. She ran up the path, past the barn, and into the meadow, where she collapsed in a heap and sobbed. Shep, the younger of the two blue-heelers, came bounding across the field and nuzzled her, licking her face. Jessica tried to push him away and spoke angrily, but when Splash joined in, she couldn't resist. She rolled with them in the grass until she was laughing as she pushed and rubbed them, then chased and tackled them, finally collapsing again, this time contented after having worked out her anger and frustration. The dogs licked, nuzzled, and lay down beside her in the warmth of a late summer sunset.

*   *   *

When Jessica returned to school on Monday morning, she sat alone at her desk in the back of the classroom and tried not to look at the youth who had joined her at lunch on Friday, trying to ignore his occasional glances and his smile. But all morning she wondered if he would come and sit with her again. The excitement she felt seemed childish, and she knew it was a sign of her incredible loneliness. She wanted to kick herself.

Don't be silly. Why would he want to talk to a pregnant whore?

But he did. Friday repeated itself on Monday lunchtime, and when it happened again on Tuesday, Jessica put down her cutlery, leaned forward, and looked the boy squarely in the eyes. "It's Clark Cook, right?"

"That's right, Jessica."

"Your dad runs the hardware store?"

"For now." He grinned at her.

"What does that mean?"

"Well, it's not going very well. You see, business has been down ever since the Walmart opened. Dad doesn't talk about it much, but we didn't do anything at all this summer—you know, like vacations or trips and stuff— and I think he's having a hard time making ends meet."

Jessica nodded and returned to her food. They didn't speak again, but the ice was broken.

Jessica had never noticed Clark before, but his persistent presence at lunch made her start paying attention to him. As she did, she realized he had been in her grade for as long as she could remember. He talked and joked with his friends, but somehow just didn't stand out, and Jessica realized that she was not the only person who hadn't noticed him. He was in several of her classes, and though he sat in the middle of the room, the teachers never asked him questions. Was it the way that he kept his head down? Or the very ordinary clothes that he wore? Or the way he just completed his work and paid attention in an average kind of way? He was polite, friendly, bright, and athletic, all the things a boy should be, but somehow, he was invisible, and Jessica could not place her finger on why. Even though they must have been in school together for ten years, she knew nothing about this chameleon that disappeared—even among his friends—accepted yet independent, able to come and go as he pleased. She was intrigued. Halfway through their lunch together on Wednesday, Jessica put down her cutlery and looked at him again.

"Why do you keep sitting with me?"

"I don't know."

"Don't be stupid, of course you do." She looked down and poked her food, and after a few moments, spoke again in a whisper. "It's not true, you know. I'm not like that."

"Like what?"

Jessica raised her eyes and studied Clark, for the hundredth time in a week trying to figure him out. His tan hair was floppy and not well-combed; his clothes were not neat, though nothing he wore was out of place; and he wore heavy-framed glasses so that only when she established eye contact with him could she see that his eyes sparkled with wit, intelligence, and compassion. Looking closely at him, Jessica found to her surprise that he was actually quite handsome. She spoke again, a little louder this time, but not enough to be overheard.

"All that stuff about me doing... doing, you know... doing *it* for money. That stuff I'm supposed to have done this summer. You know... the affair and all of that, everything. I'm not like that, really, I'm not."

"Really, I know." His tone was gently mocking, but he smiled sweetly and endearingly at Jessica, then looked down to put a forkful of meatloaf into his mouth.

His smile!

Jessica was taken aback, and something wriggled inside her. She hadn't been expecting that to happen.

"How do you know?"

It was Clark's turn to put his knife and fork down and lean forward. "Jessica, I don't think you noticed, but we were in the same first-grade homeroom. I've seen you grow up, and I've seen how careful you are with guys, like you pretty much won't have anything to do with them. The only reason you're letting me sit here right now is that you've had a row with Alison and all your friends have abandoned you. I don't know what happened over the summer, but I do know it wasn't... *that*." Decisively, he picked up his knife and fork and continued eating.

Jessica was embarrassed. She had been afraid that he was after easy sex with the school slut, but she had apparently completely misjudged him.

"I'm sorry."

"You don't have anything to be sorry, Jessica. I'm sure your life is pretty tough right now, and you've got your guard up. I'd just like to help you... if you want help, that is. If not, I'd just like to sit here with you." Jessica watched him scoop up his mashed potatoes and felt a warm pleasure welling up in her belly. It was not sexual attraction in the way she had experienced it with Colby, but comfortable, a new set of clothes that immediately fit, a soft toy that felt good, and she realized that she was content just to have Clark sit with her. He didn't need to talk or do anything, just be there.

"I am pregnant, though."

What are you thinking?

Her mouth had run ahead of her mind once again, and she looked around to make sure no one else had heard. She was glad to see that they hadn't, but more important was how Clark—her new hope for companionship—would react to this bombshell.

"Is that so?" He lowered his cutlery and looked up.

"Yes." Jessica nodded nervously, biting her lip. She wanted to scream, to bang her head against the table. One solitary soul had reached out into her lonely misery, and her self-destructive response had been to try to drive him away, first by offending him and then by telling him her ugly personal secrets.

Clark looked at her in intense silence, apparently composing his thoughts, while Jessica burned. Her heart was in her throat when he finally spoke.

"I don't want to dismiss it casually, because it's got to be the most important thing in your life right now, and I'm sure you've got a complicated and disturbing story about how it happened." After a silence that seemed to go on forever, Clark shrugged and returned to his food. "But I figured you probably were."

Jessica's insides squirmed again, and her heart pounded. Who was this guy, and how had she not noticed him all the years they had been in the same grade? And what had she done to deserve this unexpected kindness? She wasn't sure what she felt.

Over the next few days, the amount of time they spent together grew. Their quiet lunches became conversational, and they started to walk around the schoolyard during skipped periods, talking and laughing. Jessica arrived at school a little earlier every day, and they hung out together in the mornings before class started. On Saturday morning, they met up at the gas station to sit on the fence and eat MoonPies and drink Cokes. It was good to have someone to talk to again, and Clark listened, silent and serious, as Jessica told him about Colby, about her abandonment by parents and church, and finally about Alison's treachery.

"She's a good friend to you, you know," Clark said, speaking for the first time since Jessica had begun her tale of woe. Jessica was shocked at his defense of this traitor, and she jumped off the fence and turned, hands on hips, to unleash her fury on him, but when she looked inside his glasses, she saw something that cut off her tongue. Uncertain, her arms fell to her side and she waited.

"You're not going to like this," Clark said, "but you need to know. She didn't really tell people anything. You did that." He nodded at Jessica's inarticulate protestation. "You came to school with your hair all gone and behaving like a royal bitch, and everyone who knew you said that you'd been hiding for the last month. Something had obviously been going on, so when Alison slipped up and said one stupid thing—I bet no one can even remember what it was now—the rest of the class jumped on it and blew it out of proportion."

Jessica stared at the grass at her feet. She had been planning to bite Clark's head off, but deep down, she knew that he was right, and she felt terrible. After a long silence, she kicked a stone and asked the grass, "What should I do?"

Clark waited, as if to give the grass a chance to answer, but when it didn't, he offered his thoughts. "I can't tell you what to do, but I think Alison feels really terrible, too, and my guess is she'd love to be friends again. But if you want that to happen, you'll need to talk to her, maybe even apologize."

After they talked a little longer, Clark needed to leave to fulfill a promise he had made to help his Dad at the store and give the regular assistant the afternoon off, but he and Jessica agreed to get back together the following afternoon after Clark had been to church.

Jessica spent the rest of Saturday in a dreamy mood, oblivious to the concentrated, almost physically oppressive rejection that her parents radiated. This was the first weekend she had enjoyed for a month, and Sunday morning, while her parents were at church, Jessica luxuriated in her privacy, taking a long bath, putting on her best dress. She was outside playing with the dogs, ready to go and meet Clark, when she heard a rumble of gravel and realized that it must be almost lunchtime and that her parents were already home. She had meant to leave before they arrived back from church and stood up, preparing to beat a hasty exit, hoping she wasn't late for Clark, but she sensed that something was wrong. She stopped to listen. It took her a moment to realize that the noise was too loud to be a single truck.

She ran her fingers through hair that now showed the beginnings of a bob, straightened her dress, and walked around the house to see a flotilla of vehicles, led by Dad's truck, dragging a cloud of dirt up the track to the farmhouse. In Dad's dusty wake she could make out the same seven or eight vehicles that had visited the previous Sunday, and which she knew contained the church elders. Jessica stepped into the middle of the driveway, planted her feet firmly, placed her clenched fists on her hips, and held her head high. She was sure that this convoy had come to visit her and that they were not bearing glad tidings, but she was equally sure that she needed to face it. Dad's truck pulled to a stop several yards short of her, and her parents emerged, taking short, nervous glances at each other and at the throng emerging from the assorted trucks and cars behind them. They were thrust to the fore of the crowd that pressed toward Jessica, who waited, defiance coursing through her veins.

Dad looked terrible, as if he were suffering from a debilitating disease, and his head hung in what Jessica read as shame. Ma, on the other hand, while neither comfortable nor confident, seemed more in tune with the situation. She stepped forward from the crowd that formed a semicircle in front of Jessica and spoke. "Jessica, everyone at the church cares very much for you, and we've talked about what's best for... our problem."

Jessica bristled but bit her tongue, and Ma continued, oblivious.

"The elders have decided we need to deal with this once and for all. You're going to have a child—everyone knows that now—that was conceived in sin, and we all want to do our best to make things right. It's the father's responsibility and right to look after you and help you raise your child, even though you're not of marrying age, but the thing is, no one knows who he is." She stared at Jessica for a few more moments, but when Jessica did not blink, she looked down at the ground.

Jessica could not tell what was going on in her mother's head right now, but she didn't really care. She looked around the group in mute disbelief, and they started to mumble into the silence left by Ma. Finally, a few coherent phrases popped out:

"Tell us the father's name."

"Yeah, who is he?

"Is he from around here?"

"Stop it!" rang out a harsh voice.

Shocked silence reigned, and all eyes turned to Dad, who stepped forward and turned to the gathered crowd. "This is no way to treat a dog, let alone a human being. This is my daughter, and I love her." He turned to Jessica, tears streaming down his face. After what seemed an eternity, he knelt down and wrapped his arms around her hips.

"Jessica, I'm sorry. The church elders have decided that you should live with the father of your child and marry him when you're old enough. That's what your mother wants, too, and it'll be real hard for all of us at first, but I think it's best for everyone. You can't have a legal wedding till next summer, so the child will be illegitimate, but at least this way, he—or she—will grow up with both parents. I know it's not perfect, but it's probably the best way. I'm sorry." He leaned forward and held her tight, his head pressed on her belly.

Jessica looked down at the top of her father's head, her mind in a whirl. She had known that the domestic and congregational crises caused by her pregnancy would come to a head, but she had not expected it to happen so quickly, or in this way. Dad was so lost, so out of his depth, that, to her surprise, she found herself feeling sorry for him, and she placed her hand on his head and stroked his hair.

"It's okay, Dad," she said gently, "we'll get through this. We always have before, right?" He choked on his tears and looked up wanly into her smile. "Besides, you and Ma were married when you were sixteen, and I know you wanted children straight away."

The crowd started to mumble again.

Jessica's desperate mind scrambled for something to hang onto, for a place to go, but it was unable to find an anchor until, unexpectedly, a memory arose.

"... there's something about him."

Why her father's words should come back now, she didn't understand, but everyone in her life had abandoned her, and while what she was about to do made no sense, born of desperation, it seemed her only choice. She looked around the expectant faces and smiled, liberated, speaking with a reckless thrill.

"Okay, I'll tell you. The father of my child is Old Sam."

Chapter Ten

Simon sat opposite his mother, listening, when she telephoned Aunt Jodi and asked her to take him in immediately for what she described as "a short while." When it became clear that Mom would not explain why, Simon tried to grab the phone, but she hung up too quickly for him. He arrived at Aunt Jodi's shortly thereafter, expecting to spend the last night of his summer vacation answering questions, but instead he was surprised by his hostess's quiet acceptance of his presence. He found this silence awkward, and was not just surprised but disappointed, for he was lost and confused and needed someone to talk to. After a couple of hours, Simon's agitation grew to the bursting point, and he volunteered everything, beginning with the discovery of his love for Peter and moving through Mom's fear that he was damned and that she would never see him again, the vitriolic sermon, and Dad's assault. Aunt Jodi listened, gently swinging in her old rocking chair, occasionally sighing "Hmmm" or grunting "Uh-huh" while she sipped her lemonade. After Simon had finished and leaned back expectantly, Aunt Jodi continued to sit, the ice in her lemonade chinking against the glass as she rocked.

"Aren't you going to say something, Aunt Jodi?"

"What do you want me to say, dear?"

"I don't know, anything. Just tell me what you think."

"What I think? Well now, I'm just a childless widow, and I don't know that what I think really matters here. You young folk, I don't know. If I tell you what I think and you like it, then it makes you self-righteous, and off you go, and if you don't, then I'm just another middle-aged fool who doesn't understand, so I don't think you really need to know what I think."

Simon was flummoxed. He faced Aunt Jodi across the small, cluttered lounge in frustrated silence, trying to read the shrunken face he loved.

After a while, Aunt Jodi grunted. "I know he's your dad," she relented, "and you love him very much—and that's the way it should be—but he's a complete brute, always has been." Aunt Jodi shook her head and spoke to no one in particular, "To this day, I don't know what your mother ever saw in him." She blinked twice, as if returning to the present, and smiled at Simon. "It'll be a long time before it's safe for you to go back there, so we're going to have to get used to living together, and that's okay, because I sure do love company. The first thing we've got to do is get some groceries in because I don't have anywhere near enough food in the house for a growing lad, so let's make a list, and then we can go to the store together. And you probably need some stuff for school tomorrow, don't you?"

Simon realized that he hadn't eaten since breakfast and was famished, so he raided Aunt Jodi's breakfast cereal to fortify him for two hours of shopping and cooking. Dinner was relaxing, and he had a good time, forgetting his woes enough even to laugh, and after eating, they worked on a jigsaw puzzle together, but when Aunt Jodi went to bed early, she left him alone with his doubt. Simon needed to know if his homosexuality would condemn him to eternal damnation, a quest which took him online, using Aunt Jodi's computer to explore gay Christian sites. He was drawn to a recurring message that homosexuality is a test and that the reward for withstanding it is in the eternal afterlife. Simon returned to his room and studied Peter's portrait, stroking the face he adored while tears misted his eyes, then stiffened his spine, wiped his face, and covered the picture with its sheet and slipped it under the bed. He must be strong, but he could not do this alone, so he knelt and prayed in repentance of his weakness and asked for God's support of his new commitment to abstinence.

On Monday morning, he awoke well-rested, and it took him a few moments to realize where he was, then a few more to throw on enough clothes to feel presentable for Aunt Jodi's kitchen, marveling that, with all his worries, he could have slept so well. Over his protests, Aunt Jodi insisted on preparing a heavy but delicious breakfast of bacon, eggs, and grits, and despite the oversize portion, he found it pleasant to begin the day with her. Simon let his food settle, then showered, dressed, and walked the short distance to the high school, unenthusiastic about facing the world and intentionally arriving right as class was to start.

He and Peter were in different homerooms, which was a mixed blessing, offsetting the pain of missing his friend with reassurance in the knowledge that he needed the separation. To his surprise, the morning was not just uneventful, but actually quite enjoyable, and the organizational sessions with which the school year always began were an easy way to break back into things, offering a lighthearted chance to over-commit for the year ahead. He had missed the open day the previous week, but had a second chance to sign up for clubs and extracurricular activities and decided on chemistry club, cross-country, and karate, thinking of his dad as he put his name to this last.

Several times during the morning, he bumped into Jake and Scott, an inseparable pair, both small-framed with underdeveloped upper bodies and matching mops of floppy, blond hair. They were members of the Baptist church, shared Simon's distaste for football, and had been in Simon's home-room and chemistry club together for years. Only Simon's closeness to Peter had prevented them from becoming good friends. After signing up for cross-country—a first for Jake and Scott, though not for Simon—they renewed their membership of chemistry club and went to lunch together, and Simon accompanied them to directly to their chemistry class afterward, where the threesome clustered around the end of a lab bench.

The intensity of the class was a dramatic change from the comfortable morning and brought home to Simon how much work he had to get through in his last year at high school if he was to make it to college. His mind was on the upcoming history class, never his favorite subject, when he went to the restroom during afternoon break, and he was not watching where he was going as he washed and dried his hands, turned, and collided with Peter in the doorway. It was the first time they had touched, the first time they had been close, since Simon's birthday celebration.

"Oops—oh, hi." Peter spoke first, his hand on Simon's chest.

"Hi." Simon stepped hastily around Peter, letting the smaller boy's hands fall to his sides, and looked around, afraid they had been seen.

"What's the matter?"

"Nothing." But Simon winced at the speed of his answer, which advertised it as a lie.

Of course something's the matter!

Peter didn't speak, and under the scrutiny of silence, Simon cracked. He looked around to make sure no one could hear and whispered, "Peter, I love you, but I can't do this. I need to stay true to God's word, and what we did was wrong." Pressure built in Simon's chest and face as he struggled to say the words he didn't want to speak, words that would break both their hearts. "We can't see each other any more, Peter."

A wave of nausea passed over Simon, and he nearly recanted when he looked at the expression on Peter's face, saw the tears welling behind heavy glasses, but he knew he must be firm.

"I'm not strong enough to resist when we're together, Peter; it's the only way."

When Peter spoke his voice was flat. "I understand. I'll miss you desperately, but I understand. Just know that I'll be here when you're ready." Simon watched the door close behind Peter's bowed back and hanging head, aching to follow him into the bathroom and hold him, but he gritted his teeth and turned the other way.

The intensity of the history class that followed the break brought Simon's mind sharply back to schoolwork and drove home how much harder he would have to work this year to keep up. He walked home to Aunt Jodi's that night with his bag full of homework which, together with his extracurricular activities, would be a welcome distraction from his sexual insecurity and the problems of his family.

Aunt Jodi cooked another working man's meal, a large helping of meatloaf accompanied by mounds of mashed potatoes and fried okra. It was delicious, but Simon insisted that if she kept on cooking for him like this, he would put on a hundred pounds before he graduated, and she reluctantly agreed to scale back on the size of his future portions. Simon retired with a full belly to his bedroom to do his homework and to try to get a little bit ahead on his history.

He spoke by phone with Mom on Tuesday night. She told him that she had picked Dad up Monday morning, after a night in the cell, and that charges were not going to be pressed. She told Simon that she was glad that he was with his aunt, and didn't have to add that it was because Dad was still furious about his son being "one of them fag pervs." Simon had little doubt that, were he at home, he would be beaten black and blue every day until he either repented of his sin and reformed or died from his father's abuse. But Dad was one of God's simple creatures, and even though Simon was only a mile away, he was out of sight, and therefore out of mind. Apparently, there were plenty of more immediate sins and sinners to which Dad could turn his judgment and anger. Simon briefly wondered whether his mother's betrayal in calling the police made her one of them, for she wouldn't really tell him that she was doing well and evaded his questions, too soon interrupting the conversation mid-sentence, whispering, "Your father's coming now; I've got to go," and hanging up. But partly out of blind terror of Dad, Simon buried that worry at the back of his mind and allowed his attention to be deflected by the more immediate challenges of his classwork. He wanted to see Mom, but she had told him that because it would be difficult to sneak away from Dad, they would have to wait a while.

By the end of the first week of school, Simon had slipped into a comfortable routine of early morning runs with a cross-country team that included his new friends, Jake and Scott, frantically full days in the classroom that often left his head spinning, a daily debate with Aunt Jodi about appropriate serving sizes for a growing seventeen-year-old boy, and heavy evenings in his bedroom doing his homework and practicing karate. He was confident that his vow of separation from Peter was the right decision, though his heart grieved every time he caught a glimpse of his best friend at school and every time he slipped the portrait out from under the bed and stole a guilty peek.

It was only a few days before Simon had his first abrupt indication that he hadn't left his troubles behind. He was walking to chemistry with Jake when a voice behind him simpered, "Is that your new boyfriend?" before bursting into laughter. Stunned, Simon turned to see a small group of seniors walking down the locker-lined hallway away from them. He recognized them but knew none of them well.

"What was that?" Jake asked, staring at Simon.

Realizing he was probably ashen-faced, Simon pulled himself together and turned to Jake with a frown.

"I've no idea."

"That's Colby Kidd and Robbie Cook; they're from your church, aren't they?"

"Yeah, but I don't really talk to them much," Simon said, anxious to distance himself. "Come on, let's get to class, or we'll be late."

They made their way in silence, but Simon was unable to pay attention in class for the rest of the day.

Is that your new boyfriend?

How did Robbie know? What had Simon done to give himself away? The rest of the day passed slowly in an uncomfortable, extended blur, punctuated by the onset of a cold sweat and skittish glances over his shoulder. The panic attacks continued intermittently, even after Simon arrived home and Aunt Jodi clucked over him at dinner, but Simon blew it off and crept off to his room to do his homework. Somehow, he managed to pay enough attention to finish, an important accomplishment, because he didn't want to fall behind on his schoolwork so early in the year.

With his homework complete, Simon read his Bible and tossed and turned into the small hours, interspersing his frantic fear with Pastor Kidd's readings from Leviticus and Revelations, until finally entering a short and troubled sleep.

The following day at school, Simon was anxious to avoid Robbie completely, but he let his guard down in the cafeteria at lunch. With Scott beside him and Jake opposite, he was eating his food and listening to his classmate's questions about electron orbitals when Jake stopped talking and looked up. Simon half-turned his head, enough to see the shadow of a tall figure behind him.

"Cassell, your boyfriend asked me to give you this."

A hand reached over Simon's shoulder and dropped a small envelope onto the table in front of him. Simon moved quickly to brush it into his lap, and in the same smooth movement turned to see Robbie Cook returning to a small group of boys chuckling in the line. To his shock, he recognized Colby Kidd, the pastor's son, who was not only among them but was glancing venomously at Simon and apparently sharing a secret with Robbie. Simon had already guessed that Mom had gone to talk to Pastor Kidd, for why else would he have given *that* sermon? Perhaps, he now wondered, Colby had overheard? Although Simon would return to his speculation later, right now, his frantic mind was interrupted by his companions.

"What was that all about?" asked Scott.

"I've no idea."

"What was it he said yesterday: 'Who's your new boyfriend?'" Jake asked. "Wasn't it something like that? What's going on, Simon?"

"I don't know. He's just picking on me, but I don't know why, because I don't even know him."

"Let's see that note he dropped on the table." It was Scott's turn to press Simon, and he reached toward the bigger boy's lap.

"No." Simon hurriedly pushed the paper into his pocket.

"Why not? What's it say?"

"I've no idea, but I'm sure it's spiteful, so I'm not going to show you."

"You're not gay, are you?" This was Jake, and Simon looked at him, not having to feign shock.

"Gay? Of course I'm not; do I look it?" Simon felt desperation in his voice as he struggled to control himself.

"No, you don't," Jake replied, "but my dad says you can't always tell. He says I need to stay on guard because Satan is always trying to creep up on me disguised as regular Christian folk, and that once he gets to know you, he makes terrible things sound okay. He tempts you to sin by making it seem like regular behavior. Dad says that fags are the worst of all."

"My dad hates gays, too," added Scott.

"So does mine." Simon voted with his friends, at the same time feeling sick as his life began to fall apart again. Soon, he would be marked out as the only gay in the school and would be ridiculed and bullied without mercy. At afternoon break, he slipped into the bathroom, locked himself in a stall with his trousers around his ankles, and let his shaking fingers open the note. A swimming dizziness descended, and his vision blurred as he read and reread:

You fag queer pervert. You are an abomination. You make me sick. Remember Leviticus? If a man lieth with mankind instead of a woman, they have both committed an abomination and shall surely be put to death. Their blood shall be upon them. Who did you lie with, gay boy? Who will you die with?

A bead of sweat dropping from Simon's forehead onto the note brought him back to his senses. He wiped his forehead and sat up straight, reconciling himself to his new future, one that contained the possibility of physical assault that had not occurred to him until now. He had foreseen that his new friendships would be torn apart, anticipated facing the school year alone and humiliated, but had not thought of his physical safety. He had not had a fight at school since the fifth grade, but approaching this as a physical challenge gave it a concrete form that, in a strange way, would make it easier. He pulled his trousers up, folded the paper, and stuck it back into his pocket. He flushed the toilet, at once terrified and resigned, and left the bathroom to face a new world.

Mom visited him at Aunt Jodi's the following night during the men's Bible discussion group that Dad attended. Simon told her about his new friends, about how hard his lessons were, and about the teachers, but he didn't bring up Robbie's note. He didn't have to work hard to steer away from the topic or to look engaged, because he was sincerely worried about her, and she was preoccupied by his homosexuality. For the whole hour, she hung her head, and her eyes, under which dark bags sagged, were dull and lifeless. He asked if she was all right and if Dad was treating her well. Her answers were full of happy words and smiles, but a spark was missing, and she continued to deflect his questions, discussing his homosexuality, repeatedly begging him to repent of his sin and reform so she wouldn't lose him for eternity. When she had gone, he locked himself in his room, recognizing that his real problems were not the intolerance of a few boys at school, but the great rift separating him from his parents. Simon wept.

The following morning over breakfast, he talked tearfully to Aunt Jodi's back while she worked at the sink. She was reassuringly pragmatic. "Your father's been a narrow-minded thug for the entire twenty years of their marriage, and he's not done anything to hurt her yet. I know she looks awful, but it's pretty much all in her head." Aunt Jodi glanced at Simon with a resigned smile and added, "It would upset her even more if she knew you were worried about her right now, so try to concentrate on your schoolwork, all right?"

"Mom told me about Skip."

Aunt Jodi stopped and leaned her hands on the counter. After a few moments, she turned her head over her shoulder, turtle like, and asked, "What did she tell you?"

Simon didn't look at Aunt Jodi but stared blankly out of the window behind her and said, "I see the kids at school with drugs all the time." Anger welled up, tears formed in his eyes, and he looked at Aunt Jodi and blurted out, "Why didn't you tell me before?"

Aunt Jodi turned off the taps, wiping her hands as she crossed the room to sit down, and reached across the table to take Simon's hands in hers. After a long silence, she moved one hand to wipe the tears from her eyes, then said, "Because I can't bear to think about it. My two brothers are gone because none of us could talk sense into them about drugs, and Joey won't even let me visit him anymore. Your grandparents, may they rest in peace, never recovered from it and carried Skip's death as their personal cross into an early grave. You know your Mom was very close to Skip?"

Simon nodded. "She told me."

Aunt Jodi paused, and Simon could feel her eyes probing, wondering, "What else did she tell you?" But she didn't ask. Instead, she continued, "Rachel took his death really hard. She was suicidal for a while, but then she jumped into the deep end with that idiot, Brandon, and ended up marrying him. At first I thought he was a good Christian boy who would give purpose to her life, but then I saw him for what he was: trailer trash." Aunt Jodi squeezed Simon's hand and smiled through her tears. "Sorry dear. I shouldn't talk about your dad like that, should I?"

"It's okay; I know you don't like him."

Aunt Jodi squeezed his hand again and continued, "He had a really violent upbringing, but you probably know that, too?" Simon nodded. "Do you know he has two older brothers?"

"I think one's in California and one's in Seattle?"

Aunt Jodi nodded. "They left home as soon as they could and went as far away as possible. They never even came home for their dad's funeral. And his mother?"

Simon shrugged.

"Leticia Cassell." Aunt Jodi shook her head and looked up. "No, he doesn't talk about her much, does he? Within a year of Bart driving into that tree, she married again. I can't even remember the guy's name, but he was another complete loser. He beat her just like Bart had done. I'd hear Brandon ranting to your mom about it; he was so disappointed, but that marriage didn't last. The guy got into trouble with the law and up and left town one night.

"Leticia's on her fourth or fifth marriage now, and they've all been the same: alcoholics with pit bulls who live in run-down trailers, get drunk every night, and beat her until they get so bored they kick her out or move on. I think Brandon sends her a little money from time to time, but he wants nothing to do with her. She lives just over the way in Ninjimana—you might want to go see her sometime."

"So how come you don't go to church?"

"I do occasionally."

"You never come to the Church of the Epistles."

Aunt Jodi threw her head back and laughed out loud. "I'd as soon pull my fingernails out with pliers! Boy, how do I answer *that* one?" She released Simon's hand and folded her own on the table in front of her with a sigh. "I've been a Christian all my life, and I still am. We were raised Presbyterian, but we went Methodist for a while, even your Mom. I've tried 'em all, honey! Then Rachel started going to the Church of the Epistles with Brandon and brought home ideas about who was to be saved and who was to be damned, acting like she was the right hand of God. She started despising people for their lack of faith, even Uncle Walt and me. She was infatuated with Brandon and got sucked into his church and its bigotry. She never had—she still doesn't have—the hatred that some of those people do, but some of the things I've heard… " Aunt Jodi shook her head. "I honestly wouldn't put it past them to kill someone in their self-righteousness."

"Like me?"

"Oh, Simon." Aunt Jodi cradled his hands, and tears welled once more in her eyes. "Oh, Simon, if only you could have avoided the curse of this family." She released his hands, wiped her eyes, and said, "But don't you listen to me." She slid her chair back as if to stand up but stopped when Simon spoke.

"You haven't answered my question. You hardly ever go to church any more."

Aunt Jodi nodded, settled back into her seat, and said, "After what I'd been through, I lost my faith for a while, but then I came to realize that what matters is the mystery of the Gospel, and that it's beyond the doctrine of any church. You can't just study the words of the Bible; you have to make them fresh and new and bring them into your life. You have to experience Jesus as God-made-flesh directly. I realized my religion was too narrow—it still is. I judge people every day, but Jesus came to live among us so he could assume our sins, and he never judged a soul. The God I worship wouldn't damn someone for eternity because he was born in Arabia and only ever heard the Qur'an or because he never truly knew that Christ died to save him, and certainly not because he didn't go to the Church of the Epistles. If we can fully accept that Christ died for our sins, we are saved, but I think that 'fully accepting' means we need to live the life of Christ, a life of tolerance and compassion. We can't use faith in the afterlife as an excuse for acting irresponsibly and selfishly in this life, and I can't go to a church that doesn't understand that."

"So you don't think I'm going to hell because I'm gay?"

"I don't think it's for any of us to know if we're going to heaven or not—actually, Jesus even tells us we can't know—and as far as I'm concerned, the person who believes he knows is an arrogant fool. I have no idea whether you're going to heaven or hell, but I do believe that whether you're gay or not will have nothing to do with it, just like I believe that whether your mother goes to heaven or not will have nothing to do with her going to that hateful place every Sunday." Aunt Jodi stood up and returned to the sink, ending the conversation with a sigh.

Over the next few days, the rumors at school grew, Scott and Jake abandoned Simon, and his isolation and anger grew. Changing in the locker room for cross-country in the morning became so uncomfortable that he stopped attending, but early morning running had become an important part of staying fit for karate—at which he found, to his surprise, he was quite good—so that he started every day with a run in the logging trails in the woods behind Aunt Jodi's house. He concentrated on his schoolwork, and every evening, after finishing his homework, he studied the DVDs that his parents had given him for his birthday, practicing until he could follow along with his eyes closed, gaining confidence and ability in his art.

Although the barbs at school directed at Simon's homosexuality made him angry, he retained his composure. But when his sparring partner in an evening karate lesson whispered, "So what kind of demon mother has a gay son?" Simon lost his temper. Rather than lashing out immediately, though, he breathed slowly and deeply and waited for his opportunity, and when the moment presented itself, he threw the boy onto the mat at an awkward angle. There was a crunch, but before the cry of pain had even reached his ears, Simon had fallen on his opponent, his elbow ramming hard into the boy's solar plexus.

Too late, a rush of guilt overwhelmed Simon, and he pulled himself to his knees beside his victim, hands clasped and whispering, "Oh, my goodness, are you all right? I'm sorry, Josh, I'm so sorry." The instructor rushed over to the cries of pain and pushed Simon aside, knelt beside the boy, and quickly diagnosed a broken collarbone. The injured youth told the instructor that it had been an accident, and Simon was reprimanded for his carelessness and warned that the school had not ruled out an investigation. But it was not fear of this that troubled him on the walk home that night, but rather a deep sense of shame. He had thought himself above the aggression of his family but now knew that he was not, and he vowed in future to use his karate as a means of controlling and channeling anger, not as a vehicle for expressing it.

Chapter Eleven

Old Sam brushed his hands through the leaves of the bean bush one last time and looked at the remaining seedpods. He decided they would need to grow a little more before being picked, so he straightened up and stretched, then lifted the wicker basket from the ground beside him and started back toward his trailer home. Sam's gait had the slow, measured pace of a man in no rush, a man with time to enjoy every footstep and to attend to the song of a nearby thrush. He swung his foot over Bess, the sleeping black Labrador, climbed the three steps that led to the front door of his modest home, and stepped in, placing the basket on top of the washing machine that faced the door before going around it to use the bathroom.

Sam's home was fourteen feet wide—or so the salesman had told him when quoting the external measurements—and the bedrooms at each end of its fifty-foot length sandwiched a compact living area, kitchen, and bathroom. He washed his hands and stepped out of the bathroom, picked the bean basket up from where he had left it, and turned past the washing machine and into the kitchen to rinse the beans in the sink.

Bess barked, and her tail thumped the floor twice.

With his back to the open door and the water running, Old Sam couldn't hear what had attracted the placid dog's attention, so he turned off the tap, raised his head from the sink, and turned to look through the door. He heard the deep hum of a large number of cars.

Old Sam lived at the end of a quiet road, one that occasionally attracted a joy rider who wanted to open up a motorbike or Trans Am, but never in his five years in the trailer had he heard anything quite like this. As he listened, the sound grew louder and closer, and eventually, a fleet of vehicles turned onto the gravel of his short driveway. He picked up a dish-cloth and walked to the threshold, drying his hands and watching a gaggle of folk pour out of the cars, murmuring among themselves. They jostled forward to ring the steps of the trailer and thrust a young girl forward from the crowd, her head buried into hunched shoulders and looking around as if to find a way back into the pack. Her attention seemed concentrated on two people who Sam surmised were her parents. Sam, too, studied them, and his heart ached with the emptiness and sorrow they projected. By the time he looked back at the girl, her attention had shifted to him, but as his eyes met hers, she dropped her gaze from his face to her feet, which she began to shuffle. Sam looked around the group and could smell poison in the air. He recognized Emily Betts and Roger Jamieson, who had been elders at the Church of the Epistles when he had attended many years ago, and several other faces were familiar. Why was the leadership of the church he had left so many years ago bringing this girl to him?

A cry emerged from the crowd, "Go on, let's hear it," and it was joined by murmured assent. The girl's shuffling continued, but eventually, she lifted her head toward Sam and looked full at him, revealing the empty heart of a lost, lonely child. Sam's own heart bled as tears welled in his eyes, and he reached out to her with his soul.

"Sam, I know I promised I'd never do this, and I'm real sorry, but the folk at the church, even Ma and Dad," and here, she broke eye contact for a moment to glance over her shoulder. "Well, they all say you need to take on your responsibility. You see," she said, looking at her feet again and dancing as if she were on hot coals, "I'm pregnant, and I told them you're the father."

"Is that so?"

Sam was unfazed, for he had already seen in her eyes anguish that no child should be asked to bear, and two decades of meditation and deep spiritual practice had opened up his heart to the point that he couldn't refuse. He lived as a hermit to protect himself from the intensity of human suffering all day, every day, but when it came to it, he had no choice but to help. Looking around at the hungry, expectant faces of the church elders and the terror of the poor child, Sam's decision made itself. He didn't have time to think before the words flowed naturally from his lips.

"Well, if that's the case—and if your father says it's okay—I guess you'd better come and stay with me so I can look after the both of you." Sam looked up at the man he had guessed to be the father and took advantage of the silence to confirm his assessment of him as a sheepish and heartbroken man.

"So you really are the father?" A voice in the crowd quavered in disbelief.

Sam eyed the crowd, and his gaze settled on his new charge. "Come on, sweetie, let's get you out of this heat. I'm sure you could use something to drink." He held his hand out to Jessica and looked at her with a happy smile. She didn't move for what seemed a long time but finally broke into a grin from ear to ear, ran toward him, and threw her arms around his neck, then stepped past into the living room. Sam smiled broadly at the crowd and said, "Thank you all for bringing her over. I'll take good care of her and the baby. Have a good day now, everyone. Come on, Bessie, let's go in." Sam waited for Bess to enter the house, then pulled the door closed behind them and stepped into the living room, where Jessica was bouncing up and down, her hands clasped in front of her face, exclaiming, "Oh, look at them! They've no idea what to do now. Oh, this is so cool, it's just *so* cool. Oh, it's you." Jessica stopped hopping, and as she turned to face Sam, her hands fell to her sides, and her shoulders sagged once more. "Thank you. When they're gone, I'll leave you and be on my way."

"Where will you go?"

Jessica shrugged and looked defiantly at Sam. "I don't know, but no one here wants me, so I'll go and find someone who does."

"I told your folks I'd look after you, and I intend to." After a pause, he spoke again. "If I'm going to be the father of your child, we probably ought to know each other a little better. Please have a seat. Can I get you a drink? Ice water, perhaps?"

Jessica frowned.

"You'll have to get used to a pretty simple lifestyle here," Sam said, smiling broadly, "but I've got a couple of sodas in the refrigerator for special occasions, and I guess this counts. I'll get you one if you like."

"Actually, ice water is just what I want, thanks."

"Good. Please sit down."

Sam returned a couple of minutes later with two drinks, handed one to Jessica, now sitting at the small dining table, and sat down opposite her. He sipped and considered her quietly while she stared around the room.

"Is that the bedroom through there?" Jessica gestured with her head at the doorway behind her.

Sam nodded, not taking his eyes from her face. "That's actually the guest room, and, it's empty right now, but I'll get another bed and move in there. The master bedroom, which is where you'll be sleeping, is the other end of the house. We'll have to wash the sheets and clean it out, of course. What's your name?"

"Jessica. It's Jessica Jackson, sir."

"Just call me Manny. Or Sam, whichever you prefer, but don't start calling me Sir or treating me with respect; I won't know what to do."

Jessica gulped her water and stared at her host over the brim of the glass, unsure what to make of this stranger. On the one hand, he had treated

her with unbelievable kindness, fulfilling wild romantic hopes born of desperation about the kindness of a mad hermit, and yet… and yet when she
had first laid eyes on him those few minutes ago on his doorstep, she had
wondered if she had come to the right place. He looked like a derelict, and
when she had leapt into his arms, she had almost been overwhelmed by the
unexpected smell of stale sweat. She was sure she had cuts on her face from
his beard: The man must not have showered or shaved in a month. But his
trailer was clean—immaculately so—and as she adjusted to his company,
she could not help being drawn to the brilliant eyes buried in the nest of hair
and creases, eyes whose wisdom and compassion were so far beyond anything that she had ever encountered that she hadn't even noticed their color.

"How old are you, Jessica?"

"I'm fifteen. I'm sorry to barge in on you like this, but you have no
idea what those people are like. It's been terrible." She dropped her eyes and
shuddered.

"I used to be one of them, so I do have some idea. More to the point,
I assume you used to be one of them, too, until very recently."

Sudden realization descended, and Jessica reeled as if hit by a physical blow. "I could've gotten you in trouble with the law there, couldn't I?"

Sam's laugh surprised her. "So you're, what, Jessica, a little less than
sixteen?" When she nodded, he chuckled and said, "I figured as much. I
think North Carolina regards sex with a minor as statutory rape, but you
forget that I've been around those folk a lot longer than you have. They
were more likely to lynch me than turn me over to the police." He shrugged
off her repeated apologies and said, "Tell me what happened."

Jessica didn't want to revisit her tale again, but as she sat with Sam's
peaceful silence, looking up occasionally from her glass of water at his
patient smile, her reluctance crumbled. She felt safe here and found that she
wanted to confide in this man, so she put her glass on the table, folded her
hands on her lap, and began.

"It started almost two months ago. I was in the barn at home when
Colby—that's Pastor Kidd's son—came in. He sat next to me, and we fed
the kittens. Sorry, those are the newborn ones that Maisie's just had.
Maisie's our cat. Oh dear…" Jessica's hands flapped, and she rocked back
and forth in her seat. "I'm rambling, aren't I?"

"That's okay; we've got all day, just tell me as it comes out." Sam's
voice was reassuring, and somehow Jessica knew that not only was it okay
to tell Sam what had happened and that he could be trusted, but that he
would make everything all right.

"Well, I was worried he'd want to look in my cedar chest, but he
didn't. He just sat next to me and we… Well, I made the first move, but then

he... we *did* it, you know?" Jessica glanced at Sam and was reassured by his composure. "And I couldn't tell Ma and Dad... but then Ma found me and made me shave my head, and... oh, it was awful." Jessica buried her head in her hands, vaguely aware that Sam was sitting patiently with her.

Eventually, she wiped her eyes, said, "Sorry," and smiled meekly. "So anyway, I'm pregnant, and my best friend hates me, and everyone thinks I'm a slut and I'm damned, even Ma and Dad," Jessica choked as she struggled to vocalize the worst part. "They've decided they don't want me at home any more."

"That's a terrible, terrible thing for them to do. I know this won't help you right now, and it doesn't justify their behavior, but for what it's worth, I do remember how I used to think when I was a member of that church, and I'm confident that this is truly breaking their hearts, too. Anyway, you said the church elders confronted you and told you to confess, and you told them I was the father?"

Jessica nodded. "It was an awful thing for me to do, and I'm sorry. I didn't know what else to say, though. Even if anyone believed that Colby was the father, they'd want me to live with him, and I just can't do that. Oh, Sam, everyone talks about you like you're some kind of weirdo, but somehow you've always sounded like a good man to me, and... I don't know, I didn't mean to say it, it just kind of came out. I'm sorry, I really am; I've turned you into a terrible person. They probably all think you're a monster who has sex with teenage girls all the time."

Sam threw his head back and laughed, and before she could stop herself, Jessica was laughing too. When Sam finished, he spoke again. "They've thought I was a terrible person for a long time, so let's not worry about that. Now, you're obviously staying here for a while. I guess the idea is that we get married when you're old enough?"

Jessica looked up at Sam, who still wore a wide, innocent smile on his face, and nodded sheepishly.

"Well at least we've got a little time to get to know each other first. And I've just realized how rude I'm being: I should introduce myself before we go any further. You know my name, and I live here with Bess." He gestured at the dog. "We've been here for five or six years now, and we're mostly self-sufficient—I grow my own fruit and vegetables—but I'm pretty handy and make a little money on the side. I haven't been inside a church since my father's funeral six years ago, but I'm a deeper Christian now than I've ever been. I'm not used to having people around, so having you live here will be quite an adjustment for me, and you'll need to be patient." Jessica had heard stories of Old Sam's patience, although they were mostly of his kindness to animals rather than people. "I probably have rules, but I don't know what they are, so when I think of them, I'll tell you. I'm pretty sure I've developed a lot of horrible antisocial habits living on my own for so long, so you'll have to help me to correct them, too. If I leave the toilet seat up or keep my toothbrush in a bad place or need to shower more often, please tell me. We're in this together, at least until you're old enough not to need me any more, so if anything bugs you, let me know. I may be a pig, but I'm a pretty thick-skinned one, and you won't offend me. Can you think of anything else?"

"I don't want to be a bother, Sam, really I don't." Sam's kindness overwhelmed Jessica with guilt and she decided that it was time to leave. She hadn't heard the posse depart but was confident that they must have by now, so she started to stand. Not sure where she would go, she nonetheless said, "I'll just be on my way."

"Oh no, you won't." The stern tone in Sam's voice took Jessica by surprise, and she stopped, her hands pressing on the chair, to look at her host, uncertain, while he continued, "Those people left you in my care, and I'm not about to let you run off and disappear. If you thought they were upset with me before, you wait and see how they react if you run away. No, young lady, for better or for worse, I've taken you in, and until you're an adult, you're staying with me. Is that clear?"

Jessica had not realized until now how little she had thought through the consequences of her actions. Sam was right; she couldn't leave him to deal with her disappearance, so she had no choice but to stay with him. Unsure if the churning in her belly was resentment toward Sam or self-recrimination, she crossed her arms, sat down, and listened to him.

"There's one more thing we might as well get out of the way, and that's picking up all your stuff and getting you settled in. I probably don't have as much room as you, so you might have to leave some things behind. Here, let me show you around." Sam led the way into the adjacent room, whose only contents were a round, red cushion on a purple mat, and said, "This is where I do my morning devotional every morning. Actually, it's not so much a devotional as meditation." With a shrug, he turned and walked the length of the trailer and into the master bedroom, which was almost as sparsely furnished, containing just a single bed with sheets and a blanket, a Bible on the bedside table, a small, unadorned chest of drawers, and a simple desk and chair. A large statue of Christ crucified stood on the chest of drawers, and a framed painting of the Madonna and Child hung on the wall opposite the bed, the only things bringing color and life to the space.

"This is your room now, so let's strip the bed and wash the sheets, and you can move my clothes down to the closet in the other bedroom while I clear my other stuff out of here."

"What will you sleep on?" Jessica asked as they stripped the bed, and later, "Don't you need a desk?" as Sam stacked up his writings with loving care and carried them to his new bedroom.

"Don't you worry about me," Sam said, and Jessica would soon get used to this constant refrain.

Forty minutes later, they had finished moving Sam's things and each eaten one of his early apples. Sam took Jessica's apple core, opened the door, tossed both his and hers into the woods, and said, "Okay, let's go pick up your stuff. Do you want to call your parents and let them know you're coming?"

Jessica shook her head, a surge of panic rising.

Sam's voice was smooth and comforting as he said, "I know this is going to be hard, but it'll get more difficult the longer we wait." He held out a hand and helped her rise, then gave her a hug. Jessica clung to him desperately. She hadn't thought she had a heart left to break, but the idea of collecting her belongings and formally moving out of her family home was devastating. After several minutes, Sam spoke again. "If you think about it, you've already moved out. All we're doing now is clean-up, so let's get it over and done with." He gave her a squeeze and released, and Jessica looked up at him with a forced smile. There was something profoundly reassuring about being with Sam. He smiled back and said, "Perhaps we can stop off for an ice cream or something on the way home?"

"I don't know that I'm in the mood."

"You don't want to do something fun?"

"I don't have any money."

"I've got a little," Sam said in a mock-defensive tone.

"I don't."

"You're my responsibility now, Jessica, for richer, for poorer. I've got enough to take care of you, and besides, it's about time I started working a little harder and pulling my weight. I'll have to clean up, though, and I'd gotten used to this," he rubbed his bushy beard with the fingers of one hand and then burst out laughing. "Come on." He walked through the kitchen, picked up his keys, and jumped into the cab of his beaten-up old pickup. Bess jumped in, too, hopping up on the bench close enough to Sam to leave plenty of room for Jessica. "You're navigating," he said as the engine coughed into action and he reversed down the gravel drive.

Ten minutes later they pulled to a stop in the Jacksons' farmyard, turned off the engine, and clambered down from the truck. Ma emerged from the kitchen and Dad from his workshop, and, without taking their eyes from Jessica, glided toward each other as if pulled by magnets, until they stood side by side, facing their visitors. Ma stood with her arms folded across her chest, wearing a severe scowl, and Dad's arm rose and wrapped around her shoulder.

Jessica put on her bravest face, though she was quaking inside. "We're just here to pick up my stuff, so we won't be long. Come on, Sam, let's get this over and done with."

Sam reached into the cab for the roll of garbage bags he had brought and obeyed. In her bedroom, he tore small holes in the bottoms of the garbage bags, grabbed armfuls of clothes from her closet, and slipped them inside the bags with the hanger hooks protruding through the holes. He piled up the black-shrouded packages of clothes and carried them outside in a few trips, then moved on to empty the chest of drawers. Jessica began with her desk and sat down to open a drawer full of old diaries and notebooks. As she touched the wood, she remembered the surprise of waking up on her birthday morning and finding the desk already in her room. She had had no idea Dad had even been making it. She stroked the varnish and remembered the first time she had opened the drawer and found inside a princess diary, a corny gift for a twelve-year-old girl, but still perfect for Jessica, a symbol of the love and understanding with which Dad had designed and built the desk for her. It was too much for Jessica, and she collapsed into tears, hands covering her face. But then the chair slid back, and Sam's comforting presence appeared, kneeling in front of her, offering his open arms, and she fell into them, crying her heart out onto his shoulder.

She had no idea how long she cried, but when Sam asked, "Didn't you say something about a chest?" she wiped her eyes, took him to the barn, and helped him carry it to the truck, then led the way back to her room to finish the grim task of collecting her schoolbag and sorting through her other belongings. There was much that Jessica decided to leave behind, for Sam didn't have a lot of room, and she did not foresee her dolls and few ornaments bringing her the pleasure they once had, but she cleared all of her toiletries out of the bathroom and worked around her room, picking and choosing, placing that which she wanted in trash bags that Sam carried out to the truck. More than once, she broke down, and each time, wordlessly, Sam squeezed her shoulder or stroked her back, transmitting to her through physical contact the strength she needed to keep going. Finally, she was finished, and she looked at Sam with a forced smile. "Okay, I'm done."

"Almost," he said, and Jessica frowned. Instead of explaining his comment, Sam gestured toward the bedroom door with his hand, nodding for her to leave first, which she did. She heard Sam fall in behind and let her feet guide her toward the kitchen door. It wasn't until she stood on the threshold that she realized what "almost" had meant: She still had to say goodbye. She stopped and took a step back toward Sam, bowed her head, and tried to pass him, but he didn't move and caught her shoulder loosely.

"You have to do this, Jessica," he whispered.

Jessica nodded, though she kept her head low as she allowed herself to be directed toward the kitchen. Once inside, she stopped and looked up at her parents, who were sitting side by side at the table, facing her but staring at their clasped hands. The moment was so horrible as to seem fantastical, an illusion. But when they noticed her presence, Ma and Dad leaned back, their hands falling apart, and their eyes were terribly real. Sam squeezed through the doorway and stood beside Jessica in the uncomfortable silence.

Jessica felt the reassurance of his presence, watching her and waiting, and spoke first. "Well, I guess this is it. Bye, Ma. Bye, Dad." But instead of leaving, she stood staring at her parents, not allowing herself to hope but hoping nonetheless, hoping that they would tell her everything was okay, that it was all just a bad dream, a misunderstanding, hoping they would say, "Let me help you get your things out of that truck." She knew they wouldn't, but she stood there anyway, just in case, and she stood there because she didn't know how to say goodbye. Finally, Dad rose and walked over to her with tears running down his cheeks and hugged her. He buried her head in his shoulder as he rocked her, whispering "Bye, Jess," again and again to the daughter who hung limp, as if lifeless, in his arms, finally squeezing her before releasing her, wiping his eyes, and looking at Sam. "I don't have a lot," he stuttered, "but I'll mail you a check for what I can once a month."

"Mr. Jackson," Sam said with a serious tone that commanded Jessica's full attention, "what this girl needs is love and a family, not your money. Please keep it."

"I... I... I insist," stammered Will Jackson.

"If you mail me checks or give me money," Sam replied firmly, "I will return them to you. You can't buy my loyalty or your daughter's love."

Will Jackson's jaws flapped and his cheeks blanched, and eventually, his gaze drifted from Sam to his wife, who moved to his side.

"Now you listen here," she began, her pointed finger jabbing at Sam's chest. "She's our daughter, and it's our responsibility to make sure she's brought up right. Your run-down trailer isn't fit for a teenage girl, let alone her baby. She's may have sinned against our Father, but Jessica is still our daughter, and we want our grandchild to have a chance." Her fierce finger skewered Sam's chest one last time as she finished speaking.

Sam looked down at the finger, waiting for it to be removed, and when it was, he looked up and spoke with infinite patience. "Mrs. Jackson, when you dropped your daughter off at my house, you made it very clear that she is my responsibility. I am inexperienced in raising a teenager or a baby, but

I'm quite confident that together, Jessica and I can figure it out and that we'll do just fine. Unless you're willing to invite Jessica back into this house with open arms—and even if you do so, I don't think you should be too confident that she will want to come—then as far as I'm concerned, you've no place telling me what to do. I will take my guidance from what Jessica wants and needs and from the direction our Lord provides. Now, if you'll excuse us, we've got some unpacking and grocery shopping to do. Jessica, I'll be in the truck."

Jessica was dumbstruck, and so, she could see, were her parents. But although she saw fear on their faces, she experienced elation, felt herself floating, light as a feather, as her unexpected hero departed, leaving her behind with the strength to face her parents. As the door closed, she snapped out of her reverie and called after him, "I'll be right there, Sam," then looked at her father and said, "It's going to be all right, Dad." And for the first time in a long while, she really believed it. She kissed him on the cheek, then looked at Ma, not sure what to do. Finally, she said simply, "Bye, Ma," smiled at her, and kissed Dad again.

She let Sam help her up into the cab of the truck and laughed. She closed her eyes and held Bess's collar as the dog sniffed and licked Jessica's face.

"You knew that was going to happen, didn't you?" she asked.

"I had a pretty good idea," Sam replied, starting the truck and reversing to turn it around.

Jessica's parents had stepped outside, Dad's arm around Ma's shoulder, to watch her leave, and she waved at them. Dad's hand gave a halfhearted response, but Ma just stood there, arms folded.

"I'm sorry. I don't know how they could be so rude."

Sam laughed. "You don't have anything to be sorry for. It's not you who's building a personal living hell; it's your parents who are doing that. They've given you a chance to be happy. It'll take you a while to see it, but it's there."

But when Jessica looked at Sam, she saw distress in his eyes and asked, "What's wrong?"

"It's your parents. What they're doing to themselves is just so awful. They're dying inside, but their misguided sense of self-sacrifice won't let them open their hearts to love. It's so terribly unnecessary and so terribly sad." He glanced at Jessica's confused frown and explained, "Do you remember in *Peter Pan*, how every time someone says, 'I don't believe in fairies,' a fairy dies?" Jessica nodded, and Sam continued, "Well, it's a little like that. Your parents are refusing to believe in love, and so a fairy—

their relationship with you—has died. Eventually it'll be their own fairy, and they'll be hollow carcasses, zombies, wandering this earth without life.

"But that's pretty morbid." His broad smile returned. "Let's go get that ice cream, then we can go home and unpack the truck, and I'll leave you to make your little nest while I go to the grocery store."

Chapter Twelve

Dwight's vacant gaze followed a cardinal's flight across the creek and onto a branch overhanging the babbling water, where the bird hopped from branch to branch before disappearing into the woods in a flurry of scarlet and green. Dwight's eyes followed it, unseeing, into the shadows, then drifted back to his lap on which lay the Biblical narrative describing God's punishment of man's first sin.

The night of vodka and cards two weeks ago had been a welcome relief from misery that had been intensifying for months, but Dwight's descent from that high had been precipitous. Reeking of alcohol, cigarettes, and Darlene, he had hoped to sneak into his house, take a shower, and act as if he'd gotten up early for work, but instead, he had been confronted at four in the morning by Cheryl sitting at the kitchen table. Guilt had knocked him back on his heels even before his wife had looked him up and down with contempt and then gone to bed in silent, stony disgust. The following night, unable to face Cheryl, he had taken his Bible, beer, and cigarettes to the creek, and his nightly routine of reading Genesis had begun. The first sip of beer had so revolted him that he had poured it all in the creek for the fish to drink, and he had thrown his cigarettes in while the beer was still frothing. He had been clean ever since.

Dwight forced himself to concentrate on the text in front of him. He flicked from "In the beginning God created the heaven and the earth" to "Now the serpent was more subtil than any beast of the field which the Lord God had made." After two weeks of reading and rereading, he was becoming increasingly aware that Genesis chapter three was more than a story of forbidden fruit—a fruit that Darlene had offered him, and of which he had eaten hungrily—and that what he had always taken as the literal meaning of the story was simply his own superficial understanding. He realized, too, that the deepest meaning was to be found not in active analysis of the text but through letting the story soak into the fiber of his being, by letting the message itself do the work on him. A swirling dark cloud of ideas had formed in his head, and while it was swirling around, he was beginning to distinguish the nameless universal forms of consequence and responsibility and to see at their center the particular serpent that had tempted him—his pride in the hardware store.

His identity was so heavily tied to the family business that he could not conceive of life without it, and yet the business was dying. He had failed his father, who had left the store to him and trusted him to run it and had failed his family by letting a reliable income dry up, but most painfully, he had failed himself by not living up to his self-image as the rock solid, reliable father and favorite son. But although Dwight was beginning to realize the source of his suffering, he did not want to confront his serpent and instead kept returning to the words on the page, at once both a mask and a mirror.

"... that the tree was good for food, and that it was pleasant to the eyes... " The words took his mind to Darlene, and he remembered her lying naked in front of him, her hands and voice guiding him over the soft skin of her writhing body, his fingers and tongue doing things to her that he had never even dreamed of until finally, urgently, she had pulled him on top of her.

Darlene!

He loved her and he hated her. She had given him pleasure he had not known was possible but had exposed him to unbearable consequences.

Oh, Darlene!

What had she done—and why?

But how could he blame Darlene? Had he not paid her to remove her bra, pulled her to him of his own free will, eagerly accepted the fruit she had offered him?

Dwight craved a cigarette.

Sitting on the rock, sweat pouring as the pressure of guilt and craving smothered him, Dwight thought of the son he had pushed away, the wife he had alienated, and the younger son who was now hiding from him, and he felt sick in the pit of his stomach. The misery of his business failure had already driven him to drink, but now he had violated everything that he held dear and had betrayed his wife in the time of her greatest need, had been weak precisely when he needed to be strong. His mind drifted from cigarettes to the half-full bottle of vodka and carton of orange juice that remained in the refrigerator in the back room of the store, and he was grateful that it was not closer at hand.

Dwight shook his head and rose to trudge back to the house and to bed. As he passed through the kitchen, a small pile of papers in the middle of the table caught his eye. He leafed through the handful of envelopes that represented the day's mail and sat down, a surreal numbness descending, as if the statement from the credit card company, the two mail-order clothing catalogs, and the letter from Walmart were going to tell him something profound. He opened the credit card statement, calm yet expecting the worst, and was not disappointed. The bill was about the same size as usual, and the expenses—he ran his eye down charges for groceries, school clothes, and parts for his truck—were not excessive, but he knew he could not afford to pay it. He dropped the statement on the table and reached for the envelope from Walmart, wondering what they could want, and when he tore it open, a check fell out, face up, on the table. Above his wife's signature, he read, in her familiar script, the amount of one hundred twenty-two dollars and fourteen cents, but his eyes were drawn to the garish red stamps. He teased the accompanying letter out of the envelope, feeling sick in his stomach, and not needing to read the letter to know that the check had bounced.

What the heck was she doing at Walmart?

It was over. Unable to deny the Cooks' financial predicament any longer, Dwight buried his face in his hands and wept into the small hours of the morning, then joined his wife in the bed they still shared—though they barely spoke—and tossed and turned without sleeping. In the morning, he rose early and waited at the kitchen table with an untouched glass of orange juice until Clark had left for school, then asked Cheryl to sit down with him. Even as distant as they had become, he could not do this without her support, and to gain it, he needed to have the conversation that until now, despite all his efforts by the creek at composing a speech, he had not known how to begin.

"Cheryl, you have no idea how hard it is for me to say what I'm about to say," he said, then paused and looked at her. The disinterested, vacant expression staring back at him made it even more difficult for him to continue, and he needed a long time to steel himself. Eventually he said, "I'm going to have to close the store."

There: It was off his chest! He had expected to deliver a long monologue, but it had really been very simple. He studied Cheryl expectantly, but she said nothing, and more than that, she barely moved. Confused, Dwight tried to fill the uncomfortable silence by explaining, "I've been losing money for a year now, and we've been living on savings. I kept hoping that it was just temporary, that things would turn around, but it's just getting worse, and we just can't keep this going. Cheryl, I'm so sorry; I should have told you this before, but I just couldn't bring myself to."

After another long pause, Cheryl asked, "That's it?" When Dwight nodded, she said, "Well, as far as I'm concerned, the quicker you close it down, the better." Without further ado, she stood and walked out of the kitchen.

Dwight was stunned. Cheryl had just thrown away his life's work with a shrug of the shoulders, and long after her back had disappeared, he stared at the empty doorway in disbelief. Unable to understand her behavior, he had little choice but simply to accept that he had her permission, and eventually, he pulled himself together and made his way to the store in a daze. He had already opened up when Darlene arrived.

Ever since their Monday night together, Dwight's guilt had made him very self-conscious around Darlene, and this morning was no exception. He couldn't be near her without remembering the disgrace he had felt facing his wife's contempt that Tuesday morning, but what made it worse was how much he had really enjoyed being with Darlene and how much a part of him wanted to lie with her again. When he looked at her, he remembered the softness of her smooth, young skin and the smell of perfume and shampoo. He remembered how gentle and understanding she had been of his inexperience and how patiently she had guided him. He remembered, too, how much pleasure she had felt: He had not known it was possible for any human being to experience the ecstatic highs that she had reached.

She had told him many things while they lay on the floor of the store, smoking cigarettes while she let him stroke her body. She had said that she had known for a long while that he couldn't afford to keep her on payroll and would completely understand if he fired her the next day. She had expressed gratitude for the stability of her job at the store, which had helped her to settle down from her recklessly wild teenage years and to weather the storm of a whirlwind marriage and divorce and had said that Dwight's sad, roaming eyes had told her the right way to say thank you for all he had done for her. Their night together was her very private thank you, as was the unspoken permission she now gave for him to roam her body with his eyes.

She greeted him this Thursday morning the same way that she had greeted him the morning after she had changed his life: "Good morning, Mr. Cook; you look terrible." He, in turn, replied the same way he had that day, with a cold laugh.

"What's wrong, Mr. Cook; has someone died?"

Dwight laughed again, realizing for the first time how messed-up his priorities were. He thought with shame of talking to Cheryl as if the store were the most important thing in his life. If only he could have that moment back, tell Cheryl how sorry he was, how much he still loved her...

Darlene cleared her throat and brought the moment of reflection to an end.

"No, Darlene, it's nowhere near that bad. I've just finally admitted to myself what it seems like everyone around me has known for a long while: I'm going to have to close the store."

Darlene put her hand on his arm. "Oh, Mr. Cook," she spoke in a soft, sad voice, "I'm sorry. I know how much it means to you. When?"

"I only decided this morning, so I don't know for sure, but I'm thinking we spend today getting ready and run a going-out-of-business sale Friday and Saturday."

Darlene straightened and put on her business face. "We can do that. We'll have to call all the papers straight away and get ads in for tomorrow, and we'll need to get a bunch of signs printed up. We probably ought to call all of the builders, electricians, and tradesmen we can think of, just to make sure they know. I guess we'll need to be open late?"

"What do you think?"

"I say we stay open till at least ten or eleven both nights, and open up early. Are we going to be open Sunday, too?"

"It's the Sabbath, Darlene." Dwight shook his head.

"I'll bet we can clean the place out completely if we open Sunday, too." She looked at Dwight with stern resolve. "If you can't be here, I'll do it on my own."

"You've got plans for Friday and Saturday nights, though?"

Darlene laughed. "Of course I do, Mr. Cook, but you don't think I'm going to let you do all this on your own, do you? Like I told you the other night, it's the only real job I've ever had, and I'm not about to miss our busiest four days ever." She lifted her hand to his shoulder, squeezed, and, with a wink, said, "I know how hard this seems right now, but it will be fun, just you wait and see."

Darlene's eyes sparkled, and her face glowed with energy and humor, her touch and smile breaking down the barrier that Dwight had erected between them. She was right; this would be fun.

The store was quiet for the next hour, and, side by side, they leaned over the counter with pen and paper, making detailed plans: They would open tomorrow with a big flag banner outside the store reading, "Closing Down Sale – Everything Must Go"; all merchandise would be discounted "at least 20% off posted prices"; and the store would stay open until eleven o'clock Friday night, reopen at seven Saturday morning, and stay open until midnight. Dwight would try to get Clark to help them on Saturday, and, in a breach of his religion, Dwight agreed that they needed to be open on Sunday, unlocking the doors at ten and continuing until either they had sold everything or fell over on the job.

They split up. Darlene took two hundred dollars in cash and the store's credit card with her and left to get signs and fliers made and post them, not just around town, but at a list of out-of-town locations they had compiled, while Dwight stayed in the store and made phone calls. When Darlene returned six hours later, she carried a heavy, six-foot-long roll over her shoulder. Dwight wanted to look at it, but she laughed and said, "Trust me, okay? It's just the ticket. And besides, you don't have time to do anything else if it's not. Now, get a couple of ladders, and let's go outside to hang it up."

They did so, holding the sign open between them and symmetrically climbing their ladders to tie it high up on the store front. When they were done, they walked across the parking lot and turned to look, Dwight resisting the urge to look over his shoulder until Darlene told him they were far enough away. When Dwight turned, he put his hands on his hips and smiled proudly. "It's perfect, Darlene, absolutely perfect. Dad would be proud of you." He turned to Darlene and put his arm around her shoulder, and when she responded by hugging him, he planted a kiss on her lips." He was surprised and embarrassed at his spontaneous familiarity, but Darlene defused the situation by feigning a giggle.

"Why, Mr. Cook, what will people think?"

They both laughed and walked back to the store, Darlene pouring out a non-stop, detailed narrative of her success, not just in procuring a vast number of signs and posters at short notice, but in convincing the owners of a wide variety of prominent locations around town to display them. The rest of the afternoon was quiet, giving Dwight and Darlene a chance to reorganize the shelves and get some of the excess inventory out of the large storage room. They left at seven and agreed to meet up early the following morning to finish their preparations.

Driving home, Dwight realized that he was excited about his work for the first time in years. He was firmly committed to a course of action that was long overdue, and when it was completed, he would have no choice but to move on to something new. Even Cheryl's coldness and Clark's evasive silence could not deflate his evening. When he told Cheryl that he would be working very late and that she might not see him until Monday, he elicited only a terse acknowledgment, but Clark agreed to come to the store to help out most of the day on Saturday. The only cloud on the horizon was Dwight's guilt at the prospect of ending Darlene's employment after all she had done for him.

After a good night's sleep, Dwight arrived at the store before sunrise to find, to his surprise, that Darlene had beaten him in. He noticed with mild interest that she was not wearing her usual wardrobe but was instead dressed like him, in jeans, tennis shoes, and a loose t-shirt, but the warm glow Dwight felt watching Darlene move in them was testament to the very different effect that her body had on them. They spent two hours working together to get as much inventory out of the storage room and onto the shelves as possible while making sure the aisles were clear, and Dwight felt good about their state of readiness when he opened the door. He poked his head outside and looked around, disappointed that people weren't lined up outside, and his attitude worsened as the morning wore on and the antici-pated flood of visitors didn't arrive. He had brought a loaf of sliced bread, a jar of peanut butter, and some fruit so they could have lunch-on-the-go, but with the low volume of business, he instead gave Darlene twenty dol-lars and sent her out to fetch burgers.

Shortly after lunch, activity started to pick up, and by midafternoon, the store was a whirl. A handful of events stood out as memorable: The pool liner that Dwight had wondered about two weeks previously sold for $200, $100 off the listed retail price but above his original cost; for some myste-rious reason, Mrs. Collins, a diminutive and frail eighty-year-old widow, bought a chain saw; and Mr. Nickles, a man on whom Dwight had never before laid eyes, inspected the building and asked him how much he wanted for it. After a brief exchange, Mr. Nickles left him a phone number and a cash offer of $325,000.

The store started to quiet down at about eight o'clock but had a decent flow of traffic right up until it was time to lock up at eleven. Darlene turned the latch, pulled down the blinds, and leaned back against the door with a sigh. "That was some day! What do you want me to do now?"

Dwight flushed and quickly looked away, lest she realize what he really wanted, ran his eyes around the disheveled store, and said, "Well, we need to tidy up for tomorrow and get everything else out of the back, but that shouldn't take more than two or three hours. I vote we call it quits and go home to get a few hours' sleep. I'll see you back here between four and five in the morning? And I'll stop by the grocery store on the way in and get some donuts—and some coffee for you."

"That's a deal. What are you going to do with the money?" She nod-ded at the till. "There must be a fortune in there."

"I'm not going to worry about it right now. I'll just stick it all in the safe, and we can deal with it tomorrow. Come on, let's get out of here." Dwight turned out the lights and followed Darlene, watching her tight jeans gliding ahead of him into the back room and thinking of how much he would miss her after Sunday.

When Dwight arrived home, Cheryl and Clark were already in bed. He lay down on the couch so as not to disturb anyone and fell into three hours of untroubled sleep. The alarm on his watch woke him, and he took a quick shower, changed his clothes, and was in the store with the donuts and coffee by four o'clock. Darlene didn't arrive for almost an hour, but together, they had plenty of time to eat the donuts and stock the shelves for an 8:00 opening. Business started earlier than it had on Friday, and Dwight was pleased when Clark arrived at ten o'clock—not just because he was glad to have his son's help, but because it allowed him to sneak into the back office for half an hour to make a few phone calls. First he spoke to Susan Wise, the town lawyer, and then to a real estate agent he had known for years. Properly prepared, he called Mr. Nickles to counter his offer for the building at $400,000, and they settled at $375,000, with closing scheduled within two weeks.

When Dwight reentered the store at eleven o'clock, business was booming; Darlene, Clark, and he worked through lunch without pausing, and it wasn't until the day started to calm down at six o'clock that they began to think of food. Clark walked down the street to fetch pizza and then covered the store while Darlene and Dwight sneaked into the back room to eat. Once they were done eating, Clark took his leave for the night.

Darlene and Dwight were both exhausted when they closed the store at eleven o'clock. Once again, Dwight shoved the cash register in the safe, and they jumped into his truck to tour town. With stakes from the store, a sledgehammer, and their last six signs, they posted invitations that read "Come and say farewell; Cook Hardware closes its doors today after sixty years." They visited the major churches in town and prominently decorated the lawns in competition with "We're no Dairy Queen, but we do have great Sundays," "Exposure to the Son prevents burning," and other pithy calls to worship.

Exhausted, Dwight drove back to the store, pulled up beside Darlene's car to drop her off, and glanced at his watch. It was almost one o'clock and time to go home, catch a little sleep, and recharge his batteries for tomorrow, but he didn't want to let Darlene go. He wanted to hold Darlene just one more time, and his hand slipped onto the top of her thigh. Not knowing what to do and looking for guidance, he offered a wan smile and said, "Thanks for everything, Darlene," though these were not the words he wanted to say. He stared into eyes glinting in the soft glow of the nearby streetlights.

Darlene slid along the bench, turned her shoulders to him, and reached up with her mouth. As her lips met Dwight's, Darlene took his hand from her thigh and pressed it to her breast. He tasted once again the sweetness of her mouth and felt the softness of her body. When Darlene pulled away, he laid his head back, satisfied but wanting more. He watched her with greedy, guilty eyes when she gave him the conspiratorial grin he had seen before and pulled her t-shirt out from the waist of her trousers. Before Dwight could register what was happening, her t-shirt and bra were lying on the floor of the truck and her naked breasts were glowing ghostly white in the streetlights. Panicked, Dwight looked urgently out of the windows, certain that someone must be watching, but Darlene's hand touched his cheek, turned his face to hers, and then everything except Darlene's mouth and body ceased to exist.

All too soon, Darlene eased herself from Dwight's grasp, picked her t-shirt off the floor, and slipped it back over her head.

"What time do you want me here tomorrow?" she asked, assuming her business voice with discomforting ease.

"How about seven o'clock?" Dwight answered, his head spinning.

"See you then."

Dwight's eyes undressed Darlene as she walked to her car, and he watched her drive off the lot, wondering what had just happened and what she would do for a living when his twenty years of stewardship of the store came to an end tomorrow. Would she be able to find another job in Wilkeston or would she have to move? Would he even see her again?

After another short night on the couch, Dwight once again rose before his family and was in the store by six o'clock. He had secreted Darlene's bra overnight under the seat of his truck, and, with guilty glances around the empty parking lot, sneaked it into the store and hid it in a drawer in the back office. When Darlene arrived, his speech was stilted and he didn't know what to say or do, but he was soon distracted from his clumsiness by the early arrival of customers, which had turned into a flood by noon. Church-goers poured in, drawn by Darlene's signs, to snack on the cookies, iced tea, and lemonade that Dwight had bought earlier that morning and, like vultures, swooped down on the aisles to grab hardware off the rapidly empty-ing shelves as the perception of scarcity fed on itself. Dwight ensured that the more-valuable items were pulled forward and clearly visible and was willing to haggle on every deal, even negotiating five thousand dollars for all the shelves, counters, and furniture in the store and taking a twenty-per-cent cash deposit.

Finally, the moment arrived when there was not a single customer in the store. Dwight and Darlene took a breath and looked at each other.

"Mr. Cook, I think we're about done."

Dwight surveyed the store. Debris lay everywhere: a spilled carton of nails here, loose screws there, ripped packages and boxes and odds and ends of wood strewn around the floor. Although the shelves weren't com-pletely empty, there was little of value left, and a glance at his watch told

Dwight that it was already five o'clock, so there was also little chance of anyone else coming to the store. They were both completely exhausted.

"What a day—what a weekend. Why don't you lock up, and I'll get the register."

While Darlene pulled the blinds and turned off the light, Dwight removed the cash tray, turned off the register, and scurried into the back office, remembering last night in the truck as he retrieved from the refrigerator the box of chocolates and a small bunch of roses that he had bought that morning and sneaked into the store. When Darlene came in, he faced her with his gifts hidden behind his back, and when she stopped with a confused frown, he smiled and looked down, embarrassed, at his shuffling feet.

"Darlene, I don't know what I'd do without you. No, I mean you were fantastic. No... " Dwight realized he was beginning to stammer, and his face flushed at the unintended double-entendres that seemed to litter everything he said. "What I mean is that I couldn't have closed the store like this without your help. You've been great. Thanks." He extended his hands with the gifts, and Darlene exclaimed her thanks. As she took the gifts from him, Dwight whispered, more to himself than to Darlene, "I'll miss you," but the comment caught her attention. She put the chocolates and roses on the counter and placed her hand on Dwight's wrist.

"I'll miss you, too, Mr. Cook. You're so sweet." She stood on her tiptoes and leaned forward to peck him on the cheek, her breasts rubbing against the back of his hand as she did so, and Dwight flushed again; had she intended to guide herself to his hand? Back on her heels, Darlene added, "Mr. Cook, you didn't have to do this. All I wanted was to help. I'm sorry you had to close the store, but I'm glad I was here with you, and we did it right."

"Darlene, we've not just done it right, we've done it in style." Spontaneously, he added, "I'd like to take you out for a nice dinner at Susie's," and flushed again at his unexpected precocity. Nonetheless, he looked at Darlene with a spark of hope in his eye. Susie's was the only "classy" restaurant for miles around, twenty minutes' drive away across the county line.

"Mr. Cook, I've never been anywhere like that before, and I can't go dressed like this. I don't even know how to hold my knife and fork."

"You look a million dollars." Dwight smiled, taking full advantage of the excuse to run his eyes from her favorite kitten-heeled boots up her bare legs and short skirt. With a swallow, he looked down at his own attire and spoke again. "I've never been there before, either, and I probably shouldn't go dressed like this"—he was wearing jeans and a checked shirt—"but I think we deserve it." He offered her his arm. "Now come on, let me treat you." Darlene smiled and took his arm with both of hers, pressing her chest once more onto his forearm and, for a wonderful moment, resting her head on his shoulder.

The drive was pleasantly relaxing. Dwight tuned the radio in to a quiet country station, and they mostly sang along. It was a few minutes after five-thirty when they arrived at the restaurant, and seeing that they were the only car in the parking lot, Dwight was afraid that the restaurant was closed. His disappointment turned to joy when the door responded to his touch and he discovered that Susie's had opened just five minutes previously and that, although reservations were required, because Dwight and Darlene were so early and it was a Sunday, they could dine immediately. A hostess in a smart black dress escorted them to a prime table by a window, and Dwight helped Darlene to her seat before sitting opposite her and gazing down to the lake and across the mostly undeveloped valley to the rugged mountains behind. He lost himself in his thoughts, but when he noticed tracks and foundations that were the tell-tale sign of development that should have been great for his former business, the spell was broken.

He shook off his bitterness and looked at Darlene. She was still taking in the view, so he examined her fondly: the small button nose that was so cute, the delicate cheeks and soft skin, the partially open, bright red lips. How could he ever have been immune to her beauty and energy? How many hours, weeks, even months had he wasted in the last four years by not appreciating his good fortune at being in her company?

"Darlene, what are you going to do now?" he asked, his guilt at abandoning her coming to the fore.

Darlene turned back to the table, and Dwight's heart skipped.

"What, you mean for a job?" When Dwight nodded, she looked down at her hands with a shrug. "I don't know." Her reflection was interrupted by the arrival of a waiter.

"Good evening, sir. Madam." The balding man in blue blazer and tie formally inclined his head to each of them in turn, then asked, "Would you like something to drink?"

Darlene nodded and asked, "What beers do you have?"

The waiter started to rattle them off, but Dwight frowned and interrupted, "You sell alcohol here? On a Sunday?"

"Certainly, sir; this is Fenlon County."

"Then we'll have a bottle of champagne," Dwight said, shocking himself again and looking at Darlene with a start, though she seemed unfazed by his suggestion. What was it about Darlene that made him behave so spontaneously? He made his choice and handed the wine list back to the waiter, grinned at his companion, and said, "We're celebrating tonight."

"We sure are," Darlene agreed. "I don't think I've ever had champagne before."

"I'm sorry, sir; I'm going to have to ask the lady to show me some ID."

"I have it right here," she said. "It's not a very good picture, I'm afraid."

"No picture would do you justice, ma'am," the waiter replied, taking the driver's license from her and comparing the image to her face. He handed the card back to Darlene, and said, "Thank you, ma'am, would you like an aperitif?"

"I'll have a martini," Darlene replied, as if she did this every day, and the thrill of a new lifestyle coursed through Dwight's veins as he said. "Me, too."

"Yes, sir."

When Darlene excused herself to visit the restroom, Dwight stared out of the window. By the time she had returned, the drinks were on the table. After waiting for her to sit and put her napkin on her lap, Dwight said, "You were about to tell me what you are going to do next."

"Oh, I don't know." Darlene took a sip of her martini and closed her eyes. "Mmm, that's good." After a long pause, she opened her eyes and spoke again. "I guess what I really want to do," she said, removing the cocktail stick and looking at the olives, "is go to college." Dwight watched, entranced, as she teased an olive off with her tongue and munched with rich delight. "But I don't have the money, and I'll never be able to afford it working in stores." She washed the olive down with a sip of her martini and continued, "Maybe I'll move to Atlanta or Chattanooga, maybe Charlotte. I bet I can make a lot more money there, and it would be great if I could spend a couple of years just saving up."

The waiter returned with the champagne, poured them both a glass, and put the bottle beside Dwight in an ice bucket. Dwight put his barely-touched Martini aside, raised his glass, and said, "Here's to new beginnings."

Darlene chinked her glass against his, echoing, "New beginnings," and they both sipped. "Ooh, I like this," Darlene said, then put her glass down on the table and rotated it, looking up at Dwight before adding, "I thought you'd stopped drinking."

"How do you know these things?" Dwight flashed a look at her, but she simply gave him a coquettish shrug and changed the subject.

Dinner was delightful, spanning four courses and two hours. They added almost an entire bottle of Merlot to their champagne and finished off with a cappuccino, Dwight's first caffeine ever. He was intoxicated by the alcohol, but more so by Darlene's youth and conversation, and he wondered where he had been the last four years and how he could know so little about Darlene, how he had seen only her diligence on the job, how he could have resented her promiscuous display of femininity instead of admiring her beauty.

The conversation, which charmed Dwight, was as open and frank as that of three weeks before when they had lain together on the floor of the back room. She made him feel completely comfortable, listening to him, sympathizing with him, understanding him until the meal came to a natural end. As Dwight led the way out to the truck, Darlene hung onto his shoulder in a way that encouraged him to support her by wrapping an arm around her waist. After opening her door, his greedy eyes watched her slip with feline wile into the passenger seat. Once under way, Dwight realized how drunk he was and drove very carefully, but was nonetheless in high spirits for most of the drive back, laughing and joking with Darlene. As they got closer to the store, however, he fell silent and morose. He pulled into the parking lot behind the hardware store and came to a stop beside Darlene's car, letting the truck engine idle while they sat in silence.

"Well, I guess this is it," Darlene finally said. "Do you need help cleaning up tomorrow?"

Dwight shrugged. "There's really not that much to do. I just need to get the shelves cleared before that guy picks them up on Wednesday, and then I've got about a week to get out the things I care about."

"What happens then?"

"I close on the building." Darlene looked confused, and in a flood of excitement, Dwight burst out, "Didn't I tell you? That Mr. Nickles who came in on Friday agreed to buy the store."

"You sold the building? Oh Dwight, that's wonderful!" Darlene threw her arms around Dwight, and before he knew what was happening, he was pressing his lips to hers. But as his hands started roaming, Darlene pulled herself up and straightened her clothes.

"I really should be going," she said. "Thanks for a lovely dinner; it was a wonderful way to end four great years. I wish we'd gotten to know each other better before now, but… well… thanks for everything, and good luck." With a stiff back and straight face, she opened her door and extended a formal hand to him.

"Darlene, don't go. Can't we just talk a little longer? We can sit here… or we can go back into the store. I need to pay you for the last few days anyway, and all the money's in there."

"Dwight, I really shouldn't. I think we both know where this will end up, and you're married and everything…"

Dwight raised her hand to his lips, kissed it, then kissed her arm, and begged, "Please? We've got that bottle of vodka in the refrigerator, too, and it'd be a shame to waste it."

"Well, I don't know… "

"Darlene, please, you're all I have right now. My son's run away, and my wife wants me dead, and as for the Church, either they're dead wrong, or I'm already going to hell. Either way, one more night won't make any difference. Darlene…" He kissed her hand again and, bowing his head, held her hand to his forehead as if in prayer. "The last few days are the most fun I've had in years. I know I'm old enough to be your father, and if you don't want to… if it's not something that feels good, then just tell me. But the reason I've had so much fun is you, and I think you've enjoyed it too. Please." He lowered her hand and begged her with his eyes.

Darlene broke what seemed to be an eternity of silence with a laugh. "Dwight, you're not an old man," she said, "though it's true, you *are* almost old enough to be my father." She laughed again, and this time Dwight laughed with her, but his laughter turned to a whimper when she raised her hand to his cheek. He nuzzled into it and put his arm around her waist. Darlene pulled his head to her shoulder and said, "Maybe I'll just come in for just one glass of vodka, but we'll have to stop meeting in joints like this."

Chapter Thirteen

Simon returned from his morning run in the national forest behind Aunt Jodi's house energized and ready to face the day. He took a shower, dressed, and ate a breakfast of bacon, grits, cereal, and a large glass of orange juice: Aunt Jodi still insisted on preparing him a "real breakfast," but she now offered him more modest portions. On the short walk to school, he reflected with quiet confidence on the day ahead.

Simon had expected to find self-imposed isolation from Peter and ostracism from home and school a terribly lonely experience, but after a period of depression, he had found it strangely liberating. He had thrown his energies into his school work and, after only three weeks, was getting much better grades than he had thought possible, meaning that a scholarship to a good in-state university was a realistic possibility. His program of jogging and home karate practice, still following the "Master's Guide" DVDs, had improved his fitness enormously and given him a self-confident bearing that was turning reluctant heads at school. Many of his new admirers, he noticed with an ironic smile, were cheerleaders.

His first class of the day was history, and he now thoroughly enjoyed a subject that no longer intimidated him. He found the history of turn-of-the-twentieth-century China—the Opium War, Japanese occupation, and the Boxer rebellion leading to the collapse of the imperial government and the rise of communism—to be both relevant and fascinating. It was with thoughts of the implications of the hundred-year-old humiliation of China on the nation's current rise in economic power, and of the astonishingly resilient and homogeneous Chinese culture, that he wandered into the restroom. His ruminations were interrupted when the door was pushed open so hard that it slammed into the wall and boisterous voices entered. Simon didn't have to turn around to recognize Robbie's gang.

Then the chatter stopped.

Robbie broke the silence with a derisive snarl and said, "Well, if it isn't the town fag," then whispered at his cohorts behind Simon's back while Simon continued to face the wall and listened to the footsteps as Robbie distributed his henchmen. When the rustling had settled to silence, Robbie spoke again. "I've been waiting to get you on your own for weeks, you filthy pervert," he said in a voice dripping with venom. Simon heard him approaching from behind. "Now you're finally going to get what's coming to you."

Simon was standing at the urinal, his trousers unzipped and ready to urinate but holding his bladder, and though his heart pounded, he deliberately avoided looking around. Instead, he dropped his breathing and concentration to his abdomen, took a deep breath, and extended his attention behind him to the entire room. He had known that this moment would come, and he was ready.

"You might want to be careful, Bobbie. You've got a pretty face, and I'd hate to have to mess it up."

"It's Robbie, you queer, and don't you dare talk to me like that. Turn around."

"I just need to finish up here," said Simon, building up the pressure.

"I said turn around." Robbie placed his hand on Simon's shoulder.

"And I said I'm not done, but if that's what you want." Simon turned around, held himself high, and urinated down the front of Robbie's shirt and trousers. Robbie stepped back with a gasp, and his companion, whom Simon now recognized as Steven Jones, another senior, laughed out loud from the back wall.

Robbie glanced at Steven, and the laugh stopped, but Robbie's attention never wavered from Simon.

"Why you... you're going to pay for that."

He stepped forward again as Simon secured his trousers.

"I'll warn you one last time: I don't want to hurt you, but I have to defend myself."

"You prick." With this last insult, Robbie launched a fist right at Simon's head. Simon swayed back, avoiding it easily, and ducked under the next, using his and Robbie's combined forward motion to land a powerful blow in Robbie's belly. He stood up again, and as Robbie's arm lunged forward with a third punch, he grabbed it and used his assailant's momentum to throw him face-first into the wall. Robbie's shin crunched into the urinal, and his face smashed so hard into the wall that when he pulled himself upright and turned around, Simon saw blood flooding from his nose. Robbie wiped his face and examined his blood-covered hand, then glared at Simon with pure hatred. He spat a glob of bloody saliva on the floor and hissed, "Okay, the time for games is over." He looked behind Simon and nodded.

Without taking his eyes off Robbie, Simon pointed behind his back and said fiercely, "Don't move. This isn't your fight, and I don't want to hurt you."

Simon had heard of the sixth sense of mature martial arts, had even felt hints of it, but he had never experienced as clearly as today the intuitive sense of movement and location. He knew without hearing or seeing that Steven was still creeping toward him, and over his shoulder, he repeated, "I'm warning you," as he waited, watching Robbie approach him slowly from the front, fists up. When his instincts told him the moment was right, Simon leapt vertically, extending one leg sideways and, in the same movement, pirouetting over his outstretched leg and throwing a foot at the space where he knew Steven's head would be, finding it with a resounding crack. Simon completed his rotation, landed on his feet, and, with one bounce, was facing Robbie again. He heard Steven stagger into the wall behind him with a thump and slip to the floor, groaning in pain.

"Your move," Simon said, smiling at Robbie, enjoying the power that he was releasing for the first time.

Robbie rushed, and Simon waited, ducked inside the flailing fists, and brought a crushing knee up into his assailant's groin. He stepped back, watched Robbie fall slowly to the floor, then washed his hands, adjusted his shirt and trousers in the mirror, and calmly strolled out of the restroom.

"Jason, isn't it?" he asked the door guard who, wide-eyed, stepped out of his way and nodded in mute assent. "Well, Jason, you might want to go and tell the nurse that Robbie and his friend just had a fight and you're afraid they might have hurt each other."

The spring in Simon's stride felt good. The world was fresh and bright and no longer as threatening as it had been fifteen minutes earlier. He was self-assured and in control, smiling at students and teachers as he passed, indiscriminately volunteering, "Good morning," with song in his voice. The strong and self-reliant man of Peter's picture had emerged from its chrysalis at last.

As luck would have it, he saw Peter walking alone down the hall in front of him and hurried to catch up, slipping into a stride beside his old friend. Peter turned to see who was there, then looked ahead as he continued walking. "Hi, Simon, what do you want?"

"I want to talk. I want to see you again."

"You ignore me for a month and then just expect me to drop everything and... and *talk*?"

"Peter, don't be like that. I might be dead if Mom hadn't called the police on Dad. I've been kicked out of my home, and everyone at school knows I'm gay. I'm sorry I've been avoiding you, but I've had a lot to deal with. I love you, Peter, and I can't stand not seeing you any more."

"How long will it be this time before you decide you've got to be strong and that we need to stay apart again?" Peter didn't look at Simon as he spoke, but the words cut Simon deeply.

"I know I've treated you badly, but I really need you." He lowered his head, and his voice fell to a whisper. "When you... when you kissed me that first time, I was so confused. You've no idea how much of a shock it was. I didn't realize... I guess I still don't... it's all... oh, I don't know. And Aunt Jodi says, 'How do we know anyway?' How do we know who's saved, I mean. And she's... well, she's wonderful, she really is. So perhaps she's right. And... and... oh, Peter, all that matters is I'm gay, and I love you, and maybe together we can make something of this life."

They stopped walking. Peter faced ahead down the corridor, but Simon had turned to face him, his hands wringing at his sides, his head cocked in anticipation.

Then Peter smiled.

He turned his head and stole a look at Simon. "I'm sorry. I've missed you, too, and I was worried about you. I knew you'd moved in with your aunt, and I've seen what people have been doing at school."

"I'll make it. How are you doing, Peter?"

"My mom thinks we must have had an argument since we don't see each other any more, but that's all. I'm okay—and you look okay, too." He looked Simon up and down. "In fact, you look great."

"I am," Simon said. "I'm fitter and stronger, and I'm doing better at school than ever before. Aunt Jodi's cool—she thinks it's okay that I'm gay—and I just kicked the crap out of Robbie Cook."

Peter looked at Simon's chest and shoulders in awe. "You did *not*," he said, the disbelief resonating in his words.

Simon nodded decisively and said, "I just pissed all over him," then broke into an involuntary grin at his unintended pun. "I took out Steven Jones, that weasel who hangs around with him, too."

"Wow." Peter's eyes ran over Simon's upper body as if looking for a secret weapon, and his gaze mellowed into adoration as he looked back up to Simon's eyes. "I *have* missed you." He put his hand on Simon's chest.

Simon nodded and smiled back. He gently brushed Peter's hand off, said, "Not here," and asked, "Want to get together after school?" Peter assented, and Simon suggested, "How about the tree house?"

Simon floated in another world for the rest of the day. Having just defeated his nemesis, he enjoyed occasional glimpses of Robbie skulking sheepishly around, avoiding any contact, even getting up and leaving the dining room when Simon arrived. Everything went well, even the particularly difficult experiment in chemistry class that became a spectacular success. He completed his homework and his karate exercises early and told Aunt Jodi he was going out for a while. She didn't pry, simply getting him to commit to being back by half past ten, in time for a good night's sleep before school the following day.

Simon bounced on his bike down the trail, came to a stop under the tree house, and leaned his bike against the trunk. He looked at his watch, saw he was a couple of minutes early, and for the first time that day, he felt nervous as he thought about what he would say to Peter. He had a sudden panic as it occurred to him that Peter might not come, but then he heard the sound of spinning wheels and looked up. Peter's bike rounded the corner of the trail, its rider leaning on the handlebars and standing on one peddle, his free leg trailing behind, ready for a quick dismount. Simon rose, and as the bike approached, Peter stepped off and hit the ground running. Simon braced his legs and caught Peter as he came tumbling into his arms with a laugh. Simon vaguely noticed the bike clatter to the ground, its wheels spinning, but had time only for Peter's smile. His best friend was so happy, and Simon wanted to hold that joy, fill himself with it, hang on to it forever. After a timeless embrace punctuated with occasional kisses and inane greetings, the boys sat down with their backs against the tree trunk.

Peter stood abruptly and explained, "I'd better check my bike. It seemed like a good idea, and it was fun, but... " He paused and faced Simon with pursed lips and his hands on his hips. "Maybe it was a bit... reckless."

They laughed together, and Simon studied Peter's wiry frame, the cock of his head, and the flow of his stride as Peter walked the short distance to his bike, checked it over, and wheeled it back to the tree. "Nope, there's nothing wrong with it," Peter said. "It was just a little lonely out there and needed some support. Just like me."

With that, he let himself collapse against the tree beside Simon and rested his head on the bigger boy's shoulder. Simon laughed again, not speaking lest words corrupt the renewed joy of intimate companionship.

Ten minutes later they fetched the ladder and ascended to the tree house, and the next hour was one of slow movement, often no movement at all, and of few words. They touched, embraced, occasionally kissed, and expressed their mutual devotion. Simon realized how much he loved and was loved, and for the first time since he had been a small boy, he felt at home.

Ten o'clock raced upon them, and it seemed no time before Simon had to leave. With a last aching hug, a hug that vowed they would never truly be apart again, the youths hid the ladder and separately cycled home.

Chapter Fourteen

Jessica saw Clark at his locker first thing Monday morning and ran up to him, overflowing with things to say. Two hours ago, she had woken up in a strange bed in a trailer home and eaten breakfast with a bearded wild man twice her age, a man she was not sure whether to treat as her guardian or her spouse. Before she could open her mouth, however, Jessica saw that Clark was not the contented youth who had been such a comfort over the past two weeks but looked drawn, tired, and distressed.

"What's wrong?" she asked with a concerned frown.

"Nothing," mumbled Clark, burying his head in his locker and rummaging around.

"No, really, what's wrong."

"I said nothing's wrong, all right?" Clark grabbed a history book, glared at Jessica, slammed his locker, and stormed off. Jessica watched him from behind, not sure whether to be confused, concerned, or angry, then turned to the locker door, which had rebounded and was swinging freely back and forth, and, in a daze, secured the lock and followed Clark into the classroom.

The brief exchange bothered Jessica all morning, and she concluded that he must be upset at her for standing him up on Sunday afternoon, so she determined to apologize at lunch. She arrived in the dining room early and waited at her usual table, but she didn't remove her food from her tray: If he didn't come to her, she would go and sit with him today.

Clark arrived alone, and Jessica caught his quick glance at her as he stood in line for his food. When he had been served and picked up his tray, Jessica gritted her teeth and raised her hands to her tray, ready to follow him, but he made a beeline for her.

"I'm sorry about earlier," he said, offering a meek smile, sitting down and putting his food on the table, "I've just had a real bad weekend."

Jessica's tension evaporated. "And I'm sorry I stood you up on Sunday: I had a strange day, too, but I'll tell you about that later. What happened to you?"

"You know Dad was closing up the store this weekend?"

"Yeah, you were going to help him on Saturday. How did it go?"

"Oh, it went great. It looked like he was going to sell everything, even the building. The problem is he worked there yesterday, too—the Sabbath, right?—and he never came home last night."

Jessica leaned forward expectantly, not knowing where this was going, but sure that it wouldn't be pleasant.

"One of Mom's friends at church called her late last night. She'd seen Dad and Darlene—Darlene's the store assistant—together at Susie's last night. This morning, Mom went out early, and when she came home, she was livid. I think Dad and Darlene must've spent the night together and she found them."

Jessica let out a little gasp and put her hand to her mouth.

"It shouldn't be too much of a surprise," Clark continued, "because he and Mom haven't really been talking for months, and they've been getting worse. I get the feeling this has happened before."

"That's awful. I'm sorry."

Clark shrugged. "So anyway, Mom was in a terrible mood this morning and Dad wasn't home. But like I say, things have been bad for a while. I think Robbie's caught up in some bad stuff, too, and that's got a lot to do with it, but he doesn't even tell me what he's doing anymore." Clark looked up and asked, "Did you know he's moved out?"

Jessica leaned further forward and gaped. "No, you never told me."

Clark nodded and watched the gravy follow the tines of his fork as he trailed them around the plate. "A couple of times now he's gone away for the weekend without saying where. Dad got mad, and Robbie just packed his bag and left."

"Where's he been going?"

Clark shrugged, painting the gravy up to the rim of his plate. "He's my brother, and I guess I love him, but I don't understand him anymore. He seems to be angry all the time, and I mean *all* the time." Clark shrugged again. "He doesn't seem interested in talking to me any more, so I just leave him alone.

"But anyway, part of the reason Mom's been really horrible to Dad is I think she blames him for Robbie leaving." Clark's eyes were flicking around as he talked, suggesting to Jessica that his mind was also jumping, and she shook her head sympathetically, waiting for him to continue. "But it's more than that," he said eventually. "She's being real prickly, like she just doesn't want Dad to talk to her or touch her anymore, and she doesn't seem to care that Dad's closed the store at all. So it's pretty miserable at home right now." He prodded his food and heaved his chest with a snort of laughter. "If he's going to have an affair, he could do a lot worse than Darlene, though. She's got a reputation, that's for sure, but she's half his age, and she looks great." Clark raised a forkful of chicken and rice, studied Jessica, said, "She's nowhere near as beautiful as you, of course," and put the food in his mouth.

Jessica looked down at her tray, embarrassed and uncomfortable. The only person who had ever said things like that to her was Colby, and her mind flashed back to the guilt he had brought her. She had grown so fond of Clark—maybe she even loved him?—and knew that he was different, but he'd never spoken to her like this before, and she was scared. She ate a forkful of food while she recovered her composure and then changed the subject. "So what's going to happen?"

Jessica heaved a sigh of relief as Clark shrugged and let her off the hook. "I don't know," he said. "I just kind of avoid it all and spend as little time at home as I can. I eat there and do my homework, and that's pretty much it. I can't really blame Dad if he has a full-blown midlife crisis; actually, with everything that's going on right now, it's probably inevitable. Most of the time it doesn't bother me, but this morning it was just too much.

"But that's enough about me; tell me about your weekend. You looked pretty excited this morning, and I'm sure you've got a good reason why you didn't show up yesterday."

Jessica told him all about the visit from the church elders and her introduction to Old Sam, and she practically begged him to come over and meet her new guardian, whom she described in the most glowing terms. Clark agreed to visit the following Saturday and to spend the day, acknowledging that he would be glad for an excuse to spend some time away from his family. "I'd love to meet anyone who can make you this happy," he said. "Plus I'll bet by the weekend, you'll be feeling lonely again and could use the company."

Jessica laughed. She was on top of the world and couldn't imagine coming down.

But it wasn't long before she did.

On Monday night, she summoned the resolve to reconcile with Alison, and an opportunity presented itself first thing Tuesday morning. Alison was sitting alone at the back of their home room with her books on the desk in front of her, finishing off last night's homework. Jessica swallowed hard and, without giving herself time to change her mind, strode boldly forward. Alison didn't look up until Jessica was right upon her, and when she did, deep furrows cut her brow and she glared back down at her homework. Jessica turned a chair around and placed it facing Alison across the desk. She sat down, leaned on the desk to get close, and spoke quietly. "Alison, I know you're mad at me, and I deserve it. I should never have thrown that Coke at you, no matter what, but especially since the real problem was me. I've been really stupid. And I was rude, too. I'm sorry, I really am, and I miss you. I want to be friends again: Will you be my friend?"

Alison pretended to be concentrating on her writing and didn't respond.

Jessica pleaded, "Please, Alison, talk to me," and waited.

After ignoring Jessica a little while longer Alison put her pen down, folded her hands, and looked up. "I've missed you, too, Jessica. But I'm sorry, I can't be your friend."

Jessica's face fell, and she pulled back from the desk, confused.

"I'm sorry," repeated Alison. "Mom and Dad heard this weekend that you were going to have a baby and that you're going to live with Old Sam." She paused and examined Jessica before asking, "Are you? Going to live with Old Sam, I mean."

Jessica nodded.

Alison shook her head and looked away with a disgusted expression on her face. "I told them that it couldn't be true and that Colby raped you and that he was the father. We had a big argument, and they laughed at me for being so gullible. They think you've turned into a royal slut and told me not to have anything more to do with you. They think the reason we didn't see each other much this summer was that you were 'round at Old Sam's place all the time. Anyway, you've been such a bitch that I didn't think we'd ever talk again anyway, so I promised I'd do what they asked."

"You don't believe them, do you?"

"At first I didn't, but if it's not true, then why are you moving in with Old Sam?"

"Alison!" Jessica was shocked at the volume of her voice and looked around, embarrassed, before leaning forward and continuing in little more than a whisper, "The elders came 'round on Sunday, and I thought they were going to stone me."

"Don't be silly," Alison said in a voice so laden with contempt that Jessica felt herself shrivel up. "Anyway, it doesn't matter: I promised Mom and Dad." Alison picked up her pen and returned her attention to her books as if to end the conversation.

Jessica struggled with frustration and anger, eventually finding her words and forcing herself to speak gently, though her voice quivered. "But it's not true, Alison, you know it's not." Tears welled up, and she begged,

"Alison, please… you're my best friend, you're the only person I can even talk to about this."

Alison didn't lift her head as she replied, "You seem to be doing quite a bit of talking with Clark, not to mention Old Sam." Her voice had a harsh edge.

"You're going to break friends forever because your parents get some stupid, idiotic idea in their head about something I didn't do?" Jessica couldn't believe what was happening.

Alison's palms slapped the desk, and she raised her head to reveal furious eyes. "You lied to me, Jessica. And besides, we can't all run away from home and live with some weirdo hippie drop-out in a trailer. Some of us want to have a normal life at home with our moms and dads."

"So that's it; you've turned into Mommy's goody two-shoes," Jessica spat, letting spite fill her veins because she was not prepared to admit to Alison how upset she was.

"You were so mean to me that I shouldn't be talking to you anyway," Alison snapped back, fists clenched and tears appearing in the corners of her eyes. "And I've never seen Mom and Dad like this. They'd kill me if they knew I was even talking to you now."

Jessica swallowed again, trying to bring herself back under control, but she couldn't eliminate the tremble from her voice. "Well, I'm glad I said I'm sorry, but I can't believe how mean you're being. Goodbye, Alison." Jessica stumbled and nearly tripped as she rose, but she recovered and tried to maintain her dignity as she strode out of the classroom. She looked straight ahead, ignoring the stares and whispers of the handful of students who had overheard the last heated words and hoping they could not see that her lower lip was quivering. Jessica was so upset that she didn't even notice Clark slip out of the room behind her. He caught her right outside the girl's restroom, and with a smile, Jessica convinced him she'd be fine, that she just wanted to be alone right now. But with Clark out of the way and classes beginning, Jessica secreted herself in the restroom and cried for the whole first period.

Alison's rejection reopened old wounds, and by Wednesday night, it was beginning to sink in that Jessica was never going home to Ma and Dad. When she got back to the trailer home that night, she called out for Sam, but there was no reply. She searched the surrounding yard and woods, and when she realized that his truck was not there that she despaired. She threw herself headfirst onto the couch, buried her face in a cushion, and sobbed for twenty minutes. When she pulled herself up, she drifted into the bedroom and sat on the floor by her cedar chest, then lifted the lid and rummaged through the miscellany inside, taking out a friendship bracelet that

Alison had made for her in second grade, a funny birthday card from Dad, and an illustrated story she had written in fourth grade, until she could stand it no longer. She folded her arms on the rim of the chest, placed her forehead on her wrists, and collapsed in shuddering grief. She was unable to move when she heard the front door open, or even when Bess came bounding in and licked her neck.

Sam brushed Bess away and sat on the floor beside her, saying, "I'm sorry I'm late, Jessica," in a voice so soft and beautiful that it would have been soothing if her were reading the telephone directory. He rubbed her shoulder as he continued, "Someone needed a water heater repaired, and I needed to go and buy a part, and I didn't know that Cook Hardware's closed down. The job took a lot longer than I thought, and then I had to go by the grocery store to get some meat for your dinner. This family-provider thing is taking some getting used to. But listen to me just going on. Are you feeling lonely?"

She lifted her head, looked at him through her tears, and nodded.

"That's okay. It'll take a while to get over what you've been through." He smiled and wiped the tears from her cheek with his thumb.

"Oh, Sam, I don't deserve you." Jessica burst into tears again and buried her head in his shoulder, and he wrapped his arms around her, covering her with a tender blanket of love. After a few minutes, she lifted her head toward the ceiling and wailed, "Why?" She shrugged Sam off and looked helplessly at him. "Ma and Dad hate me, and Pastor Kidd's thrown me out of the church." She threw her arms wide in despair and looked up at the ceiling again. "My life used to be all about the Church and my family, and now they're both gone. I don't even know if I believe there's a God anymore." She looked hopelessly at Sam.

Sam slid toward her and with a gentle touch of his hand pulled her to him, easing her head onto his shoulder. "Do you remember when you were a little girl and you believed in Santa Claus?"

Jessica's cheek chafed on his beard as she nodded.

"Well, you don't anymore, right? Do you know why?"

"Because I know he's not real."

Sam smiled and said, "Oh, he's real enough," stroking Jessica's hair before continuing. "Santa's a metaphor for giving. He lives his whole life for the sake of others, spending each year planning for just one day of giving, even though he never meets a single person who says thank you. By the time we're teenagers, we cast off the man but not the metaphor: Santa represents the pure joy that can come from giving. Christianity's like Santa. It's an enduring, eternal message, the path to salvation, but we have to realize that the understanding we have as children won't serve us as adults. We need to take our understanding to a deeper level."

"But Christianity's not like that," Jessica interrupted. "Christ wasn't a metaphor; he was God made man, and the Bible is His divine Word. Bible-reading groups and sermons are what we use to deepen our faith." Jessica sat up and wrapped her arms around her bent legs, pulling her knees in close and resting her chin on them. She wanted to believe so very much.

Sam smiled again. "Those are very important, it's true, but they're not enough. Imagine saying you're taking up carpentry, but instead of buying tools, you just sit around with other so-called carpenters and talk about it, and none of you ever makes anything. You wouldn't be very good, would you?"

Jessica laughed halfheartedly and wiped away her tears.

"Just like we need to make things with tools and wood before we can call ourselves carpenters, we each have to live a Christian life before we can call ourselves Christians. Jesus didn't spend his time in scripture classes with the Jews; he lived an active life with fishermen and tax collectors, even prostitutes. You have to see God everywhere, not just in the Bible. Tell me, do you remember the Golden Rule?"

Jessica answered robotically, "Thou shalt love the Lord thy God with all thy heart... and thy neighbor as thyself."

Sam nodded. "Luke 10:27, the path to eternal life. That one simple verse, the one true Commandment, contains Christ's whole teaching. Everything else we impose on this Commandment is our own judgment. All our opinions—especially those we hold of others' views or worth and our conceited 'understanding' of Scripture—are presumptions against it." He had been gazing into space as he spoke, but with a blink, his eyes came back into focus, and he turned his head to Jessica. "Can I tell you a story?"

Jessica nodded. Sam inclined his head to acknowledge her permission and began. "When I first went to school in Atlanta, I was young and naïve. I'd been going to the Church of the Epistles my whole life, and I knew with absolute certainty that I had faith and was saved. When I took my first comparative religion class I was concerned that the teachers would attempt to corrupt my faith, but I decided I was strong enough, so I went along, planning to learn enough to help me spread God's Word.

"But things didn't turn out as I'd planned.

"You see, as part of that class, we had to visit the temples of other religions. I went to all those strange places thinking about how I'd come back later to save all the sinners and pagans and how worthy I'd be when I did so, but after a while, I realized that some of the pagans had something that I was missing, and that it was something I'd always thought I had: the deep, selfless love that Paul describes in First Corinthians, love that 'suffereth long, and is kind,' love that, 'beareth all things, believeth all things.' When they looked at me, it was with their whole soul, and when I opened my mouth to speak, they gave me their complete and undivided attention, even though I was an arrogant young idiot. I treated them as fools because they couldn't hear the Gospel, but they listened to me without an ounce of prejudice or judgment."

Jessica knew that sitting in a run-down trailer, listening to the heretical ramblings of a bearded drop-out should have been an uncomfortable experience, but although Sam turned what she had heard from the pulpit of the Church of the Epistles on its head, his words were powerful and resonated deeply in a way that she couldn't understand. She listened, entranced, as he continued.

"I didn't meet many people like that, just a handful, but the fact that I found them among people deeply committed to religions other than Christianity was enough to make me wonder. I even met a couple of Buddhists who had not only studied the Bible, but had as deep an understanding of it as anyone I've ever met. All of these people taught that we should love God with all our heart and love our neighbor as ourselves, and they lived their lives that way, utterly selflessly, without sparing a thought for their own needs or desires. Just being around them made me realize how incredibly narrow and selfish I'd become in my faith. I had been convinced that I'd been saved, but being with them made me see that I'd become stuck in my own private salvation without one ounce of true compassion.

"There was one teacher in particular who affected me deeply and who I visited again and again. He cared for what he called 'the myriad living beings which haven't been saved.' He even told one student—and I knew he was really talking to me when he said it—that he didn't have an independent salvation. He said that he could only be saved once he had made sure that all other beings had been saved first. I cried for hours that night."

Jessica knew that she was going to cry for hours, herself, but that everything was going to be okay. "Thank you, Sam, that was... " her voice trailed off.

"Just remember, true compassion doesn't come from God, it *is* God. He has shared it with us by breathing life and consciousness into our frail frames. Who are we to deny this, to try to gain anything from it for ourselves—even salvation? Who are we to do anything but live in wonder and perhaps do our best—recognizing it for the nothing that it is—to help others along the way?

"And that includes getting the dinner." Sam kissed Jessica's forehead and squeezed her shoulders. "Come and help me, will you? I'm not used to cooking for two, and I could use another pair of hands."

Chapter Fifteen

Peter put the plastic plate of half-finished Jell-O and whipped cream on the tray, wiped his mouth with a paper napkin, and tossed the wad of paper on top of his chicken bones and mashed potatoes. He leaned back against the Formica bench of the fried-chicken fast-food restaurant, rubbed his belly, and sighed.

"I'm stuffed."

"That was good." Simon nodded in agreement, putting the last of his biscuit and jelly into his mouth.

Peter glanced at his watch and shifted restlessly. "I need to get home. Mom's sick."

"You said earlier; is there anything I can do?"

Peter shook his head. "I just need to get home and check on her, 'cause Dad's working late tonight. This has been a great day."

Simon assembled the remaining trash and stood. Peter reached out to take the tray, but Simon beat him.

"I need to get some work done tomorrow," Simon said, "so I'll see you on Monday." He tossed the garbage in the receptacle and added the tray to the pile on top.

"I'm not sure I can wait that long." Peter held the door for Simon and, as his friend passed through, placed his free hand on Simon's back, rubbing. They crouched beside each other to unlock their bicycles, Peter aching to hold Simon close, but he couldn't, not in public in Wilkeston, so when they rose and faced each other, Peter could only reach for Simon's hand and squeeze it to say farewell.

Peter's short ride home was filled with the joy of Simon coming to terms with his true nature and the promise of a life together after high school, maybe in Atlanta or even San Francisco. He was floating in a dream when he pulled into his backyard, walked into the house, and turned on the kitchen light.

"Hi, Mom, I'm home," he called out, slipping out of his jacket and reaching up to hang it on the wall.

"Hi, Peter; did you get the bread, dear?"

Peter's hand froze by the coat hook, his jacket still in his hand. Guilt at his neglect shattered his happiness. "Sorry, Mom," he called into the house, "I forgot. I'll go and get some. Do you need anything else?"

"No, thank you. You are a sweetheart."

Peter pulled his jacket back on and stepped into the living room, where Mom was lying on the couch in front of the TV. "Are you feeling any better?"

"A little." She smiled up at her son as he sat down on the edge of the couch next to her and put his lips to her forehead.

"You're still hot. Are you sure you don't want any medicine?"

"I've got some cold medicine in the bathroom. If I'm still not feeling right on Monday, I'll visit the doctor."

"I'll be back in a little while." Peter kissed her again and stood up.

He rode his bike a mile to the grocery store and chained it up outside. After picking up a loaf of bread, he browsed the shelves and decided to treat his mother to some hot chocolate and picked up some Motrin for her fever and a cheap paperback to read—she had always had a soft spot for detective thrillers. He paid using the money she had given him that morning, dropped the supplies into his rucksack, and tossed the bag over his shoulders. Twilight had darkened into night while he had been inside, and he was anxious to get home, so he didn't pay attention to the car that pulled up next to him as he knelt, fumbling with the lock, or to the four doors that clicked open but did not close. As footsteps approached him, he paused and looked up from the bike, but he didn't raise his head in time to see who was there before a foot landed squarely on his nose. He was thrown onto his back in a brilliant burst of pain and blood.

"Wanna come for a ride, gay boy?"

The agony in his face filled Peter's entire being. He lifted himself onto his elbows and raised his head, but his blurry vision was worsened by the loss of his glasses and the searing pain, and he could only vaguely distinguish the shadowy outlines of three or four adolescent males. He started to sit up, but hands roughly grabbed his upper arms and manhandled him into the car. Before he could react, he had been wedged in the middle of the back seat of a large, American-made vehicle.

"So you're Simon's boyfriend—I've been trying to figure it out for weeks. You've been real careful, haven't you? But not careful enough: We've seen you holding hands with him."

Peter started to protest, but he was silenced by a fist in his abdomen that doubled him up, followed by an elbow to the face that just missed his nose, landing instead on a cheek freshly split by the boot. The pain was accompanied by the warmth of blood gushing from the wound and running onto his shirt.

"Careful, Steven; he's bleeding all over Dad's car. Besides, you don't want to get any of that gay blood on you. There's no telling what you'll catch.'

"Yuck! You're right, Jason, I'll be careful." Peter's companion turned to him and added, "But don't you try anything, or I'll do it again anyway."

"Where are we going?" asked a weak voice from the front of the car.

Peter was thinking the same, though his mind was in turmoil. The pain was intense, but unless he could escape, he knew there was worse to come. What could he do, though, wedged in the back of a car between boys larger than he? If only Simon were here. He would know what to do; he would fight his way out.

"Is that you, Colby?" Peter asked, but his question ended in crushing pain on the back of his bowed head, pain so great that Peter cried out.

"We told you to shut up."

"Good one, Robbie."

Peter realized he had been kidnapped by the three boys who had attacked Simon in the boys' room, accompanied by the minister's son. Where were they going, indeed, and what would happen when they got there? He was hurting like he had never hurt before in his life, and his heart was pounding in terror. Oceans of sweat mingled with the blood pouring from the gash in his cheek, and he could feel that he was on the edge of physically quaking with fear. He needed to escape and tried to calm his racing mind, tried to focus on his situation and the car, but it was hard, and he could see no way out.

Stay alert. Wait for your chance to run, to steal the car, to scream for help.

Breathing deeply from his abdomen—a trick Simon had taught him— he surprised himself by settling his panic into an alertness that cut through the pain.

"What are we going to do with him?" It was Colby again, his voice weak and trembling.

"Let's take him down by the river and hang him," said Robbie. Peter started to protest, but before his grunts could articulate themselves into words, a fist landed on the side of his face. "I'm sorry, Jason. I'll have to wipe it down in here afterwards, but he just won't shut up."

"You can't be serious?" The car swerved as Jason spoke.

"Watch where you're driving, Jason," Robbie snapped. "Sure, I'm serious. This is Simon Cassell's fag. He's a pervert, despised in the eyes of

the Lord, and he's sleeping with the jumped-up puke that broke my nose."
Peter heard the injured pride in Robbie's voice, turned his head slightly, and
saw Robbie's finger stroking the deformity that his nose had suffered when
Simon had slammed his face into the wall.

Jason pressed, "Robbie, you can't go around killing people just
because their boyfriends beat you up."

There was a resounding thump as Robbie's fist hit the roof of the car.
"This fag has sinned against nature, and he's going to die tonight. If you've
not got the guts to do God's will, then I'll do it on my own. Now take me to
the river."

Peter experienced the intensity of being that exists only on the edge of
life and death. His mind became sharp and oscillated between looking for
a way out and attempting to accept his fate. Silence reigned in the car for
the next five minutes, giving him a chance to say silent prayers of reconciliation with his Lord. He reflected on how lucky he was not to have
Simon's doubts about his sexual orientation and that he harbored no fears
of the impact it would have on his salvation. The silence was finally broken
by the sound of quiet sobbing from the front passenger seat.

"What's up, Colby? Too hot for you, is it?" Robbie goaded. "You're
just like your old man, full of fire and brimstone, but not willing to see
things through."

"Don't you talk about my dad like that," Colby shouted, but his outburst was met by laughter.

"I'll talk about him just how I like. Now, are you with us or not?"

"Robbie, I can't… "

Robbie let silence continue for a few moments, then called to the driver, "That's far enough, pull down the next road. There are a couple of pas-
tures back there by the river." Jason obeyed without comment and came to
a stop when ordered.

"Don't move, fag. Steven, beat the crap out of him if he does." Robbie jumped out, stepped into the pool of light in front of the car, and walked
across the dirt to a rusty iron gate in the three-string barbed wire fence. He
used both hands to lift the gate and drag it open, then turned, waved the car
through, and led Jason across a bumpy field to an old oak tree.

"All right, everybody out. That includes you, butt-boy. Jason, do you
have any rope?"

Jason laughed. "No, of course I don't."

"Well shit." Robbie looked around the field for ideas. "Open the
trunk, Jason."

"But, Robbie… " came Colby's plaintive voice.

"But what?"

Peter sensed Steven and Jason stopping in sympathy. The future of the lynching rested on a razor's edge, and it was up to Robbie as the ring leader to make it fall one way or the other, a challenge he took head-on.

"Didn't you hear what the pastor said the other week? Your own father, Colby! He said that gays must die and that their blood is on their own hands. And he quoted the Bible. It says right there in the Bible that it's our responsibility to kill this faggot."

Under the ferocity of Robbie's exegesis, the mob acquiesced. Jason popped the trunk, and Robbie rummaged through what sounded like a large tool bag, emerging with a pair of wire cutters.

"Steven, go and cut me a long length of that wire fence. Jason, kick him in the balls so he can't move."

Peter tried to shield himself from the attack, but it was useless and he crumpled in agony. For good measure, Jason kicked him again in the head, and Peter reeled. He had been hoping for an opportunity to jump alone into the front of the car and ride away, shortly to pull up in triumph at Simon's house, but the accumulated pain was so great that he could barely move, and the sting of blood and swelling in his eyes was enough, even without the loss of his glasses, to partially blind him and render escape an impossibility. It was time to surrender to his fate.

Mom, I'm sorry I didn't get you your bread tonight. Simon, I'm sorry... I'm sorry. Dear God, please look kindly on me, and if I'm going to die, please let it be quick.

Colby's plaintive voice tried to rise once more. "Robbie... " It was his last desperate effort to assert himself against the gang, but his resistance was swept away by Robbie's overpowering scorn.

"You want to hang out with the big boys, you gotta do what the big boys do. Now let's get on with it. Okay, Steven, let me have that." Peter couldn't turn his head to see what was happening but surmised from the noise that Steven had accomplished his task and that Robbie was cutting the wire into smaller lengths.

After a few moments, Robbie spoke again. "All right, Steven, tie his hands behind his back with that."

"But it's barbed wire."

"Then you'd best be careful not to jab yourself, hadn't you?" Robbie snorted with laughter. "Colby, you tie his ankles."

Colby's resistance had snapped. He turned Peter roughly onto his face and placed a knee in his back so Peter couldn't move. Peter's hands were grabbed, and then his feet. The pain of barbs digging in to his wrists and ankles was accompanied by occasional short outbursts as his assailants jabbed themselves, too. Peter struggled to resist, but it was useless. He forced himself to speak. "Colby, you don't have to... "

His words were cut off by another boot in the face. This time, the toe landed squarely in his mouth. He felt the crunch of teeth breaking, but there was already so much blood and pain that he had to run his tongue over the jagged stumps at the front of his mouth to know the extent of the damage. The agony was unbearable—so much so that it lost its reality and he transcended it, able to lie still, calm, yet alert, in the face of inevitable death. He relaxed his limbs and allowed the wire to be twisted tight and didn't fight as he was manhandled onto the roof of the car. Lying on his back on the roof, barbed wire sticking painfully into his wrists and back, he blinked the blood out of his eyes and watched the hazy outlines of movement with disinterested fascination. Robbie and Steven climbed up to join him on the roof and struggled to tie another long length of wire over a limb just out of reach. Finally, they managed to throw one end over and secure it with a series of twists.

"Okay, help me get this piece of shit to his feet."

Peter considered falling off, but only for a moment. He felt himself float upright as if carried on a cloud. As the wire was twisted around his neck, he thought with regret of the hot chocolate his mother would not drink tonight and of the farewell he would never be able to say to Simon. His only real—though fleeting—anxiety was about the anguish that the two people he loved most would feel when his body was found.

It was done. Steven slid off the roof, and Robbie stood back to test his workmanship. With an extended finger, he tested the wire that was tied as tightly from Peter's neck to the branch.

Peter was numb to the prick of the wire as Robbie pulled it but felt a few inches of slack as he tried to survey his lynching mob with bleary eyes. "May God forgive you," he volunteered

"How dare you, you vile piece of shit! Here, pass me that piece of wire," Robbie said, gesturing at something beside Colby's feet. "Yeah, that one," he said and reached down. He mumbled, "Thanks," and then twisted the wire into a circlet that he rammed down and twisted onto Peter's head to form a crown. Peter blinked the blood out of his eyes enough to make out the leer of hatred on Robbie's face, and his heart was filled with compassion for the loathing that was eating Robbie alive.

"Don't you dare look at me," Robbie spat out, his expression again enraged. He swung his fist again. Peter was knocked sideways against the noose and swayed but somehow avoided slipping on the metal of the car roof. He straightened up, still looking at Robbie, whose face wore a peculiarly defiant expression.

"Give me the keys, Jason," Robbie ordered, looking away and sliding off the roof.

"They're in the ignition," was the mumbled reply.

Simon heard the door click open and slam closed almost immediately and then heard the engine roar into life. The car started to move slowly under Peter's feet, and he hopped along the roof to maintain the slack in the makeshift noose, reciting the words of the Lord's Prayer with his eyes closed. A sharp pain around Peter's neck blurred into a swimming brilliance that gradually faded to pure white.

Chapter Sixteen

Jessica sipped her iced tea, turned to Clark, who was sitting on the ground beside her, and asked, "So, what do you want to do now?"

"Let's go get some ice cream."

"You want to walk, or shall I get Sam to give us a ride?"

"I hate to keep bothering him. Besides, I need to stretch my legs."

"So do I." Jessica rubbed the base of her belly and added, "That book he got me says walking is the best exercise when you're pregnant."

Jessica had just spent a sunny Saturday afternoon entertaining Clark. When he had suggested to her on Monday that after a week in her new home she would be ready for company, she had laughed at him, but he had been right. The finality of her split with Alison had been difficult, but on Friday night, with the prospect of two days at home, her separation from Ma and Dad and the familiar stone house that had been home for fifteen years really sank in. She had lain in her bed, weeping silently long into the small hours of the morning.

By the time she had awakened on Saturday, the sun had already been high in the sky, and she had cast her worries aside, jumping right into preparing for Clark's visit. Cleaning the house—despite Sam's insistence that the place was already in good order—and tidying up the yard had kept her busy all morning. Shortly after Clark had arrived, they had eaten a grilled chicken salad that Jessica had prepared, and she had walked him around "the estate." Jessica had taken great pleasure in showing off Sam's vegetable garden with which, after only six days, she was already becoming quite familiar.

"Come on, then, let's go."

They rose from the ground where they had been sitting in the shade behind the trailer and dusted off the seats of their clothes. Jessica reached out for the drink in Clark's hand, but he shook his head, took another sip, and said, "This is great iced tea. You made this, too?"

Jessica nodded, dropped her hand, led the way slowly and in silence around the trailer, and called through the open door, "Sam, we're going to town for a while." She turned to Clark and held out her hand again. This time, after relishing a last mouthful of tea, he relinquished the glass. Sam was already entering the kitchen as Jessica reached the top step, and he took the empty glasses from her.

"Okay, you kids have a good time."

Although Sam had already shaved off his beard by the time Jessica had woken up that morning, the sight of his smooth chin gave her another double-take: Her first impression of Sam the previous weekend as a bearded tramp living in peace with the animals, a wild hermit with penetrating eyes, would be a lasting one.

"Sam, you look great," she said with a smile.

"Well, I don't know about that," he said, putting the glasses down on the counter and rubbing the skin of his jaw, lingering on a small razor cut, and adding, "But even I have to admit it's an improvement, and it's long overdue. When are you going to be back?"

Jessica shrugged and turned to Clark.

"By dark, sir. And thanks for a wonderful afternoon. I can see Jessica's going to be very happy here."

"Sam. The name's Sam. Now run along and enjoy yourselves."

Jessica rested her fingers on Clark's upraised palm and descended carefully from the trailer. They walked beside each other in silence until they were a hundred yards up the road when a thought flashed through Jessica's mind and she looked at Clark.

"I've been so completely caught up in making sure your visit today went well that I haven't really thought about *you* one bit. How's it going with your mom and dad?"

Clark's laugh was tinged with bitterness. "You've not been selfish at all. The truth is, I'd rather not think about them right now. They're behaving like a couple of school kids, worse than you and Alison. Ouch!" He jumped aside to avoid Jessica's swinging fist. "No, really, it's horrible. Stop that!"

Jessica concluded her assault by shoving Clark on the shoulder and asking, "Did you ever figure out if he spent the night with that store assistant… Darlene?"

Clark nodded. "He's spending even less time at home now that he doesn't have the store. I don't know where he's going, but I imagine he's with her, and so does Mom."

"It must be awful."

"Mom's just making it worse, though. She's been ignoring him for weeks now, even before this started. I don't know, Jessica—it really is like you and Alison. I just want everyone to grow up, but I don't think there's anything I can do, so I just try to keep out of the way. Now tell me, did you really find that algebra homework easy?"

Jessica laughed. "Sure. You've just got to cross-multiply, factor out the quadratics, and cancel. It's no different, really, than if they were numbers."

"Well, I still don't get it. I'll have another go tomorrow, but you may have to give me a private tutorial."

"I'd like that."

They reverted to silence, and Jessica walked close beside Clark, her heart beating fast every time their hands brushed. She decided to take the plunge and, with a surge of excitement in her belly, grabbed his hand. His fingers closed around hers and squeezed, and after a few minutes, their fingers were interlaced.

The ice-cream shop was a family owned business in a stand-alone building next to the police station. Jessica had forgotten until she and Clark reached the parking lot that the shop also rented out movies, sold great pizzas, and did good business from the movie theater across the street. When she was younger, Dad had driven her down on Friday nights in his pickup to fetch deep-pan, double-cheese pizza with pepperoni and no tomato sauce as a weekly treat, and occasionally he had really spoiled her and rented a video as well, though Ma had never approved of this indulgence.

The façade of the building rose tall before Jessica, bombarding her with memories, and she froze in the parking lot, caught between worlds. She was only vaguely aware of Clark squeezing her hand and barely noticed him ask, "Are you okay?"

She had rented *Cinderella* and *Sleeping Beauty* at least half a dozen times each.

Where had it all gone wrong?

The shock subsided, and when Clark asked again, "Jessica, what's wrong?" she gave him a weak smile.

"It's nothing, Clark, I was just remembering something."

She was grateful that he didn't press, but instead waited patiently, his hand in hers, until she was ready to move.

"What do you want?" he asked as they entered.

Jessica replied, "A double chocolate cone," and almost choked as the name of her childhood favorite sprang from her throat as habit. Her thoughts chased the words out of her mouth, wanting to catch them, to pull them back, unspoken and unheard.

Dad, where are you?

Jessica's heart was racing, she was sweating, and she was strangely disconnected from the world in which Clark said to the teenager behind the counter, "Hi, Annie. Two double chocolate cones, please." His voice sounded slow and synthetic to Jessica. The familiar smell of hot cheese and pizza dough made Jessica's heart ache for the family she had lost, and her eye fell on movies lined up on the racks for rental: *Ella Enchanted, The Princess Diaries*, and, behind them, shelves of Disney favorites.

Where was *her* prince?

Jessica's head began to swim, and her fingers felt swollen and awkward as they accepted the cone from Clark. She rested her hand on his arm and turned with him to walk out of the store.

She didn't notice the threshold. Her toe snagged and she stumbled.

Clark caught her, but not before her knee had scraped on the concrete step and her ice cream cone had fallen to the floor, where Jessica watched it explode in slow motion, spraying Clark from the knees down. Kneeling in the debris, the front of her dress sticky and cold, Jessica dissolved in tears. Clark stepped around her and into the middle of the mess and, with chocolate squishing under the soles of his shoes, lifted her to her feet. Tears streamed down Jessica's face, and as if it were the most natural thing in the world, she stood on her toes, wrapped her arms tightly around Clark's neck, and pressed her lips to his. Clark's arms enfolded Jessica, and she disappeared into him for a timeless moment.

Slowly, she reemerged into the world, returned to the flats of her feet, and gazed up into a face that made her skin tingle, made her glow all over, made everything all right.

My prince was here all along.

Standing in Clark's arms, she knew this was where she belonged, and her heart at once yearned for him and was completely satisfied, but for a terrible moment, she panicked. Would Clark, like her parents, like Alison, leave her?

"Please don't go," she whispered, not intending for Clark to hear.

But he did hear her, and his response was as magical as the kiss itself. "I'll always be there for you," he said. "This is true love. Do you think this happens every day?" She remembered the line from one of her favorite movies, which she now knew she had never understood before. Tears streamed once more from her eyes, and she buried her face in Clark's neck, holding him tightly, not wanting to ever let him go.

Clark's soothing voice brought her back again. "Jessica, we're letting all the air out of the store. And my ice cream's melting and running down my hand."

Jessica released him with a sniffle and a laugh. "Thanks."

"Thank *you*. Do you want another ice cream?"

"I just want to sit down."

"Go on, then, and I'll join you in a minute."

Jessica floated to the bench that faced the movie theater. This time there was no question in her mind—she really had found the man of her dreams. He was not where, or what, she had expected, but he was just right. The door jingled again, and Clark sat beside her.

"Here, I brought some damp paper towels and another chocolate cone."

Jessica wiped the worst of the mess off, threw the paper in the trash can beside her, and took the ice cream. Clark put his arm around her, and she leaned into him, resting her head on his shoulder while they licked their ice creams.

"Hey," Clark exclaimed, "they're showing that new movie tonight." Jessica looked up in surprise at the sign outside the movie theater across the street and then at Clark, who glanced at his wrist and said, "There's a show that begins in twenty minutes. You want to go?"

Jessica thought for a minute before bursting out laughing and leaning heavily into his shoulder. "You knew that all along, didn't you? Sure, I'd love to."

*   *   *

"That was wonderful," Jessica said, holding onto Clark's arm as they left the theater. "How did you like it?"

"It was okay."

"Well, you're a *guy*." Jessica leaned into him and squeezed his forearm, but then she relented. "Thanks for taking me. I really enjoyed it." Jessica was oblivious to the handful of familiar faces leaving the small theater with them, floating instead in the fantasy land of the movie, her prince beside her. Instinctively, she headed toward home. They had covered fifty yards before she realized where she was going.

"I'm sorry," she said as she stopped. "What do you want to do now?"

"Let's just get you home. I promised Sam you'd be there by dark. I know we'll be in plenty of time, but since I hope we'll be doing this again, I'd like to get off on the right foot."

"Oh, we'll do this again, that's for sure, but you don't have to walk me home. It's completely out of your way."

"I'd like to, though, and not just because I don't want to go back to my own home."

Jessica was happy to have his company for a little while longer, and they walked slowly and mostly in silence, Clark's arm over Jessica's shoulder, hers around his waist. The fit was perfect, and their stride lengths matched. When they came to the gravel drive leading to Sam's trailer, Jessica stopped and turned to face Clark.

"Thank you for a wonderful day."

"Thank you, Jessica; it was just what I needed." He paused, looked at his shoes, and added, "I've wanted more than anything in the world to kiss you since we were in fifth grade, so now I can die a happy man."

"So why did you wait until now, you silly thing?" Jessica grabbed Clark's shoulder and pulled him behind an oak tree before he could answer.

Chapter Seventeen

Pastor Kidd watched Colby stir his bowl of cereal with what appeared to be absentminded violence, causing milk to splash onto the table.

"What's the matter, Colby?" his mother coaxed for the third time.

"I told you, nothing's wrong," Colby replied, his voice petulant. He dropped his spoon in his bowl with a clatter and sat upright.

Pastor Kidd's full spoon was raised to his own open mouth, but he lowered it and leaned forward. "Colby, it doesn't matter whether anything's wrong or not, you will *not* talk to your mother like that. Apologize to her right now."

"I'm sorry, Mom," Colby said without looking up, his voice surly as he retrieved his spoon and resumed prodding his cereal. Harris, exasperated, looked at his wife. She shrugged and rolled her eyes, but when she saw that Harris was about to say something else to Colby, she furrowed her brow and shook her head. Harris returned his attention to his cereal and resolved to talk to his churlish son later about this attitude, which would not help the boy become an effective pastor.

Sarah placed her hand at the nape of her son's neck and spoke gently. "Colby, I don't know what's wrong, but your father and I are here to help you, and we can't do that unless you talk to us."

Colby pulled his head toward his shoulders but was saved from having to reply by the sound of the telephone. Harris and Sarah exchanged frowns. Who could be calling this early on a Sunday morning? Sarah rose, lifted the phone out of its cradle on the counter, and as she looked at its screen, her expression filled with concern. She pressed the button and put the phone to her ear.

"Good morning… yes it is… yes, he's right here." Sarah held out the phone to Harris and said, "It's Sergeant Wilson."

As Harris stood to take the phone, he noticed Colby staring at him from a transformed face. No longer defiant, the boy's skin was white, even clammy, his eyes were wide, and his jaw sagged, pulling his mouth into an uneven circle. As Harris spoke into the phone, he once more wondered what was wrong with his son.

"Good morning, Joel; how's Linda? … Oh, I see… uhuh… uhuh… oh my goodness, dear Lord help and preserve us!" Harris leaned forward with urgency, his whole body tense. Out of the corner of his eye, he saw Sarah sit down, but he was transfixed by Colby's face, now that of a vampire's victim as the blood was drawn from it. Even the red hair on the boy's head appeared to be fading to translucence.

"No, Joel, I've no idea… yes, I will. It's the very least I can do. Thank you." His hand fell slowly from his ear as he struggled to deal with the numbness that had overcome him. When his eyes recovered focus, they drifted to Sarah, and he said, "Joel wanted to let me know that one of the members of our church died last night. Peter Anderson. Jack Summers found him in one of his fields down by the river this morning." Harris choked back a hysterical cackle, wondering as he did so why laughter arose in times of shock, and said, "He'd been hanged by barbed wire from an oak tree."

Harris jumped at the sound of the phone clattering on the table, and when he looked down, realized what had happened and wondered how it had fallen out of his hand. Though time had lost all meaning, it was only a moment before Harris's mind reengaged and he was looking at Colby. The boy seemed to be fading away before Harris's eyes, shrinking back in his seat, his bleached skin shriveling in the heat of his parents' gazes. Colby's brow was covered in sweat, and his eyes flickered, frantic, back and forth between his parents.

"Colby, you know something about this," Harris said, then held his hands in prayer and looked up. "Dear Father, please help and preserve us." He looked back at his son and asked, "Colby, what do you know?"

Colby lurched forward onto the table, buried his head in his arms, and collapsed in tears. "Oh, Dad, what am I going to do?" he wailed.

Harris Kidd's heart raced as he stepped around the table and placed his hands on Colby's shoulders. "Son, I have to know what's going on."

Colby lifted his head, though he didn't look up. He wiped the tears from his eyes, sat back, and placed his hands on his knees. Harris waited patiently for Colby to compose himself, and when the boy raised his eyes to look into his father's, asked, "Do you know what happened to Peter?"

Colby nodded.

"Please tell me."

Colby was silent, so Harris tried another angle. He knelt before Colby, placed his hands on his son's, and asked, "Were you there?"

Colby looked away but gave another nod.

"You... you didn't... you didn't... do it?"

Colby choked and sobbed, then looked at his hands. He turned them so that their palms supported his father's, and after what seemed an eternity, said, "No."

Without moving his gaze from Colby, Harris felt the tension flood out of Sarah, still sitting at the table with her food.

"Thank the Lord for His mercy. Now tell me what happened."

Colby cried and shook his head. He lifted his hands and buried his face in them.

"Colby, you've just seen something terrible, and you have to talk to me." Harris was terrified, but he had spent his life developing self-discipline. He knew how effective equanimity was with his congregation and had cultivated this eloquent tool over the years until, out of instinct, he acted with serenity in the most turbulent situations. In the face of this horror, the habit of a lifetime asserted itself, and he breathed slowly, squeezed his son's legs, and waited. Finally, Colby's sobs slowed, and he looked at his father again, dropping his hands back to Harris's.

"It was Robbie. Steven and Jason were there, too, but it was Robbie who did it."

"Robbie Cook?" Harris looked at Sarah in disbelief, which he saw mirrored in her eyes. Feeling as if he were being dragged along, an unwilling participant in a dream, asked, "Why?" The question seemed wholly inadequate to the fantastical situation, but it was all Harris could manage.

"Because Peter was gay."

The silence that followed was terrible. Eventually, Colby broke it. "He was Simon Cassell's boyfriend. Robbie saw them... It's like you said, Dad, God abhors gays and wants us to hand them over to Satan for punishment."

Harris felt Colby's words hit him as if they were a freight train, but he had had not allowed himself an emotional response in more than thirty years, and this was no time to make an exception. He inhaled deeply and turned to Sarah, just in time to see her pull back from the table, her chair flying into the cupboard behind her. She recoiled and staggered forward into the table, knocking her cereal bowl to the tile floor, where it shattered, showering Harris and Colby with drops of milk.

But no one noticed the mess. Sarah stood with her hands shaking in front of her face until Harris spoke.

"Let us pray together."

Harris felt himself starting to crack and knew that he needed the calm and quiet of introspection, out of which the strength of the Lord would bring him back under control. He kissed his son on the forehead as he stood and eased the youth to his feet, leading him a few short steps to the center of the kitchen, where he knelt, facing Colby. He released one hand and reached out to Sarah, who accepted the invitation and knelt between husband and son, clasping hands to close the circle. They bowed their heads and prayed in silence.

Dear Lord, please grant me the wisdom to see the way. Please act through me and allow me to bring your compassion to bear…

Harris tried to articulate his internal prayer, tried to stay focused, tried to hear Christ's voice, but his mind was in turmoil.

Colby, what have you done? My son, why, why?

Father, forgive Colby for what he has done, and show me what I need to do—

Colby! You are the future of this church, of my father's legacy, how could you bring this upon us? You, who were supposed to be so strong are instead a coward.

Lord, please act as a light in this time of darkness, please guide us and—

Where did I go wrong? But Colby's right; the Bible condemns homosexuality as a sin, punishable by mortal death.

Slowly, Harris's disciplined mind wrapped itself around the trauma, and at the same time, he surrendered to the Spirit, gave himself to the will of Christ, and returned to a place from which he could operate. He took a last, deep breath, squeezed the hands of his wife and child, and smiled at them each in turn, granting permission to rise. They released each others' hands.

"The Lord will give us strength to get through this, but for now, I've got a lot of thinking to do, and there are people I need to talk to, and I have a service to deliver. Colby?"

Colby looked at his dad, his face ashen.

"I think it's best if you miss the service today."

Get thee from my sight while I work out what to do with you.

"Run along to your room and stay there." Harris watched Colby scurry from the room and tried to let all thoughts of his son and the murder leave with him, for they would resolve themselves later in the day, and right now he needed to deal with his distraught wife and, after her, his sermon. He sighed and stepped toward Sarah, wrapping his arms around her shoulders as she folded herself into him.

Harris was Sarah's husband, protector, and spiritual guide all in one, and he took his responsibility very seriously. When he had first met her twenty-one years ago, she had been an impressionable nineteen-year-old, the daughter of an army officer who had just retired to Wilkeston and who, in seeking new meaning for his life, had been reborn in the Church of the Epistles. She had desperately wanted to follow her father into his newfound spiritual bliss and had submitted every aspect of her being selflessly to Harris, hoping he could do for her what he had done for her father. Harris had tried so hard to help, for the light burned bright in her, but despite his greatest efforts, she had not fully broken through and still harbored doubts about her salvation.

Harris's first love would always be the Lord, and his primary responsibility would be to his congregation, but Sarah had opened up a special place in his heart and awakened in him feelings he had not experienced for a decade. Though she was sixteen years his junior, she had soon become the first romantic dalliance he had allowed himself since his parents had left him in charge of the church and gone to Africa to engage in missionary work. He had never experienced love in the physical way that he knew other men did, and his sex drive was so low that Sarah had once joked that it was a miracle she had ever conceived. At no point in their twenty-year marriage had he experienced the romantic love that made him ache for Sarah's presence or wish to shower her with roses, but he cherished her very dearly, so in grief, he held her and poured in his strength until she was renewed and ready to stand on her own. She squeezed him tightly to let him know she was ready, and they released each other.

"What *are* you going to do, Harris?"

"I need to compose my thoughts first, and I need to deal with this morning's service before I do anything else. Once I've done that, I'll visit the Andersons and offer them prayer and consolation, and then I need to talk to Robbie and his parents."

"What about the police?"

"That's one of the things I need to work through, but not until after I've offered compassion to the bereaved and gotten the facts straight. But right now I've got a service that starts in…" he glanced at the clock, "a little over two hours, and I need to compose myself and get dressed."

"Okay, Harris, you run along to your study and get to work and let me know if you need anything." She pulled a bucket and sponge from the cupboard underneath the sink, filled the bucket with hot, soapy water, and turned to the broken plate and spilled cereal.

Harris, watching her fondly, whispered, "Thank you, dear. God's kindness in giving you to me was indeed unbounded," before turning and leaving the kitchen. He tried to force his mind to turn to the sermon that he would soon need to deliver. But no sooner had he closed the door to his study than Colby sprang back into his mind. Harris's eyes fell on the dark blue leather armchairs in the corner, and he remembered Jessica confronting him there a month ago. "Colby raped me," she had said. "I have talked to Colby," had been his reply, and indeed the boy had, but surely Jessica's anger had merited further inquiry? Why had he chosen to brush over her accusation, to accept Colby's indignant dismissal of the claims? Why had he not really talked to Colby?

He had dug no further because it had not occurred to him that he needed to, for his son was not just of the cloth, a minister in training, but had deep faith and was saved. The Kidds did not—could not—behave in the way that Jessica had asserted, for they were holy people, messengers of God. Harris's father had been a pastor before him, and his grandfather before that, and both Harris's siblings were, too. It was simply understood that Colby, Harris's only child, would succeed into the Church of the Epistles ministry, but Colby's admission that he had stood by while a horrible crime had been committed hade woken Harris to a truth that he realized, with a jolt, that he had already known: Colby was not shaping up into the compassionate, centered minister that Harris expected but was instead arrogant, spiteful, and cowardly. Harris looked deep into his heart and wondered if his son could be a rapist and a murderer.

Dear Christ, help me, help me in this, my darkest hour.

The Old Testament and the Apostle Paul alike condemned homosexuals, but Pastor Kidd could not condone murder. He fell into the chair behind his desk, rested the top of his balding head in his hands, and wept. His hand reached out and picked up the phone to call his younger brother for counsel but froze with the phone in midair. Russ would not understand, and he still harbored resentment that Harris had become pastor in Wilkeston, leaving him to go to seminary and build his own congregation in West Virginia. No, Russ was too petty to help. Harris returned the phone to its cradle and his head to his hands. He had never been able to approach his sister. If only he could track down his father in Africa…

Harris had grown up the oldest of three children in a devout Church of the Epistles family. Like so many families in the church, the oldest male child had been the apple of his parents' eye, and by the time he was in his early teens, Harris had recognized the extent of the favoritism that had accrued to him. The greatest of its many advantages was his inevitable ministerial succession within Wilkeston's Church of the Epistles. His brother had resented this, Harris knew, not just because of the undemocratic selection process, but because Wanda, the youngest of the three and the most spiritual child by far, would be passed over. From the earliest age, Wanda had not only memorized Scripture with apparent ease but had also intuitively teased out deeper meaning, had brought joy and wisdom beyond her years to the most difficult of situations, and had been adored throughout the community. Yet even now, in the full knowledge that he needed her wisdom, Harris could not reach out to Greensboro, where Wanda, the mother of three and wife of a cigarette factory worker, ministered to a large Baptist congregation.

Although Russ had left at eighteen for seminary, full of anger and resentment toward Harris, Wanda had remained content with her lot. She had wanted to live out her days in Wilkeston but been persuaded to attend a small college less than a hundred miles away, and while there, she had fallen in love with Brad. Upon graduating, she had moved to Greensboro to be near Brad when he returned home to the family design business. Within a year, however, in a whirlwind turn of events that Harris had never understood, everything had changed. Wanda and Brad had separated, and shortly thereafter, Wanda had married Jack, an uneducated laborer, become assistant minister to a Baptist church, and announced that she was pregnant with her first child. But through it all, she had retained her equanimity and had never spoken of Brad with anything other than compassion and love. Wanda's indomitable spirit and everyday spirituality were the only things apart from the Lord himself that had ever humbled Harris, and just thinking of her shamed him. How could he call and expose his unworthiness to her?

Harris's mind rebelled again, and he was glad of the sanctuary of his office, for his composed façade was about to shatter. He knelt and prayed for a long time, opening himself up in complete surrender. Slowly at first, but with increasing power, he felt Christ reach inside him and give him the strength to continue, and though he didn't hear a clear answer, with the renewed faith that comes only from direct communication with the Spirit, Harris rose, confident that the Lord would be present when he really needed Him. An hour later, he had completed preparations for the service and had dressed and gone to the church.

He saw that the Andersons were absent. His heart went out to them. He would visit them later, but what was he going to say? "Your son was murdered because he was gay and is damned to spend eternity in hell"? Dwight Cook was absent, too—something strange was happening in that marriage, which he would have to explore soon—but Dwight's wife and sons were there. He would need to talk to Cheryl about her oldest boy later today, too.

When the service ended, Harris sensed the tension in his congregation and knew that the rumors were spreading, but he was not ready to deal with them. He had an obligation first to get the facts and to talk to the bereaved.

Sarah had also missed the service, and when he arrived home, she looked up from the sink, hope in her eyes. He shook his head and continued to the stairway. He did not yet have the answer, and he needed to talk to his son. His knock on Colby's bedroom door was answered by a quick, "Yeah."

Harris pushed the door open. Colby was lying on his bed, reading the Bible, and looked up at his father's entry. "Colby, I need to know something."

Colby closed the Bible on his finger and sat up.

Harris sat on the edge of the bed and searched the worried face of his son for an answer. Finding none, he asked, "Did you rape Jessica?"

"Dad, you asked me that a long while ago, and I told you—"

Harris cut him off and barked, "Did you rape her, yes or no?" This was the first time that anger had slipped through Harris's guard that he could remember, and he saw shock in his son's eyes. A surge of guilt rose and subsided, but Harris relinquished his weakness and, recovering his composure, said, "Tell me what happened."

After a tense pause, Colby spoke hesitantly. "Well, I didn't rape her, but… " He started to wriggle and looked away.

"Go on."

"Well, you see, she was in the barn and we were playing with her kittens. She started touching me, 'n' stuff, and then… " Colby looked at his hands and then shut his mouth.

Harris, the patient, calm listener, outwaited his son, who eventually cracked under the pressure of silence and said, "We kissed, all right?" The words spurted out like water from a burst pipe, violent and sudden. "We kissed, and then we lay on the ground, and then… then she… then we… did it."

"You made love?"

"Yes."

Where did this defiance come from? Why so spiteful, so mean?

"But did she consent?"

"She was there with me." Colby's voice was angry, his face twisted. "She didn't stop me."

"She didn't resist you?"

"Sure, she did, but that's what they all do, right? They want to keep teasing you, play hard to get. But she didn't try real hard. I mean, the house was right there, and it was obvious that she really liked me."

"Colby, you fool." Harris clenched his fists and gritted his teeth, momentarily paralyzed, then released his tension and stood, speaking abruptly. "Come to my office in ten minutes," he said, "I want you dressed and ready to go out."

"Where are we going?" Colby looked confused.

"I don't know, son, I don't know," Harris said, and hoped that he hadn't shown the helplessness he felt.

When Colby knocked on his door ten minutes later—punctually, Harris noticed—he was ready for the boy. He had thought through the issues in front of him and had decided on a course of action.

In the light of Colby's disclosure, Harris had revisited Jessica's underage sexual promiscuity and unwillingness to repent and the outrage this had stirred in his congregation. Harris did not think he could redirect this outrage, deciding that it would be unhelpful to try, and further that the situation offered an opportunity for cleansing. Every community needs an occasional scapegoat for the sins it most fears of itself, and he concluded that the best interests of his church were served by sustaining the casting out of Jessica, however unjust it may seem.

As for yesterday's murder, homosexuality was a sin that revolted his congregation—Joel Wilson possibly more than any other—and he knew that they would regard the killing of a gay who had practiced his perverted sexuality in their midst as just retribution, but although the punishment was sanctioned by Scripture, it was a violation of Harris's moral framework, and there was also the practical matter of the law to deal with. He did not yet know what he would do with this situation but resolved to investigate and listen to the facts with an open mind.

"Come in," he called out through the door, and when Colby opened it and stepped in, Harris waved his son toward the desk. Colby closed the door and stood opposite Harris with his hands behind his back as the pastor studied him.

"Colby," he said at length, "I've been thinking about what to do. I am very upset that you didn't tell me more about what happened with Jessica—very upset."

"Yes, sir."

"But from what you've said, I will accept your word that it wasn't rape. I see no reason to undo what we have done."

"Thank you, sir."

"However, it is an act so unbecoming a minister of this church that, as far as I am concerned, you need to forget any ambitions you may have of becoming one."

"But—"

"I know, I had hoped—no, I had expected—that you would take over this church from me, as I did from my father, but I see now that it's not to be. Believe me, it's more disappointing for me than it can possibly be for you." Harris watched his son's face as the youth bit his lip and stood tall. At last, the boy was showing some backbone—such a shame that it was too late. Harris composed himself and continued, "As for the murder of Peter, I've told you a thousand times before that it is not acceptable to simply stand by and watch when you know that what's happening is wrong. It's your obligation to step in."

"But—"

"I haven't finished." Harris surveyed the boy with a cold eye. "Homosexuality is a terrible sin that revolts me as much as it does you, but while killing gays is certainly permitted in Scripture, you should know an action that radical is inappropriate. The murder has robbed Peter of the opportunity for repentance and ultimate salvation. While I am glad you didn't play a role in it, I am more disappointed than I can possibly tell you that you just stood by and let it happen. It's almost more than I can bear."

Colby faced him in silence. Was he hiding something else? Harris let silence work for him again, but this time Colby didn't offer up anything new.

"Very well. Now we're going to visit Robbie Cook and discuss—"

"We?" interrupted Colby.

Harris nodded, looking up sharply. Colby's interjection had been abrupt and nervous, so he studied every nuance of the boy's facial expression until he was sure that the moment had passed and that he would learn no more. Whatever had made Colby jump was once more under control, and Harris continued, "That's right: *we*. And then we're going to visit the Andersons."

"Yes, sir."

"Is there anything you want to say?"

"No, sir."

Harris studied the boy once again. The terror that had painted Colby's face that morning was still present, but Colby was showing fortitude of which Harris had until now not thought him capable. With reluctant pride in his son, Harris rose, took a deep breath, and tested his resolve and poise. He was ready.

"Then let's get it over with."

The journey to the Cooks' house passed in near silence. Although Colby told Harris on the way that Robbie had moved out after an argument with his father, Harris nonetheless felt it best to approach the young man through his parents. Cheryl opened the door, and Harris watched her face race through multiple emotions in the space of a heart beat: happy surprise and the spontaneous, joyous exclamation, "Minister!" were immediately replaced by a worried scowl and an unspoken, "What's wrong?" and then by confusion as she glanced at Colby. There was no way of cushioning the blow of a minister visiting in a formal capacity.

"Won't you come in, Pastor Kidd? Colby?" Cheryl shepherded them into the living room. "Can I get you anything to drink?"

"No, thank you, Cheryl." Harris settled himself comfortably and authoritatively in the master chair, looked around, and asked, "Is Dwight home?"

Cheryl had perched on the edge of the armchair, and with her hands folded on her lap, she looked at the ground. "No, Pastor. Dwight and I... Dwight's not here much these days."

"I'm sorry to hear that, Cheryl."

He had known something was wrong even before noting Dwight's absence at the morning service, and Cheryl's manner made him fear the worst. He should have talked to the Cooks sooner, but now was not the time to worry about marriage counseling, even though Dwight's absence inter- fered with his immediate plans, so although he felt obligated to say, "I'm available to help you and Dwight any time," Harris didn't give his hostess time to respond before continuing. "Cheryl, something happened last night that we need to discuss. A young man was killed."

Cheryl jerked upright.

"I'm here because..." Harris paused, glanced at his son, then looked back at Cheryl and said, "I'm here because I think that Robbie was involved."

Cheryl blurted out, "My Robbie?"

Harris nodded and said, "I'm afraid so." He waited for Cheryl's thoughts to race and the shock to pass while Colby wriggled in obvious dis- comfort.

Cheryl eventually composed herself enough to ask, "What hap- pened?"

"Peter Anderson—that's Bo's boy—he's seventeen, wiry, wears heavy glasses?" Harris waited for Cheryl to nod acknowledgement that she knew him, then continued, "Well, he was hanged from a tree with barbed wire last night down at Jack Summers' place.

"Dear Father, help and preserve us." Cheryl gasped and put her hands to her mouth. "And you think Robbie... my Robbie... you think Robbie was involved?"

Harris nodded. "I do. Peter was gay, and I think Robbie believes he was acting out the Lord's will. As his pastor, I need to talk to him, and I wanted you to be involved."

Cheryl didn't question Harris's presumption that he would take the lead, but simply said, "Robbie doesn't live here any more."

Harris nodded and said "I know, but I thought it would be best for us to visit him together."

Cheryl nodded. "Let me put on some shoes and get my bag."

Colby had scooted into the back of the car before either of the adults reached it. Cheryl was a bag of nerves, stammering incoherent and conflicting directions to Robbie's residence, and when they pulled to a stop in the drive of a small, rundown house just outside of town, she burst from the car like elastic bands out of a bag. Harris and Colby followed her to the door and stood patiently while she rang the bell and hopped from foot to foot, glancing at her watch. She gave Harris a nervous smile.

"He lives here with a couple of his friends," she explained and rang the bell again, pounding the heel of her fist on the door before the sound of the bell had faded.

A gruff voice muffled by the door called out, "All right, all right, I'm coming, don't knock it down." The door was opened by a young man in t-shirt and boxers. He ran his fingers through wild hair as if to confirm he'd only just got up, said, "Hello, Mrs. Cook, please come in," and turned to walk back down the hall without waiting. "Robbie, it's your Mom," he yelled, scratching his crotch un–self-consciously and ambling down the hall. After a couple of moments, Robbie appeared, barefooted and doing up the button on his jeans underneath a loose t-shirt emblazoned with a crucifix above the phrase, "Jesus Saves." He stopped dead in his tracks when he saw his pastor, his face turning white.

Cheryl broke the silence. "Robbie, something dreadful happened last night, and we want to talk to you to see if you know anything about it."

Robbie laughed spitefully and said, "Isn't it Dad's job to poke his nose into other people's business?"

Cheryl's awkwardness gave way to sudden anger, and she spat out her response. "Your father loves you, Robbie, and you've broken his heart. I'll thank you not to laugh about it. Now let's get out of this hallway so we can talk in privacy."

Harris looked back and forth between them, examining the family rift to which he needed to attend—later.

With a shrug and a modicum of humility, Robbie waved them through a doorway that led into the living room. He closed the door behind them and sat on the floor with his back to the TV, facing his mother and pastor, who sat on the couch, but concentrating his attention on his school friend, who was hunched up in the armchair, staring at his hands. Pastor Kidd sat back to watch and crossed his legs, wearing the robe of calm and patience. When the silence became too uncomfortable for Cheryl, she spoke.

"Someone died last night, Robbie, and I need you to tell me what you know about it."

"Mom, lots of people died last night." With a mischievous grin, Robbie looked around the faces in the room.

"Don't you get smart with me, young man," snapped Cheryl. "Were you at Jack Summers' place last night?"

"I can't tell you what I was doing last night."

Cheryl leaned forward, the fire in her eyes projected in her voice, which was a flamethrower that made Harris Kidd's hair stand on end. "I watched you do this to your father and, to my eternal shame, I didn't support him. I'm not going to let you do it again. With God as your witness, were you at Jack Summers' place last night?"

Robbie's petulant demeanor became submissive. After a pause, he said, "Yes."

Harris watched the conversation with dispassion, aware of Colby squirming in the armchair, his face contorted with anxiety. He could sense Cheryl's insides churning with the effort she was making to control herself. "What happened, Robbie?" she asked in a hushed, quaking voice.

After a long pause, Robbie sat upright, threw his arms wide, and, in an impassioned voice, cried out, "He was gay, Ma. He was a perverted, God-hating sinner. He was acting in sin with Simon Cassell, and it had to stop. God commands us to punish abominations." He turned to Harris. "You said so yourself: 'They must be put to death; their blood will be upon them.'"

Harris felt a twinge of pain as his words were thrown back at him, but at the same time, he felt a thrill as he saw Robbie's passion. He needed to address the great wrong that had been committed, but at the same time, he wanted to harness this ardor and turn it to the needs of the congregation, to the work of the Lord, rather than excise it from the community.

Robbie stood up and paced in front of the TV like a caged animal. "It was disgusting... revolting... horrible. He had to die. I couldn't allow him to offend God's sight any more. If I hadn't dealt with his sin, I would have been guilty of it myself." He stopped and faced his minister. "It says so in Ezekiel."

I have made thee a watchman... When I say unto the wicked, Thou shalt surely die and thou givest him not warning... his blood will I require at thine hand.

Harris reflected on the words of Ezekiel 3:17 and 3:18 for a long moment and this time ended the silence himself. He spoke slowly and deliberately. "Son, homosexuality is an abomination, and unrepentant homosexuals are damned, of that there's no doubt, but for you to go out and kill this boy without giving him an opportunity to repent, a chance to turn to the light, that's wrong, Robbie. But what's done is done. Your acts will ultimately be judged by our Lord and Savior Jesus Christ, and it simply falls to me to prepare you for the End of Times. Why don't you tell me exactly what happened?

"How about it, Colby?" Robbie said, laughing. "Shall we begin at the part where you stuck your knee in the fag's back and tied barbed wire round his wrists?"

Colby hung his head, and his face turned as red as his hair. Harris looked at Colby, his composure threatening to crack, and demanded, "It that true?"

Colby didn't return his glare. Instead, he raised his face defiantly to Robbie and snapped, "It was all your idea. You made us help, but you know it was all your idea."

"Hold it," Harris interrupted, using his authority to calm things down. "Let's start at the beginning. Robbie?"

Robbie took the lead in narrating, slowed only by brief outbursts from Colby, and the story was laid out for Harris. When Robbie had finished his story, three faces turned to Harris, eyes wide in submissive expectation, and Harris quaked. He had appointed himself earthly guide to the spiritual salvation of his flock and had commanded their unquestioning obedience for more than thirty years, yet now, when these three people really needed his leadership and guidance, he did not know what to do. Should he turn four youths over to the police, giving up his son, fracturing his community, and losing Robbie's passion from his flock, or should he turn a blind eye and enlist Sergeant Wilson's hatred of gays to attempt to mislead and misdirect the police investigation? Harris wanted to fall to his knees and pray for guidance, but the faces staring at him needed his strength and wisdom.

What should I do, Lord? Please give me a sign.

Whatever path he chose, Harris knew he would not sleep for days and that keeping up the façade of discipline and control from which his authority flowed would exhaust him. He wanted to go home to Sarah, to kneel before her and cry, ask her to hold him and give him strength, but he did not have that luxury. He would need to stand tall and lead his home and his church with confidence, and he still needed to inform Bo and Meryl Anderson that their son's soul was damned. As Harris swallowed hard and waited for the Spirit to speak through him, he felt his stomach churn. By great force of will he kept his exterior wall of calm erect, but he felt a quiver under his right eye as it twitched.

Chapter Eighteen

Because he had no early morning school activities on Monday, Simon went for a long run and took his time in the shower and over breakfast. It was a beautiful day, and he enjoyed the smells and sounds of late summer on his short walk to school, arriving just in time for his first lesson, experimental chemistry, which was his favorite. He was happy, and he knew it, but as he walked down the bustling school corridor to drop off his bag, fragments of student conversation caught his ear:

"... poor bastard... "

"... hanged by barbed wire... "

"... murder... "

Something terrible had happened. He slowed down and paid more attention.

"... Peter Anderson—he was gay, you know."

Simon grabbed the wide-eyed freshman by the shoulders, spun him around, and demanded, "What happened?"

"He... he... he was killed. On a tree."

Simon shook him. "Who?"

"Peter Anderson," the boy squealed.

"No, not Peter. It couldn't be Peter. You're wrong. You're wrong." Simon shook the youth again, and when he realized what he was doing, he released the younger boy, freeing his hands to tear at his own hair. The teen stepped back, almost in tears, and rejoined his friends, who stood together, staring at Simon and whispering among themselves before scurrying off and disappeared into classrooms like cockroaches running from the light.

Simon was in a daze, his world spinning dark and incomprehensible. He was oblivious to the crowds still milling in the hall and the curious looks he received as people stepped around him. He was insensitive even to the supportive hands that were placed on his shoulders, to the occasional Are you all right?, Do you need to go to the nurse?, and Can I help you? Simon slipped from beneath the last hand, barely even recognizing his chemistry teacher, Mr. Davis.

The door swung open at his touch, and Simon fell out into the school-yard, where he stumbled down the steps and across the grass before collapsing with his back against the trunk of a tree. Gradually, he became aware of a voice beside him, that of Mr. Davis, who had followed him and crouched next to him, a concerned expression on his face. Simon concentrated and with effort made out the words coming from his favorite teacher's lips.

"Simon, Simon, what's the matter?"

"They say he's dead. He can't be dead, can he?" Simon looked up at his teacher hopefully, but Mr. Davis lowered his eyes. Simon's mind drifted off to gray shores under dark mountains, a land of despair with no room for Mr. Davis.

"Simon, you need to see the nurse. Come on, try to stand up and wrap your arm around me."

Something registered subconsciously, and Simon's body obeyed the instructions. He let Mr. Davis haul him to his feet, hung his arm over the man's shoulder, and swung his feet mechanically.

*   *   *

When Simon opened his eyes, he frowned at the unfamiliar ceiling; where was he? Feeling groggy, he looked around, his eyes taking in a woman's plaid jacket draped on the back of a chair and a white coat hung on a girl's shoulders. It must be a lab coat, for didn't he have chemistry class today?

But something was wrong. The girl's hair was gray, the legs that protruded under the seat weren't a teenager's, and the desk wasn't part of the chemistry lab. Vague familiarity dawned and grew into recognition. Simon was lying behind the school nurse, Miss Patts—why?

Dull confusion yielded to a flash of recollection, and he sat bolt upright, his head on fire. "Peter!"

Miss Patts looked around at him and smiled. "Hi, Simon. Are you feeling better?"

Simon looked through her. "Peter. Peter's dead."

A serious expression came over the nurse's face. "I'm sorry, Simon. I know he was a good friend."

"You don't understand, I love Peter." Simon was numb but couldn't lie still. He needed to run, needed to scream, and he stood and started to walk out of the room.

"Simon, please don't. Lie back down and let me get you something to drink."

But Simon didn't respond to her request. He moved slowly, giving Miss Patts plenty of time to intercept him and close the door, pressing her back against it and gripping the handle firmly.

"Simon, you can't leave here right now. You're not well, and you might hurt yourself—or someone else."

Gently but firmly, Simon pulled the nurse's resisting hand off the doorknob with one of his own and turned it with the other. Against the weight of her body, and her increasing resistance, he pulled on the door, easing it open. Paying no attention to Miss Patts's pleas, Simon slipped through the crack and walked toward the main door of the school with the nurse on his heels, begging him to come back. Unheeding, Simon walked out of the door and off the school premises, where Miss Patts eventually abandoned him.

*   *   *

A tray with a bowl of banana pudding, a plate of fried chicken and mashed potatoes, and two large Cokes landed on the table opposite Simon, who looked up in a daze.

"You look like you need to get something inside you," a kindly voice offered as a fat hand took the pudding and slid it across the table toward him. "Here, eat." The familiar, portly frame of Officer Hayes fell onto the seat across the modular table from Simon and pushed a Coke toward him. For the first time since he had heard the news of Peter's death, Simon came to himself.

"Where am I?" he asked and, looking around, realized the answer to his own question. He turned back to Officer Hayes. "We used to come here for dinner. He used to sit right there where you are, Officer," Simon pointed, "and now he's gone." He took a sip of his Coke and sat back, tears welling in his eyes as reality set in.

The officer managed to speak clearly while gobbling down his potatoes. "Beth—she's the store manager," he waved a leg of chicken at the counter behind him. "She called the station 'cause you were causing such a commotion. You know how you got that stuff all over your shirt?"

Simon looked down, saw the smears and blotches, and shook his head.

"You walked straight into some woman who had a tray of food. Spilled it everywhere, you did, over you, over her, but Beth says you didn't even notice, you just walked over here and sat down like a robot." After a few minutes of silent munching, Officer Hayes spoke again. "Are you going to eat that?"

Simon looked down at his pudding for a moment and shook his head. With a grateful nod, the policeman pulled the dessert across the table and dived in.

Simon gestured lazily with his hand and asked, "Who did it?"

"Hmm?"

Simon leaned forward, suddenly alert, his eyes boring into the uniformed man. "Who did it, Officer Hayes, who killed Peter? Have you caught the murderer?"

Hayes finished the dessert and put the empty bowl on the tray. He spoke around the back of the hand that wiped his mouth. "Can't tell you anything about that, I'm afraid, son; that's official police business. We can't go telling everyone about the case. That could compromise our investigation, see?" Hayes puffed out his chest.

Simon was now sufficiently aware to realize that a more pragmatic approach was called for and asked, "Can you at least tell me the public version of what happened?" He leaned his elbows on the table and listened in horror as the murder scene was described to him. When he had pulled himself together again, he shook his head and spoke, his whisper barely audible. "Why would anyone want to kill Peter?" After a pause, he spoke more firmly. "Who's in charge of the investigation?"

"That would be Sergeant Wilson."

"Well, I want to see him. Can you take me?"

Officer Hayes laughed. "The sergeant's a busy man, especially right now. He doesn't have time to talk to everyone who knew Anderson."

"I didn't just know Peter, I loved him. I knew him better than anyone else. I know who did this, and I want to make sure they fry."

Officer Hayes stared at Simon with cold eyes while he picked his teeth with the tine of his plastic fork. "Right now, you need to be back at school, Simon."

"If you take me to school, I'm just going to leave again, and I'll go find Sergeant Wilson on my own, so why don't you save us both the trouble and take me to him?"

The officer scrutinized the plaque on his fork, then began to work on the other side of his mouth, still staring at Simon. After a few moments, he nodded, offered a shrug, and stood up with the tray.

"That means you'll take me?"

"He's probably not there, and even if he is, I can't promise he'll have time to see you."

"Thanks," said Simon, following the officer out to the car with new-found purpose. Hayes pulled out of the parking lot, picked up the handset to his police radio, and called for the sergeant. He received a call back within moments.

"Sarge, I've got a kid here says he knew that Anderson boy real well. Seems to think he might be able to help us in the investigation."

"Who is it?"

"Simon Cassell. He goes to the high school. He says... " Officer Hayes looked at Simon as if unsure, and continued awkwardly, "He says he loved Peter."

Simon nodded, and they waited for the sergeant's response. "I'll be back at the station in half an hour," he said. "Bring him in, and I'll see him when I get there."

Officer Hayes clipped the handset back to the dashboard and turned to Simon. "You're in luck."

Simon nodded and mumbled, "Thanks."

Simon had never been in a police cab and knew that he would normally be examining the array of electronic devices and gadgets, but today his mind was elsewhere. He had a sinking feeling that he not only knew the identity of Peter's murderer but that his own behavior had provoked the fatal outburst of violence. In beating Robbie Cook up, he had left Robbie hungry for revenge, and he must have let Robbie see his affection for Peter.

Simon's curiosity was finally aroused when they entered the station, which he had passed a thousand times without ever being inside. He was asked to wait in a steel-framed chair behind the door, and from there, he looked around the small reception area. A cheap, veneer countertop, peeling at the edges, split the room in two, on the far side of which sat Rose Waits, a large girl who had graduated from high school three years before and had been the receptionist, secretary, and administrative support for the force ever since. Behind her was a desk on which a clunky, cream-colored computer, with unfamiliar brand labels and coffee stains, sat. While Simon was waiting, an officer—Officer Jacks?—entered through a side door behind the counter and handed Rose a pile of forms and a floppy disc.

Simon looked around the badly stained, off-white walls. A glass-covered wall panel beside him contained statutory notices, and opposite it hung three large portraits of sergeants—including the incumbent—and a smaller, framed photo of the six-person force, arrayed in front of a gleaming police car. Simon felt a twinge of disappointment. He had expected to be ushered into gleaming halls of efficiency and technical mastery, not a dilapidated fraternity house.

The side door opened again, and Officer Hayes's head poked around. "The sergeant will see you now," he said, holding the door open for Simon, who followed the officer into a long corridor. They turned off into the second office on the right, a small, grubby room with an old Formica desk, a small computer monitor, a mound of floppy discs, and several untidy piles of forms. A head of wispy, yellow hair hung over the desk, so low, Simon thought, that it was in danger of being jabbed in the eye by a pen wielded by an arm as thick as most men's legs. Sergeant Wilson looked up from the form that he was completing.

"Simon, come in. Have a seat." Sergeant Wilson rocked back in his chair, his comb-over slipping and clinging to his greasy jowls. He raised his hands to wipe back his hair, then placed his elbows on the arms of his chair and twiddled his pen. He raised a heavy boot onto the desk and spoke.

"Officer Hayes tells me you think you can help with our investigation into the murder of Peter Anderson."

"Yes, sir." Simon looked at the hulk in front of him. He had seen the sergeant regularly at church, but never this close or in his uniform, and had never noticed the man's power before. He must be six foot two and over two hundred and fifty pounds. The short black sleeves of his uniform bulged, and his face was seamed with experience. He had a reputation around town as someone who always got his way, and not just on matters of law enforcement.

"Why don't you go ahead?"

In the face of the sergeant's calm confidence, Simon wondered whether to back down, for he had no real evidence for what he was about to say. But he was seeking justice for Peter and knew he was right. His heart raced.

"I think it was Robbie Cook," he said.

Words that a moment ago had been no more than thoughts now lay, exposed, for the world to see. He bounced his heel and tapped a finger as he awaited the policeman's response.

Sergeant Wilson coughed. "Robbie Cook. You mean Dwight Cook's son?"

"His dad ran Cook Hardware."

"Uh-huh, that's Dwight." The sergeant's face wore an amused smile, and Simon could feel himself getting flustered. "So what makes you think Robbie would go and kill someone?" the sergeant asked.

Simon had prepared himself to divulge his sexual orientation—had already hinted at it in the car—but nonetheless found it very uncomfortable.

"Well you see, he hated gays, and Peter and me, well, we… "

The sergeant pulled his foot off the desk and rolled forward to lean on it with his elbows. "Are you trying to tell me that you're gay?"

Simon nodded.

"You were Peter's... boyfriend?" The sergeant's voice was poison, as was the contempt in the man's eyes, but Simon could only nod again. "And because Peter was gay, you think Robbie killed him?"

Simon nodded. "Yes, sir."

The sergeant rolled back, returned his foot to the desk, and resumed twiddling with the pen. "That's it?"

"Yes, sir," Simon said, but then frowned. "Well, no, sir, there's more. I broke his nose."

The sergeant emitted another short laugh. "You're telling me that you assaulted another boy?"

"No, sir, he attacked me." Simon was flustered, and he wanted to curl up and die, but he was here for Peter, so he persisted. "Robbie attacked me, and I acted in self-defense. But he was real upset."

The sergeant scrutinized Simon's body in apparent surprise before looking up and summarizing. "So let me get this straight: Because you're gay, and because you broke Robbie's nose, you think Robbie killed Anderson. Is that what you came here to tell me, son?"

"Yes, sir, it is." That was precisely what he had come to say, but Sergeant Wilson had made the whole affair sound ludicrous. Simon wriggled in his seat, wanting to explode.

The sergeant leaned forward again, held Simon's eyes, and said, "Simon, I have to tell you that's one of the most ridiculous stories I've ever heard—and I get a lot of them. I shouldn't tell you this, but you obviously... cared for Peter... " the sergeant sneered, "so I'll give you a little inside information. But you've got to keep this to yourself. We can't afford to have any leaks, okay?"

Simon nodded, mute, and the sergeant winked.

"Good. Well the thing is, you see, there's been an increase in drug activity in this part of the state. Some of the gangs from out east are coming up to the mountains, and we've known for some time that they're coming into Wilkeston." He sat back and twiddled his pen. "Filthy business, drugs; the scumbags kill each other all the time. Anyway, that's who did this."

Simon was confused. "But Peter never had anything to do with drugs."

"It's often hard to tell, son. You'd be surprised how many murderers or child molesters or drug traffickers are husbands and fathers who love their kids. And fags, well... " He gave Simon a knowing, contemptuous, smile and paused before finishing his sentence. "We all know fags are the worst. Besides, even if he didn't use drugs—and we're waiting for the autopsy results—it doesn't mean anything. People stumble into criminal activity and get caught up in it by accident all the time. No, all of the evidence points to drugs, Simon. Thanks for coming by."

The sergeant bowed his head and returned to his form.

The interview was over. As Simon rose, the sergeant repeated, "Not a word, Simon, not a word."

Simon walked into the reception area with his head in a spin. Had the sergeant just given him the runaround because he hated gays? Had Simon turned the investigation against the love of his life by disclosing his sexual orientation? When he leaned on the counter for support, Rosie smiled at him and asked, "Are you all right?" Simon nodded, but she slid her chair back, saying, "You look pale. Let me get you a glass of water," and left through the door at the back of the office.

The name Anderson written on the tab of a folder on the counter caught Simon's eye, and with a nervous thrill, he glanced around the room, then leaned over to flip the cover back. Atop the small pile of papers was a sheet covered with letters, numbers, and names, but all Simon noticed was the name Anderson and a pattern in the middle of the page that looked like a fingerprint. Simon knew that the word "fag" would never enter the folder but decided that a homophobic police force with ancient equipment would never avenge Peter and that if he wanted justice, he would have to act himself. He closed the file and, with the adrenalin rush of a first-time thief, folded it in half and stuffed it down the front of his shirt, then slid it down and tucked it into the waistband of his trousers. He was just sitting down, his heart pounding, when Rosie returned with a glass of water. Simon smiled and said thank you as he took it, then sipped, grateful for the refreshment and for Rosie's lack of suspicion.

When Officer Hayes emerged from the side door, he once again needed persuading not to take Simon back to school. This time it was easier for Simon to convince the policeman to drop him off at Aunt Jodi's. As he got out of the police car, Simon saw the curtains twitch and knew that Aunt Jodi was wondering why a police car was pulling up outside the house and that his emergence from the car filled her with anxiety. He exchanged a courteous farewell with the officer, raced to the house, and closed the kitchen door behind him.

"Hi, Aunt Jodi," he said. "I guess you're wondering what's going on?" Aunt Jodi nodded silently but patiently, her arms folded, and Simon continued, "You remember me telling you about Peter?" His aunt nodded again, and Simon said, "Well, he's dead."

Aunt Jodi's face dropped, and her arms fell open. "Oh, Simon, that's awful. What happened?"

"He was hanged from a tree with barbed wire down at Jack Summers' place."

Aunt Jodi reeled, reaching out for the countertop with one hand for support, while the other covered her open mouth. She felt her way to the table and collapsed into a chair.

"How horrible. Oh, Simon, I'm so sorry."

"I know that Robbie Cook did it, Aunt Jodi, I just know." Anger rose in Simon at his humiliation by Sergeant Wilson and at the lack of justice Peter would receive, and he spoke with ferocity. "The police say it's drug related, but that's ridiculous. And they won't try to solve it anyway 'cause he was gay. If they're not going to figure it out, then I will. I'll make sure Robbie gets what's coming to him."

"What did you say?" Aunt Jodi's brow furrowed and she looked severely at her nephew.

Simon looked back unflinching, his head raised and his jaw set, and spoke firmly as if making a vow. "I said that I'm going to get Robbie Cook for this." He reached down his shirt and pulled out the police folder.

Aunt Jodi didn't break eye contact right away but eventually shook her head and buried her face in her hands. Running her fingers through her hair, she composed herself and spoke. "Revenge is a terrible thing, Simon. It will fill you with loathing until it's all you live for, all you are, so that when you finally get it, there's nothing left." She reached out for his hand. "Simon, nothing can bring Peter back, and I'm not going to let you dishonor his memory by turning your life into one of hate."

"But Aunt Jodi," Simon protested, "I loved Peter, and now he's dead. And the police aren't doing anything about it. What am I supposed to do?"

"Well, your Uncle Walt worked with a couple of FBI agents when he ran the bank; why don't you let me call them up and see if they can help? But let's leave it to them, Simon. Peter would want you to cherish and honor his memory, not get yourself in trouble by interfering." Simon started to protest, but Aunt Jodi put her index finger on his lips to stop him. "I'm not going to talk about it. Now is a time for grieving, not for arguing. Let me have those." She took the police folder from his hand, put it on the counter by the stove, and commanded, "Pray with me." She slid onto her knees and held out her hand for Simon.

Chapter Nineteen

Special Agent Nic Horn pushed the door of his small, single-story suburban home closed behind him and kicked off his shoes before tossing them into the closet. He dropped his soft leather briefcase on the hallway floor, where it sagged against the wall, hung his jacket on the hook by the front door, and walked into the kitchen. A quick glance at the clock as he opened the refrigerator told him it was eight-thirty; he wanted to stop working so late, but his group supervisor had given him yet another "opportunity to prove himself" that involved little more than late night Web-surfing. He was becoming evermore convinced that it was a mistake to follow the criminal mind into the Internet. With a sigh of resentment, he slammed the refrigerator closed, popped the top off his beer bottle, and looked at the phone. The flashing light told him that three messages awaited him, so he dropped the mail on the counter and leaned beside it, pressed the play button on the phone, and flicked through a small pile of envelopes and catalogs.

"Hi, this is Alison. I have great news for you: You've been selected for a full house satellite… "

Nic pressed the delete button. The tone of the first few words had fooled him into thinking for a moment that it had been a live voice, someone he knew. Prerecorded telemarketing was, in his mind, a far greater public harm that the vast majority of the junk he had to pursue on the Internet.

"Hi, Nic, it's Anna. Listen, I had a wonderful time on Saturday night, and I was wondering when we could get together again. Umm… I know someone who can get us real good tickets for concerts, so maybe we could do that one night? Or maybe we can go out for dinner? Or maybe we can just have a quiet meal 'round at my place, and, you know, well… " There was a girlish giggle before the voice continued, "Like, curl up in front of the TV. Why don't you call me? My cell number is ——. Bye, sweetie."

Nic's hand hovered over the buttons, and a smile appeared on his face as he thought back. After a tedious day meeting with the ATF and hearing about their lack of progress on the abortion clinic bombs, he had gone out for a drink on Saturday with his partner, Jeff, and picked Anna up in a singles bar. He found out later that Jeff had ditched her friend, who had been both boring and ugly, but Anna had been cute, and she had a lot of energy. They had performed sexual acrobatics on his living room floor late into the night, then retired to his bedroom after an intermission for the second act, and when he had risen, tired, for a morning shower, she had joined him for an encore.

Anna was young and entranced by his gun and badge. Although Nic didn't have the patience for a long-term relationship with an adoring twenty-something, Anna had a gorgeous body, and he was certainly not going to turn down great sex. He pressed replay while he scrambled for a pen and pad, then scribbled down the number and deleted the message.

"Agent Horn, this is Jodi Garrett from Wilkeston. You probably don't remember me, but I'm sure you remember my husband, Walt. He was Chairman of the Board of the First National Bank of Wilkeston, and he worked with you on a couple of money-laundering cases. I want to talk to you about the murder of someone who's very dear to us. The police seem to be a little out of their depth, and... well, please call me. The number here is ——. Thanks."

Nic frowned and let his finger drift from the notepad to the delete key. He regularly received calls inviting him to interfere in local police affairs and generally ignored them, but he did remember Walt, who had given him really good leads and offered a lot of cooperation in two of Nic's first white-collar cases at the Bureau, both of which had been great successes. Calling Mrs. Garrett would be a complete waste of time, he was sure, but he owed her husband a favor, so he wrote the number down. After finishing his survey of the day's mail and discarding it, he visited the bathroom, tossed his empty beer bottle, and fetched a fresh one from the refrigerator. He took the pen and pad from the counter and the phone from its holder and fell into his favorite chair in the living room. Another glance at the clock on the way told him he had twenty minutes before his favorite show, which should be plenty of time. He dialed the number on the pad.

"Mrs. Garrett? Hi, this is Nic Horn."

"Hi, Agent Horn. Thank you for returning my call so quickly."

"No problem. I really enjoyed working with your husband; he's a real prince of a guy. How is he?"

"He died six years ago."

"Oh, I'm sorry. He was a good man."

Six years? I've been in this dead-end job, treading water, for over six years!

"Thank you, Agent Horn."

"Just call me Nic, Mrs. Garrett."

"Okay. Well, like I said in the message, we've had a murder up here, and the local police seem to be out of their depth."

"Uh-huh."

"Well, actually it's worse than that. They seem to be headed in completely the wrong direction. Are you homophobic, Agent Horn?"

"Just plain Nic is fine, Mrs. Garrett. No, I'm not homophobic. Some of my best friends are gay, and one of the things I do for a living is to protect civil rights, including those of homosexuals. Why do you ask?"

"Because if you'd said 'yes' this would have been a short conversation. You see, the boy who was murdered was my nephew's boyfriend. Simon—that's my nephew—is convinced that Peter was murdered by someone he knows who hates gays."

"You said 'boys,' Mrs. Garrett. How old are they?"

"Seventeen."

"And your nephew thinks this was a hate crime and that he knows the murderer?"

"Yes."

"You've talked to the local police, and they aren't being helpful?"

"They told him that it's a drug-related murder. But Agent Horn—Nic—Peter has never had anything to do with drugs, nor has anyone in his family. It doesn't make sense. And Simon thinks that the police sergeant is a homophobe."

"Well, I'm sure the police know what they're doing and that they wouldn't let prejudice interfere with their investigation, but if it would make you feel better, I'd be happy to call up there and see what I can find out. Why don't you describe the particulars of the murder?"

Nic took notes, and the call was winding up when Mrs. Garrett said, "There's one more thing… " Her confident tone had been replaced by a nervousness that intrigued Nic.

"Yes?"

"Well… you see… "

"Mrs. Garrett, this is a confidential call between old friends. If there's something you want to say… "

"Thank you, Nic. I don't know if they're of any use to you, but I seem to have come into some fingerprints."

"Is that so? Well, I'll bear that in mind, Mrs. Garrett."

Nic smiled and hung up. He sat back in his chair, sipped his beer, and held the phone to his forehead. It was probably nothing but the paranoia of an old lady, but something didn't feel quite right. He looked at the clock. If he called the Wilkeston police, he would miss his show, but he was no longer in the mood for TV. He took another sip of his beer, leaned forward in his chair, and dialed the first number on his notepad.

"Nic?" The voice was muffled over loud background noise.

"Yeah. Hi, Anna."

Damn that Caller ID—he really had to pay the phone company to block his number.

"Nic. It's good to hear from you." The muffled music and background noise faded and Anna's breathing quickened, and Nic guessed she was covering the phone with her hand and walking out of a bar to talk to him.

"You left a message about getting back together?" he said.

"Yeah?"

"I'm kinda in the mood tonight. Are you free?"

After a brief pause, Nic was rewarded by an enthusiastic, "Sure."

"Wanna come over to mine? There's another bottle of that wine, and I've got some really good movies."

"I know you have." Her chuckle had a dirty undertone. "I can be there in twenty minutes."

"That'll be great. See you then."

Nic pressed the red button and ended the call, his face split by a satisfied grin. Though not tall, Nic was graced with a chiseled face and elegant hands, and he worked out and invested in his clothes and his hair, all to lure women. His relationships usually ended quickly among accusations of his deceit and chauvinism, but that suited Nic, and he knew that it was precisely these attributes that allowed him to toss around great chat-up lines in the first place. He was also aware that simply being an agent imbued him with an additional air of mystery and romance, but even so, he never ceased to be amazed that women ten years younger than him and drop-dead gorgeous would fall for his charms.

Just one more call, and then he would be ready to host Anna. He pulled the pad toward him, dialed the number that Mrs. Garrett had given him, and picked up his pen.

"Wilkeston Police Department, can I help you?"

"Hi, is Sergeant Wilson there?"

"The sergeant's off duty, sir. If this is a routine matter, you can call back during business—"

"This is Special Agent Horn of the FBI, and I'd like to talk to Sergeant Wilson right now. Would you please see if you can find him?"

"Sir, he's gone home, and I don't think—"

"I can assure you he'll want to speak with me." Nic pressed the pen into the pad and carved heavy circles. "Perhaps you can give me his number? Or better yet, why don't you call him right now and have him give me a call back here." Nic gave his phone number and hung up. He had just enough time to visit the kitchen to swap out his empty beer and return to the comfort of his armchair before the phone rang again. The caller ID told him the area code was Wilkeston, and he made a note of the number and answered.

"This is Horn."

"Special Agent Horn? Hi, this is Sergeant Wilson of the Wilkeston Police Department. I understand you wanted to talk. How can I help you?"

"Thanks for calling, Sergeant. I'll cut right to the chase: I understand you've had a violent murder up there. I'm doing some routine inquiries on an Atlanta-based case, and I need to get some more information to see if there's a connection."

Nic felt the sergeant's frown in the pause before he answered.

"We've had a strange murder, Agent Horn, and that's for sure, but I hardly think that there's a link with Atlanta."

"Why's that?"

"Well, sir, we're a small community up here, and it seems pretty unlikely that anyone from out of town would have anything to do with this."

"It sounds like you know who did it, then?"

"Actually, we don't yet, but we're making good progress on the case."

"Do you have any suspects?"

"None that we feel able to name at this time."

"Hmm. Doesn't sound to me like you've got a lot, Sergeant. What was the motive?"

"That's a tough one, Special Agent. It was a pretty violent crime, so it looks like a feud of some kind, but the boy's family seems pretty quiet."

Nic smelled a lie and decided to risk tipping his hand.

"Is it drug-related?"

A "yes" answer would suggest interstate crime, potentially opening up the case to FBI jurisdiction, whereas a "no" would contradict Mrs. Garrett's story.

"We thought of that, but we don't have any organized crime up here. Could be local drugs, of course, but we've got a pretty good handle on that. No, up here in the mountains, folks have long memories and feuds run deep. We think it's most likely an old dispute that the Andersons had with another family, but either way, we're confident it's a local matter and that we'll get to the bottom of it."

"Well, Sergeant, this has been really helpful. It certainly sounds like you've got a good handle on it."

... and my head's spinning so much from the smell of all this bullshit that I'm about to pass out.

"Thank you, Special Agent, I'm glad you think so."

"I've got just one more question for you."

"Uh-huh?"

"Do you have any prints?"

"Huh?"

"Fingerprints. Footprints. Do you have any?"

"Well... of course, we've investigated the scene, and we've gathered whatever we can, and—"

"Sergeant, this is an informal inquiry right now. I'm just checking things out for a friend, and I don't want to open a case file on this, but I need to see what you've got before I can walk away."

"I didn't know that the Agency did favors for friends, Agent Horn. Mind if I ask who's interested enough to call you?"

Nic kicked himself for the slip and recovered with, "It was a figure of speech, Sergeant."

"Well, like I said, this looks like a local affair, Special Agent. If we find anything that opens it up or links it to Atlanta, we'll be sure to let you know, but for now, I think we need to handle it ourselves."

The dislike Nic had taken to the sergeant turned to outright animosity when the man tried to blow him off. He thought quickly and decided that for now, instead of pressing without success, he would follow up with Mrs. Garrett.

"Sergeant, I hope there's not more here than you're letting on, because if there is, I *will* find out. Good day." He cleared the line, grinning, and made another call.

"Mrs. Garrett? It's Nic. Listen, I'm sorry to disturb you so soon, but did you say something about fingerprints? Do you have a scanner at the house? Good. Would you mind emailing them to me? Use my home address, Nic.Horn@———.com. Yes, I'll be very discrete, Mrs. Garrett. No, I don't have anything yet. Yes, as soon as you can. Thank you, Mrs. Garrett."

Nic sighed and tossed the phone onto the table, where it clattered and rolled to a rest against the TV remote. He took a sip of beer and, with a mischievous grin, picked it up again to make one last call. The phone was answered at the first ring.

"Forensic lab, this is Stephanie."

"Hi, Steph, what are you doing there at this time of night?"

"Nic?"

"Hi, Babe."

"I love my job, man. You should find something you enjoy doing."

"Oh, I already have. Problem is, they don't pay me for it, and it's illegal at the office."

"You're too old for all that wild-living crap, Nic. Besides, you know it just makes you miserable. You need to break down and have a real, honest-to-goodness, midlife crisis."

"I would, but I need someone like you so I can have a good time while I do it, Steph."

"Oh, you're so full of shit, Nic. And besides, you probably have some hot chick there right now. What are you calling me for?"

"I need a favor, Babe. No paperwork just yet; this is a quickie."

"That's what they all say, honey."

"Yeah? Well, I've got some fingerprints coming in from bumfuck country that I need you to check against the current caseload. Just do the southern Appalachians; I don't think these guys know their way out of the county, let alone the state."

"Sure, what's the deal?"

Nic heard a car pull into the driveway and its engine cut out. He needed to hurry up and finish the call.

"I'm not sure. It started as a favor for an old friend, but something doesn't feel right with this one. My instincts... "

He was interrupted by a laugh. "Your instincts couldn't get you into a whore's underwear."

"They worked well enough with you. Will you do it?"

"That was a long time ago."

"Please?" Nic regretted his comment, wondering if he'd overstepped the line.

"They're coming in tonight, you say?"

Nic smiled. He could get into Steph's underwear again tomorrow. He would have to catch up with her next time he was in Washington and see if they could recapture some of the old magic. "I'm going to email them to you within the hour, with love."

"If you wonderful agents didn't keep giving me late-night work I might just have to leave this place and find something else to do. But since I love my work so much, and because the only guys I meet are sleaze balls, I'll look at them tonight for you."

"Thanks, Babe. Hey listen, do me a favor and don't ask where the prints came from, all right? This is all off the record."

"What's going on, mystery man?"

There was a ring at the door. "I'll tell you later, Babe. I owe you one... another one."

"Is that your latest conquest I hear?"

Nic laughed. "It's the pizza guy. Talk to you."

He strolled to the front door, dropping the phone off on the way. The thrill of a developing case was the best aphrodisiac he knew, and when he opened the door for the well-endowed twenty-something waiting outside, he didn't intend to spend long on foreplay.

*   *   *

It was still dark when movement and noise interrupted Nic's sleep. He had the nighttime reflexes of a disturbed dog and was immediately wide awake, his hand on the butt of the gun under his pillow, his head raised.

"Sorry, honey, did I wake you?"

Nic released the gun, rubbed his face with his hand, and rolled toward the voice.

"What time is it?"

"Six o'clock. I need to get off to work. I've got a change of clothes in the car outside, so I was just looking for your bathrobe."

"It's in… " Nic began, before chivalry took over. "Your clothes are in your trunk?"

"Uh-huh?" The twenty-something sounded hopeful.

"Why don't you go jump in the shower while I go and fetch them."

"Thanks, honey." A warm body pressed against him, and a pair of lips found his.

Anna turned on the bathroom light, and Nic watched her body through the open doorway for a few minutes before rousing himself. He was a very lucky man. He walked naked to the kitchen, grabbed a towel from the pile of clean laundry, and, while he looked for Anna's keys, wondered idly if she always had a change of clothes in her trunk. He found the keys on the counter, tied the towel around his waist as he walked to Anna's car, took her clothes bag indoors and threw it on the bed, and returned to the kitchen to make some coffee. He was leaning against the counter, drumming his fingers while his first fix of the morning dripped through the filter, when the phone rang. He looked at it, recognized Stephanie's number, and snatched up the receiver.

"Hey, Babe, you go to bed last night?"

"Nah, I was too busy working," was Stephanie's reply. "You?"

"Read some poetry, said my prayers, and was in bed by ten o'clock."

"Bullshit. Listen, I looked at those prints. You're not going to believe it, but your instinct paid off for once. We've got a match on Whatbom."

"You're shitting me!" Nic lurched upright.

"Who came up with that name, anyway?"

"What?"

"Whatbom."

"You like it? Have you any idea how hard it is to come up with good names in that dumb-assed naming convention? It stands for Women's Health, Atlanta. So what've you got?"

"I bet you never name another bomb in what's left of your very short career. Anyway, it looks like your bumfuck subject was in the neighborhood, 'cause his prints were on the gatepost of the abortion clinic when they dusted down the morning after the bombing. I'll email you the specifics."

"Damn. I owe you big, angel. Real big."

"Where did you get those prints?"

"I told you, it's off the record. We never had this conversation, Steph. I'll pay you back, I promise. You need anything right now?"

"Just a man who's sex drive is slower than Mach seventeen. Run that motor down and call me, okay? By the way, how old was she?"

"Who?"

"The girl who came by last night."

"Baby, what do you take me for?"

"I know you, shithead, and well enough to know that it was a dumb question. You probably have no idea, but I bet she's thirty with collagen lips and a big pair of silicon tits. Do you even know her name?"

"Steph—"

"Call if you need anything more. The email's on its way."

"I love you."

The line went dead, and Nic jumped for joy. Finally, he had a break, and he was going to really enjoy it. The coffee forgotten, he turned for the bathroom, let his towel fall to the floor, and stepped into the steaming shower to join Anna.

After Anna left, Nic gloated over a cup of coffee, then at seven-thirty sharp dialed into the daily joint task force briefing call on the bombings. His participation was usually passive, and today was no exception. He let his mind wander back several weeks to when he had pulled onto the chic Atlanta side street that was home to the Women's Health clinic to find it already a Christmas tree of yellow ribbons and flashing red, white, and blue lights. He had had to park a full block away and show his badge half a dozen times before he could get through to the scene of the bomb blast, only to see Bart Dixon of the ATF, the man leading the conference call that he was ignoring right now, waving his arms around and directing activities. Nic had bitten his lip so hard it had bled.

He did not understand how, at a time when counterterrorism was the top priority of the FBI, when the nation was looking to the Bureau for protection, a sister organization with a fraction of the resources should be invited to the party at all, and yet there it was, first in line. The Department of Alcohol, Tobacco, and Firearms, created by the Department of Treasury to enforce the collection of taxes on imported whiskey, had somehow managed over the course of two centuries to become the national authority on explosives, and although it was now—rightfully—a division of the Department of Justice, it still refused to accept the natural leadership of its umbrella organization. The Bureau rarely ceded a high-visibility case, and certainly did not do so without a fight, but for the second time in six months, Nic had had to play second fiddle.

The first time, when Nic had tried to assume control at the scene of the first Atlanta women's clinic bombing, his boss, a career bureaucrat whose primary interest was in avoiding visible mistakes—which in turn meant taking no unnecessary risks—had undermined him. Mike DiRoma had not only agreed that the ATF should have primary jurisdiction but had also, in front of Bart, advised Nic that it was "neither expedient nor in the public interest to compete with a sister department." Nic still wondered how Mike had gotten away with taking this position, wondered who within the Bureau he had pictures on, and had fumed as he reflected on his role as FBI liaison to the joint task force, first limited to Rosebom—named after the floral display in the yard of the first women's clinic bombed—and now including Whatbom. He bitterly resented the endless hours of briefing meetings he had had to attend with Bart to hear after the fact what the ATF had done, both men knowing that Nic would have to endure painful follow-up meetings with Mike to relay what he had just heard and, in turn, bring his boss's unhelpful suggestions back to the ATF to be laughed at.

So later that morning, when Nic picked up the phone to place the call his boss that he anticipated would turn the tables on the ATF, he was smiling broadly.

Mike was angry to hear that Nic had not mentioned the Wilkeston lead on the briefing call and was anxious to pass the information on immediately, but Nic slowed the conversation down. He asked for permission to drive up to Wilkeston to do some discrete reconnaissance first and, if it checked out, to allow Mike to introduce the topic at a higher level. This would, he argued, avoid embarrassing the Bureau if his intelligence was poor, and it was an argument Nic knew would prevail, though it took longer than he had expected for Mike to realize that it was a course of action that gave him higher visibility and lower risk. When Mike agreed to consult with the Assistant Special Agent in Charge, Nic smiled, as he always did, at

Mike's deliberate pronunciation of the acronym ASAC, wondering why generations of agents placed the emphasis on the short first letter.

Nic held Dunn, the ASAC, in high regard, and was confident he knew where Mike's conversation with Dunn would lead. He had already contacted Jeff, his partner, and they were sitting together in a coffee shop, packed up and ready to go for a week out of town, when Nic's cell phone rang. Nic looked at the number and winked at Jeff. He opened the clamshell, pressed the speakerphone button, and held the phone at an angle so Jeff could overhear.

"Where are you?"

"Surfing the Websites on that list you gave me last week."

"What the hell… you bring this crap to me, and then you sit on your ass. I want you in Wilkesboro by lunchtime, and I want a personal report at five o'clock."

"Yes, sir. Can we make the report at six o'clock, sir? I'll probably still be interviewing at five."

"Well… okay."

"And I took the liberty of calling Jeff—"

"I guess that's okay, too. Now get your ass moving. And Nic?"

"Yes, sir."

"For Christ's sake, be discreet. The last thing we need is publicity before we're ready."

"Yes, sir." Nic closed the clamshell, muttered, "Asshole," then grinned at Jeff. "We've got ourselves some real work, brother."

"Let's go get 'em."

Jeff was ten years younger than Nic and, with a lean face, broad shoulders, and sweeping blond hair, was strikingly attractive. While for now Jeff appeared happy to follow in Nic's wake and "learn from the master," Nic knew that this could not last. Jeff would outgrow Nic's crusty ways, and unless Nic got a break, Jeff would—like Darren, his previous partner—move on to another assignment and leave Nic older and no wiser. But for now, fresh from good sex, with a hot lead and the prospect of over two hours in the car to show off to his sidekick, Nic was on top of the world.

Nic drove while Jeff examined Stephanie's email on Nic's laptop, asked Nic a lot of questions about process, and listened while Nic recounted tales of his past successes. After reviewing the facts, the agents each spent an hour on the phone calling colleagues and contacts to find an informal relationship that they could use to work more effectively with the Wilkeston police force. To Nic's chagrin and personal embarrassment, they came up empty. Wilkeston was, indeed, a small town in the middle of nowhere, with no apparent ties to the outside world, except for a single set of fingerprints. Finally, with no other options, Nic called Sergeant Wilson. The station got him on the line straightaway.

"Special Agent Horn, what a pleasant surprise. How are you today?" the sergeant's tone was cold, even hostile.

"Very well, thank you. I've also got some good news for you: After we spoke, I reassessed the situation and discussed it with my supervisor, and we concluded that I need to come up for a quick look around."

The silence at the other end of the line seemed interminable. Nic glanced from the road to Jeff, covered the mouthpiece, and laughed silently.

Finally, the sergeant replied. "I don't understand. This is a local affair."

"For right now it is, but there are facts that I can't disclose to you which require us to look at the Anderson murder more closely before closing the file."

After another pause, the sergeant spoke in a resigned voice. "So you're coming to Wilkeston? Well, I don't know that we've ever had FBI agents in Wilkeston before. This is a rare honor, Special Agent, a rare honor. And when do you think you'll be arriving?"

"In about ten minutes." Nic thought he would die laughing during the pause that followed.

"Well that's fine, mighty fine."

"We thought we'd meet you at the crime scene; I'm sure you've got it well-preserved. Is it easy to find?"

The sergeant gave what turned out to be very simple instructions, and Nic hung up.

"The damned hick took so long answering my questions," he laughed, "that I thought we were talking by satellite."

"You *are* a son-of-a-bitch, though, calling him out of the blue like that."

Nic shrugged. "Just keep your eyes open for three grain silos and an abandoned gas station. We turn left immediately after the gas station, and a mile further on, we'll see the field on the left."

The murder site was easy to find, and within fifteen minutes, Nic pulled up behind a police cruiser. A uniformed bruiser leaned against the car, his arms folded and his ankles crossed—Nic wondered whether it was in defiance of the authority arriving from Atlanta or out of habit from a previous career as a nightclub bouncer. When he turned the ignition off, both he and Jeff retrieved jackets from the back seat, slipping them on and pulling out their badges as they covered the short distance to the man they took to be Sergeant Wilson.

Without standing upright, the sergeant appraised them. "Good morning. The body was found in there." He tipped his head to the field on his right. "We preserved the scene, as you can see, but we've removed the victim."

Nic nodded and asked, "You took photos first?" The sergeant went to the passenger door of his car while Nic surveyed the scene. A rusty iron gate lay open before him. Beyond it, a single tree, from which dangled a length of barbed wire, stood in the middle of the field. Nic was interrupted in his study of the scene by a stack of photos that appeared at his elbow. He thanked the sergeant and leafed through the photos, Jeff looking over his shoulder, to see a small, young man who had been badly beaten and then hanged. Nic expected that the coroner's report would show multiple broken ribs and facial bones and probably a number of lost teeth.

"The beating occurred…?" he asked, handing the photos back, stepping over the police tape, and walking into the field.

"Right here, under the tree." Sergeant Wilson sped up to overtake Nic and pointed to an area just to the side of the suspended wire. "There's blood—all the victim's—and we found a couple of his teeth."

Nic and Jeff looked at the ground, then up at the tree.

"And the wire…?"

"Cut out of the fence over there."

Nic's eyes followed the pointed finger. "Wire cutters?"

The sergeant nodded. "We didn't find them, though."

Nic looked around under the tree. He pointed at depressions and flattened grass, marks that were too indistinct, he feared, to yield much detailed information, and asked, "Those were made by a car?"

Wilson shrugged. "We think so. Anderson's feet were only about two feet off the ground when we found him. Allowing for slack in the wire and the bending of the branch, we figure he was standing on the roof of a car that drove off and dropped him."

"You said you think this was a family vendetta?" When the sergeant nodded again, Nic continued, "I don't think BS—that's our Behavioral Sciences guys in Washington—will agree, Sergeant. I'm not the expert, but it looks like the level of violence was… let's just say it was excessive, suggesting real anger or hate. Cutting wire from the fence suggests that the murder was not premeditated, and the number of times the wire was twisted around the boy's neck is far more than was necessary. No, Sergeant, I think what you have on your hands here is a hate crime, probably done in the heat of the moment." After a pregnant silence, Nic asked, "Do you know anything about the victim that would make him the target of a hate crime?"

The sergeant took a step forward and placed his hands on his hips. His bulk towered over Nic as he spoke. "Special Agent, perhaps you'd like to tell me what's going on here."

Do you really think you can bully me into backing down, you fucking hick?

Nic looked up at the sergeant with distaste and offered a smile laced with contempt. "Sergeant, what's going on here is that you have a chance not to be reported for interfering with the FBI. Now perhaps you'd like to cool down and answer the question."

In the brief silence that followed, Nic studied the sergeant carefully as he answered, but not quickly enough: "Maybe. We believe Anderson was gay."

Nic kept a cold stare on the sergeant until the officer stepped back and glanced away.

"Shall we go to the station?" Nic asked. "I'd like to take a look at your files."

"Follow me."

Back in the car, Nic asked, "So what do you think?"

"Hate crime is right," Jeff answered, "this was pretty brutal."

"Which reminds me: Can you talk to Quantico later? You know Mike's going to want the BS on this. But what do you make of the sergeant?"

"Slippery character, huh? Why would he want to hide something?"

Nic shrugged, impressed that Jeff had picked up on the nuances so quickly and confidently. "Right now, it beats me, but I don't think he wants this one solved. Our job is to see if we can figure out why by six o'clock."

The police station lived down to Nic's expectations. He and Jeff were ushered into a small conference room with a single, vintage phone and a clunking 486 computer, the likes of which Nic hadn't seen in years. Five minutes later, Sergeant Wilson came in.

"Would you guys like coffee?" He led the way to a coffee pot in the reception area, took his time pouring, then said, "Let's go to my office."

Nic rolled his eyes at Jeff but followed. He sat in one of the chairs facing the desk, and Jeff took the other. The sergeant lounged back comfortably and sipped his coffee, surveying his visitors. Nic pretended to ignore him and scanned the office, taking in the absence of technology, the array of awards collected over twenty years of service, the handful of family pictures—a wife and two teenage boys, enjoyment of hunting and fishing—the Bible on the credenza, and the crucifix on the back wall.

Eventually, the sergeant adjusted his seat and said, "I'm sorry, Agent Horn, but it looks like our files are a bit disorganized right now. We can pull everything together for you to review, but we won't have it ready till later today, maybe tomorrow. You can wait here, or we can call you."

"I think we'll get you to call us. You have my number?"

Sergeant Wilson nodded. "I'm sorry, but if you'd let us know earlier you were coming, we could've gotten everything ready for you."

"That's okay. I think we're best off interviewing people anyway. Perhaps we can start by having you tell us who you've talked to?"

The sergeant leaned forward.

"Agent Horn, what are you doing here?"

Nic studied him with cold distaste. "*Special* Agent Collins and I are here because we saw some similarities between a case we're working in Atlanta and the Anderson murder, so we wanted to look at a little more closely."

"You're investigating a hate crime?"

Nic nodded.

"And you already thought that the Anderson murder might be a hate crime?"

Nic nodded again: The sergeant was smarter than he let on. Nic anticipated where this was going and prepared his answer.

"So how come you knew this was a hate crime, Agent?"

"The FBI has many eyes and ears, Sergeant. We didn't *know*, but preliminary information suggested circumstances that might be of interest to us. Now, can we talk about the interviews?

After Nic deflected a couple more attacks, the sergeant gave them the addresses and phone numbers of Peter's parents, of Jack Summers, the owner of the field and the discoverer of the body, and of a couple of high school teachers. Nic thanked him for his help, shook his hand, and started to leave. In the doorway, he turned around and looked hard at the sergeant, who was already absorbed in the pile of papers on his desk.

"One more thing, Sergeant."

The head lifted.

"Do you know if Peter was a member of a church?" Nic saw the quick flicker of deceit he was looking for in the man's eyes before he received an affirmative answer. The sergeant rustled on his desk and read off the Pastor Kidd's name, along with an address and phone number.

"You're a church man yourself?" Nic asked, indicating the cross on the wall.

"Yes, sir, that I am."

"I saw a lot of churches when we drove into town, so I'm sure you're not associated with this... " Nic looked at his notes to read the name, "this Church of the Epistles that you just mentioned?" He looked up.

The sergeant's eyes shrank as he scrutinized Nic. "I guess it's a small world, *Special* Agent."

"That it is, Sergeant, that it is. Call us when the files are ready."

On the way out, Nic asked the oversized young woman at the front desk for a lunch recommendation.

"Flo's is my favorite. She does great burgers and onion rings," was the answer.

Nic looked at her bulging waistline and wondered how often she ate there but said only, "That'll be fine," and asked for directions.

Flo's, operating out of a converted trailer, was a lubricating experience for the visitors. Over a quick lunch on the deck, the agents exchanged disparaging speculations on such matters as the average biomass and IQ level of the local constabulary before returning to business.

"That was pretty sharp, Nic, making the church connection like that. What do you think it means?"

Nic shrugged, "I don't know yet, but I'm beginning to become a believer in coincidence. It's no accident that we have an uncooperative asshole at the station and a brutally murdered gay who both go to a church I've never heard of. I think we're going to have a long chat with this Pastor Kidd. But we ought to get a little background first. Why don't we start off with the farmer and then talk to the Andersons?"

After learning nothing new from Mr. Summers, Nic and Jeff found the place that Peter Anderson had once called home, which was, like so many others in town, a 1,600-square-foot ranch house set on a large, well-maintained lawn and surrounded by mature hardwoods. The front door was opened by a small, gray-haired woman who was visibly struggling to hold herself back from a nervous collapse.

"Mrs. Anderson? Hi, I'm Special Agent Horn of the FBI, and this is my partner, Special Agent Collins. We're here helping the local police." They both held up their badges. "We'd like to talk to you about your son. May we come in?"

The lady shuddered, nodded, and walked slowly back into the house. Jeff and Nic stepped in after her and closed the door. They entered an open area that combined living room and dining room, waiting in the doorway while Mrs. Anderson approached a kneeling man from behind. His hands were clasped and his head bent in prayer, his shoulders convulsing. Mrs. Anderson spoke to him with a fragile voice.

"Bo, it's two detectives to talk about Peter." She rested her hands gently on his shoulders, and he slowly lowered his hands and rose to face the officers to give them a wan smile.

"I'm sorry, it's just, well, oh…" He choked back a sob and smiled again.

"No, it's us who should be sorry," Nic responded, "we're interrupting you in your time of grief. But we're going to have to talk to you about your son's death, and it will be easier for all of us if we do it before too much time passes."

Mr. Anderson nodded. "Please take a seat."

He lowered himself onto the couch, and his wife sat close to him, her leg pressed against his and her hand on his knee. Nic and Jeff pulled hard-backed chairs from the dining table on the other side of the common area and sat facing them. Jeff took out his pen and pad while Nic leaned back and used body language to try to put the Andersons at ease.

"I know this is hard, but I have to ask you a few questions. First, can you tell us how you found out about your son's death?"

"Sergeant Wilson called us on Sunday morning."

"What happened after that?"

"We were too upset to go to the service—and Meryl was sick anyway—but Pastor Kidd visited us afterwards and we talked for a long time."

"That was Sunday afternoon?"

They nodded.

"When was the last time you saw Peter alive?"

Meryl Anderson took this question. "He rode to the grocery store on Saturday night to get me a loaf of bread." Her frame crumpled, and it appeared hard for her, taking a long time, to add, "He's dead because I sent him to the grocery store." Nic waited as her husband put his arm around her shoulder to console her.

When Mrs. Anderson was somewhat composed, he continued, "What store would he have gone to, Mrs. Anderson?"

"The Piggly Wiggly."

Jeff interjected with, "How did he get there?"

"By bike."

"I assume the bike's still at the store?"

She shrugged.

Nic received a nod from his colleague and resumed. "Did Peter have any close friends or enemies?"

Bo Anderson answered, "He had one real close friend, Simon Cassell." Mrs. Anderson wailed and collapsed in tears again.

After an appropriate pause, Nic asked, "How about enemies?" When they shook their heads, he asked, "Do you have any idea who might want to kill him? Or why?"

Both parents began to sob. Nic sat patiently, waiting for an answer. Eventually, Mr. Anderson choked out, "Peter was a homosexual." When it became clear that he was not going to say anything further, Nic nudged him.

"Please go on."

Mrs. Anderson held her husband's hand, which seemed to give him strength. "We had no idea until Sunday afternoon," he explained. "Pastor Kidd told us that Peter was dead and that we needed to pray real hard for his soul because he was gay. Unless there's a miracle, he's going to hell, and we're parted from him for eternity."

"How do you think Pastor Kidd knows that Peter's gay?"

The Andersons looked at each other, obviously not having thought about this. "I don't know," Mr. Anderson finally said, "but he's the Lord's servant, and he has vision and knowledge."

"Thank you for your time and patience, Mr. Anderson. Mrs. Anderson." Nic nodded his head at each in turn. "I'm sorry to impose on you in your grief. We'll see ourselves out, and we'll try to leave you in peace, but we may have some more questions later." Nic looked over his shoulder as he left to see the couple, hand in hand, slip off the chair and kneel at the coffee table again.

Back in the car, Nic observed, "I'd bet a lot of money that someone involved with the Church of the Epistles not only knows what happened Saturday night, but knows a lot about Whatbom, too."

Jeff nodded. "I guess we need to go see the preacher?"

"Good call, hotshot. Tell me the way." He fired the engine up and, with a crunch, rammed the gearshift into reverse, spraying gravel up the drive.

A drab woman with a wide, flat face and heavy glasses opened the door of the Kidd residence. When Nic and Jeff introduced themselves, she ushered them through to a well-appointed study and said, "The minister will be with you shortly."

Nic spent ten minutes looking at the books on the shelves before the minister appeared, his resentment at being made to wait growing, and with it, his dislike Pastor Kidd. The eventual exchange of names and handshakes did nothing to soften Nic's demeanor. He settled in a leather chair facing Pastor Kidd across the desk and began, "We're investigating the murder here last weekend."

"I'm sure the local police are very grateful for your assistance, officer. We're just a small town, and you must be a great help."

As Pastor Kidd settled in, Nic noticed him making the most of his large frame and higher chair, and he recognized and resented the cheap power play as well as the subtle sarcasm.

"Peter Anderson was a member of your church?"

Pastor Kidd steepled his fingers and nodded. "He was one of my flock, and I'm afraid I failed him."

"How so?"

"Officer, I think that's obvious."

"It's Special Agent, Pastor. Do you mean you failed him by letting him die?"

Pastor Kidd studied the two agents before answering. "Special Agent Horn, Peter has been my responsibility for seventeen years, and to have him snatched from us—and from his dear parents, Bo and Meryl—at this unripe time is nothing short of a tragedy."

Nic examined his subject minutely, looking for any crack in the façade, but the minister was implacable, a picture of calm and control.

"Pastor, how did you know that Peter was gay?"

The question did not raise even a flicker in the pastor's eyes, and he poured out his answer with comfortable ease.

"I am his pastor, and it is my business to know. I know who in my flock is having marriage problems, who is sick and dying, whose children are getting involved in drugs. It is my responsibility to pay attention and listen, Special Agent; it is my calling to lead my people to the Lord. How can I do this if I don't know about their lives?"

"What is the view of the church on homosexuality, Pastor?"

"Views of homosexuality within the Church are as diverse as the Lord's sheep, Special Agent. But of course, you mean the view of my church, the Church of the Epistles. We regard homosexuality as a sin, and unrepentant homosexuality as an offense that will place one firmly within the fires of hell.

"You asked earlier about how I failed Peter: My true failure was in allowing him to die an unrepentant homosexual, for he is damned. You may find that harsh, Special Agent Horn, but we believe the Word of the Lord is clear on the matter."

"Life is harsh, Pastor Kidd. Do you believe the Bible supports killing homosexuals?"

"It certainly contains language to that effect, Special Agent, but it also provides the Sixth Commandment: Thou shalt not kill. If an unrepentant homosexual is killed, he has been robbed of the chance to repent and therefore find his place in heaven, so, no, Agent Horn, it is not the policy of this church to murder homosexuals."

"That was not my question."

"The intent of your question was to determine if I preach the murder of homosexuals. I do not." The Pastor did not move as he held Nic's gaze clear and fixed. He remained tranquil, the very picture of comfort and peace.

"How about abortion?"

The Pastor waited and eventually smiled.

"Abortion?"

Nic almost smiled, too. The Pastor was an accomplished adversary who had not only seen through Nic's use of silence but had also let Nic know by replying playfully with an expert card, a question.

"Yes, Pastor Kidd, abortion. What is the stance of your church on abortion?"

"I see. You're here because you're trying to tie the murder of Peter Anderson to the abortion clinic bombings in Atlanta."

Nic tried to not to let his surprise at the Pastor's insight show.

"As you've noticed, Special Agent, we are a small community without the resources of Atlanta—I assume that's where you're from, though you haven't properly introduced yourself—but we do get newspapers, and many of us can read them. But to answer your question, mine is not a church of hate. I do not stand in the pulpit on a Sunday and admonish my flock to go forth and murder. We love each other, and we love the Lord, Special Agent, and that is what we practice—love. We try to keep ourselves to ourselves and to lead good lives."

Nic's dislike for the minister was increasing. The man was smooth as malt whiskey, calm as the eye of a hurricane. Nic sensed deceit beneath the veneer, but he couldn't put his finger on it. He was just about to give up when he caught a glimpse of a tell. Looking closely, he saw it again.

The pastor had an eye tic.

The lower eyelid on the pastor's right eye had briefly twitched with an involuntary spasm. Pastor Kidd tried to mask it by offering Nic his profile, but it was too late.

"Very good, Pastor Kidd, thank you for your time."

The minister rose, grinned broadly, and exuded confidence and warmth as he shook their hands. "I hope this was of some assistance. If I can do anything else to aid your investigation, please let me know."

"We will, Pastor, we will."

In the privacy of his car, Nic punched the steering wheel and blurted out, "That shit knows he's got a murderer and a bomber in his congregation, and he's hiding the bastard."

"He was a slippery customer, that's for sure, but I don't see how you figure that, Nic." Nic glanced at Jeff's furrowed brow and explained the eye tic. Jeff joked, "I thought you didn't believe in instinct."

"I don't care if it's good detective work, instinct, or divine intervention, I just know that he's hiding our murderer. We'll find the son of a bitch if we have to fingerprint every member of that church to do so."

"You think Mike'll go for it?"

"Not unless he has no choice. Get the BS shrinks in Washington on the phone: I want an indication from them that both of these cases are hate crimes performed by religious extremists. We need to paper this so there's no way Mike can cover it up, so while you're on the phone, I'm going to start to write a 302. Get me a juicy quote from BS, Jeff, and I'll slip it in the report and submit it before we talk to Mike at 6:00. Once we've done that, he'll be in a box.

"And we've got control, Jeff. It's our case. The ATF will find out tonight, and they'll show up tomorrow lunchtime scrambling for a toehold, but we'll be in charge.

"Now, where can a guy go to get laid in this bumfuck town?"

Chapter Twenty

On Sunday morning, Jessica had been bouncing restlessly around the trailer, missing Clark after their wonderful time together Saturday, and yet scared of the emotional commitment that she realized she was making to him, when Uncle Bo had called to tell her of Peter's murder. Jessica had been too numbed to respond, so she had held the phone for a moment in silence, then abruptly hung up. Although she had seen Peter at school several times since Pastor Kidd's vitriolic and inflammatory sermon, she had never stopped to talk, and her last memory of her cousin would be veiled in prejudice.

But she was hurt most by a deeper stress that was not about Peter.

She had been overwhelmed by the loss of her dream of Colby, of her virginity, and of her family, and now, just when she was getting back on her feet, she had lost her best friend. Fear of further loss, that of Sam and Clark, constantly hovered on the edge of her dreams, and the news of Peter's death made it even more real. She was guilty and defiled; how could she expect Clark's loyalty when she was going to have someone else's baby? Clark had quoted from *The Princess Bride* on Saturday night, and their first kiss had surely been one of the "six great kisses," but would it be enough to make him stay? He had declared his love for her, but Colby had already shown her what a boy will say for a female favor. The feelings of rejection that she had been hiding had burst through, and she had hidden in her room and wept.

Old Sam, God bless him, had heard her and crept into her room to hug her, talk to her, even sing to her. His lullabies and silly songs had made her smile and cry and eventually allowed her to sleep. Without Sam's unquestioning acceptance and unconditional love, she didn't know how she could have coped.

.Jessica had spent the whole of Monday staring out of the classroom window in a daze. Her lunchtime and breaks had been passed with Clark, whose silent companionship had supported her and given her hope. School on Tuesday had been just as bad as Monday, and Wednesday not much better, but finally, on Thursday morning, she was beginning to settle down. When she entered the school, however, she knew something had happened: Although it was a clear, sunny day, a pall hung over the building. Her home room was hissing with conspiratorial whispers, and suspicious glances flashed like concealed knives. She looked for Clark, but he had not yet arrived, so she sat on her own and waited. It was only a few moments before he appeared in the doorway, looking terrible. His eyes were hollow, and there was desperation in them as they roamed the room. When they found hers, he tipped his head and turned to walk away. Jessica hastened after him.

"What is it?"

"It's Robbie."

"Your brother?"

Clark nodded. "They think he killed Peter."

"Heaven protect us!" Jessica swayed with shock, then collected herself. "They?"

Clark shrugged and pushed the main door of the building open. "The FBI, I guess." Jessica followed him through the doorway. "I don't really know what's happening. Some guy in a dark suit came to the house right as I was leaving. He asked me who I was, then waved a badge at me and told me to make sure I come home tonight."

"That must be what everyone's whispering about."

Clark threw his bag by the base of a tree and collapsed on the ground. "He's my brother, Jessica. He's always been wild, and I knew he was up to no good, but this… They think my brother's a murderer."

"Oh, Clark," Jessica said, dropping to the ground beside him, "Clark, I'm sorry." She took his hand in hers and held it on her lap, laying her head on his chest. After a lengthy silence, she remembered something and said, "You know it's Peter's funeral today?"

Clark looked up, startled. "I can't go."

"It's right after lunch, remember. We were going to go together?"

"I can't, Jessica, not after this."

She squeezed his hand and said, "Just go for me, okay? He's my cousin, and my parents might be there: I need your support. And it's the best thing for you, too, you know it is."

Clark's silence was the answer Jessica needed. She let it sit for a while, then squeezed his hand again and said, "Come on, class has started, and you've got that algebra that you can't afford to miss."

Clark smiled, and she pecked him on the cheek.

Presiding over the funeral that afternoon, Pastor Kidd gave the feeling that he was acting out a hopeless exercise for the damned. He offered the briefest of comments about Peter's childhood and spoke of the importance of repentance before it was too late, a comment Jessica suspected was directed at her.

Jessica looked around the dreary gathering: Peter's parents were there, but only a handful of others, including a reporter from the local newspaper and an older boy she vaguely recognized from school standing with an older lady. Peter had been abandoned in death. Even Jessica's mother, who was Auntie Meryl's sister and Peter's aunt, was absent. Jessica was appalled. It was ridiculous, she knew, to feel complicit in the absence of parents whose judgment had resulted in her own eviction, but nonetheless, she felt vicarious guilt of her parents' presumed judgment of Peter. Jessica's face flushed with shame as she considered the misery Ma's self-imposed isolation was bringing to her and Dad. Even after years of holding her sisters at arm's length, how could Ma not be with Auntie Meryl when she needed her the most?

Jessica didn't have to look at Clark to feel his pain; the clutch of his hand on hers told her everything, and she knew it was only the pressure of her hand that kept him under control. After the service was over, the small gathering wandered out of the church. Jessica silently hugged her aunt and uncle. Unable to articulate or even understand the sickness that filled the pit of her belly, she reached out for Clark, and they left the desolate scene, hand in hand, in silence.

After Clark's misery on Thursday and the desolation of Peter's funeral, Jessica had another restless night and was unable to concentrate in school on Friday. The sound of her own sigh brought her attention back to the history class, and she turned from the window out of which she was staring, ready for the teacher's wrath. Fortunately, the room was filled with the noise of book bags rustling and books slamming on desks, and the teacher had noticed neither her distraction nor her sigh. Jessica wiped the tears from her eyes and glanced at her neighbor's book, opened her own to the same page, and gazed without enthusiasm at a chapter on the Civil War.

The class didn't last much longer, and Jessica was released once more to her daydreams. She would ask Clark later what she had missed, but for now she would drag down the hall to her next class. She recognized a melancholy face coming toward her and spontaneously said, "Hi," adding as the older boy paused, "Didn't I see you at Peter's funeral?"

Simon glanced at her dismissively. "What of it?"

Jessica turned and fell in beside him. "I'm Jessica Jackson, Peter's cousin. I used to go to the Church of the Epistles, but it all went kind of wrong. I don't know how well you knew Peter, but sometimes it's good just to talk. So, you know, if you want to, let me know, okay?"

The youth stopped walking and looked down at her, surprise written on his face. "Thanks."

Jessica nodded and scrutinized him: A plain boy who looked like he should play football, he would be handsome if he combed his hair. She smiled, said, "Well, I'll see you around," and turned to walk back to the classroom, refusing to look over her shoulder to see if the youth was still staring after her in disbelief, though she knew he was. She scowled to herself.

What was I thinking?

Jessica was a teenage girl about to have an illegitimate baby. *She* was the one who needed support and understanding. The last thing she needed was to be reaching out to help complete strangers. Why had she just made such a ridiculous offer?

Sam.

She realized the answer with surprise. She had just acted exactly the way Sam would have done, spontaneously helping those in need. Jessica puffed her chest out with pride, until she realized what a silly and contradictory response this was and fell once more into confusion. When she arrived at her class, she immersed herself in the difficulties of geometry and put the whole thing behind her.

Lunchtime came around fast, and she took her usual place in the corner, waiting for Clark to join her, but when a tray slid onto the table opposite her, it was not Clark's. She looked up at the sound of an unfamiliar voice.

"Hi, Jessica, I'm Simon Cassell. Listen, that was really nice what you did earlier. I thought I'd sit down and get to know you a little better—if that's all right?"

Jessica nodded.

"It's okay if you don't want to, you know." Jessica realized with a start that she had looked away, desperately seeking Clark's company, and she saw disappointment on Simon's face as his tray was withdrawn.

"No, please sit down," Jessica gestured energetically, embarrassed at her rudeness, "I'd like that a lot."

"You don't have to worry about me wanting to, you know... *do* anything," he said as he sat down. He leaned forward and whispered, "I'm gay."

A possibility arose in Jessica's mind and she asked, "The sermon the weekend before school started...?"

Simon nodded, and a knot formed in Jessica's stomach. Over Simon's shoulder, Jessica saw Clark pick up his full tray and turn from the food counter. She caught his attention and waved him over, but he smiled at her and shook his head. Jessica scowled, then noticed Simon glance over his shoulder and look back at Jessica with a question in his eyes, his hands reaching for his tray.

"It's okay, that was just a friend." Jessica forced a smile and put her hand on his to stop him leaving. For an awkward moment, she realized how unhelpful her comment had been, but didn't know what to add, and as the moment stretched, the silence became increasingly uncomfortable. Eventually, Simon put his knife and fork down and leaned forward.

"I've heard about your... situation. Well, actually, Peter did. He was so sensitive, he always paid more attention to other people than I did. Did you ever see his paintings? They were... "

Jessica saw tears welling in Simon's eyes, but Simon pressed fingers to his eyes and changed the subject.

"I think he said that you'd... " Simon looked embarrassed. Instead of completing his sentence, he said, "Actually, I'll probably get what he said wrong. Something happened between you and Colby?"

"He raped me." It was harsh, but it seemed the best way of summarizing what had happened.

"Little shit," Simon spat in disgust, gripping his cutlery firmly. After a pause, he relaxed, took a mouthful of chicken, and spoke. "Without Peter, I have no one to talk to. My parents kicked me out, and I live with my Aunt Jodi now, and she's wonderful, but... but it's difficult."

"My parents kicked me out, too."

"I think Peter said you told everyone that Old Sam was the father and that he took you in." Simon smiled through moist eyes and lowered his fork.

Jessica laughed. "Yeah. I was kind of desperate. They all wanted the father to accept responsibility and kept on nagging me to tell them who it was. They wouldn't believe me when I did, and I couldn't marry Colby anyway." She looked down at her hands and shook her head. "Poor Sam. I was incredibly selfish, I see that now, but I didn't know what to do." Raising her eyes again to Simon's, she said, "I've been incredibly lucky; he's an amazing man. You know what he did?"

Simon shook his head.

"When I said that he was the father, he said, 'Is that so.' That's it: In front of all those people, he just said, 'Is that so,' and invited me into his home. Oh, he's been so wonderful." Jessica stared into space.

"If you live with Old Sam, you must be on Old Charles, right?"

Jessica nodded.

"Then we live real close to each other." Jessica's eyes widened with surprise, and Simon nodded. "Aunt Jodi's on Oak; it's the next street over."

Jessica recognized the street name. "You must come around sometime, maybe one night after school?"

"That would be nice. I might just do that." Simon grinned broadly and pushed himself back from the table. "Well, Jessica, it's been a real pleasure. Thanks."

"Thank you," Jessica replied, though after speaking, she wondered, *For what?* Simon picked up his tray and left her to finish her dessert alone, but before she could start eating, another tray landed in front of her.

"Why didn't you come and sit with me?" she asked Clark sternly, eyeing his mostly finished lunch.

"I didn't want to interrupt you two."

"What do you mean? We weren't saying anything private," Jessica snapped.

Clark laughed. "I know that," and looked around before leaning forward to whisper, with a tone of mock conspiracy, "He's gay!"

Jessica laughed as Clark sat back comfortably, playing casually with the contents of his tray. She couldn't stay mad at Clark, who was in much better spirits now then when they had last spoken.

"I didn't know you knew Simon," he said, chasing a runaway pea with his fork.

"I didn't until this morning. I don't know what came over me. I just went up to him during break and spoke about Peter. I told him to come and talk if he wanted. How do you know he's gay?"

Clark skewered his pea and examined it. "You know things like this if you go to the Church of the Epistles and your brother is a murderer." He snorted, then shifted his gaze to Jessica, and his scowl softened. "Maybe you should throw a party for Church of the Epistles' rejects and invite him over. We can get Dad to come, too." He put the pea in his mouth.

"Don't forget Darlene," Jessica added with a mischievous smile.

Clark cocked an eyebrow. "That's right, I'd forgotten she used to go there, too." He captured another pea.

"Actually, it turns out he lives on the next street over. He said he might come around sometime," Jessica added in a defensive tone, dropping her dessert spoon on the empty plate.

"Well, good. Something tells me we're going to need all the company we can find. You ready?" He tipped his head at her empty plate. Jessica nodded, picked up her tray, and led the way to the tray return hatch and out of the hall.

Chapter Twenty-One

"You shouldn't be worrying about what to do right now, Dwight. What you've just done took a lot of courage, and you've got cash in the bank and time on your hands. You should stop for a while and think."

"Maybe you're right, Darlene," Dwight said to the ceiling, "but when I get up in the morning without anything to do, I feel like something's missing from my life." After a pause, he turned and spoke to her profile. "Heck, something *is* missing; that store *was* my life. And it's worse with all that's going on at home right now." He huffed, folded his hands behind his head, and stared back at the ceiling.

"I wish that I had money. It gives you so many options." Darlene reached out to the bedside table, pulling a cigarette from the pack and lighting it, then balanced an ashtray under her naked breasts and put the cigarette in her mouth. Her eyes followed the smoke that trickled up from her lips before she tapped off the ash into the ashtray and turned her head to face Dwight. "Maybe it's different when you're used to running the show—and I guess you are—but I really think it would do you good to take some time off. You should take a trip, maybe go to the beach or something."

Dwight smiled and rolled onto his side. He tucked the pillow under his armpit and rested his head on his hand. "You know what's doing me good right now? You are. You really are beautiful when you smile." He reached out and touched her lips. "In fact, you're irresistible."

He slid his hand from her lips to her cheek and stroked it with the tips of his fingers, then gently cupped her face in his whole hand and leaned forward to kiss her on the lips.

"Maybe I do need to go to the beach. And maybe I'll take you with me."

The idea thrilled him. He saw Darlene running in the shallows, felt her wrapped around him in the sea, making secret love, and imagined quiet dinners under the stars with wet hair. Dwight closed his eyes tightly and pressed his lips to Darlene's. His tongue tasted fresh cigarette that her mouth transformed into an intoxicating aphrodisiac, and he slid the ashtray onto the bed beside her, pulled her warm, smooth weight on top of him and held her tightly to fill an empty ache. Their legs entwined, and the sheet slipped further down her body. He ran his hands ran over her back and thighs and pulled her closer. Something wonderful happened to him when he lay with Darlene, and he didn't want it to end.

But Darlene pulled her mouth away from his. She folded her forearms on his chest, slid the ashtray across the mattress toward her, and picked up her cigarette. After she had taken a drag, she turned it around and placed it between his lips. He sucked and inhaled, and out of eyes half-closed against the acrid smoke, he gazed through Darlene's hair at her foot waving in the air like a palm tree in a tropical breeze.

"I'd love to come to the beach with you, Mr. Cook, but you're never going to take me. And I don't know about you, but I've got things to do this afternoon." She retrieved her cigarette, kissed him one more time, and sat up with her feet hanging off the bed.

"I know I've got to sort things out at home but I will, Darlene, I promise I will..." Dwight wanted to continue his protest, wanted to convince himself that he would soon be ready to take her, but his insides were in turmoil. He still loved Cheryl, though he couldn't see how life with her was possible anymore, and he still had the church and his boys to think of. He was lost. His eyes flicked around the room, mirroring his restless mind, and settled on the clock. "Goodness, is that the time?" he asked and ran a quick mental check to make sure that the attaché case in the kitchen contained everything he would need to close on the sale of the store building that afternoon.

"Yeah," Darlene replied, starting to stand.

"Great." Confident that he was prepared for the afternoon, Dwight reached out and grabbed Darlene's trailing wrist. "I've got over an hour before I have to leave. Come back here." With playful roughness, he pulled her toward the bed and tossed her onto her back beside him, her arms flopping above her head.

Darlene laughed. "I know you're making up for years of neglect, but I think you've had enough for now. Come on, we need to get some lunch in you. I don't want your stomach rumbling in the middle of a big real estate deal." She rolled once more into a sitting position.

Dwight stroked her back and asked, "You're busy tonight?"

Darlene nodded. "And tomorrow, and the day after. But it's almost the weekend, and you ought to try to spend time with your family. Especially Clark."

Dwight knew she was right, but he hated it. He didn't want to spend the weekend without Darlene, but above all didn't want to have to deal with his dysfunctional home. Cheryl's animosity and Robbie's absence reflected the ideological chasm that was opening up between him and his family, and Clark's vanishing acts were placing his younger son on the same side of it as his mother—and the church. Dwight faced the most important people in his life across a gap that was becoming too wide for him even to shout across. His only solace was his favorite rock by the stream, and since he had quit drinking—again—even that did not offer him much relief. He was being pushed out but lacked the courage to either face that reality or fight it. No, he wanted to stay here with Darlene and hide.

His hand fell from Darlene's back as she stood, and he admired the flow of elegant curves as they walked to the bathroom. He tried to feel positive about his good fortune—a beautiful young woman on his arm and the imminent final step of a surprisingly substantial economic windfall—but the sickness of losing everything he held dear would not go away.

"Come on, let's get some lunch," Darlene said, wrapping a short dressing gown around herself. Dwight started to rise but was interrupted by the sound of the Rolling Stones from the floor. It was Cheryl's ringtone. Embarrassed, he glanced at Darlene, but she continued walking toward the door as if nothing had happened. Dwight lunged for the floor, rummaged in his clothes, and managed to retrieve his phone from the pocket of his trousers before it stopped ringing. Surely Cheryl was not really calling him? But he glanced at the screen and saw the ten digits that he had associated with home for twenty years. He flipped his clamshell open and looked up to see Darlene standing in the doorway, scowling, her hands on her hips. Dwight pressed the phone to his chest and cocked his head at Darlene, silently pleading.

"Hmm." Darlene grunted and, with a kick of her bare heels, was gone.

Dwight put the phone to his ear. "Hello?"

"Hi, it's me."

"Hello, dear," Dwight said instinctively, immediately regretting his habitual familiarity.

Cheryl brushed off his faux pas in a business-like manner. "Listen, those FBI agents were just here to search Robbie's room, and they walked off with that pile of papers from his bedside table—you remember, 'God hates Sweden' and all that? They asked me where he was the night of the Atlanta bombing. Dwight, I think they may… "

"Cheryl," Dwight interrupted, "I don't think we should have this conversation by phone."

"Don't be so silly. They already think he did it, just like you do."
Cheryl's voice was cold. "Where are you, by the way?"

"Cheryl, I don't know what he's done, but I can't help him if he's not
going to tell us. I'll always love him, but he has to follow the law. If he's
committed a crime…" Dwight paused, reflecting on what it was safe to say
on a phone that might be tapped, and Cheryl spoke into the silence.

"You're with that slut who used to work at the store, aren't you?"

"Cheryl! I'm on my way to the closing for the sale of the store building. Why don't I come by afterwards, and we can talk about this."

"That may be where you're going, but that's not where you are right
now."

"Cheryl, please don't do this." Dwight's jaw was tight, and his face
was red. "I'll talk to you after we're through the closing."

"Dwight, we've been married for twenty years. Don't you think I can
tell when you're hiding something? I don't know what's happened to you,
Dwight. I always admired you because you were so strong and upright, but
now… now you're just a weak, cowardly old man. I'm sorry I called. Goodbye, Dwight."

"Cheryl!"

Dwight jerked upright, but the phone was dead. He lowered it from
his ear and cradled it in both hands, aching with emptiness.

When he entered Darlene's kitchen, it was empty. He finished tucking
his shirt into his trousers and sat down at the table. Darlene appeared
moments later with the mail in her hands. "Oh, hi," she said, glancing
briefly at Dwight as she shuffled envelopes while walking. She dropped a
couple of letters on the table and tossed the rest in the trash can under the
sink.

Dwight was torn between the beautiful woman in front of him and
Cheryl, his wife of twenty years. He wanted to make things right. "Darlene,
she knows about us, I just need to—"

"I don't want to hear about it. You're cute and fun and I like being with
you, but you're never going to leave her. Now what do you want on your
sandwich, Mr. Cook? How about ham and cheese, and maybe some potato
chips?"

Call me Dwight.

Dwight knew she called him Mr. Cook to create distance and to nee-
dle him, and he wanted to protest both this and his intent to handle Cheryl,
but he felt sick to his stomach. He was paralyzed: Although his home life
and rejection by Robbie and Cheryl were intolerable, he was unable to tear
himself away, unable to fully enter an alternative life with Darlene. On top
of this, he had his salvation and the church to think about, and now Robbie
was the target of an FBI inquiry. It was all too much.

He watched his fantasy woman cruise the cabinets and assemble lunch supplies on the counter, wishing he could find a way to just be with her, wishing the pain of Robbie and Cheryl would go away. Darlene opened a cabinet over her head, stood on her toes, and stretched up to retrieve the potato chips. The spectacle of her taught thighs and the short bathrobe riding up her naked buttocks jolted Dwight from his reverie, and he wanted to make love again. But Darlene didn't, so he tried to content himself with watching her at work from behind.

"Tell me," he said, the question arising spontaneously, "how is it that you figured it out in your teens but I'm over forty and I still haven't got a clue?"

Darlene looked briefly over her shoulder with a frown and asked, "Figured out what?" before returning to preparing lunch.

Her question confused Dwight, and he frowned. "I don't know… How to be happy, I suppose."

"Dwight, I haven't figured anything out. I'm just as confused as you are; maybe more so." Darlene turned around with a plate in each hand and the bag of potato chips dangling from her fingers. She walked over to put the sandwiches on the table, opened the bag, giving Dwight a healthy handful of chips, and added, "I don't know that I'm particularly happy." From the pitcher on the table, she poured them each a glass of lemonade and sat down.

"Well you certainly look a lot happier than I feel."

Darlene laughed and said, "I guess I just don't worry about things like you do. Life's too important to take it—or yourself—too seriously." She assessed the sandwich in her hand and took a big bite.

"Don't you ever wonder what it's all for… you know, and whether you're going to be saved or not?" Dwight watched Darlene chewing and nibbled on his chips while he waited for her answer.

Darlene's eyes wandered, as if she wanted to speak but was unable to do so through a mouthful of food. Finally, she swallowed and said, "Billions of people around the world read the Bible, and they all think they're saved, but it means something completely different to every one of them. There are Catholics and Jews, Baptists and Methodists; how can I know who's right? Especially since the only guide I've ever had is Pastor Kidd, and he's a complete prick."

Dwight couldn't suppress a snort of laughter, and having just taken a chunk out of his sandwich, he had to cover his mouth to stop himself from launching it out of his mouth. As he had become more intimately acquainted with Darlene, she had let her language become more relaxed, and after being shocked at first by her colorful vocabulary, Dwight simply found it funny. He recovered his composure and mumbled through his mouthful, "Pastor Kidd isn't that bad."

"Yes, he is. He's a narrow-minded bigot. He's only a preacher because he inherited the family business. He's a thug without any real authority, and yet the folk at that church think he's God's agent. No, I think I'll stick to Christianity without prejudice, thank you very much. Besides, I don't have time for any of that shit: I need to work." Darlene took another bite of her sandwich as if to end the conversation.

Dwight chewed on his sandwich in silence, deeply jealous of Darlene's ability not to worry, until it came to him that her simple, carefree life carried a different stress—that of being one paycheck away from poverty. It occurred to him how wonderful it would be if she didn't have a financial guillotine hanging over her head, and he suddenly felt ashamed. He owed her much and was in a position to help her, yet had not done so. Why not bring the college degree she wanted closer to reality? With a lightheaded feeling of liberation, Dwight stood up and walked to the counter where his attaché case lay, reached inside it, and said, "Darlene, I'd like to give you something."

"What's that?"

Darlene was concentrating on the remains of the sandwich that she held in her hands when Dwight turned, checkbook in hand, and answered, "You were the only one who was there to help me close down the store, and without you, I doubt if I could have done it." Dwight returned to the table, sat down, and pushed his sandwich aside to replace it with his open checkbook. "Here, consider this a bonus or a sales commission. Buy yourself something nice, maybe, but save most of it up for that college degree."

Darlene looked at the check that Dwight slid across the table, her eyes sparkling. She protested, politely, although at the same time the check for $10,000 was slid off the table and into the pocket of her bathrobe.

"I really want you to have it," Dwight said. "You didn't just help me in the store… " He looked down at his hands before continuing, "You gave me something to hold onto when everything was falling apart. It means a lot, a whole lot to me, and I want—"

But Dwight never finished his sentence. Darlene had stood and was walking slowly around the table, a look of raw passion on her face, the hem of her short bathrobe swinging with her undulating hips, and her fingertips trailing on the table behind her. She put her hands on Dwight's chest and pushed gently until he slid his chair back, then swung one leg over his and sat down on his lap. The tie on her bathrobe tugged itself loose, and Darlene shrugged the garment from her shoulders. Dwight breathed in Darlene's hair, her flesh, her heat, and his body throbbed in anticipation.

*   *   *

Susan Wise joined Dwight in the conference room within minutes of his arrival at her office. They were reviewing the settlement statement together when Mr. Nickles' arrival was announced. Susan confirmed that Dwight was comfortable with the numbers and closing process, then buzzed to let the out-of-town visitor enter. Her assistant brought in Mr. Nickles and fussed around, hanging up coats, fetching drinks and cookies, and making sure everyone was comfortable, a show of hospitality and introductions that took a full ten minutes. The formality of the closing rushed by in less than twenty minutes, and the transaction finished in another extended celebration of handshakes and conversation that Dwight endured for ten more minutes before he felt he could politely leave.

He stepped out into the fresh air and inhaled deeply, listened to the birds and insects as if he were being reacquainted with long-lost friends, and with a spring in his step, he strode along Main Street a free man. Only in its complete absence did he realize what a burden the store had become. He wanted to celebrate... with Darlene.

His heart sank. He would not only not see Darlene for the next couple of days but had no choice other than to go home.

Home.

He laughed at the hollow ring of the word. Still, Darlene was right: He was a married man, and although his hormones drove him in another direction, what he wanted above all else was to reconcile with Cheryl. He also had the FBI's apparent assertion of Robbie's complicity in the bombing to address, and he wanted to make sure he didn't drive Clark away as he had done his older boy. The lightness gone from his step, Dwight plodded back toward his truck, which was parked outside Susan Wise's office, jumped in, and turned the ignition. He stared for a while at the hood with his hand hanging on the steering wheel before finally dropping into gear and pulling away.

When he walked into the house a few minutes later, he tried to ignore his wife's desultory snort and asked, "Where's Clark?"

"It's Thursday." The derisive message in her voice was palpable: *You oaf, you may have left, but the rest of us are soldiering on.*

Cut deeply, Dwight tried to recover. "So what time do you expect him home from school?"

Silence.

Speak to me, you witch!

But Dwight's infidelity with Darlene now shared the blame, and he had lost the moral high ground. He tried a different tack.

"Cheryl, can we talk?"

"What about?"

"About us. About this family."

The desultory snort was repeated, followed by silence. Dwight waited, and finally, Cheryl turned to face him. "You make a spectacle of yourself around town with that… that painted whore, and then you come here and want to talk about '*this family*.' " The venom she projected made Dwight physically recoil. "You humiliate me and then come back as if nothing had happened. How dare you!"

Cheryl turned back to face the sink, shaking, as Dwight stared at her back in horror. He hadn't expected this and didn't know what to say. Eventually, the first tremulous words trickled out. "Cheryl, I'm sorry; truly, I am." Once the dam was broken, a flood of stream of consciousness poured from his mouth. "I'm sorry, Cheryl, I didn't mean for it to happen. I want this family to work; really, I do, and I've tried, the Lord knows I've tried. I tried to turn that store around, and I tried to bring those boys up right, but Robbie's turned bad. I know you don't want to hear it, Cheryl, but he has. We both know he's involved in those bombings, and no amount of us interfering with the FBI will help.

"And then there's you and me, Cheryl, what's happened between us? We used to be so close, and now we hardly say anything to each other any more. You can't blame Darlene for that: We stopped talking a long time ago. You've got ideas that don't make sense to me. Maybe I could deal with them if I could understand them, but I can't. Life was so easy when we believed the same things, but I don't think that we do any more, Cheryl, and I don't know how to handle that.

"I'm sorry." Dwight looked down at his hands, feeling hollow. Sitting in the kitchen where he had eaten breakfast and dinner for twenty years, he wanted more than anything to reconcile with Cheryl and have Robbie home, but in his heart, he knew some things could never be undone, and he still physically yearned for Darlene. Lust and loyalty battled for his soul, and he squirmed with guilt.

Cheryl responded with silence, but there was something different about it. Dwight looked up, hopeful. Some of the stiff pride had dissipated from Cheryl's back, and she hung her head as if struggling to find common ground with her life partner. Eventually, she turned to face him.

"Why? Why did you do it, Dwight?"

"Cheryl, I'm sorry, I truly am." Tears welled in Dwight's eyes as he gazed at his wife. "I'm weak, Cheryl, I always have been. It's always been you who kept me going, and I feel like you're changing, growing away from me." It hit him again just how beautiful she still was and much he still loved her. In her soft eyes, her angular cheeks, her fine chin, he saw the woman he had fallen in love with, the mother of his boys, the woman he had sworn before God and family to have and to hold, " 'till death do us part." He wanted to hold her close until the sadness evaporated from her face, to hold her forever.

But then Cheryl said, "A lot of what I believed before was wrong, and we need to be strong to hold true to God's will." Though her voice was gentle, the gentle spell was shattered.

"What does that mean?" Dwight asked, sickness filling his stomach once again.

"I'm still not sure, but I do know it's about following God's Word even if we don't understand, like Abraham offering his only son to the Lord."

"Cheryl, you're not suggesting that it's okay to kill people?"

Cheryl shook her head, waved her hands in the air, and sighed. Her hands fell to hit the side of her legs with a slap, and she said, "Dwight, I just don't know anymore." Confusion evaporated from her face and was replaced by an intensity that verged on joy. This looked like the Cheryl with whom Dwight had fallen in love, but when she spoke again, it was with the voice of a stranger. "Following God's will sometimes means fighting against society. It means doing things that are unpopular, maybe even illegal. We each have a calling, and I can feel mine coming, but I don't know what it is yet. God will reveal it when He's ready."

Cheryl's words drew back a veil, and Dwight could no longer hide from the enormity of their differences. "You're saying that it's okay for Robbie to go around bombing abortion clinics and killing people, aren't you?"

Cheryl's relaxed demeanor hardened. "You have no idea what he's been doing, and nor do I, but the Lord is a hard master, and He punishes those who disobey Him. It's a terrible sin to take the life of the unborn, and His judgment on those who do so will be harsh."

"But what of the Sixth Commandment, 'Thou shalt not kill?' How can you go against the Commandments?"

Cheryl's stern face grew quickly red as she clenched her fists. "How about the Seventh Commandment? Or the Fourth? Or the Tenth? It looks to me like you're working your way through them one at a time. Robbie may have a temper, but he's justified by faith and he's exercising the judgment of the Lord as it's laid out in Scripture. Robbie hasn't succumbed to greed, or cast aside his vows to his God and his wife. How dare you stand here stinking of that... that *woman* and lecturing me about obedience to the Commandments!"

Dwight didn't know whether the revulsion he felt arose from the violence of Cheryl's manner, from her terrifying support of radical activism, or from her litany of his sins, but it didn't matter: Cheryl had just thrown his world of more than twenty years onto the ground and trampled it into the dust. Although he had feared the worst, until now he had held out hope that he could salvage his old life. Unable to avoid the stark truth any longer, he sat, helpless and paralyzed, wide eyes locked onto Cheryl. She alternately clenched and opened her fists as she simmered, then threw her hands into the air with a despairing wail and stormed out of the kitchen.

Dwight had just been served an eviction order to leave his own life, and he shook for several minutes after Cheryl had left the room. Finally, a convulsion ran from his head to his toes, and he recovered his senses enough to go to his truck and rummage around in the glove compartment, hoping to find the pack of stale cigarettes from dinner at Josie's with Darlene. Once he had found it, he walked to the stream to smoke while his nerves recovered, wondering what he would do now, where he would go. He laughed bitterly: He had nothing to do, nowhere to go.

Nowhere to go.

The words were shocking in their simplicity and their naked truth. He was homeless. The thought of moving in with Darlene flitted through his mind, but he dismissed it. He had hoped she would be his new life, but now it came to it, he realized what he had known in his heart all along, that the last thing a beautiful young woman needed was an unemployed, married man living with her. Until his separation with Cheryl was final, Darlene wouldn't dream of letting him that close. And because his community was the Church of the Epistles, alienation from Cheryl meant alienation from his friends.

Nowhere to go and the rest of my life to get there.

For a brief moment, a feeling of freedom made him feel lightheaded, but then the hollowness of his victory hit him: He had been freed from the very things that made his life meaningful, and freed to do... nothing. He felt sick as he put his cigarettes in his pocket and stood up, attempting to kid himself that he was ready to leave. But ready or not, it was time, and he hopped into his truck, driving to the county line, where he sought out a small anonymous bar from which he bought a bottle of bourbon. Then he drove to the Walmart, parked in the far corner of the wide-open tarmac lot, and lay in the back of his pickup, watching the sun set and the stars rise until he passed out.

Chapter Twenty-Two

Jessica spread the cream cheese on her bagel with slow strokes, savoring her anticipation of its texture and taste. The short wall next to the Piggly Wiggly, on which she now sat, had replaced the fence by the gas station as her favorite hang-out, and it had neither the gas station's now-unpleasant association with Alison nor the leering presence of Shawn Hickman. More importantly, the grocery store sold excellent bagels, Jessica's current, pregnancy-induced, craving. She ate one for breakfast most days—Sam kept the trailer well-stocked—and when she could, she enjoyed walking into town and paying a modest premium to select a fresh bagel from the wide range at the grocery store's bakery counter. But she usually brought a knife and her own cream cheese from home to offset the extravagance.

"Clark, I don't see how you can ever set foot in that church again," she said in a matter-of-fact voice, placing her knife on the wall beside her and holding her bagel high in a two-handed gesture of reverence. To emphasize her point, she said, "I really don't see how you can," before taking an impossibly large mouthful and turning to look at him, her chipmunk cheeks bulging.

The murder of the week before and the abrasive presence of the FBI were becoming a part of everyday life in Wilkeston, but the disappearance of four high school students was challenging loyalties and causing an undercurrent of distrust. Jessica knew Clark had been as revolted as she had been by the mockery of Peter's funeral and that the suspected complicity of the minister in the disappearance of the murderers festered within him, though he hadn't wanted to discuss it. He had finally snapped just before coming to meet Jessica, when he had told his mother he wouldn't go to church with her tomorrow.

"Jessica, I feel so guilty. When I left this morning, she looked so lonely. First Dad, then Robbie, now me; we've all left her."

"You haven't done anything of the sort. You've just told her that you can't go to a church run by murderers."

Clark smiled. "It's not run by murderers, Jess."

Conflicting emotions raged inside Jessica for a moment: anger at Clark's defense of the Kidds played against her happiness that he could still smile. But by the time she had finished her mouthful, the conflict had subsided.

"Clark, I know you feel terrible that Robbie's involved, but there's nothing you can do, and you're right to avoid the church. You know what Colby did to me, and now it looks like he's involved in Peter's murder, and Pastor Kidd has to be involved, too. I know he lied about what happened with me. Heck," she tore off another chunk of bagel with her teeth and spoke through the cream cheese, "I bet both he and your mom know where Peter's killers are. That church is sick, Clark."

Clark hung his head, and Jessica ate in silence. Several minutes passed before either of them spoke again.

"You're right, Jess. It's just… I don't know what to do. I mean, Mom's all alone without me, and whatever he's done, Robbie's my brother." Clark lifted his head and spoke with passion. "He's my brother, Jess, my own flesh and blood. We used to throw baseball in the backyard and go to the pool together. We used to talk. What should I do?"

Jessica finished the last mouthful of bagel, licked her fingers, and hopped off the wall, knowing that nothing she could say right now would help. She cleaned the knife with her lips and dropped it into the plastic bag that contained her tub of cream cheese and the bag of bagels she had purchased to take home.

Clark flopped down to join her, a wilted flower. Jessica didn't speak, but instead stood on tiptoes, reached forward with her lips, and kissed him on the cheek, then turned and started walking back to the trailer. Clark fell in beside her and reached out to touch her hand, silently offering to relieve her of the grocery bag. She acquiesced, and Clark switched it in his hands to lock fingers with her.

As they got closer to the trailer, Jessica's thoughts drifted to her guardian, whom she had grown to love very much in a short time. She had been astonished at how caring he had turned out to be, at how naturally he had assumed the responsibilities of fathering a pregnant teenager. He had shaved, cleaned himself up, and was doing whatever odd jobs he could find for six or seven hours a day to keep Jessica in clothes, food, and school supplies.

She walked hand-in-hand with Clark up the gravel path to the trailer, delighted that Clark was going to spend the afternoon with her, but having no particular plans. There was no sign of Old Sam in the yard, but his truck was parked beside the trailer, and his constant companion, Bess, lay across the threshold of the open door, so Jessica knew he was home. The dog lifted her head and panted at Jessica's approach, her tail thumping on the floor of the trailer. Moments later, Sam appeared in the doorway, a smile from ear to ear.

"Hi, Sam, what are you doing?"

"Oh, I've been meditating."

"What, the whole time?"

Sam shrugged.

When Jessica had departed for the grocery store two hours before, she had left Sam sitting cross-legged on the cushion in his room, facing the wall, and from his dismissive answer, she knew he hadn't moved while she had been gone. It amazed her that he could sit still for so long. She had tried meditating a couple of times when he wasn't around, but the pain that had arisen in her legs and the distraction of her monkey mind swinging from thought to disconnected thought as if between branches in the jungle had driven her nuts. Sam had told her that she was no different than anyone else, that only by sitting with herself in stillness could she ever really see the behavior of her mind, and that when she did, it would start to settle down like a glass of muddy water. She had vowed to keep trying, because Sam had assured her that daily meditation had become important to his own spiritual and religious practice, but she could not see herself ever reaching the comfortable and compassionate peace of her guardian.

Sam turned to Jessica's companion. "Clark, it's lovely to see you. Will you be staying for lunch?"

"He's probably going to be here for dinner, too." Jessica was looking at Clark when she spoke and was glad to see the surprise that could have turned into a protest instead become a smile.

"Wonderful," Sam clapped his hands in glee. "I do love to have young people around."

Sam not only loved young people; his joy was infectious. Clark had brightened up, the weight that he had borne back to the trailer forgotten in the radiance of Sam's beaming face. Jessica remembered something that Sam had mentioned a few days ago and suggested, "Hey, why don't we walk up to Anna's for lunch?"

"You've just eaten, Jess," Clark objected.

"That was just a snack. And besides, I'm eating for two. Isn't that right, Sam?"

"I think Anna's is a wonderful idea. Let me just put on some shoes. Oh, and I guess I need to get some money." He disappeared, only for his head to reemerge momentarily like a child's to offer, "I'll be right back."

He reappeared a few minutes later with a slightly awkward expression on his face, removed Bess from the doorway, and pulled the door closed behind him. Jessica didn't understand his unusual expression until she noticed his clothes.

"Why, Sam, you look great. That's a really nice shirt, and those are new jeans, too, aren't they?"

Sam didn't answer her straight away and wouldn't meet her eyes, so Jessica cocked her head and caught his arm as he descended the steps.

"Sam?"

When he looked up, his face broke into a radiant smile. "I didn't want to keep embarrassing you by going around in the scruffy old clothes I usually wear, so I bought some new ones."

"Oh, Sam." Jessica released Clark's hand and gave Sam a hug. "You're so sweet. Thank you." She gave him a kiss on the cheek. "I'm so lucky to have two handsome men to take me out," she said, looking back and forth between her companions. "Are you ready?" They both nodded, and she turned to lead the way.

Anna's was a small diner occupying the ground floor and deck of a largish house on the shore of a nearby reservoir. Most of the handful of restaurants in Wilkeston had acceded to the popularity of the buffet and offered a selection of soggy, over-cooked vegetables and deep-fried meats. Even the Chinese restaurant had succumbed, although it distinguished itself by livening up a couple of its otherwise bland meat-and-vegetable combinations with cashews. Anna's menu, on the other hand, had not changed in thirty years. It served the best burgers for miles around, along with a selection of grilled sandwiches, all accompanied by onion rings and fries. From Sam's place, it was a two-mile walk directly away from the town along the creek that flowed down from the reservoir.

Sam punctuated their stroll by pointing out a pair of red-tailed kites and a kingfisher, animals at which Jessica would not normally have looked twice, but which, viewed with Sam's enthusiasm, assumed incomparable beauty. They arrived at Anna's before the main lunch crowd swarmed into the parking lot, chose a table on the back deck, and luxuriated in the Indian summer. Hungry after their uphill walk, they ate their food silently and relaxed afterward, sipping Cokes to cut through the grease that now coated their throats.

Sam sighed. "That was good. I could get used to this eating out."

"Sam isn't used to going out for food," Jessica explained to Clark. "He's quite the farmer and cook—but you know that." She looked across the lake, her eyes were drawn to three turkey vultures circling the trees. She gazed at them while listening to Clark and Sam chatting idly, and when the possibility occurred to her that Sam's wisdom might help Clark with his current problems, she changed the subject.

"Sam, Clark's brother's gone missing. Actually, four boys have disappeared. It looks like they're the ones responsible for that horrible murder I told you about and that the Church of the Epistles might be helping hide them."

"You mean that boy who was hanged last weekend?" Sam asked. When Jessica nodded, he added, "You told me that he was killed because he was gay, right?" Jessica nodded again, and Sam shook his head sadly as he leaned forward heavily onto the table.

"Hate is such terrible thing; it causes so much pain. If only people would stop and look, they'd see how it's their own insecurities that cause their hatred... " His voice drifted into silence as he stared at the table, tears welling in his eyes, which had swollen and turned red. After a few minutes, he shuddered and wiped his eyes, and with a smile looked up at Clark to say, "I guess you're torn between your loyalty to your brother and horror of this crime? And if the church is hiding the boys, I guess you're confused by the church's support of murder—and rape?"

Clark nodded, glanced at Jessica, then looked expectantly at Sam.

"All you can do, Clark, is be true to yourself—and I mean your real self, the one that you occasionally feel deep inside. Look deep. What does it tell you?"

Clark paused before answering quietly, "That all of this is terribly wrong and that I mustn't have anything to do with it."

Sam nodded. "Then that's how you must deal with it. It's easy to get caught up with what other people want, even loved ones, but if you can keep in touch with your true self, you won't go wrong."

Clark stared at the table, strangely silent. Jessica reached out for his hand. He responded with a quick glance and a smile but looked back at his empty plate. As the silence extended, Jessica's chest started thumping and her brow furrowed. "What's the matter?" she asked. A mockingbird landed on a fence post behind him. Clark still didn't speak, and Jessica tensed, leaned forward, and asked again, "Clark, what's going on?" Eventually, he squeezed her hands and looked up.

"Right before Robbie left home, Dad found papers or something in his room that made him think Robbie bombed that abortion clinic in Atlanta."

Jessica let out a horrified squeal and put her hands to her mouth.

Clark smiled weakly, apologetically, and mumbled, "Sorry, I should have told you before." He turned to Sam and asked, "So what should I do now?"

Sam shook his head. "You're not having an easy time of it right now, are you, son? What to do indeed. Well, first off, as a general rule, everything you do has unintended consequences. We have the tendency to act without thinking things through, and inevitably, we're surprised at the result. How much more true it is at a time like this. Anything you do will cause huge ripples. I've found over the years it's best to be sure before you do anything to understand how it will affect others."

"But, Sam," Jessica interrupted, "everything you do is spontaneous."

Sam shrugged and grinned at her. "I know. It doesn't make sense, does it?" He looked back at Clark, serious once again. "Clark, you need to take some quiet time with this. If it were me, I would meditate and the answer would gradually become clearer, but if you're not used to meditating, then pray. Kneel down, pray your heart out, and then listen. The key is the listening—that's really all meditating is. God will reveal the answer to you if your question is sincere and if you really listen for His answer."

After another long silence, Jessica asked the table, "Could Clark stay with us for a while?"

Clark protested, but she cut him off. "Your home is a mess and your family's even more screwed up than mine."

They fell into a sullen silence.

Sam looked back and forth between them for a while and eventually said, "The problem, Jessica, is that it's not my decision. If Clark needs the clothes off my back or the roof over my head, then they're his, but I can't take him away from his family, however dysfunctional they are." Sam turned his attention to Clark. "You have to work this through yourself. There's an old saying in Eastern religions about leaving home while still living at home. You have to try to help your family but not get involved. If you want a haven or a friendly voice, my door is always open, but you can't run away completely—at least not yet.

"Anyway," Sam's voice brightened, "right now it's a beautiful day and we've got all afternoon with nothing to do and nowhere to go, and it's downhill all the way back." Sam's infectious smile once more split his face, and Clark and Jessica couldn't resist returning it. "I tell you what," Sam said to Clark, "Jessica's told me about your dad. Why don't you call him and see if he wants to come over this afternoon? I'd love to meet him."

"Oh, Clark, that's a wonderful idea!" Jessica clasped her hands in front of her face in glee.

Clark looked back and forth between his companions, and a smile broke across his face. "I'd like him to meet the both of you, as well," he agreed

"Great," Sam replied. "There's a phone inside, why don't you see if they'll let you use it? We'll just enjoy the view while we wait."

Chapter Twenty-Three

Dwight was awakened by the sound of his cell phone. He groaned as he stirred and wondered who could be calling. He slipped out from under Darlene's leg, letting the fingers of one hand linger on her hip while reaching with the other to the floor to pull the phone out of his trouser pocket. The number on the screen was not familiar, so he dropped the phone on the floor, let the call cut to voicemail, and snuggled up against Darlene's warmth. It had been only twenty-four hours since the last time his phone had awakened him, still drunk, in the back of his pickup, twenty-four hours since Darlene had told him that her weekend plans had changed and she wanted him to come over Friday night. Curled up against her this morning, he was so happy that he pushed aside questions of whether her behavior was related to his contribution to her college fund. All that mattered was the wonderful way she had satisfied his every unspoken desire.

His phone rang again, and, seeing the same number, he decided not to ignore it. Rolling onto his back, he snapped it open and put it to his ear.

"Hello?"

"Hi, Dad, it's me."

"Clark!" Dwight exclaimed, louder than he would have wished, and jerked upright. He glanced anxiously at Darlene, saw with relief that his outburst hadn't woken her up, and whispered into the phone, "Clark, it's great to hear from you, but it's so early."

"Dad, it's lunchtime! But you sound like you're busy. I'll call back later."

"No, I'm up," Dwight said, reaching out with his voice. After a moment of silence, he added, desperately, "Clark?"

"I'm still here, Dad."

There was a pregnant pause during which Dwight's panic subsided and was replaced by guilt. His son needed him, yet here he was, at midday on Saturday, a dirty old man sleeping with a woman young enough to be his daughter. Dwight was filled with self-loathing and a belief that he was no longer worthy to help Clark. And yet, though he felt responsible for everything that had gone wrong with the family, he was the only father Clark had, and it was his responsibility to respond—and God knows his heart ached to be with the boy. He summoned the courage to speak.

"So how are you, Clark?"

"Fine." Another long pause followed, during which Dwight struggled to find something to say. Eventually, Clark broke the silence. "How are you, Dad?"

"Oh, I'm fine too," Dwight answered. After an uncomfortable silence, he laughed. "Clark, I'm sorry; this is silly. Your mom and me, we... well, we—"

"I know, Dad."

"And what with your brother and... " Dwight's throat constricted, and tears filled his eyes. He could not bring himself to talk about Robbie, but this time, Clark didn't fill the cavernous silence. Eventually, Dwight forced himself to continue, "Clark, I... you... it's been difficult. I haven't known what to say, so I guess I haven't said anything."

"Me, too."

"Clark, I miss you. It's difficult for me to be at the house right now, what with your ma and all, and with Robbie gone. You're all I have left to call family." He wanted to say more, but it took a long while to summon up the courage. "I love you, Clark."

Boy, that was hard—but why?

"What are you doing this afternoon, Dad?"

Dwight felt a thrill of anticipation as he answered, "Nothing."

"I've got a couple of friends I'd like you to meet. They're cool, and I think you'll like them. What do you say?"

"I'd like that a lot, Clark. I'd like that an awful lot."

"Do you know where Old Sam lives? Down Old Charles toward the end on the right?"

Dwight started to picture the road, but just then, Darlene rolled over beside him and raised her arm above her head. The sheet slid back, exposing skin that shimmered in the sunlight streaming through the bedside window. Her breasts seemed to shine as her chest rose and fell with her breathing. Confident that he could find his way, Dwight let his mind drift from Clark and grunted, "Sure."

"You want to come over in about an hour?"

"That's great, I'll see you then."

The phone lingered against Dwight's ear for several moments as he watched Darlene. He had lost Cheryl, and Robbie was going to jail—or worse—but there was still hope for Clark. He needed to be a father to the boy, needed to give him an alternative to the extremism of his mother and his elder brother. And he needed to leave Darlene. He reached out with his hand to shake her gently, to wake her, to say goodbye, but she was so beautiful, her body so immaculate.

His hand, instead of rocking Darlene's shoulder to wake her, smoothed her hair away from her ear. He closed the phone in his other hand and dropped it onto the floor behind the bed, then nuzzled up to Darlene's neck, nibbling gently, while his hand slid under the sheets. Darlene simpered and rolled onto her back, casting the sheet aside and opening her eyes, and Dwight sat up and gazed at her as she lay, patient and inviting.

He might be a few minutes late meeting Clark.

*　　*　　*

Dwight drove slowly up the dead-end road that he thought led to Old Sam's place, peering through the woods that lined both sides of the road to look for a driveway. He regretted his earlier craving for sex, which had prevented him from paying attention to his son's instructions, and he knew from the clock on his phone that it was almost two hours since Clark had told him to arrive in an hour. He was lost, and not knowing how to get hold of his son, Dwight was sweating in his panic, his mind racing. Years ago, he could have called operator services, and they would have known who Old Sam was, but now, heck, 411 was probably based in India.

The woods on his right ended, revealing a house, but the hope that sprang into his chest disappeared almost immediately; the building was run down and surrounded by scrub and long grass. Besides, didn't Sam live in a trailer? The road was petering out, and Dwight's heart was sinking again when he caught a glimpse though the tree trunks of a gravel track just ahead that ran off to the right toward a trailer. He mopped his brow with the forearm of his shirt, brushed his damp hair back with the palm of his hand, and pulled in, heaving a huge sigh of relief as his son stood up from the small group of chairs in front of the trailer and walked toward him.

Dwight stopped behind Sam's truck, turned off the ignition, and stepped out six feet from Clark. The driver's door slammed behind him as he faced his son, both of them motionless and expressionless. Dwight didn't know what to say, and the pregnant pause stretched as he waited for his son to speak. After what seemed like an eternity—though it could only have been five seconds—he said, "Hi, Clark," and took a step forward.

"Hi Dad," Clark said, stepping forward too.

They fell into each others arms, father and son reunited in a brief but emotional hug. When they parted, Dwight put his hands on his son's shoulders and said, "It's good to see you, Clark."

The noise of a door closing interrupted Dwight, and he looked up to see someone walking toward him from the trailer. Dwight had expected to see Old Sam, but this stranger was clean shaven and well dressed, so, confused, Dwight asked Clark, "So why don't you introduce me to your friends?"

"Oh, sure." Clark turned, his father's hands slipping from his shoulders. "That's Jessica," he said, pointing at the seated form, "and this is Sam," he added, turning and gesturing at the most recent arrival, who had fetched another chair from the trailer. Sam placed the chair with the others and continued to walk toward Dwight.

"I know Dwight," Sam said to Clark and then spoke to his visitor. "It's good to see you."

As his host approached, Dwight was finally able to recognize him. "Hi, Sam," he said, "You're looking really well." He experienced an inexplicable lightness of being as he shook hands and looked into Sam's sparkling eyes.

"Why don't you come over here and sit down with us?" Sam started to turn but stopped in his tracks. "Oh, this is Bess," he said, putting his hand on the head of the black dog who had strolled over from the chairs, tail wagging wildly, to sit down beside him. Her tongue hung out, and she looked up at her owner expectantly.

Dwight knelt down and extended a hand. "Hi, Bess. My, you're a good dog, aren't you?"

"Go on, Bess." Sam raised his hand and clicked his fingers. "You can say hi."

Bess sprang forward, her tail still sweeping in 180-degree arcs, to receive an ear-and-neck rub and then followed Dwight back to the chairs to sit down between his legs. Dwight rubbed her ears, relieving his stress and distracting him from his nervousness.

"Do you want some tea, Dad?"

When Dwight nodded, Clark poured a glass from the pitcher on the small plastic table in front of him. Dwight raised his glass and squinted over the top of it at the girl sitting beside his son. "I recognize you, Jessica. Have we met before?"

"You probably know my parents, Will and Jane Jackson?"

"Of course, you're members of the Church of the Epistles. Will and Jane are fine people. You live on that farm just the other side of town, right?"

"Well, actually, I live here with Sam right now."

A wave of nausea washed over Dwight as he remembered: This was the girl who had been cast out of the church for fornication. Involuntarily, his eyes fell to her belly, which she covered with her hand as if to protect it from his gaze. Dwight fought to recover his composure, but he could feel the sweat streaming down his temples. He put down his glass, with two hands swept the sweat back into his hair, and said, "I'm sorry. I know... "

But he stopped in mid-sentence as a terrible thought struck him. He turned to Clark with his mouth wide open and furrows across his brow. Clark met his eyes, but Dwight didn't know what to say. He nodded his head sideways at Jessica and frowned an unspoken question.

Clark and Jessica looked at each other and burst out laughing. Dwight's confusion increased, and his lower jaw worked as he looked between them, embarrassed and flustered, until Sam helped him out.

"Come on, now," he said, "that's no way to treat our guest." He turned to Dwight and said with a soothing voice, "I think I understand your concern. The paternity of the baby is a matter of dispute, but the child is not your son's. For right now, let's say I'm the adoptive father and Jessica is living here as my responsibility. Now, would you like some brownies? They're fresh; I just made them." He picked up a plate from the table beside the tea and held it out to Dwight, who took a piece. He forced a smile as the chocolate melted in his mouth.

"Well, I seem to have jumped in with both feet, haven't I? I'm sorry."

The laughter had settled, and in the silence that followed, Dwight ate his brownie and studied Jessica while she stared, distracted, into the distance, perhaps looking at a bird roosting in a tree, perhaps at the tree itself. She was a pretty creature, with soft features and a little button nose in the middle of a narrow face. Unlike so many of the teenagers he saw around town, her eyes weren't heavy with makeup, though she obviously lavished attention on her black hair, which shone brilliantly. But Dwight was not a fan of the short, boyish hairstyle she wore, though it seemed to be the vogue these days.

But she was carrying someone's illegitimate child.

Dwight's conscience squirmed. Intellectually, he understood the hypocrisy of his situation—he was sleeping with a woman out of wedlock—but in his heart, he knew a great sin had been committed here. What was Clark thinking? Dwight looked at his son, who was watching Jessica with big eyes, and realized that he no longer knew the boy. He had no idea what was going on inside Clark's head and no idea what his son enjoyed and what motivated him. Clark had been using his ability to disappear without anyone noticing for so long at home that Dwight had lost touch with his own son. But then, Robbie had obviously been foreign to him as well, and Dwight realized Clark's alienation should not surprise him.

"Jessica, I think Clark needs a few minutes alone with his dad."

His reverie interrupted by Sam's voice, Dwight looked at Jessica's adoptive father and felt a tingle run down his spine. This was the man who had intuited Dwight's family problems in the store ten weeks ago, and he seemed to be reading Dwight's mind again.

"Why don't you come and help me start preparing dinner?" Sam continued. "I think we might have company tonight, and I'm going to need potatoes and beans. Can you fetch a basket and get some from the garden?"

"Sure." Jessica rose and turned to the trailer.

Sam put his arm around her shoulder, and as they strolled slowly along, said, "Let's see what we can do with that chicken we've got in the refrigerator."

Dwight watched their backs disappear into the trailer and then turned his attention to his son. He had ignored the boy for the last few weeks but loved him desperately, and now that he was with him, he wanted to hang on.

"She's a lovely girl, Clark," he said. It had presumably been important to Clark that Dwight make a good impression on Sam and Jessica, but by being late and rude, he had blown it, he knew, and beads of sweat popped onto his forehead. The thought that his son's affection was for a girl carrying another man's child returned, and the beads turned to a flood. Dwight wiped his forehead with the palm of his hand while Clark stared at his tea without speaking. "Clark, what's on your mind?" he asked, but still Clark didn't speak. Dwight sensed a pressure cooker building, and said, "Clark, I'm sorry, I—"

"What's going on, Dad?" Clark interrupted, his voice taut, his fists clenched. "Just when we all need you, you run away. You get drunk, you sell the store, you shack up with Darlene. What kind of dad are you, anyway?" He shook his head and glared at his glass.

Dwight was shaking inside, the inadequacy of his parenting laid bare. With a couple of deep breaths, he composed himself enough to start speaking, and once he had begun, the words poured out. "I've not been there for you—for any of you—recently, and I know the family's fallen apart. I'm sorry, I really am, but it's a lot more complicated than you think. Maybe you're right, maybe I should have done a better job as a dad, especially when Robbie was younger, but I didn't. The Lord knows I did my best, but Robbie just turned out bad. And your mom won't come right out and say it, but I swear she thinks it's okay to bomb abortion clinics. We just can't talk to each other anymore. I've not made any money at the store for two years now, and it doesn't seem to matter to her. We just don't care about the same things. I want to be a better father to you, Clark, but I don't have the strength to do it alone. I need your help. I need your help to quit drinking—I've tried, but I keep slipping back—and smoking, too."

"And Darlene," Clark added.

Dwight saw a flash of hate in his son's eyes and wanted him to understand. "She's not a bad person, Clark. Believe it or not, she's helped me a lot." He saw anger glowing deep in Clark's eyes when his son looked up at him. "It's not her fault. Clark, I need you. Please?"

Clark let the silence linger so long that Dwight thought that they would both explode. But when Clark finally spoke, he was surprisingly calm. "Dad, I can't go to the Church of the Epistles anymore. I told Mom this morning and I know it's really upset her, but after what they did to Jessica and then the way they handled Peter's funeral, I just feel sick even thinking about Pastor Kidd."

Dwight presumed that Clark meant Peter Anderson, and though he had no knowledge of the funeral and no idea why Clark would have attended, Clark was waiting for him to speak to his concerns about the church. Not sure where this conversation would go, he said, "The church is at the root of what's separating Mom and me, too, but she's your mom, Clark. She's your mom and she loves you just as much as I do. She needs love and she needs help, Clark, and you're the only one she has left who can give it to her."

"So I've got to help Mom while you go and live with Darlene and see me on Saturdays?"

Clark's anger hit Dwight as a physical blow, and he reeled in his seat before replying, "Darlene wouldn't let me live with her even if I asked. I won't lie to you: I sleep over there sometimes, but mostly I sleep at home. With everything that's going on, though, I'm not sleeping well, and I just don't feel comfortable at home, so I'm usually up and gone before you get up."

"Where do you go?" Clark's eyes still smoldered, but his voice was calmer.

"Till a couple of days ago, I used to go to the store and hang out. Even after I closed up, it needed cleaning out before I sold it. But now..." Dwight shrugged. "I guess I'll spend a lot of time at McDonald's. Maybe you could join me one morning."

Clark turned his head to watch Jessica in the field as the air between them began to clear. This time the silence was comfortable.

"She's a lovely girl, Clark," Dwight repeated, following his son's gaze.

Clark grunted and, after a pause, called out her name. When Jessica turned to him, he said, "Why don't you come and join us."

"Sure. Let me take these in to Sam first."

After watching her walk back to the trailer and ascend the steps with a basket of vegetables, Clark turned to his father and said, "I really hope you like her."

"I'm sure I will." Dwight smiled from the heart, and it felt good. It was the cleanest he had felt in weeks.

Jessica bounded out again with a fresh pitcher of tea in her hand. She topped up Dwight's glass first, then Clark's. She reached out for his hand, and Dwight glimpsed the hand squeeze and the quick, reassuring nod Clark gave her before she sat down. It was only moments before Sam rejoined them, too, and, quickly assessing the situation, spoke. "Well, Dwight, I hope you'll stay for dinner."

"That's very kind." Dwight looked at Clark, who nodded his permission, and said, "If you're sure you've enough to go around, I'd love to."

"We've got plenty," Jessica answered for her guardian. "Now tell me, where are you living these days? Oh!" Her hand leapt to her mouth. "Sorry, I didn't mean… It's just, well, Clark's told me about you and his mom, and I just assumed… "

Dwight laughed, more comfortable after his conversation with Clark, and reassured in the knowledge that others could make social faux pas, too. "That's fine, Jessica. You're right; things are pretty rocky at home right now, and I was just telling Clark that, now I've sold the store, I really don't have anywhere to go. I guess I need to get a little place of my own."

The table fell silent for a few minutes, then Jessica piped up.

"Hey, Sam, isn't that house next door for sale?"

"What, that run-down, overgrown place?" Dwight interrupted, an edge of disdain in his voice.

Sam nodded, his face a picture of slow, considered wisdom. He didn't speak immediately, but when he did, his words were heavy and seductive. "There was a sweet old lady used to live there: Mrs. Douglas was her name. Her husband died years ago and her kids all moved away, so she lived there alone. She died three years ago and her son hung onto the place for two years, thinking he'd become a real estate tycoon in the mountains. Well, he never did, and last year, he finally decided to sell it. Only he won't put a penny into it. I used to help Mrs. Douglas around the house, so I know it pretty well. It'll need a lot of work, but it's a good little place, and if you were interested, I'm sure you'd get a great price. I'd enjoy helping you fix it up, too, and it'd be kind of nice to have a neighbor again."

"Dad, that's a great idea. You've got all that money from selling the store, and Jessica would help, too, and I could come and stay with you, and… " Dwight watched his son's gaze flicking between him and Jessica and smiled. It might just be perfect, a place he could call home, a place where his son could come and visit, albeit because of its proximity to his girlfriend. And there was something special about Sam, too. Dwight would enjoy having him as a neighbor.

"There's no harm in taking a look, I guess."

"Let me call the real estate agent," Sam offered, "and see if he'll meet us there after dinner."

Chapter Twenty-Four

Nic drew an emphatic red line on the whiteboard then turned to face his team of nine FBI and ATF agents. With his back to the charts, sketches, and pictures that covered the main wall of the bed-and-breakfast cottage that the FBI had established as their command post for the Wilkeston manhunt, he asked, "Okay guys, is there anything else?" He scanned the faces, placed his marker on the shelf under the whiteboard, and, to give the agents time to think, strode behind them to the coffeepot in the small buffet kitchen.

As recognition for his initiative in finding and tracing the lead that brought the operation to Wilkeston, the ATF had—reluctantly—accepted FBI leadership for this portion of operations and given Nic the break he had been seeking by placing him in charge in the field. He picked up a bagel, surveyed the faces one more time, and sipped his coffee. With a grimace, he exclaimed, "Why can't anybody find any decent coffee?" and threw his half-full paper cup in the trash.

His big break, indeed! Three weeks ago, the interviews and evidence had identified four missing youths as the prime suspects, but he was no closer to finding them than he had been then, and he didn't think he could stand being cooped up in Wilkeston for one more day. He knew the boys were being helped, but he couldn't find a crack in the local community to help him.

"It's gourmet coffee, man," answered Jeff, one of the team. "I found some at that Wriggly Piggy store while I was getting the bagels."

"Then I guess I should have asked, 'why can't anybody *make* a decent cup of coffee?" came the bitter retort. "Well, if there's nothing else...?" He looked around the table one more time and finished with, "Okay, let's just keep doing what we're doing. We've got the right surveillance points, and if we just keep plugging away, one of these little shits will show up eventually. Go get 'em."

The agents grunted and grumbled as their chairs scraped on the floor and they rose to their feet. The two agents who had spent another night manning a helicopter equipped with sophisticated acoustic and infrared heat-seeking equipment left quickly for one of the adjacent bed-and-breakfast cabins to get some sleep while everyone else topped up their coffee, sifted through the assorted bagels, and dispersed. After an extended period of chatting and engine revving outside—a cigarette- and social break—the cars departed for their assigned surveillance duties.

"So why don't you show me how to make coffee?" asked Jeff.

Nic played to his reputation for having no sense of humor and didn't acknowledge that his younger partner was needling him. He took a bite of his bagel—choosing not to admit that it was excellent—and put it on the table before going into the kitchen to pick up the bag of ground coffee.

"This looks like the real thing," he said, "which is a good start. Now unless the water here is complete piss, we should be able to get something going." He lavished attention on rinsing out the old pot and measuring the coffee scoops into the filter, knowing how this would antagonize Jeff. "There," he said as he added water, "let's see what that tastes like.

"You know," he said, turning to his partner and changing the subject, "You'd think we would have learned something from Eric Rudolph and Saddam Hussein, wouldn't you? We're looking for four boys who couldn't survive a week on an Outward Bound course, and yet we've got an army of agents and helicopters equipped with multimillion-dollar technology scanning the mountains all night. What are we thinking? I'll bet they've never been more than a hundred yards off a paved road."

"Who do you think we'll get first?"

Nic thought about this for a moment before replying, "Well, that Robbie strikes me as a tough cookie. If he were the only one we're looking for, I'd be a little more worried, but Philips and Jones won't last too long. And you know, although his dad's a complete son of a bitch, my money says that the preacher's boy is a pussy." He nodded decisively and said, "Yup, I'll bet we get Colby Kidd first."

"I agree. Why don't we concentrate everything on him for a couple of days?"

Nic's eyes sparkled. "He sounds like a spoiled little puke, too, so if we do get our hands on him, he'll crack pretty quickly. And his dad's an arrogant prick; I'd like nothing better than to take him down a peg or two." He nodded more energetically and said, "Yes, let's do it." The coffee forgotten, Nic strode back into the living room and looked at the board of names and assigned tasks.

"We've got Jack and Penny watching the preacher's place, which is good: Nothing's going to slip past them easily. But we ought to extend the radius and put a tail on the mother. I'll bet she's leaving food and supplies for the boy. And I'll call Mike and see if I can trade in those stupid helicopters for some dogs. Why don't you call Jack and see if he knows where the mother is?" He pulled out his cell phone, looked with disdain at the words 'No Signal,' and turned again, this time to walk into the communications room to call his boss.

Nic's conversation with Atlanta didn't improve his temper. Mike was unwilling to seek additional agents and was unwilling to make the call himself on providing dogs, based primarily on budget issues. He insisted on involving the Atlanta Special Agent in Charge and thought he might need to go "up the chain" from him to DC, causing further delays. "Fucking bureaucrats," Nic cursed as he rejoined Jeff. "They'll send us a couple of dogs, but it'll be at least three days before they can get them up here, and we can only have them for three days, and we're SOL on additional agents." He shook his head, and asked, "So where's our mark?"

"She's at home. Jack says she hasn't been out of the house for almost three days."

"By my book, that means she's overdue for a trip." He went back to the board and scanned his list of officers. "We can't take Penny and Jack off the house, and Fran... Hell, Jeff," he turned to his partner, "how do you fancy a surveillance job?"

They each poured themselves a large cup of coffee for the ride and took another bagel. Nic poured an enormous amount of sugar in his coffee, topped it up with cream, and enthused, "Mmmm, now *that's* what I call good coffee." He wondered absently if Jeff was smiling at or with him, picked up the car keys, and tossed them at his partner with the instruction, "You drive." Ten minutes later, they pulled into the parking lot of a small bank and Jeff turned off the ignition. They were facing Main Street toward the dead-end road on which the Kidds lived. Sarah would come into view if she were to drive anywhere other than her immediate neighborhood.

It was a long morning, during which Nic remembered with distaste when stakeouts had been his bread and butter. For five years, it seemed that he had spent most of his waking hours—and many of his sleeping ones—sitting behind the wheel of a parked car, on the boundary between boredom and insanity, and never quite sure which side of the line he was on. It was a little after two o'clock when the radio crackled into life.

"Nic? Jeff? You guys there?"

Nic brushed away Jeff's hand and picked up the mic himself. "Sure, but make it quick; we're pretty busy out here."

"Your tail's on the move. She's driving her own car, a blue Saturn."

"Thanks, Jack. Anything unusual?"

"No. She walked out of the back door into the garage, and next thing I know, she's driving out."

Jeff turned on the ignition as he and Nic sat up.

"Okay, Jack, we've got her now."

The blue Saturn pulled out and turned left in front of the bank. Jeff put the car into gear and slipped out a vehicle behind it. They made directly for the Piggly Wiggly, where the Saturn pulled into the nearly vacant lot and parked close to the door of the store. Jeff drove past the main entrance to the parking lot, slipped in at the far end, and came to a stop fifty yards away from his target, his view partially obstructed by the car behind which he parked. Through its windows, Nic watched Sarah Kidd get out and open her trunk, pull out a large blue sports bag, slam the trunk, and walk into the store.

"What on earth is in that bag?" Jeff asked.

"I've got a pretty good idea," Nic replied, then turned to his partner. "She's less likely to recognize you than me. Put on your hat and pull it over your eyes. Follow her into the store, and don't lose that bag even if she leaves without it."

"Lose the target but keep the bag?"

Your instincts couldn't get you into a whore's underwear!

Nic remembered Steph's words, and he smiled. *I'll show you, I'll show all of you.*

"That's right."

"Okay, boss." Jeff reached over onto the back seat and grabbed a loose hooded jacket and a grubby baseball cap. He stuck the hat on his head, pulling the peak low, and stepped out of the car. As he slunk across the parking lot, he zipped up his jacket and pulled the hood over the top of the cap. Nic nodded his approval: Jeff looked like a grubby manual laborer. So long as he didn't have to open his mouth, he wouldn't be noticed hanging around in the store.

Nic walked around the car and slipped in behind the steering wheel. He adjusted the seat and mirrors, readying himself for a quick getaway, then sat back and studied the trickle of customers in and out of the grocery store, sipping his cold coffee, and listening to talk radio. His coffee finished, he tossed the cup onto the back floor and continued to wait. A little over an hour later, he saw Sarah Kidd leaving, looked around for Jeff, and cursed. Where was his partner? Then he remembered, looked back at Sarah, and realized that although she had a couple of plastic bags of groceries, there was no blue sports bag. He radioed Jack and Penny to let them know she was on her way home, then called Francis and Rio to join him at the grocery store and be ready to help with the tail. He gripped the wheel in anticipation, his heart pounding as he watched Sarah drive away.

Your instincts had better be right...

Ten minutes later, Jeff crossed the parking lot at a fast walk. Nic turned the ignition and looked around. A middle-aged woman had preceded Jeff out of the store, pushing an overfilled trolley, and if Nic was not mistaken, he had caught a glimpse of blue fabric at the bottom.

"So you got yourself another coffee while you were waiting?" He nodded at the cup in Jeff's hand as his colleague closed the door behind him and pulled off his hood.

Jeff ignored the jibe and said, "I think we've got something."

"Red sweater and jeans?"

Jeff nodded. The woman glanced around as if afraid someone was following her, then opened the trunk of an old Chevrolet Impala and piled in a large number of grocery bags, followed by a big blue sports bag.

"Kidd bought a ton of groceries. Basic stuff: bread, pasta, canned food, as well as paper towels and plates. After she'd paid for them, she took a couple of bags of groceries with her but left the shopping cart with everything else in it by the door. That's when I went and got my coffee. I didn't see the red sweater come in; she may have been in the store for a while."

"She didn't go in while I was watching," Nic interjected, putting the car into gear to follow the Impala.

Jeff nodded and continued, "I didn't notice her till after she'd checked out. She walked up to the blue-bag cart, dropped two bags of groceries into it, then pushed it out the door; it was as simple as that."

Nic picked up the radio, pressed the button, and said, "Steve, I need an ID on a car."

"Go ahead." Steve was in the operational communications hub at the bed and breakfast. This would give him a welcome break from monitoring a dozen tapped phones.

"Nineteen eighties Chevy Impala, NC tag Bravo Foxtrot Tango Seven Two Niner."

"Okay, let me work on it." When Steve came back on the radio a few minutes later, Nic had taken two left turns and was headed out of town. Nic had also radioed Fran—who had not arrived at the store before the Chevy had pulled out—to tell him their route.

"It's registered to a Michael Hawkins, 402 Paluka Drive here in Wilkeston."

"Where's that?"

Jeff pulled out a map and raced Steve to find it but lost.

"It's just off Main Street, right downtown."

"Then why are we driving out into the boonies with the groceries?" asked Nic rhetorically. "Tell me about Hawkins."

Steve's answer was interrupted by Jack, who called in to let Nic know that Sarah Kidd had arrived home. When Jack had finished, Steve started again. "Age forty, married to Bertha, and get this: They're members of the Church of the Epistles."

"We've got the bastards," Nic said, thumping the steering wheel with glee.

The Impala left the city limits on the main road and after two miles turned off down a paved road. Jeff was following their progress on a detailed map and told Nic, "This is Nabana Road. It looks like it winds 'round in a loop that's maybe ten miles long."

A mile later, the car took another turn and Jeff clapped his hands, looking up from the map with a huge smile on his face. "This is Poke Creek," he said. "It's only about a quarter of a mile long and deadends into the creek."

Nic slowed as he continued on Nabana past the end of Poke Creek, slowing to read the sign and confirm Jeff's navigation. He turned the car around quarter of a mile further on and pulled onto the side of the road to watch the end of Poke Creek, not wanting to alarm Bertha Hawkins or the fugitives. If he was right, there would be plenty of time to get the full team in and surround the boys later. He gave Francis a radio update, then dropped the radio speaker into Jeff's waiting hand.

"Steve, tell me about Poke Creek," said Jeff. "Look up the power company."

"Okay." A few minutes later, Steve came back on with news. "Well, we've got seven houses on the grid. Five of them are current, one is overdue, and one looks like it hasn't had service in the last two years."

"Jeff, we've got ourselves four murderers hiding out in an empty house." Nic had a grin from ear to ear. He took the microphone from Jeff and said, "Steve, bring everyone in and figure out a way to surround this place. And wake up our helicopter techies. We need that high-tech shit out of the bird and onto a four-wheeler, and we need their asses over here with it now. Have them bring over the warrants, too. And I need to get on the phone to Atlanta."

Thirty minutes later, the blue Impala reappeared, and Nic watched Bertha drive away. Francis and Rio, who had arrived twenty minutes previously, pulled out to follow. Nic had instructed them to make sure they didn't let the car out of their sight because he wanted to be sure no one was lying in the back. He sighed and, in a whisper, wished Bertha all the best for her last few hours at home with her husband, Michael, on Paluka.

Chapter Twenty-Five

Jessica was straightening the collar of her cotton shirt in the bathroom mirror, preparing to spend the weekend decorating Mr. Cook's house, when she heard muffled conversation. Clark had arranged to meet at her at his dad's house, but she was a little late, and he must have grown impatient. She ran a brush through her rapidly growing hair, still damp from the shower, and was stepping out of the tiny bathroom into her bedroom when there was a knock on her door.

"Send him in, Sam. I'm almost ready."

It was hard to believe that in only three weeks since she had first met him, Mr. Cook had already closed on the purchase of the house next door—at an incredibly low price—and moved in. After three years of neglect, the four-acre yard was wildly overgrown, but the house was solidly built and in surprisingly good shape. Last Saturday, the weekend after Dwight had moved in, a small army of helpers had descended at the crack of dawn, and by late in the afternoon on Sunday, they had had scrubbed the place from top to bottom. Jessica, Sam, Simon, Clark, and Darlene had agreed to return and decorate this weekend.

"Jessica, it's Pastor Kidd."

Jessica scowled, her blood boiling. She surged at her door, opened it, and glared at Sam. "How dare he! What does he want?"

"Calm down, Jessica." Sam took her palms loosely in his. "For all his faults, Harris is a man of God, and he's not going to come around here unless he's got a very good reason. And remember the problems he has in his own life right now." He kissed her on the forehead and squeezed her hands gently before letting go. "I'll be in the living room if you need me, but he said it was you he needed to talk to." Jessica inhaled deeply, straightening her shoulders and forcing a smile. Sam was right. Although she despised Colby, the incarceration of his son must be a devastating blow for

Pastor Kidd, and the trauma within his congregation must be consuming him. But it was Sam himself who fortified Jessica. She could face anything if he was beside her.

Pastor Kidd was standing a few feet from the bottom of the steps, staring out across Sam's vegetables with his hands comfortably clasped behind his back when she arrived. He released them and turned at the sound of Jessica clearing her throat. His minister's robe swung with the motion, and he looked up the steps at her.

"Hi, Jessica, it's been a while. You're looking well." Jessica stood silently and waited, watching her former pastor closely. She felt some measure of reluctant awe that, despite his trials, he bore himself with the same composed confidence that she remembered. He strode toward the trailer and rested a foot on the lowest step. "Have you found yourself a new church yet?"

Jessica continued to wait.

Pastor Kidd sighed and said, "Jessica, I have some bad news for you. May I come in?"

"No."

The pastor retrieved his foot and stood up straight. "Very well," he said, "I suppose I shouldn't be surprised. You should probably sit down, though." He paused, but Jessica deliberately leaned her shoulder on the door jam, crossed her arms, and waited, making it clear that his simple advice was going to be ignored. Pastor Kidd sighed again and said, "I'm sorry Jessica; it's your father. There's no easy way to say this... He's dead."

"Dead?" Jessica snapped to her feet, her hands jerking out to hold onto the doorframe. The visitor nodded slowly, watching her. "How?"

"Your mother—God bless her—found him first thing this morning. When she woke up this morning she realized he hadn't come to bed last night, and she went looking for him. He was in the workshop, lying under his pickup. All the doors and windows of the shop were closed, and the ignition of the truck was turned on. We think he left the truck running and died in the night of carbon monoxide poisoning."

"Oh my goodness." Jessica swayed.

Pastor Kidd added, "We're afraid it might have been suicide."

"How's Ma?"

"She's not well, but her faith is still strong. In time, she will heal in Christ, but this is a bitter blow."

Jessica did not need to hear any more. She straightened herself and slowly closed the door. Pastor Kidd's last words crept through the crack just before the latch clicked. "The funeral's tomorrow after the service."

It was several minutes before she could turn and walk slowly, unevenly into the living room. Sam stood up from the couch to meet her and envelop her in his arms. She didn't respond immediately but soon placed her head on his shoulder. It was not long before her arms were tightly around his back and her tears were flooding his shirt. Eventually, she sat down and Sam fetched a glass of water for her.

"I never had a chance to say goodbye. What am I going to do? Oh, Sam." She buried her head in his shoulder again, slopping water from her glass over his back. Sam's patient presence was deeply reassuring, and eventually, Jessica managed to pull herself into a sitting position, Sam's hands on her shoulders, and smile at him.

"Well, I guess I should call Ma."

"Jessica, that sounds like a nice idea, but I'm not sure it's wise right now."

After a moment's thought, Jessica replied, "I know she'll be upset, but it's what Dad would want me to do." She gritted her teeth and walked over to the telephone that Sam had recently—and reluctantly—installed, picked up the handset, and, with pounding heart, dialed the familiar number.

There was a click.

"Hello?"

Jessica recognized with a surge of excitement a voice she hadn't heard in over a month, and blurted out, "Ma, it's me." The only reply was silence. After what seemed an age, she tried again: "Ma, it's me, it's your Jessica."

As the silence hung, Jessica's heart ached. She realized that Sam had been right, that this had been a bad idea, but she forced herself to continue.

"Pastor Kidd just came 'round and told me about Dad... it's awful. Oh, it's... " She swallowed hard and stammered in confusion, her voice cracking under the restrained need to cry. "Ma, I'm sorry—no, I mean... Ma, I miss him." She could contain her emotions no longer and blurted, "Ma, I miss you. I need you, Ma. Ma?"

Not so much as a breath came down the phone. Ma was either made of steel or had her hand over the mouthpiece. Jessica tried again.

"Ma, I need you."

She waited, but Ma offered her no release.

"I love you, Ma. I'll see you at the funeral tomorrow. Ma?"

The buzz of dial tone followed a click. In a daze, Jessica let her hand fall to her side, then slowly raised it again to replace the phone receiver. Sam's arms gently turned her around, and she fell into his chest, adding a deluge of salty tears to his already-soaked shirt.

"I should be there with her. It should be Ma who's hugging me, not you."

After a long time, and outside, sitting on the step with Sam and sipping her water, Jessica eventually pulled herself together.

"I'm sorry. After all you've done for me, you must think I'm terribly ungrateful," she said. Sam simply smiled and squeezed her leg. A little while later, Jessica said, "I think I'm ready to go 'round to Mr. Cook's."

"Are you sure?"

Jessica nodded firmly.

Sam studied her and finally spoke. "Okay, if you're sure you want to, Jessica."

"I think it'll do me good. Besides, Clark will be there."

"Then let's go." Sam reached inside the door and grabbed his tennis shoes, slipped them onto his bare feet, and tied the laces. He closed the door and walked without speaking down the driveway with Jessica on one side and Bess on the other. Jessica was surprised to see no cars, not even Mr. Cook's pickup, in their neighbor's drive, but the front door was open, so they went in and called.

"Hello? Is anybody there?"

"Hi," echoed down from upstairs, and a clatter of footsteps brought Clark careening down. He tumbled to a stop in front of them and looked at Jessica with concern. "Are you all right?"

The question was enough to set her off again. The tears started to flow, and she barely managed to choke out, "Dad's dead," before falling into Clark's arms and hanging from him, limp and helpless. Eventually, Jessica raised her head, wiped her eyes, and said, "Sorry." She looked around the hallway, and before Clark could speak, added, "I'm so glad you're here. Where's everyone else?"

"Simon's not coming till this afternoon, and Dad's gone out so that he doesn't kill anyone."

The words shocked Jessica, and she stepped back so she could look at Clark's face, her hands holding his. Until she had met Mr. Cook three weeks ago, she had held him in some measure of contempt, for what Clark had described showed him to be a weak man, but having now spent time with him, she had come to know Mr. Cook as a charming, smart, and witty man who loved Clark deeply. He was torn up about his wife and older son and was really trying to quit drinking—he had been dry since she met him. She couldn't see Mr. Cook killing anyone.

Clark shrugged to dismiss her unspoken question. "I'll tell you later."

"No, please go on." She squeezed his arms.

"Well… okay. This morning he went 'round to pick up Darlene and found her in bed with someone else."

Jessica snorted a laugh, then raised her hand to her mouth in embarrassment. "I'm sorry, I didn't mean that. It's just, well, it's such a *shock*." But as soon as she had spoken, Jessica realized that it was not a shock, and tried to cover her tracks. "How's he taking it?"

"Not very well."

Jessica was relieved that she had not offended Clark, and she encouraged him to continue. The tale was a welcome distraction from her own troubles.

"I only spoke to him on his cell phone, so it's not very clear, but here's what I think happened: He'd been to buy some paint and supplies in Baxton. There's a really nice coffee shop there, so he got a cup of coffee and a muffin for Darlene's breakfast." Clark's eyes lost focus and gazed vaguely upward. "I can see him now, happy as a clam that everyone's going to come and help him with his new house, and feeling really pleased with himself at getting a nice surprise for Darlene. He would have been on top of the world." Clark's eyes snapped back into focus. "But then he got to her house. I guess there were a lot of cars there, or a lot of noise; maybe the door was open. He guessed it was the tail end of a party that had been going all night and let himself in. He looked for Darlene and didn't see her. Her roommates must not have been around, either, because if they had been, they would have stopped him right there. Dad went into Darlene's bedroom with the coffee to wake her up. The way he tells it, he just opened the door and went in, and there she was, in bed with someone else. I think they were... you know... doing it. But Dad didn't really tell me. He just choked up, told me he'd be home later, and hung up. That was an hour ago. I've tried to call him back a couple of times, but he won't answer."

Clark shook his head and continued in a lighter tone. "But that's enough about my family. We're a mess, but Dad will be okay—eventually. How about you: How are you?" He put his hands on her shoulders and squeezed.

"Not very well." Jessica smiled weakly. "I called Ma and spoke to her, but she wouldn't say anything to me. I couldn't even hear her breathing."

"Oh, Jessica."

Clark wrapped his arms around her again, and they stood together in silence, Jessica's head buried in his neck. Eventually, she stepped away from him, sniffed, and said, "I'll be okay. Right now I just need to do something." She looked around to ask Sam whether he wanted to join them, but he had already discretely vanished to find his own chore. She faced Clark again and said, "Let me go to the restroom and wipe my face. Where will you be?"

"Upstairs, in the master bedroom."

Jessica washed and dried her face and looked at herself in the bathroom mirror. She saw the reflection of a spick-and-span room behind her, and for a moment, she yearned for a bathroom like this herself, but she brushed the thought aside. Right now, she wouldn't give up Sam and his tiny trailer for anyone or anything. She turned into the room and smiled as she remembered how dirty Mr. Cook's house had been when they had descended on it to clean last weekend, then chuckled out loud as she looked at the bath and recalled Darlene and her housemate Roxie arriving at the dinner table together that evening, giggling. Jessica had known of their arrival—although she hadn't seen them—when frequent splashes and shrieks had begun emanating from the downstairs bathroom that Jessica was now in, the cleaning of which they had obviously taken on as their task. When the girls had arrived at the dinner table, Jessica had looked with distaste at their wet clothes and hair and wondered whether they had accomplished anything other than making themselves and the floor wet. At the time, she had been very upset but had bit her tongue, and a little while later when she had excused herself from the table, she had been surprised at how clean the bathroom had been, though the bath had been full of water.

Jessica joined Clark upstairs. He had collected the small amount of furniture into the center of the room, covered it with throw cloths, and had started to roll paint onto the ceiling. He fetched a second stepladder for Jessica from another room, and they spent the morning together painting ceilings throughout the house. They encountered Sam occasionally, sanding woodwork and touching up the worst chips with primer. By lunchtime, when Mr. Cook arrived, Jessica's nerves had settled, and she and Clark were ready to paint the walls with the paint Mr. Cook had purchased that morning.

Although Mr. Cook was visibly upset, he was a lot more composed than Jessica had feared and jumped into the task at hand. Simon arrived shortly after Mr. Cook with pizza, and after a quick lunch break, the enlarged team returned to their work. By the end of a very long day, they had made substantial progress.

Clark or Sam must have spoken of Jessica's bereavement, because during the course of the day, with a minimal exchange of words, each of Jessica's friends hugged her and offered to take a break from painting Mr. Cook's house to attend the funeral the next day at lunchtime. Walking home in the dark with Sam, Jessica's mind returned to the father she would never see again, and she started to cry. She finally slipped into a fitful sleep at three in the morning.

*   *   *

The following day, Jessica and Sam pulled up in the parking lot of the Church of the Epistles and waited in the truck with the engine idling, separated by wooden white walls from the community that had once been so important to Jessica's life. Distress at her father's death was juxtaposed with nervousness, both at the thought of being seen by those who had so recently judged her—particularly Ma—and at the very idea of entering the sanctuary. A hearse was parked by the vestry door. Presumably, her father's casket had already been taken into the building. Jessica realized with shock that she didn't know who her father's pallbearers were to be or who would speak at the service.

She turned her head toward movement and saw Clark and Mr. Cook approaching the church steps dressed in somber black trousers, jackets, and ties. Simon, similarly attired and with his aunt on his arm, was walking across the parking lot on a converging path. Jessica turned to Sam, who cocked his head, questioning. She nodded and looked down at her hands. Sam walked around the truck to help her descend and she leaned on his arm as they crossed to where her friends tried to smile and hugged her wordlessly.

The door of the church opened, indicating the end of the service, and a few people drifted out into the daylight. The six companions took their cue and entered, Jessica, clinging to Sam's arm, in the lead. The majority of the congregation remained for the funeral service. At the head of the aisle, Pastor Kidd was working with the funeral-home staff to arrange the coffin. Even in her distress, Jessica couldn't miss the sideways glances and the whispered conversations as she walked up the aisle and followed Sam into a pew halfway up the church. Clark slipped in after her, and with Clark's hand on her lap, his fingers entwined in hers, and Sam on her other side, Jessica waited as patiently and calmly as she could.

When Pastor Kidd finally spoke, his rich voice filled the church, and the quiet murmur in the congregations subsided. "Dearly beloved, we are gathered here today to say farewell to a good man," he said. "Will Jackson was a member of this church, and a good husband and father. He was a good friend to many of us." Pastor Kidd stepped forward, shaking his head and continuing more quietly, "This has been a very difficult year for Will and Jane Jackson, and it surely took its toll on both of them. They had difficult choices to make, choices that would have tested the faith of the strongest believer."

Jessica looked down angrily and breathed deeply.

"But through it all, Will was a loyal and committed husband to Jane, and he always found time to retool himself in his workshop." Pastor Kidd broke into a chuckle, and his tone became conversational. "Boy, did he love that shop. It seemed like every time I went 'round to visit the Jacksons, I'd find him on his back under the truck. It will be a permanent mystery to me when he ever found time to work on the farm."

But then the pastor stiffened his back and his tone as he said, "We will never know for sure what happened on Friday night. Did he just fall asleep while he was working, or did he leave the engine on with the intent of killing himself? Will Jackson was a strong man with strong faith, and he was deeply committed to Jane, so we have good reason to hope that it was an accident. When you pray for Will, be sure to remember this."

Jessica looked up, confusion pushing her anger aside. What had Pastor Kidd said yesterday? Something wasn't quite right, though she had only registered his words subconsciously, and she had to work hard to remember. But when the words came back, they hit her hard.

"… It might have been suicide."

Suicide.

Jessica's world swirled into darkness. Her mind spun, and the room filled with shadows. She heard no more of the eulogies or readings by life-long friends, was oblivious to the helping hands of Clark and Sam that guided her back out to the truck for the funeral procession, and was unaware of the formality of the burial itself.

Suicide.

If her father had taken his own life, he was damned, and it was her fault. The man who had raised her, the man who—despite the wonderful time she was having with Sam and Clark—she still loved more than anyone in the world, had been driven by her sin into the eternal fire. All the wonderful moments they had experienced together were gone forever, expunged in the instant he decided to take his own life. Jessica's terror was unspeakable.

Although she didn't pay attention to the burial, she knew when it was over. As the assembly started to dissolve, she broke away from Clark's consoling arm and made her way to Ma, who was being comforted on the shoulder of a church elder in the front row of the small graveyard gathering. Jessica knelt before Ma, put clasped hands on the older woman's knees, looked up into a tearstained face, and said, "Ma, I'm sorry."

Jessica just wanted to be with Ma, wanted the exile to end. Her grief was larger than the mortal death of her father—it was for his eternal damnation, and for the pain and aching emptiness that she knew was as unbearable for Ma as for her. Not knowing what to say, she repeated what she always said when she knew she had upset Ma. "I'm sorry."

But this time Ma didn't wipe the tears from her eyes and smile down, didn't lose her fingers in Jessica's hair, pulling her daughter into a hug. This time, she sat motionless, her lips curled down at the corners in disgust. This time, the eyes that stared at Jessica's hands resting on her knees narrowed, and the brow above them furrowed.

Pastor Kidd stepped forward and said, "Jessica, I don't think this is the best time to remind your mother of what you've done." His voice was soothing and the touch of his hands on her shoulders gentle, though it made Jessica want to scream at him to leave her alone. She couldn't resist his mesmerizing tone of voice, though, and the pressure of his hands, and she stood.

The spell was broken by Sam, who interrupted roughly, replaced Pastor Kidd's hands with his own, and said, "I don't think Jessica needs to be subjected to any more insinuations of guilt."

Jessica looked over her shoulder as if waking from a dream and saw Sam's intense gaze concentrated on Ma. He said, "Mrs. Jackson, please permit me to offer you my condolences, which are of the gravest kind. I know your grief must be unbearable. I sincerely hope that, with time, it will heal, and that you will come to realize your salvation cannot be found by continuing to punish yourself and everyone who loves you.

"Now we should leave you in the comfort of your community. If there is anything Jessica and I can reasonably do to help ease your pain, you need only ask. Good day, Mrs. Jackson. Pastor Kidd." Sam nodded formally to Jessica's mother, then to Pastor Kidd, slipped his arm around Jessica's shoulder, and turned toward the truck.

But they were stopped by a question.

"Sam?"

"Yes, Pastor Kidd?" Jessica felt Sam's balance shift as he turned his head to look over his shoulder.

"Do you think we might have a word?"

"Of course. Clark, would you?"

Clark slid comfortably between Sam and Jessica, his arm seamlessly slipping around her shoulder, and led Jessica toward Sam's truck while Sam turned to face Pastor Kidd.

*   *   *

Pastor Harris Kidd had been in internal turmoil for weeks. His pastoral relationship with the youths responsible for the murder of a member of his congregation and the officer presiding over the investigation had burdened him with deciding what to do for all of them, and he had chosen a path which promised to be relatively easy and popular, one that would cause minimal conflict and allow the passage of time to wash the incident away. But when the FBI had come to town, Harris's passivity had been compromised, and he had been forced to actively obstruct justice. The investigation had also reawakened in him feelings of guilt that he was responsible not just for protecting the murderers but also for inspiring their actions through his teachings. When he had seen the youths arraigned and held without bail and had heard the coroner report on the suffering Peter must have undergone as he was brutalized, his heart had cracked, and when he had realized that his wife was to be charged with harboring a fugitive from justice, the crack had widened to a chasm. He didn't think he could bear any more vicarious pain.

And now Will Jackson had died, likely by suicide.

He had shared in Jane Jackson's suffering, grieving deeply at the possible loss of Will's soul, but it was not until the girl had stepped forward that the full weight of responsibility had fallen on him. He had ignored Colby's weakness for too long, and when he had sustained Jessica's expulsion, albeit for the good of his church, it had not occurred to him that his acts could cause Jane and Will suffering of a magnitude that would lead to death and damnation. If he had listened to and really cared for these souls, he would have found out the truth and acted differently, and Will would still be alive. Harris had sent Will Jackson to hell.

As he walked away from the gathering and Sam fell in beside him, Harris asked, "How's Jessica doing?"

"She has good days and bad days, but she's a strong girl, and she'll be fine."

Harris sensed Sam waiting and breathed slowly to compose himself. In the years since he had last spoken to Sam, the passionate evangelist who had been one of the bright lights of his father's community had matured into a man barely known to Harris. The pastor was acting out of instinct rather than any premeditated logic, and his stomach churned uncomfortably, but Sam was the guardian of the child whose life Harris had ruined, and it was time to start to make amends. He breathed deeply to compose himself and said, "I didn't know at the time, but now I do. Colby's the father of Jessica's child."

Harris had no set expectation for a response, but now that his message had been delivered, he waited for a pointed jibe, a sarcastic laugh, perhaps just a grunt. But none of these was forthcoming. Instead, Harris felt in the silence that followed an infinite patience. He glanced at Sam and saw warmth in his eyes, a compassion that was grieving with him, not judging. Under the power of the love that emanated from Sam, Harris needed all of his discipline and self-control to turn inward for strength, to compose himself so that he could eventually continue speaking. "I thought what I did was best for everybody," he said, "but I was wrong. I've been so wrong. It's time for me to accept my mistakes and try to heal them."

He was hoping that Sam would take the lead and tell him everything would be okay, but still, Sam waited. They reached the edge of the cemetery and stopped walking, turning to face the gathering from afar and standing side by side in silence. Still, Sam waited. The guilt of his actions weighed down on Harris, and after a long silence, he said, "Sam, I want to invite Jessica back to the church and confess my mistake to everyone. I want to do what I can to make amends." Harris looked at Sam's profile anxiously, waiting for the man's judgment, wondering what was it about Sam that engendered a respect that Harris had never felt for any person other than his sister.

After a long pause, Sam turned to face Harris, his eyes soft and misted with tears. "Pastor Kidd," he said, "what's done cannot be undone, but that doesn't mean you can't help. I don't underestimate your offer or the transformation within you that makes it possible, but I'm afraid I don't think it would be helpful to convey it to Jessica right now. She harbors great bitterness for the church and for you, and she grieves desperately for her father's death and her mother's absence."

The hope in Harris's stomach sank. He knew that Sam was right, but he ached to do something, to help Jessica.

"Time and love—Clark's love, an unborn baby's love, and, to the extent she'll have it, my own love—will heal Jessica. But there is a far greater good that you can do."

Sam paused, and Harris felt the depth of his gaze.

"Your ministry has followed the way of your father toward judgment and intolerance. It was this judgment that led you to close your heart to Jessica, to allow hatred and prejudice to fester within the hearts of certain members of your church until it exploded in murder, and to allow those you love to go to jail for hiding four murderers. True repentance can only come if you center your ministry on compassion and universal love."

Tears welled in Harris's eyes, and the hair on the back of his neck rose. It was all he could do not to collapse on his knees before Sam. It was not just his pride and the proximity of his congregation that prevented it, but the humility that Sam exuded, and the realization that his own obeisance would embarrass the man. Instead, Harris bowed his head, a sense of relief and purpose filling the emptiness of his heart, and said simply, "Thank you, Sam."

*   *   *

Jessica was standing beside the open door of the truck, facing Clark when she looked over his shoulder to see Sam approach. Clark squeezed and released her hands, bowed his head, and slipped away. Jessica's forlorn gaze followed the youth for a moment, then turned to Sam, who helped her up to the passenger seat, clambered in on the driver's side, and turned on the ignition.

"What was that about, Sam?"

"Oh, it was nothing, nothing at all. How are you doing?"

Jessica looked down at her hands.

With one hand, Sam reached across the cabin and massaged the base of her neck.

"You haven't done anything wrong, Jessica. None of this is your fault. It's a terrible day, but we'll get through it."

Jessica shook off his arm and slid away to curl up against the door of the truck, eyes wide with terror. "It was suicide, Sam, "she said. "Pastor Kidd said they thought it was suicide. My father's going to hell, and it's all my fault."

"None of this is your fault, Jessica," Sam repeated, rubbing her calf. He slipped the truck into reverse and looked over his shoulder as he backed out. "Besides, why do you say your father's going to hell?"

"Because suicide is a sin. It says so in the Bible."

"Where does it say that?"

Jessica opened her mouth but then realized she didn't really know the answer. After struggling for a moment, she tried, with less confidence, "Thou shalt not kill?"

"Actually, that's a poor translation from the Hebrew. It really means something more like, 'You mustn't murder.' No, I haven't found any evidence that the Bible condemns suicide. As best as I can tell, it's doctrine created by Saint Augustine and Saint Aquinas, and it never made sense to me, because a lot of the Catholic saints—arguably even Jesus—effectively committed suicide by goading the authorities into killing them."

"But everyone knows that it's a sin punishable by eternal damnation."

"Just like everyone knows about purgatory and the Trinity and souls ascending into heaven, even though none of them is discussed in the Bible. Jessica, even if he did kill himself, would the God that you believe in and love really damn your father based solely on that one act?"

Jessica struggled with the question. It didn't make sense that He would, but equally, she knew that the fickle, even arbitrary, power of God was far beyond her comprehension.

Sam pulled out of the church parking lot, turning for home as he said, "Besides, even if that doctrine were true and your father were to go to hell, I'll be there to help him."

"Sam," Jessica said in a sharp, disciplinary voice, "Don't be silly, you're not going to hell."

Sam shrugged his shoulders. "You don't think I'm going to heaven to have a good time if there's anybody in hell who I might be able to help, do you? Now, shall we get back to Dwight's and finish that painting?"

Chapter Twenty-Six

When Jessica left the church in a daze to go to her father's graveside, Simon didn't leave the church to support her because he had problems of his own.

When had he sat down in the pew behind Jessica, he had been immersed in her grief and not noticed his mother's presence in the church. It was only after Pastor Kidd had begun to talk that Simon's eyes had wandered and seen her on the other side of the aisle, two rows in front of him. She had stared straight ahead as if pretending he wasn't there, but Dad, sitting beside her, had thrown angry glances over his shoulder. Simon had nudged Aunt Jodi and pointed. She had nodded, indicating that she had seen them, too.

The sight of his parents had teased Simon's attention away from the service, and he had become increasingly distracted. He had tried to study his mother but because of the angle and the intruding heads, he hadn't been able to get a clear view. Restless, he had let his eyes roam around the congregation and had realized that he did not dislike these people. Rather, he had fond memories of good folk that he had known all his life, parents striving to do the best for themselves and their children, concerned citizens working for a better world, souls striving for salvation. Sure, there were bad apples—and he counted his father as one of them—but these were the exception rather than the rule. It was a shame that they had so poisoned the barrel that he couldn't stay here.

When he had noticed Peter's parents, he had smiled. They were such lovely people and had been so kind to him over the years; what must they have thought when Peter and he had stopped seeing each other? Perhaps they had attributed it to an argument, maybe even rivalry over a girl. Had they even known that Peter was gay? They must now, of course, because of Pastor Kidd's words at his funeral. Did they miss their son as much as Simon did?

Simon's gaze had moved on, and he recognized Clark's mother. Simon had thought his fragmented family had borne a unique struggle, but seeing Mrs. Cook, he realized this was not so. And there was so much more. He saw suffering, strife, and fragmentation in what before he had always seen as a harmonious, homogeneous community. Mr. and Mrs. Hunt, Darlene's long-suffering parents, for example, who sat quietly at the back of the church. Simon had wondered what kind of relationship they had with a daughter who had been embarrassing them for almost a decade, even after having left church and home. And Mark Pocock sat alone, without the wife who had left him amid rumors of his antics at strip bars in Atlanta, and without the children she had taken with her to live with her mother in Asheville.

But the known troubles were only the tip of the iceberg. How much more distress and pain were hidden from him under the veneer of salvation sought and attained, of Sunday's best and devotional music? Simon had found himself resonating with the unease of ordinary human suffering. He had realized that, despite the grace that had descended on this community, they were all still ordinary people who got sick, whose children got in trouble, who were tempted by sin. He was not alone.

The noise of quiet conversation and movement accompanying a mass exit disturbed Simon's reflections: The service was over. Mr. Cook, who was sitting next to Simon, stood up to join Clark when his son stepped out from the pew in front, but Simon looked across at his mother and waited, Aunt Jodi sitting patiently beside him. Mrs. Anderson nudged her husband as they passed Simon and raised her hand in a friendly gesture, and Mr. Anderson smiled and nodded. The Andersons' faces, though, carried an emotion that Simon had not seen before.

As the congregation filed out, Simon waited, as did his parents, until they were the only four people left in the building. A palpable tension filled the air, and Simon's mind flashed through memories of Gary Cooper readying himself to face Frank Miller at high noon, of the gathering of forces at the OK Corral, scenes from movies he had seen with Uncle Walt and Aunt Jodi many years ago. He rose and started to ease into the aisle but was restrained by Aunt Jodi, who squeezed his arm and whispered, "Be careful." Simon's father had also stood and was trying to shake himself free of Simon's mother's efforts to hold him. It was during this struggle that Simon got his first clear view of his mother and was shocked by a face that was pale, haggard and drawn, the face of a sick woman. Catching his eye, she looked away in embarrassment, giving up as she did so any residual hope of restraining his father. Simon was drawn to her, and he eased Aunt Jodi's hand away from his arm, a surreal calm descending on him. He was poised and knew that whatever happened would be okay.

Dad bulldozed out of the pew and stopped in front of Simon, shoulders hunched, elbows bent, and fists clenched, his leering face and furrowed brow thrust toward his son. Simon's reactions were sharpened and his confidence improved by his intensive karate training, and he ducked around his father, brushing aside the older man's efforts to restrain him as no more than a phantom, and leaving him standing alone, his jaw hanging, in the aisle. Simon slid along the pew to sit beside his mother, who turned her drooping head away from him. He gently put his hand on her chin and tried to tilt it toward him. She raised her hand and shook her head in token resistance but quickly succumbed.

At first, she wouldn't raise her eyes, but when she finally did, Simon saw into the depths of a sorrow that was beyond his comprehension. As his heart ached and tears sprang into his eyes, he wrapped his arms around her in a silent embrace.

A rough hand on Simon's shoulder interrupted the touching of souls and shattered the moment. Simon allowed himself to be pulled away and faced his father from the pew.

"Get your hands off my woman, you disgusting pervert."

"Dad, I have no argument with you. Please don't do this," Simon said, his tranquil stillness permeated—though not disturbed—by a growing melancholy. How could these two people he loved so much—for, yes, he acknowledged to himself that he still loved his father—make their lives so miserable?

"Come here."

"Brandon, don't," Simon's mother called in a desperate plea, grasping the back of Simon's shirt as his father grabbed the front of it to pull the youth into the aisle. Simon didn't resist his father, and the grip on his back loosened and fell away. Simon rose and stood calmly in front of his father, who released his shirt, looked him up and down, and said, "I should beat the living shit out of you right here and right now."

"Brandon," Simon's mother cried out in a horrified voice, "you're in a church!"

"What better place to punish a sinner than in the presence of his Lord," Brandon replied, not glancing at his wife as he spat the words at her.

"Simon," Aunt Jodi said gently from behind him, "your father is a violent and dangerous man. You should leave before he does something he will regret."

"It's okay, Aunt Jodi," Simon answered, not taking his eyes away from his father's. "I need to handle this." Simon realized that this confrontation with his father was different from his prior beatings, for he was no longer cowed by their father-son relationship or by his conviction that he was an

undeserving sinner succumbing to his father's just punishment. Not only
had Simon's karate skills improved vastly but, for the first time in his life,
he saw his father as small, weak, and morally wrong.

"Yeah, it's okay," Dad snarled. "He's going to repent for his sin and
come back to the Lord."

"Dad, I never left the Lord, and I still love you and Mom. Your hate is
the only problem here, and I can't stand to see it making both of you so miserable."

"It's not me who's making her miserable; it's the abomination she calls
her son."

"Brandon, stop it!" Mom was almost screaming, choking. She slid
along the pew and reached out to intercede, but her husband knocked her
hand away. Her attempt rebuffed, she turned to Simon and pleaded, "Please
go before he hurts you."

Simon smiled at his mother, keeping Dad in the corner of his eye, and
said, "It's okay, Mom, he's not going to hurt me."

"Boy, you're going to burn in the fires of hell, and it's going to start
right now," Dad said, his red face showing that his anger had reached boiling point. He lunged toward Simon.

Simon neatly swayed away from the punch and informed his father in
a deadpan voice, "Dad, you're not going to be able to hurt me. I wish you
wouldn't try." But this only intensified his father's anger, and the older man
threw himself at Simon with the ferocity of a cornered bear. Even knowing
that his father would be ineffective, Simon was surprised at the ease with
which he could evade the assault. Simon's confidence grew as he avoided
or blocked his dad's punches and sidestepped increasingly desperate lunges
to grab him. He propelled him into pew-ends or tumbling on the floor.
Twice, Dad managed to grab Simon, but before he could take advantage of
his success, Simon skillfully twisted a joint to apply controlled but excruciating pain to his father to release himself.

Dad stood, shoulders stooped, arms sagging, and stared at Simon,
panting. "What kind of demon are you?" He leaped forward in a last, desperate effort that was no more successful than the others, ended face down
on the ground behind Simon, exhausted and demoralized, and called out in
a pitiful voice, "Your mother wants only one thing: She wants to be with
you in heaven when you both die. Can't you just give her that one thing?"

"Dad, this is taking me time to get used to, as well, but you need to
understand that whether I'm gay or not has nothing to do with whether I go
to heaven. I'd be far more likely to go to hell if I had hit you just now."

Simon looked around and realized the distance they had covered in
their confrontation. He walked back to the pew where his mother and her

sister were now sitting beside each other holding hands. Aunt Jodi stood to make room for Simon to sit beside his mother, who was slouching, her face hidden in her hands.

"Mom, can't you understand? I'm not going to hell just because I'm gay." He sidled to her so that their bodies and legs touched and let his hands rest on hers.

"No, Simon, I can't." Mom's head lowered further, and her lips quivered. "Unless you repent, you're damned, and that's all there is to it. I'll lose you forever. Oh, Simon," she lifted her hands and grabbed him as if in desperation, wrapping her arms around his neck, clinging to him as if it were the last time she would see him. "Please repent, please come back to the Lord—to me—while there's hope."

"Mom, I'm gay, and that's all there is to it. Jesus said on the mountain, 'whosoever looketh upon a woman to lust after her hath committed adultery with her already in his heart.' It's the same for me. Even if I did decide never to have a relationship with another man, every time I was attracted to one, I'd be guilty of homosexuality. There's no way around the fact that I'm gay. All we can do is hope that's okay—but isn't hoping all we can do anyway?

"But, Simon," his mother started to cry, "I can't stand that you're gay and that I won't see you in heaven."

"Mom, you must stop saying that. Jesus said 'Judge not, that you be not judged.' He also said that no one can know about the Day of Judgment: 'Of that day or that hour knoweth no one, not even the angels in heaven, neither the Son, but the Father.' None of us can know, no matter how great our faith, that we are truly saved. You've just got to completely trust Him and let Him live in you as you live your life. You know that you love me and I love you, and all we can do is trust and live our lives as best we can."

"But it says in the Bible—"

"Mom, I've been thinking a lot about this, and I've realized that the world's full of people with completely different faiths who all believe they're saved. They are just as certain as we are. So why are we so sure we're right and they're wrong? How can our tiny little minds be sure we've really understood anything? We're only human, so surely we have to make room for a little doubt?"

His mother burst into uncontrollable tears and wrapped her arms around him. "Simon, there *is* only one Truth. Please come back to the light."

Their embrace was interrupted when Simon's chastened father said, "Come on, Rachel, let's get home," and pried one of her arms from Simon's neck. She pulled herself together enough to clamber into the aisle, turned to look at Simon one last time, and then, sobbing hysterically again, collapsed onto her husband's shoulder to cling to him for support as he dragged her up the aisle.

Simon despaired as he watched. Aunt Jodi slid back into the pew next to him, and he said quietly, "There's nothing left for me in Wilkeston; I need to move on."

"Simon, you're only seventeen. There's plenty left for you here."

"No, there isn't. I'm an outcast at school, and even my own parents think I'm damned. No one will have anything to do with me."

"Please stay here through the end of the year and graduate, even if you just do it for me. You've put in so much work already this year, and if you keep it up, you'll be able to get a scholarship to a good school. After that, you can do what you want. And you've got those nice new friends in the house behind us to keep you company, too."

As he watched his parents leave the church, Simon nodded: Aunt Jodi was right. He would stay in Wilkeston for her until he graduated, but not for one day longer.

Chapter Twenty-Seven

Nic Horn sat in the second pew of the Church of the Epistles in a t-shirt and jeans, listening to the background chatter of the assembling congregation.

Two months earlier, the FBI had surrounded and stormed the house on Poke Creek, and Pastor Kidd's son had been one of four fugitives taken into custody. Within twenty-four hours, emerging circumstantial evidence had placed Robbie Cook and Jason Phillips in Atlanta at the time of both Rosebom and Whatbom. A few days later, Mrs. Kidd and Bertha Hawkins had been arrested for accessory after the fact and for harboring a fugitive, and Nic had suddenly achieved celebrity status. The US attorney in charge of the investigation, and his own ASAC and special agent in charge, had flown into Wilkeston on a private jet for a press conference, and Nic had appeared with them on national TV. Within days, Nic had left the clean-up in Wilkeston to others and gone home to Atlanta and to new opportunities.

But there was one loose end, a piece of business to which Nic wanted to attend: He wanted to make sure that Pastor Kidd joined his family behind bars.

Nic had spent his last official days in Wilkeston interviewing the pastor and revisiting prior conversations, trying to find evidence that would bring charges to bear on Pastor Kidd, but he had not been able to find a crack in the man's armor. In the hundreds of hours of interviews now on file, no one had said anything that clearly implicated Pastor Kidd, and the attorney general was not inclined to indulge Nic's determination to continue until someone did. Nic could not rationally explain his initial intense dislike for the pastor, but he had hoped that it was reciprocal, that by riding the pastor hard, he could goad him into making a mistake, and it was with this in mind that he had driven to Wilkeston six times in the past two months to attend the Sunday service and to make himself as visible as possible. Nic was more confident than ever that Pastor Kidd had attempted to cover up Peter Anderson's murder, and he suspected that the acts of religious terrorism that he had been investigating had occurred, if not with the sponsorship of the Church of the Epistles, at least with Pastor Kidd's tacit approval.

The congregation settled down as the elders entered and sat on the pew in front of Nic. Pastor Kidd entered the sanctuary very soon thereafter from the side and looked at Nic with bright eyes and a brilliant, open smile of joy. Nic didn't have time to react before the pastor turned his head away and opened his arms expansively to welcome the faithful and invite them to "Make a joyous noise to celebrate the glory of the Father, and to invite His light to shine on us in these difficult times in which so many of our dear friends face federal charges."

The congregation rose, and the enthusiastic middle-aged woman on Nic's left joined in to sing along with the popular number in a powerful voice. She leaned into him, then threw her arms around his neck to hug him while a young man swayed energetically to Nic's right. After two months, Nic was no newcomer to this, but he still felt intolerably awkward. He tried his hardest to avoid physical contact with his neighbors, but after a while, and against his better judgment, he found himself beginning to rock, even to sing along, to songs that were becoming familiar.

Nevertheless, he heaved a sigh of relief when Pastor Kidd brought the music to an end and invited the children to leave for Sunday school. The excited young faces were now familiar to Nic, and as Pastor Kidd moved through the weekly announcements, he realized that he felt strangely at home. He recognized the Andersons, of course, but also the Hibbards, the Newsoms, and many other families whom he had come to know as he had actively socialized after his visits to church. He had initially treated their welcome with cynicism, for he couldn't believe they didn't resent him bitterly for bringing charges against nine members of the church, but although he squirmed at the proselytizing subtext of their conversation, he had experienced astonishing warmth, and a sincere—though oppressive—desire to save his soul.

Nic was relaxing comfortably when he was caught off guard. Pastor Kidd had invited visitors to stand up and introduce themselves, an invitation that Nic ignored, as he had done on each of his previous visits, but this time, Pastor Kidd pointed him out and mentioned him by name. He pressed until Nic raised his palms to decline an introduction.

"Special Agent Horn is a little shy, which I can understand after recent events, but I do want to acknowledge his presence. It takes a brave man to follow his convictions, even more so when his life is on the line, but this is something Nic Horn does every day. God has brought him to us today, as he has many times over recent months, to serve a purpose which only He knows. I am deeply grateful to Nic, for although his duties have brought me—brought us—great suffering, in the trauma of difficult choices and separation from loved ones, he has been God's instrument to help me rediscover a humility I had lost. Through my suffering, I have opened myself up to Christ as never before, and the commandment to love thy neighbor as thyself has come alive for me. Every morning, I wake up and feel truly blessed that I have been given another day to preach the Gospel of love and salvation. I pray that the Lord will reward Nic for his role in this inspiration by bringing him to the light, but I will not presume." Pastor Kidd turned to face Nic and addressed him directly. "Agent Horn," he said, bowing slightly, "welcome to the house of the Lord. May you receive all His blessings, and whatever happens after today, you will always have my deepest gratitude."

Nic's hands gripped the seat of the pew as if to hold on as one more layer of his preconceptions was ripped aside. For two months, he had been looking for words of hate and exclusion at the church but had yet to find them; rather, after a couple of awkward weeks, he had been invited with open arms into the spirit of joy and brotherhood that the community shared. And now Pastor Kidd, who surely knew that Nic's only reason for attending was to throw him in jail, was thanking Nic. The FBI agent's suspicious mind scrambled to find the duplicity that he was sure must lie behind the pastor's words long after Pastor Kidd had broken eye contact and let his eyes roam the church. Nic was reflecting on the meaning of the words "whatever happens after today" when Pastor Kidd spoke again, interrupting his thoughts.

"I want to tell you about my journey," Pastor Kidd said in a soft, gentle voice. Nic knew something huge was about to happen, for not only was the preacher uncharacteristically bowed at the shoulders, but the elders in the front row shuffled uneasily, stealing glances and whispering among themselves. After another lengthy pause, Pastor Kidd straightened himself up and began speaking.

"One morning many weeks ago, the phone rang, and Joel Wilson told me about the murder of Peter Anderson. That was a terrible start to a terrible day, but instead of going to the heart of the great evil that had happened, I allowed myself to become caught up in the discovery that my son, who I thought would be your pastor when I was gone, was a weak and spiteful child not up to the task. This blow hit me hard, for I had become complacent in my office and in my belief that leading this church is the exclusive right and responsibility of my family." Pastor Kidd lowered and shook his head, allowing several moments of silence to hang. When he looked up again, he had tears in his eyes. "Would Christ have allowed Himself to indulge in this kind of hubris?" he asked. "Would He have blinded himself in the way I did? Would He have allowed Himself to cause so much suffering, and would He have sent two souls to hell?"

Pastor Kidd paused and looked around the congregation, his arms open before him. Even though Nic was emotionally hooked, he couldn't help smiling at the rhetorical skills that flowed so naturally from the preacher. "Of course He wouldn't," Pastor Kidd continued," and I can no longer continue my mission under the cover of a veil of lies and deceit. I hope one day to return to this community in Wilkeston that has been my life, and that you will invite me to serve you once again, but I need you all to know what has passed." Pastor Kidd turned to face Nic and said, "Special Agent Horn, I plan to give you the information that you seek. I pray that the Lord will give me the strength to complete what I have set out to do today and that He will give you the courage to use this knowledge wisely."

Nic leaned forward in his seat and licked his upper lip, then, realizing what he had done, closed his mouth, concentrating intently. The moment he had been waiting for had come at last, though not in the manner he had expected, and he wasn't going to miss a word. But as the pastor held Nic's gaze and he saw tears well in the soft green eyes, he felt a stirring of love and freedom and compassion that he had not experienced since he had shared a year of his life with Steph more than five years before. He frowned, confused, and Pastor Kidd turned away.

"I convinced myself for weeks," Pastor Kidd continued, "that I was afraid of what would happen to you without me to guide you to the Lord. Can you believe that?" He looked around with a wide grin and eventually broke into laughter. "I thought that you couldn't find your salvation without me to lead you there?" He patted his chest and added, "Me, this conceited, nasty little man standing before you. What nonsense! A moment's rational thought would have told me how ridiculous the idea was, but I was blinded by my delusions of grandeur. I couldn't see that each of you has a salvation that is yours alone and that you have a wonderful community to nourish you whether I am here or not. When the police take me away to repay society for my crimes, none of that will change." Pastor Kidd stopped talking for a few moments to look around, then with tears running down his cheeks, choked out, "I'll miss you, but you deserve better than this."

Nic, too, looked around the faces of the congregation and saw for the first time that these people had found something that completely eluded him, a belief in their salvation. With bitterness, he contrasted this with the hollow ache of resentment at the center of his own life. He tried to push the insight aside and concentrate on the task at hand, but as he sat in rapt expectation, he couldn't push aside a darkness that was swirling around in the back of his mind, shrouding a place that he had never noticed before, but one that he was beginning to see contained glimpses of a different way of life.

After what seemed an eternity, Pastor Kidd pulled himself tall, breathed deeply, and said, "I am responsible for the death of Peter Anderson and for the bombings of two abortion clinics. I am responsible for ruining many lives and sending two souls to hell. It is my teaching, albeit it well-intentioned, that lies behind the horror in which we are now all engulfed." He stood tall and proud, and Nic saw in him the resolve and fortitude of a noble in the French Revolution being marched to the guillotine to meet his death. The congregation bubbled with whispers and the elders shifted uneasily, but Pastor Kidd only waited, eventually holding up his hands, palms forward. When the noise had settled, he continued, "It is a rare man who is strong enough to truly act only in the interests of others, and I'm afraid I am not one. Where I should have been preaching Christ's message of love, I was instead teaching fear. Instead of following Christ's life, which was a lesson in compassion, I was teaching you hatred of difference. And instead of practicing forgiveness, I was encouraging bigotry.

"I now realize that when my grandfather first named our community of worship the Church of the Epistles, it was out of respect for the practicalities with which Paul, as founder of so many churches, had to deal. Our name was intended as a warning that, although a church is a place of community that requires compromise and governance, we should remember the underlying message and not get caught up in the rules. It is in this that I have failed you. I have allowed the regulations to take on their own form and have allowed conformity and exclusion to govern, where Paul's intent was for wisdom and compassion to be brought to bear in an infinitely flexible manner to provide a harmonious setting for us to live Christ's gospel.

"Were this an error of ignorance, it would be easier to bear, but it is an error of arrogance, and for this reason, I wanted to share my experience with you so that you might learn from my mistakes and not repeat them. That very first day when I discovered the murder and decided that it would be best for the church—for *my* church and my dynasty—to cover up the crime and help the perpetrators escape, I was bowing to conceit. Not content with damning Peter by teachings which led to his murder, I decided to avoid the civil consequences of the crime, thereby encouraging all of you to believe the murder of homosexuals is justified, even though I did not believe it myself."

Pastor Kidd hung his head and sighed, then wiped his tearstained cheeks and looked up with helpless eyes. "What was I thinking?" He shook his head. "And at the same time, I discovered the truth about Jessica Jackson—that my own son had raped her and that his seed was growing inside her—and rather than deal publicly with this truth, I left a family to suffer so much that, eventually, a loving husband and father, a beloved member of this congregation and a wonderful man, found his waking hours so dark that he took his own life. By my arrogance and failure to deal properly with the situation, I condemned Will Jackson to hell." Pastor Kidd turned and approached the altar, where he fell to his knees, his shoulders shuddering.

Nic was not just stunned by the confession but, more than ever before, realized that he was drawn to Pastor Kidd. He had convinced himself that he was visiting the church to nail Pastor Kidd to the cross of the law, but he was now able to acknowledge that there was another, deeper reason from which he was hiding: Pastor Kidd was a living expression of a power that Nic didn't understand. Nic hated himself for his weakness, for allowing this chicanery to affect him, but, nonetheless, he was drawn to it. He knew that the wall he had spent a life building to defend him from even the possibility of spiritual onslaught was being dismantled by Pastor Kidd faster than he could reinforce it, yet still he came to listen. He resisted the message, though in his heart he knew that something wonderful was happening, something he could not understand.

Eventually, Pastor Kidd rose to stand, facing the altar, and the babble of chatter in the congregation subsided. He turned to face the congregation with a smile, a new man, and said, "I came here today to confess and to preach to you one last time, and I want to conclude by reminding you of the wonder of the Gospel. You are not all as weak as me, but I beg you to take to heart how strong our petty conceits are and how, if we let them take root, they can grow out of our control. Maybe we want our daughter to win the cheerleading competition or our son to take over the family business as a preacher." He chuckled. "Maybe we want our wives to be more grateful for the extra effort we put in cutting the lawn on Saturday or our husbands to tell us how nice our new dress looks. These are little things, but once we let them take root, they grow, and in time can lead to the murder of other cheerleaders—I know you've all seen that happen in the news—or, in my case, the avoidance of my responsibilities as a preacher. They can lead to conflict in a marriage and a host of other family problems. In short, they can lead to misery and suffering, and to a diversion of our lives to personal goals and possessions, rather than to the glorification of God.

"We cannot escape the simple fact that we are all sinners, condemned to a fragile, mortal life in which we continue to err, to make mistakes, and to sin—yes, to sin. The only way out is eternal salvation through Christ the Lord; Christ, the only perfect human being; Christ, who was God made flesh."

The cognitive dissonance in Nic's head and heart was building to a crescendo, the wall inside him now only paper thin.

"But Christ made it easy for us. By His living example, He showed us how to live our lives, and when He died on the cross, He opened the gateway for our release from this fallen state, the path to our salvation. Christ died to atone for our sins, and all we have to do to be saved is to fully accept that sacrifice. This is the Good News, the Gospel, and it is the decision of the elders, with my full support, that from here forward, this church should be guided by the Gospel of the path to salvation, rather than by the letters that interpret it. It is with this in mind that we have decided to change the name of our church to the Church of the Gospel." Pastor Kidd's voice reached out in a passionate tremble, accompanied by clenched fists and arms quivering with emotion, tearing holes in the flimsy fabric of Nic's defenses. "Accept the sacrifice of the crucifixion and let Christ into your life; accept the sacrifice and find salvation; accept the sacrifice and be born again. I beg you, listen to the Gospel, accept Christ's sacrifice, and enter a new life in Him."

Nic's resistance collapsed, and his world turned upside-down. He saw everything anew, brilliant and fresh. He looked at the congregants and saw each of them as a person of excruciating beauty, a divine creation. He saw God in His fullness playing out His will in every move that His congregants made, every breath they took, for each eternal minute. For the first time in his miserable, selfish life, Nic understood the power of the Gospel.

His mind flashed over the weeks he had spent caught up in the emotional rollercoaster of solving this crime: the excitement of the Atlanta bombing; the frustration of the ATF takeover; disgust at the pettiness of his circumstances; another high when he recognized the value of the information from Mrs. Garrett; helter-skelter, with a rush of energy, to closing in on "the gang," and the thrill of national TV; and most recently, on to deflation and hatred in the depression of loose ends. Though Nic had returned to Wilkeston to tie up the biggest of these—the pastor standing in front of him—he now realized instead that *he* was the loose end and the source of the hatred. Nic had spent the last decade of counter-crime rewarding his successes and drowning his sorrows in alcohol and sex, never seeing how self-centered his life had become. He had come to convict Pastor Kidd of his involvement in murder and terrorism, but he had instead been convicted of his own sin and had received his first glimpse of a spiritual life. He had been defeated by a pastor at the very moment that he should have been celebrating his own victory, but he realized that this was insignificant, for the greater battle had been raging in his soul, and his ego had lost its first real encounter with the spiritual message. He had seen for the first time the profound love that was possible for the spiritual heart and now recognized that his previous hatred of the Church of the Epistles—now the Church of the Gospel—was really discomfort at being around people whose conviction of salvation completely empowered them and yet was totally inaccessible to him.

"I know this is rather abrupt, but that's all I have to say today," Pastor Kidd said before turning to Nic. "Special Agent Horn, I have made my confession before this congregation, before God, but also before the civil authorities which you represent. I submit myself to each of this trinity, and I place my physical self in your care. I will wait for you in the sacristy." He turned and walked through the side door, leaving Nic sitting numb while the church emptied.

When Nic eventually left the church, it was through the main door, with no thought of arresting Pastor Kidd. Rather, he was in a new state of awareness, conscious that something was different. He knew that salvation was not inaccessible. He heard the song of birds as if for the first time and turned, with a broad smile on his face, to stroll into the woods.

Chapter Twenty-Eight

Jessica heard a knock at the trailer door and the warm exchange of greetings that followed between the two men in her life. The younger called to her through the crack in the partially open bedroom door, "Are you dressed?"

"I'm just changing Willy's diaper."

"So I can come in?" Without waiting for an answer, Clark's head appeared around the door, and he said, "Hi."

Jessica looked up from the floor with a broad smile. "It's good to see you; thanks for stopping by."

"You look beautiful."

"Thanks." She nodded in gratitude and returned her attention to a box of wipes and the baby's bottom. It really did mean a lot that Clark would visit this morning.

Clark stepped into the room, pushed the door closed behind him, and walked around behind Jessica. He crouched a little, looking over her shoulder, and said, "Hi, Willy," extending a finger toward the chubby, bare-bottomed baby. Willy was not yet old enough to reach out, so Clark nestled his index finder in the baby's tiny hand and was rewarded with firm pressure on his finger. Jessica sealed the diaper, flipped the bottom of the white cotton onesie out from under the baby's bottom, and slipped out from beneath Clark's arched body. Clark rolled forward onto his knees.

"Why don't you finish dressing him?" Jessica asked, pulling a primary-colored outfit with matching hat and socks from the top drawer of the dresser.

"This is nice," Clark asked. "When did you get it?" He picked up the boldly patterned shirt that Jessica had dropped beside him and examined it.

Jessica smiled and thought how sweet he was to notice these details, then kissed him on top of his head, stepped back, and folded her arms to watch. Clark made cooing noises and tickled the baby, then reached down to the snaps on the bottom of the onesie.

Jessica thought, "What a fine father he'll make," then bit her lip as her presumption registered. She spoke as if to help her leave the thought behind. "I'm going into the living room. Bring him out when you're ready." She walked out of the small bedroom and sat on the couch next to Sam, who put his arm around her shoulder.

"Are you going to be okay?"

"Sure," she answered, but she felt the tremor in her voice and knew Sam must realize she was not as confident as she pretended to be. Sam let her snuggle up and rest her head on his shoulder, her hand on the front of his waist, and she put aside the responsibilities of motherhood to be an emotionally insecure teenager for a few moments. But it was not long before the sound of Clark bouncing the baby and singing to him made her smile and sit up. Clark's toe appeared around the door to hook it open, and he stepped into the living room. Jessica enjoyed seeing him in this role, and it clearly brought him pleasure, too.

"What do you remember about your dad from when you were a kid?" Jessica asked absently, once again mentally projecting Clark into that role for Willy.

Clark shrugged. "I don't know. He's my dad, and I've always loved him, no matter what. I guess he loved me, too, but he was pretty rigid, and I never really had much fun with him."

"He seems pretty laid-back now, though," Jessica said, standing up. She smiled at the baby and offered him her finger.

Clark nodded. "Life's good for him."

It had not been good for the first few months after Jessica had met him, though. Dwight's torment at separation from Cheryl and discovery of his son's crime had been compounded by discovering Darlene sleeping with another man and by his wife initiating divorce proceedings. The terms of the divorce had been quickly agreed to, and the legal proceedings were now finalized. Other than $100,000 cash that Mr. Cook retained—together with the small number of checks he had written to Darlene—Mr. Cook had given all the family assets, including the proceeds of the sale of his business, to Cheryl. His small nest egg had covered the deposit on his house with enough left over to open the first Christian bookstore that Wilkeston had ever known, only a couple of blocks from the arts, crafts, and furniture store that had once been Cook Hardware. Mr. Cook had said this was a way of rebuilding a life gone astray, and the experiment in retail had turned into a flourishing avenue for Mr. Cook's own spiritual growth: He had become his own best customer.

Mr. Cook was now reconciled to life as a bachelor. As far as Jessica could tell, he recognized his continuing—though intermittent—relationship with Darlene as non-committed fun, and a fairly expensive hobby, but he was committed to his younger son. He had also acquiesced to Clark's request to set aside one room in his house as a sanctuary in which a small religious community led by Sam celebrated Christ every Sunday morning in the tradition of the first churches. The congregation had recently declined by one when Simon had left for college, anticipating majoring in chemistry, but he had been a faithful attendant until then and promised to be back at Christmas and for the long summer—though from his correspondence, he seemed so happy that Jessica wondered if he would return.

She pushed aside a wistful desire for Simon's presence today and attended to Clark's question: "Why can't I come with you?" Her face became serious, and she aged three or four years as she took back on the role of responsibility.

"Clark, we've been over this before: It's going to be stressful enough dealing with my mother without having to explain why you're there, too, and giving her something new to worry about."

"But why would I worry her?"

Jessica was patient because she knew how much this meant to Clark and because she had grown to love him so very much. "Clark," she said, "Ma's already hopelessly confused about my life, and you being there would just make it worse. Now please, I've got enough to worry about without having to go over this again."

"Okay, you're the boss. But if you change your mind—"

"Clark!"

"I know, I know. You do look beautiful, though."

Jessica stood up, took her son from Clark, and handed him to Sam, who carried the baby outside. She turned to Clark with her hands hanging at her sides.

"Thanks for coming over."

"No problem. It's a big day, and I want to make sure it goes well. I feel kind of useless, though, since there's nothing I can do to help."

"You're so sweet. Hold me."

They slipped comfortably into each others' arms and hugged for a long time before Jessica lifted her head to press their lips together. Clark was wonderful to her, and she couldn't bear to think what the last year would have been like if he hadn't come into her life. She placed her hand gently on his cheek. "Thank you—for everything."

Clark didn't answer but just smiled and kissed her again.

But Sam was waiting outside in the car with Willy, and they were already late: Ma would be getting anxious. She put her hands on Clark's chest and turned to leave, her fingers touching Clark's until, at the last possible moment, they fell apart. She climbed into the truck's cab, checked that Sam had strapped the baby properly into his backward-facing carseat, which had been a present from Mr. Cook, and put on her own seatbelt. "Okay, let's go," she said as Bess, who had accepted the need to cede her seat to Willy and lie on the floor, placed her head on Jessica's lap.

During the short drive, Jessica fretted about Clark. He had been so much a part of Willy's life that it didn't seem right to exclude him from the baby's first visit to his grandma, and yet she knew it would be a difficult reconciliation. As they approached their destination, however, thoughts of Clark faded and the butterflies took over. When they had arrived, Jessica needed Sam's hand to give her the strength to climb down from the cab. He even took out little Willy, wrapping the baby in his shawl and placing him in her arms, before picking up the diaper bag. She looked up, expecting her mother to step out and welcome them, then cursed under her breath at her mother's absence.

Why is she making this so difficult?

Sam rubbed her back and whispered in her ear, "Don't worry, and remember, she's as nervous as you are."

Jessica didn't answer, but just having Sam with her helped. She summoned every ounce of her strength and strode purposefully to the front door of the house that she had called home until a year before. The door opened almost as soon as Sam's hand hit it.

"Hi, how are you?" Jessica asked, speaking first.

Ma replied, "I'm fine," though all her attention was focused on Willy. "So this is my grandson," she said. "Hello, Will. May I?" She held out her arms and looked at Jessica, who nodded, ignoring her mother's abbreviation of the baby's name, and helped Ma take the baby.

"Aren't you a pretty little thing? And so alert. Look at those eyes; he looks just like his grandpa. Come on, shall we go in?" Without waiting for an answer, she turned and walked into the living room.

Jessica had wondered how she would feel returning to the house after an absence of a year and was surprised at how comfortable she was. The smell was the first thing that hit her—a familiar cocktail that she had never consciously noticed before. She identified the tang of old wood and polish, hints that must be Shep and Splash—though they never used to be allowed in the house—and oil and sawdust from the workshop, and under it all was a familiar, complex mix of several lifetimes of good Southern cooking and the faint odor of Ma's obsessive cleanliness. The delicate watercolor land-scape that Jessica had forgotten hung, as it always had, in a heavy and inap-propriate baroque frame on the wall opposite the front door; the ugly blanket that she had never liked adorned the only couch her parents had ever owned; a thousand little things combined to given her a special feeling of being home. She hooked her arm under Sam's biceps and let him lead her into the living room, where he insisted she sit beside her mother. He went to the far side of the room to sit in an upright chair beside the window, ignoring the closer and more comfortable winged armchair that had once been Dad's—presumably, Jessica assumed, out of respect.

Ma Jackson cooed at her grandchild, oblivious to the world around her. Eventually, she looked up at her daughter in a precious moment that transcended their differences. "Jessica, he's beautiful. I just want to hold him and never let go."

Jessica and her mother talked about sleeping and feeding patterns, the wonders of disposable diapers, and the bliss of being able to sleep through the night. Jessica occasionally glanced at Sam, who sat quietly and watched. After an hour, Willy started to fuss and, over a period of fifteen minutes, wound himself up to an intermittent cry.

"He's hungry," Jessica explained, sitting up and undoing the lateral snap-fastener on the front of her nursing blouse—another present from Mr. Cook—and putting a cushion on her lap. As Jessica reached to take the infant from her mother, Ma acknowledged Sam for the first time since they had arrived by scowling as if to tell him to leave the room.

"It's okay, Ma; he can't see anything, anyway."

But Sam stood and turned to look out of the window. Jessica directed her attention to the crying infant, whom she laid on the cushion. After adjusting herself over him, she put a hand under her blouse and helped Willy find the nipple.

Ma did not appear reassured at the appropriateness of Sam's presence, and Jessica enjoyed a brief rebellious thrill as she watched out of the cor-ner of her eye as Ma squirmed. But after a couple of minutes, Ma had begun to relax again, and when Jessica raised her eyes, Ma was once more study-ing the baby, enthralled. Jessica switched breasts and, after Willy had latched on, stroked his cheek in private rapture.

"Have you thought about when he's going to be baptized?"

Ma's question abruptly interrupted Jessica's peace, causing her to jerk her head up in surprise. "What?"

"Baptism. Have you thought about when Will's going to be baptized?"

"No, I haven't. Why would I worry about that until he's old enough to make that decision for himself?"

"Well, you know, he was, well… umm… "

Jessica was too stunned to speak and looked back down at Willy, steam coming out of her ears. When Ma didn't press the issue, Jessica resumed stroking the infant's face to help herself calm down. By the time Willy had finished eating, she had relaxed enough to look up.

"Sam, pass me a burp cloth, would you?"

He turned back from the window and retrieved one from the diaper bag while Jessica adjusted herself and secured the front of her blouse. When Sam had laid the cloth across Jessica's shoulder, Jessica lifted the baby to it and rubbed his back. Sam stood behind her and massaged her other shoulder for a bit before speaking to Ma.

"The truth is, we haven't thought about baptism, Mrs. Jackson, what with him being so young." Jessica tensed, but the pressure of Sam's hand told her to calm down. He must know what he was doing, and she had grown to trust him absolutely. "What did you have in mind?"

"Well, since you ask, I was with Pastor Kidd the other day, and we got to talking about young Will… "

It's Willy!

"… and, well, we had this idea that it might be nice for him to be initiated into the Church of the Gospel afore he gets too much older."

Jessica felt her hair stand on end and her legs tense with the instinct to jump up and scream at her mother, but the mysterious hold of Sam's touch stopped her.

"That's a very nice idea, Mrs. Jackson, it really is. Let us think about it, and we'll let you know. But right now, we really ought to get going. I'm sure you remember how babies are: Willy's going to want his nap, and I'm pretty sure Jessica could do with a little rest, too."

"Thanks for stopping by, Mr.… Is it okay if I call you Sam?"

Jessica smiled—Sam's surname had been completely forgotten, even by himself.

"Of course it is."

"Well, thanks. Are you sure you need to go so soon?"

"Yes, I'm afraid so. Come on, Jessica, let's get Willy to bed." Sam started to help Jessica to her feet.

The movement threw Ma into turmoil. She jumped up, swirled around stammering, and finally stood in front of Jessica to blurt out, "I'd be happy to help you look after Will, you know, like when you need a babysitter or… " The unfinished sentence hung awkwardly, and she glanced at Sam with obvious discomfort before adding, "Your room's just the way you left it. If you wanted to come back with him and stay—just for a few days, of course—that'd be fine, too."

Jessica couldn't restrain herself any longer. "His name's Willy, Ma, and I can't... "

But Sam's hand clasped firmly to her arm, his reassuring presence cutting off her protest. "I think we should leave now, Mrs. Jackson. Thank you for your hospitality; we'll see you soon."

Sam picked up the diaper bag and pressed Jessica toward the door. Once they were outside, he helped her into the truck and strapped the baby's seat in.

As they pulled away, Jessica hit the dashboard and unleashed her anger. "How dare she! We come all the way over here to let her see her grandson, and the first thing she says is that I need to give him up to Pastor Kidd. And then she invites me to move back in so she can get her hands on the baby herself. Of all the... " Jessica slammed her head back into the headrest and let out a growl.

"Your mother has a lot of suffering to deal with, Jessica, and—"

"She sure does," interrupted Jessica, "and it includes mine—and Dad's. She's been doing nothing but manufacturing suffering for as long as I can remember. And now you're siding with her, Sam. Why?"

Sam waited a moment before answering. "Does it really matter to you whether Willy's baptized as an infant?" he asked.

"I don't understand," Jessica said, frowning. "When he's ready, I want you to baptize him."

Sam snorted a laugh. "I don't know about that; I wouldn't know where to begin. But put that aside for now: If infant baptism doesn't mean anything to you, why does it matter?"

"Sam! It's just wrong. He needs to decide to do it for himself."

"And he will. How could it hurt him to let someone splash some water on him when he's a baby if it doesn't mean anything? Unless you're afraid there's some kind of magic potion in the water?"

Jessica couldn't help chuckling at the image of Pastor Kidd mixing potions and reciting incantations in a dimly lit, smoke-filled laboratory to create holy water that would draw heathens to him. But she also considered Sam's question. Perhaps he was right; perhaps she *was* being silly.

"I don't know, Sam." She squirmed. "It just *feels* wrong."

"What harm would it do if you let your mother win this one and let Willy be baptized as an infant into the Church of the Gospel?"

"I just don't want him raised in that environment. They can't just change the name and expect everything else to change with it." Jessica spoke forcefully. "Besides, I want you to baptize him."

"Well, let's say I promise to figure out how to do that when he's ready to decide for himself. Now, can we please deal with the issue at hand? He wouldn't be raised in 'that environment,' Jessica; you're his mother, and you would still be raising him how you want. And I spoke to Pastor Kidd before he changed the name of the church, and I believe that it's more than symbolic. Anyway, I'm not sure the old Church of the Epistles did you any real harm."

"It was horrible, Sam, you know it was."

"They treated you terribly when they found out you were pregnant, but up till then, you knew you were saved and that Pastor Kidd was preaching the Way, the Light, and the Life, right?"

Jessica nodded slowly, reluctantly.

"It brought you great happiness and purpose. It did the same for me. But you and I, we both had experiences that made us outgrow that community and understand Christ in a bigger way—just like we both outgrew Santa Claus. Pastor Kidd is a holy man, and there's nothing wrong with the teaching of the Church of the Gospel—particularly since the name change—as long as you understand its limitations. Besides, your mother is really trying, in her own way, to bridge the gap. I dread to think what she had to pull to get Pastor Kidd to agree to the infant baptism of an outsider."

Jessica hadn't thought of that, and it made her pause, but after a moment of reflection, she frowned. "It's just wrong, Sam."

"Why? This isn't about you, Jessica. Try to think of this as doing something for your mother. Why is it wrong to give her something that doesn't matter to you but means the world to her? And young Willy, too: It might even give him a grandmother—and a grandfather. Is that so wrong? Please at least think about it."

A grandfather!

The thought was not new, but it still jarred. Pastor Kidd was Willy's grandfather by blood, though she didn't expect him ever to accept that responsibility. She put the thought aside and promised, "I will," though she still didn't agree.

They drove in silence the rest of the way home. By the time they arrived, Willy had fallen asleep. Jessica took him out of his seat and held him tightly. She climbed backward out of the truck and looked for Clark, though she knew he was long gone, then went to her room, laid Willy in the bassinette, and curled up on her bed, looking at her son through the rails. Seeing Ma had reawakened feelings of love and estrangement, remembrance of both the joys of home and its difficulties. Ma was a cold woman but was capable of enormous sacrifice. Perhaps Sam was right; maybe it would be good for Willy to have a grandmother.

Watching her sleeping baby through the bars of his bed, Jessica wept.

CPSIA information can be obtained at www.ICGtesting.com
Printed in the USA
LVOW120332190112

264532LV00002B/168/P